## THE ERIMUS MYSTERIES

# THE ROMANOV RELIC

### JOHN REGAN

Copyright © 2025 John Regan

All rights reserved.

# ACKNOWLEDGMENTS

It goes without saying that no one finishes or begins a novel without influence from other people. Having always loved the English language in general, words and their meanings in particular, and fast approaching my fiftieth year, I decided to do something about it.

My writing bug took hold when I enrolled in a creative writing class held in Middlesbrough on a Monday evening. Encouraged not only by the teacher but enthused by the other members of the class, the genesis of this novel began.

After the classes had finished and I had taken a brief interlude away from writing, I found myself drawn back towards this story and completed it.

Finally, as I'm sure everyone knows, we are the total of the experiences we go through in life, good and bad. So, to anybody I've met, laughed with, cried with, and travelled further along the road on life's journey with, whose influence, however small, manifests in some way in this book, many thanks.

John Regan, January, 2025.

JOHN REGAN

# DISCLAIMER

Many of the places mentioned in this book exist. However, the author uses poetic license throughout to maintain an engaging narrative. Therefore, no guarantee of accuracy should be expected. The characters depicted, however, are wholly fictional. Any similarity to persons living or dead is accidental. The beliefs and opinions expressed by the characters in this book are not necessarily those of the author.

This book was revised in 2024/25 to reflect the author's continual improvement as a writer.

# PROLOGUE

**1950 – Saltburn-by-the-sea, north-east England** – The man removed items from the washhouse, placing them in the small yard one by one until one last piece lay in the corner, covered with an old blanket. He lifted the cover, revealing the statue of The Virgin Mary beneath. Tilting the figure to check its weight, he heaved it up in his arms and tiptoed outside, placing it carefully down along with the other things.

His wife came outside carrying a mug and held it out to him. 'I've got you a cup of tea, Harry.' She studied his handiwork. 'Having a clear-out?'

'I am.' He took a sip of tea. 'What do you want me to do with this statue?' he said, nodding towards it. 'It's the one our Billy sent home.'

The woman shook her head as her eyes filled with tears. 'I don't know.' She shrugged. 'Give it to a local church. Billy's gone, so he won't come looking for it.' She pulled a hanky from her apron pocket and blew her nose.

He put his arms around his wife. 'Don't go upsetting yourself. I'll get rid of it.'

**1944 – Holland** – The German soldier stumbled through the trees as voices from behind shouted for him to stop. Reaching for his pistol, he paused for breath as his eyes scanned the area he had come from. He eased his backpack off, lowered it to the floor, and hid behind a large tree. A British soldier came into view, and the German aimed and fired, the bullet whistling past his pursuer. The British soldier dived to the floor and rolled into a ditch for cover as a second British soldier appeared, dropped onto one knee and fired his rifle at the German, hitting him in the neck. He slumped to the ground, clutching at his wound as copious amounts of blood spurted from it. The two soldiers, with their rifles raised, crept their way across to the stricken man and looked down at the dying German. They watched as he tried to speak, but his words stalled in his mouth and were forever lost. Gradually, his movement ceased, and his eyes fixed in a vacant, lifeless stare.

'He's SS,' Billy said. 'Check his backpack while I keep an eye out. There may be more of them hiding.'

His friend held something aloft. 'I've found his knife. This one's mine, you had the last.'

Billy glanced around. 'No problem. You shot him. All's fair in love and war. Is there anything else?'

'There's something heavy in his knapsack wrapped in sacking.'

'Quick put it in mine, Arthur,' Billy said. 'Someone's coming.' Arthur opened his friend's backpack and dropped the parcel in.

More British soldiers came into view. 'Over here.' Billy shouted. The soldiers raced towards them as Billy turned his head to face Arthur. 'I'll hide it, and we'll see what it is later,' he whispered to his friend.

Billy crept away from the farmhouse and headed off into the darkness while his compatriots slumbered behind him. The full moon, dressed in a starry night, brightly illuminated the surrounding countryside as he paused and scanned the area behind him before moving on. Stopping a short distance away, he dropped to his knees and started digging, the soft earth quickly piling up next to the hole. He located the item he sought and, placing his hand inside the hole, removed the package. Billy held it up, and juggling the object between his hands, he put it on the floor and unwrapped the sacking. Billy glanced around again, surveying his field of vision. Satisfied, he picked up the statue of the Eagle and held it in front of him, smiling as he gazed at its beauty. He paused and snatched at a breath as footsteps broke the silence behind him.

'Billy,' a voice said. 'It's Arthur.'

'Arthur, come here,' Billy said as Arthur located his friend's position and hurried across to him.

Arthur's eyes widened as he spotted the statue. 'Let's have a look,' he said as Billy handed it to him. Arthur juggled the Eagle in his hands. 'Christ, it weighs a bit,' he said. 'What do you think it's made of?'

'It looks like silver,' Billy said.

'Silver?' Arthur gasped. 'It must be worth a fortune. What are we going to do? How the hell are we going to get it back home to Blighty?' he said, handing the statue back.

'Don't know yet,' Billy said. 'I'll have to give it some thought. I may have an idea, though.' He tapped the side of his nose with a finger. 'A way of getting it back across the channel.'

'Great,' Arthur said. 'Has it any markings on it?'

Billy turned the statue over, showing Arthur the base. 'Have you a match?' he said, and Arthur fumbled in his pocket, pulling out a small box. He took out a match and struck it on the side, the glow from the flame bathing them in the light. They stared at the base of the statue and at the small symbol of two crossed keys engraved on it. Below this were two strange letters, and underneath this, a crest. Billy wrapped it back up in the sacking, deposited it in his backpack, and covered it over with clothing.

Arthur held out his hand. 'Fifty, fifty?'

Billy smiled. 'Fifty, fifty.'

Arthur and Billy headed into the darkness away from the camp, and Arthur placed a hand on his friend's shoulder. 'Did you manage?'

Billy nodded. 'I did. Wilf said he's heading for the coast tonight. Should be there tomorrow.'

Arthur frowned. 'Can we trust him?'

'Wilf's my cousin and as straight as they come. He's got a friend that's going back home – took a Jerry bullet in the leg. Wilf said his pal will smuggle it back to England and take it to our mam and dad's.'

'What happens if he finds it in the statue?' Arthur said.

'He won't. It's well hidden. I've told Wilf to tell him it's for our local church.'

Arthur nodded. 'Good.'

'I've given him a letter for Mam and Dad asking them to look after it until I return.'

Arthur grinned. 'What are you going to spend your half on?'

Billy rubbed his chin. 'I Haven't really thought about that, but I'm going to ask Mary to marry me when I get home. It might come in handy for the wedding.' He winked at his friend. 'I'll be looking for a best man.'

Arthur patted him on the shoulder. 'I'm available.'

'I thought you might be,' Billy said.

**1940 – Warsaw** – The man pushed the wrapped parcel under his coat, slipped along the narrow street, and, stopping at the door to the pawnbrokers, he knocked. The door opened a little, the hinges creaking with age.

'What is it?' a voice said.

The man glanced left and right along the street. 'I have something to sell, Mr Vagna.'

Vagna grunted and pulled the door open fully. 'Maric,' he said, smiling. 'I didn't recognise you. Come in, my friend.'

Maric followed the man into the shop, and the pawnbroker locked the door behind the two of them.

Vagna pulled out his spectacles and balanced them on the edge of his nose. 'What have you got for me?'

Maric opened his coat and pulled out the cloth-covered object. He slowly removed the material to reveal a statue of an Eagle. 'Well. What do you think?'

Vagna's eyes widened. 'Where did you get this?'

'From old man Rashnik's place.'

Vagna gasped. 'You stole it from a dead man?'

Maric scowled. 'I found it after the Germans had been.' He spat on the floor. 'The Bastards took poor Rashnik outside and shot him in broad daylight.' Maric leant in closer. 'It was underneath some floorboards. The German scum must have missed it. What use would he have for such things now when he's dead?'

Vagna nodded slowly. 'True, but even so.'

Maric spat on the floor again. 'Better in our hands than the Nazi murderers.'

Vagna nodded again. His compatriot's comments beyond criticism.

'What's it made of?' Maric said. 'Silver?'

Vagna lifted up his glasses and put a small magnifying glass to one eye. 'Not silver. Platinum, maybe,' he said, studying the hallmark.

Maric's eyes widened. 'Platinum. It must be worth a lot.'

Vagna pulled the eyeglass from his eye and tapped the base of the statue. 'Klyuchi Kross.'

'Klyuchi Kross?' repeated Maric, frowning.

'It's Russian. Klyuchi Kross was a famous goldsmith of high renown. Look here,' he said, tapping his bony index finger at a symbol on the base. 'The crest of the Romanovs.'

'How did it get here?' Maric asked.

'I don't know, but it has great value, though. How much were you looking for?'

Footsteps sounded from outside, and somebody thudded on the door.

'Open up!' a voice from outside said.

Vagna pushed the Eagle back across the counter towards Maric. 'You idiot. You've been followed,' he said, waving at Maric. 'I want no part of this.'

Someone banged on the door again. 'Open up!' shouted the voice again. Louder.

Vagna shuffled across to the door and unlocked it, and three Polish soldiers pushed their way past him, followed by a young German SS officer, smoking a cigarette, who stepped past the other men. The German stood erect with one arm behind his back as he looked around the room. 'Maric Balisch,' he said. 'I'm arresting you for looting. A crime punishable by death,' he said, nodding towards the soldiers who grabbed Maric.

'Please,' Maric said, dropping his head. 'I didn't know it was wrong. I needed food for my family. We're starving.'

The officer's eyes fell on the Eagle. 'What's that?' he said, tapping it with his stick.

Vagna nodded towards Maric. 'He brought it here,' Vagna said. 'It has nothing to do with me.'

'Take them both,' the German officer said. 'Shoot them outside. Let everyone be aware of what we do to thieves and their allies.'

Vagna struggled as one of the soldiers took hold of him. 'But I had no part in this. I'm guilty of nothing.'

The officer sneered at Vagna, his top lip curling as he spoke. 'You're a Jew. That's crime enough,' he said, dropping his cigarette butt at the feet of Vagna.

The German officer picked up the statue as the soldiers dragged the two men away and lifted it up to the light for a better view. He studied it as gunshots broke the silence of the night.

**2015 – Durham** – Anne Jacobs sat in the office of The Crossed Keys Insurance and Financial Services, tapping on her computer keyboard as the office phone rang. 'Crossed Keys,' she said.

'I've got a lead.'

'On what?'

'The Eagle,' the voice said.

'You're kidding.'

'No. Someone's been asking around. A private detective named Hockney.'

'Right,' she said. 'Has this Hockney found it?'

'No, but he knows all about Parchester.'

Jacobs sat back in her chair and drummed her pen on the desk. 'We need to arrange a meeting with Mr Hockney. He may be able to assist us in locating its whereabouts.'

'Should I give him a ring? I could arrange an appointment for you.'

'Yes, you do that, but be discreet. We don't want the fat man and his friend finding out.'

**Two Weeks Earlier** – Private detective William Hockney sat behind his desk at the office of *The Erimus Detective Agency*. All was silent except for the scribbling of his pencil on a betting slip as someone tapped on the door.

'Yes?' he said.

Kim, his secretary, strolled in. 'There are two men to see you, Bill. Mr Green and Mr Sleen,' she said and held the morning post out to him as he continued to write out his bet.

'What about?'

She smiled. 'What am I, Bill? A bloody mind reader? They said it was a private matter.' Kim looked back towards the door. 'They look like a pair of dodgy characters if you ask me. One's a big, fat bloke, and the other's a little goggle-eyed guy.'

Hockney sat back in his chair and smiled. 'Yeah, well. Those dodgy characters might be paying your wage next week. We aren't exactly snowed under at the moment, are we.'

'Hmm.' She tossed the morning post onto the desk and pouted at Hockney. 'I'll show them in, shall I?'

'Big smile, Kimbie,' Hockney said.

She pulled a face at him and exited, returning moments later with two gentlemen. 'Misters Green and Sleen,' she said, enunciating their names as her broad Teesside patois echoed around the room. Kim nodded at Hockney, scowled at the men and left, closing the door behind her with a resounding thud.

The fat man sat on a chair in front of Hockney's desk – the item of furniture groaned resentfully beneath his massive weight. 'Delightful girl,' the fat man said. 'I would ask for a refund from that charm school, though.'

'Ignore her,' Hockney said. 'Boyfriend troubles.'

'Ah, affairs of the heart. Always problematic.'

'So, gentlemen,' Hockney said, putting aside the betting slip. 'What can I help you with?'

The fat man hauled himself forward and leant across the desk, offering his chubby hand to Hockney. 'Rupert Green,' he said, and this is my associate, Sleen.'

Graveney glanced at Sleen. 'Doesn't he have a first name?'

'He does, but we tend to call him Sleen.' Green brushed a speck of dust from his jacket. 'I need your help in acquiring an antique for me, Mr Hockney.'

'What sort of antique?'

'A statue of a bird. An Eagle, in fact.'

'And this bird is where?' Hockney said.

Green chuckled. 'If I knew its whereabouts, Mr Hockney, I wouldn't be employing you.'

'Fair enough. But I will need something to go on.'

'Yes, of course you will,' Green said, playing with the huge ring on his finger.

'Nice ring,' Hockney said.

'Ah, yes. The ring,' Green said. 'It's a club I'm a member of. *The Crossed Keys.* It's rather exclusive.'

Hockney smiled and took out a notebook. 'This statue? Worth a lot of money, I suppose?'

'Indeed, and I'm willing to pay handsomely for its recovery.'

Hockney looked up. 'Can I ask you why you picked this agency?'

Green pinched his chin with his finger and thumb. 'At random, Mr Hockney.'

Hockney put down his notepad and fixed Green with a stare. 'The telephone book, was it?'

Green lowered his eyes. 'Yes, I believe it was.'

'So, how do I go about finding this statue then?'

Green placed his hands on top of his huge belly. 'There's a gentleman, Mr Stankovich, who has some information regarding its location. Unfortunately, I don't know the whereabouts of Mr Stankovich.'

Hockney picked up the pen and wrote again. 'This Stankovich. What do you know about him?'

'He owns a nightclub in Middlesbrough. *Abandon.* Have you heard of it?'

'Vaguely, I'm a bit long in the tooth for such places.'

'I'll give you some out-of-pocket expenses,' Green said, clicking his fingers at his companion. Sleen put his hand into his inside pocket and pulled out a wad of notes. 'There's one thousand here,' Green said, 'and plenty more if you can locate the statue.' Green slowly rose from his chair, like some giant creature emerging from an African river.

Hockney stood and offered his hand. 'I'll see what I can do, Mr Green.'

Green held out his sweaty, chubby paw. Reaching into his pocket with his other hand, he pulled out a card and pushed it across the desk towards Hockney. Green's eyes narrowed. 'Has anyone else been enquiring about this statue?'

Hockney met his stare and shook his hand. 'No. And if anyone does?'

Green raised an eyebrow. 'Let me know, will you?' he said as the two men turned and left.

Hockney walked over to the window and looked outside. He waited until they had left the building before returning to his desk and picking up his phone.

'Mr Stankovich,' he said. 'It's Bill Hockney. I've had the fat man and his sidekick in here asking about you and the statue.'

'What did you tell them?' Stankovich said.

'Nothing,' Hockney said. 'But why would Green come to me? I'm not in the phone book or Yellow Pages. They must be aware that I know you.'

'We should meet, Bill. I'll phone you later.'

**Three Weeks Earlier** – Hockney showed Stankovich into his office, indicating for him to sit on one of the chairs in front of his desk.

Hockney opened the top drawer of his filing cabinet. 'Drink? I've only got malt, but it's quite a good one.'

'Malt's fine.'

Hockney handed him a glass. 'So, you said you had a story to tell.'

Stankovich took a large swig from the glass and began. 'All stories have a beginning, and mine's no different. It starts in St Petersburg during the rule of Tsar Nicholas II.' Hockney leant back in his chair as Stankovich continued. 'On the outskirts of the city lived a humble boy called Gregory Stanislav. At sixteen years of age, Stanislav was apprenticed to a goldsmith named Stankovich.'

'A relation?' Hockney said.

'Yes.' Stankovich smiled before resuming. 'Stanislav, whose mother had died while he was young, lived with his father. Over the years, his father had become increasingly ill, relying on Gregory to look after him. While visiting the local marketplace, Stankovich spotted Gregory with his father and was impressed by the little handmade trinkets they were selling. After enquiring who had made them and having been told by Gregory's father that he had been making them for over forty years, having learned the trade from his father, he had passed his skills on to his son. Much to his father's delight, Gregory had shown a high aptitude for it, possessing an ability way beyond his father when he was young.'

Hockney lifted the bottle and held it towards Stankovich. 'Another?'

He nodded his head and continued as Hockney replenished his glass. 'Stankovich spotted the pair many times over the years, watching Gregory grow into a young man. Sometime later, on his usual walk through the old part of the city, Stankovich had chanced upon Gregory once more. Now, about sixteen years of age, Gregory was without his father, who he informed Stankovich, was too ill to come along with him anymore. Stankovich had no children of his own, and spotting the boy's potential offered him the opportunity to work at his shop. Gregory's father's illness worsened, and he was now being cared for by a relation of Gregory's, so Stankovich seized the opportunity and set about training the boy. Over time, his father's health declined further until he passed away several months later.'

Stankovich took another mouthful of his drink and placed the empty glass on the desk. 'Stankovich and his wife, Petrova,' he continued, 'had grown to love Gregory as their own, and as the boy grew into a man, Ruben and Petrova Stankovich retired from their business and passed it over to their now adopted son. A little later, Gregory met and married a local woman called Magda and settled down into domestic bliss. The Stankovichs, after retiring, moved to the coast and rarely visited the old city. Over time, the old pair became increasingly infirm and were happy to let Gregory look after the Goldsmiths. Gregory and his wife, Magda, would visit them occasionally when their business allowed, and letters from his adopted mother and father and vice versa were regular treats. Magda fell pregnant in 1881 with twins and gave birth to twin boys who they named Josef and Janik.'

Hockney sipped his drink. 'How do you know all this?'

'Janik Stankovich was my great-grandfather.'

'How does this fit in with the Eagle?'

Stankovich smiled. 'I'm coming to that, Bill. May I continue?'

'Please do.' Hockney sat back in his chair.

'The two boys showed great aptitude in their father's profession – soon surpassing his expertise – and in 1901, the old man decided to retire. He handed the business over to his two sons, giving each of them a silver-plated key to the property as a symbolic gesture. The boys, being ambitious, moved to a larger workshop closer to the centre of the city and renamed their new premises Klyuchi Kross. *The Crossed Keys*.' Stankovich pushed a small piece of paper across the table to Hockney.

Hockney glanced at the design. Two crossed keys and some lettering beneath this. 'Is this their hallmark?'

'Yes, indeed.' Stankovich smiled and carried on. 'The two brother's reputations continued to grow, and their name became well-known far beyond the city limits. It was said that their ability rivalled Faberge himself. About a year after they'd moved to their new premises, Josef met a woman called Helena Matronovich. By all accounts, she was stunning and much admired by the men in the city. Josef pursued her relentlessly, and according to his diary, she finally agreed to marry him in 1904. At first, their marriage was a happy one, and as the business grew, everything seemed perfect. In 1905, while working at their shop, a gentleman by the name of Illanonovich Bukarin arrived and introduced himself as a high-ranking official in the court of the Tsar. After the 1905 revolution had been crushed, Bukarin decided he wanted the brothers to make a keepsake for the Tsar in commemoration – an Eagle made from palladium. The brothers were overjoyed. It offered them an opportunity to enhance their growing reputations further.'

Stankovich paused and then resumed. 'After receiving the necessary amount of precious metal, the brothers set about fashioning it. However, when the work was finished, Josef became ill with a fever, and after his wife and brother nursed him, he eventually started to recover. According to his journal, he awoke one night in his bed feeling much better and ventured downstairs, but as he approached the front room of the house, he heard a noise inside. Unsure of the time and at first thinking that burglars had broken in, Josef crept towards the door. Unable to see into the room without making himself known, he peered through the crack in the doorway and through the mirror. Josef saw his brother and wife in each other's arms.' Stankovich took a sip of his drink and continued.

'Shocked by this, he made his way back to bed and spent a sleepless night remembering what he had seen. The next morning, unsure if he had dreamt the whole episode, he mentioned nothing to his wife or brother. As the days passed, though, his paranoia grew until, gradually, an enmity between himself and his brother took hold. One night, after drinking heavily and drunk on vodka, he confronted the pair of them. A fight ensued, which ended when Josef stabbed Janik before fleeing the scene with the Eagle. Janik died of his injuries two days later. Josef, who had been pursued by the police and Bukharin's men, was found dead in the forest on the outskirts of the city, his head smashed in and the Eagle gone. The Eagle had claimed its second victim.'

Hockney held up a finger. 'Are you saying there's a curse on it?'

Stankovich laughed. 'Of course not. I don't believe in such things myself, but you'd be surprised how many do.'

'And the Eagle?'

'The Eagle remained lost until 1941 when it resurfaced in Warsaw.'

Hockney glanced at his watch. 'I'm sorry, Mr Stankovich, but we'll have to continue this story later if that's okay? I'm due at Teesside Magistrates.'

'No problem. Perhaps lunch tomorrow at twelve-thirty? I'll send my driver.'

'Twelve-thirty is fine,' Hockney said. 'I'll see you then.' The two men shook hands, and then Stankovich was gone. Hockney looked at a brown envelope with his name written across it on his desk, which Stankovich had apparently left for him. On opening it, Hockney, to his delight, found it contained five hundred pounds, so, putting the money into his inside pocket, he picked up his betting slips and headed off.

**The Next Day** – Hockney, escorted by the waiter through the other diners, arrived at a table. Stankovich rose and offered his hand to Hockney. 'Bill. So glad you could make it.'

Hockney laughed. 'Free lunch? My mother didn't breed any idiots.'

'Quite.' Stankovich smiled. 'We'll have a spot to eat before we get down to business.'

'Fine by me.'

'Can I get you a drink, sir?' said the waiter, who had remained at his side.

'Whisky with ice.' The waiter nodded politely at Hockney and left.

Hockney and Stankovich enjoyed an excellent lunch, the pair of them chatting about various subjects, and as the restaurant gradually emptied, Stankovich rose from his seat. 'If you'd follow me. We need a little more privacy.'

Hockney accompanied Stankovich upstairs and through into an office. Stankovich closed the door indicating for Hockney to sit. He sat opposite Hockney and handed him a glass of Whisky.

'Who owns this place?' Hockney said.

'I do. Well, a large part of it.'

Hockney sat back in his chair. 'Where were we?'

'I was telling you about the history of the Romanov Eagle.'

'You said it re-surfaced in Warsaw. In—'

'1941,' Stankovich said. He put his hand in his jacket pocket, pulled out a tattered black and white photo and pushed it across the desk towards Hockney. 'What do you see in this picture?'

Hockney took hold of the snap and studied it. 'It's a photo of Heinrich Himmler and a German officer.'

'The German SS officer is called Otto Klaus. He came from Munich and lived in the same suburb as Himmler before the war. This photo shows Himmler at Klaus' house in Holland during the occupation. Klaus married, and Himmler was the guest of honour.'

Hockney handed back the photo. 'Interesting.'

Stankovich waved his hand over the photo. 'Take another look.'

He studied it for a couple of moments. 'What am I looking for?'

Stankovich sat back in his chair. 'On the mantelpiece behind the two men. What do you see?'

'A statue of an Eagle?'

Stankovich grinned. 'The Romanov Eagle.'

Hockney frowned. 'How can you be sure it's the same Eagle?'

'I have all the drawings from Janik and Josef's workshop. They had every piece catalogued. It's the Eagle, all right.'

'So, you know Otto Klaus had the Eagle. Where did it go from there?'

'Otto Klaus commanded a panzer division, and in 1943, his unit was involved in fighting with the Allies. After the Market Garden operation failed, his division was all but destroyed, and Klaus fled along with a couple of others.'

'Where too?'

'Across Holland. Trying to escape the Allies. He was shot dead by a British soldier in 1944.'

'And the Eagle?' Hockney asked.

'His house in Holland was captured by the Allies, and they made a record of everything they found there. There was no mention of the Romanov Eagle.'

Hockney took another look at the snap. 'Are you suggesting he took the Eagle with him?'

Stankovich smiled and took a large swig of whisky. 'Let me put it this way, Bill. If it had been discovered by anyone, why hasn't it resurfaced?'

'Maybe a collector has it?'

'Otto Klaus loved antiques. His house was full of items from all over Europe. Items he'd stolen. If he wanted something portable, with great value, what better?'

'I see your point. An eighteenth-century nest of tables wouldn't do,' Hockney said. 'Still a big leap of faith. Surely anyone gaining possession of the Eagle would just sell it.'

'The soldier that shot Klaus was called Arthur Parchester.'

Hockney's eyes widened. 'You've found him?'

'I'm afraid not. Arthur Parchester died in Holland in 1944. He was killed along with most of his platoon when a shell from a tank hit a house they were taking cover in.'

'So, let me get this straight. You think Parchester obtained the Eagle from Klaus?'

'Yes, I do,' Stankovich said.

'So where is it?'

'That's where the trail goes cold.'

Hockney rubbed his chin. 'I think you're wasting your time. He could have buried it in Holland. The Eagle could be anywhere.'

'I won't accept that. I managed to trace a cousin of Parchester's. Sadly, he was in a nursing home and not in the best of health, but he remembered helping Arthur Parchester to smuggle a statue out of Holland and back to England. Unfortunately, he passed away in the nursing home soon after I met him.'

'The Eagle?'

Stankovich ran a finger around the rim of his glass. 'A statue of The Virgin Mary.'

Hockney frowned. 'The Virgin Mary?'

'He described it to me. It was large enough to conceal something inside.'

'An Eagle, perhaps.'

'Precisely.'

'Still a big leap,' Hockney said. 'You may be wasting money on a long shot.'

Stankovich smiled. 'Bill. Find the statue, and there's a six-figure sum in it for you.'

Hockney raised his eyebrows, and Stankovich nodded. 'That's right,' Stankovich said. 'A cool half million. The statue itself is valuable, but given its provenance, its worth is enormous.'

Hockney put his glass on the desk and sat back in his chair, rubbing his chin again. 'How come you haven't pursued this yourself?'

'I employed someone else to do that. Unfortunately, the man I hired was a little overzealous, shall we say, and the family of Arthur Parchester is unwilling to assist us. They may not know anything anyway. I thought a new approach, someone like yourself, with a background in the police, may be a little subtler.'

'I see?'

'Expenses are no problem. Even if you have to travel overseas.'

'When would you like me to start?' Hockney asked.

'As soon as possible.'

'Is there anything else I should know?'

Stankovich thoughtfully sipped his drink. 'I'm not the only person looking for the Eagle.'

Hockney glanced at the photo again. 'Oh yes.' Hockney looked up. 'Who else is?'

'A woman called Anne Jacobs and a man named Rupert Green.'

'And they are?'

'Green's a rich businessman.' Stankovich ran a finger around the edge of his glass again. 'For a time, he and I worked together to find the Eagle, but we had a fall-out, and Green decided to go it alone. He's a distant relative of mine. His great-grandfather was Josef Stankovich. Josef had an illegitimate son with a woman, and Green is the descendant of that boy.' Stankovich laughed. 'He claims that he is the rightful heir because Josef was the elder of the two brothers.'

'I take it you don't agree?'

'I'm not bothered about the claims of Green. As far as I'm concerned, this is a race, and its winner takes all.'

'What does he look like?' Hockney said. 'In case I meet him.'

Stankovich smiled. 'You can't mistake Green. He's huge.'

'And the woman?'

'She's related to the man who commissioned the piece.'

'Bukharin?'

'Yes,' Stankovich said. 'Well remembered.'

'She does have a point. After all, it was her ancestor who paid for it.'

'He intended to give it to the Romanovs,' Stankovich said, 'and if he had, it would almost certainly have been seized by the communists during the revolution. No one from the Romanovs is around to claim it.'

'You're right, I suppose.'

'If you have any reservations, Bill, say so now. I could always employ someone else.'

'I have no problem at all.' Hockney smiled. 'My conscience is up for grabs – at the right price.'

Stankovich nodded and got up from his seat. 'Keep me informed, Bill. Especially if Green or Jacobs show up.'

Hockney stood and offered his hand to Stankovich. 'I will.'

# CHAPTER ONE

**October 2015** – Hockney staggered through the dark streets, his eyes darting back and forth. Passing revellers on a night out, he paused in a doorway. He rechecked his inside pocket and pulled an envelope from it. He looked around, nervously, scanning left and right before continuing on. Stumbling past darkened buildings and lively bars as detritus from the day's shoppers blew about the pavement in the gentle night breeze.

Turning into a side street, he passed the old municipal building reincarnated into a swanky restaurant-come wine bar. He stopped again as shooting pain in his side pushed hard for his attention, he put a hand on his injury and stared at the wet stickiness which coated his hand. He needed to be quick, he reasoned and opening the envelope, Hockney pulled out the postcard – yellowed with age, its corners crumpled, a photo of a field of tulips on the front – and turned it over. Written on the back in capitals were the words: OUR LADY NO. 346. He folded the postcard in half, pulled a key from his trouser pocket and placed it between the fold of the bent card. Pushing both into the envelope, he sealed it and headed across the road searching for a post-box. Finally spotting one further up the street, about fifty yards away, he made for it. As he reached it, he paused and slumped against it, his injury sapping his strength. Looking around and sure he wasn't being watched, he popped it into the slot and set off again, his injury slowing him down considerably.

Turning a corner, he heard voices up ahead. Hockney ducked into an alley, and hopeful rather than certain he had not been spotted, he retreated into the darkness and backed away from the road. Here he waited, hardly daring to breathe as his heart rate increased with another jolt of adrenalin, reacting to the loss of the precious fluid. A figure stopped at the end of the alleyway – the streetlight illuminating the man in a silvery glow as he looked about and listened. He glanced down the alley, turned and peered along its length into the inky blackness concealing the end of it. Hockney stopped, his back now pushed up against the building at the far end. There was no way out. A wall to his left and a high metal fence to his right thwarted any hopes of escape. Even if he had not been injured, Hockney doubted his ability to scale either of them. He waited and hoped, but as the man turned as if to leave, Hockney slipped, and his right foot kicked a can on the floor as he fell. The noise in the silence was deafening and Hockney groaned as the man moved along the length of the alleyway towards him. Stopping halfway, he lit a cigarette, his features briefly illuminated by the lighter. Hockney sighed and slumped onto the floor, his strength and energy all but spent. The man drew closer, the knife in his outstretched hand glinting in the moonlight.

'I believe you have something of ours, Mr Hockney?' he said.

Hockney struggled to stay conscious. 'It appears death doesn't always come armed with a scythe,' he said to himself as the figure loomed over him, his last view before he passed out.

Inspector Clive Comby sat in the passenger seat of the Vauxhall Vectra parked at the rear of Middlesbrough police station. He was eating a somewhat disappointing bacon and egg sandwich, coupled with an average cup of milky tea he had purchased from the café across the road. Comby, in his late fifties, wore the sort of face not so much lived as squatted in. He sighed as his middle-age spread pushed alarmingly at the buttons of his ill-fitting shirt, looking like the Hoover Dam attempting to hold something akin to the Atlantic Ocean back. Comby, in a feeble attempt at restoring some sort of order to his person, had wetted and brushed flat his hair. Despite this, he still looked like a man who had all but given up on his appearance. The driver's side door opened, and DS Mick Hardman, a portly figure himself, got in, allowing the vehicle to reach some sort of equilibrium.

Comby stared at him. 'Remind me never to go to that café across the road again.'

'You say that every time, guv, but you keep going back for more. You're like a culinary masochist.'

'I mean it this time.' Comby groaned. 'It's only its close proximity to the station that makes it appealing. If you hadn't taken all this time, I could have gone over to Sheila's and got a top-notch breakfast.' He glowered at his junior. 'What took you so long anyway?'

Hardman winked at Comby. 'I was talking to the lovely WPC Fernley.'

Comby grunted. 'Let's put your lusting aside, shall we,' Comby said. 'We've got a body over the border that looks like a stabbing. Follow the flashing lights.'

Hardman started the engine and drove off as Comby poured the rest of his tea out of the window before tossing the remnants of his bun over his shoulder into the back to join the remains of many other long-forgotten meals.

They arrived moments later at the crime scene, and the two podgy figures clambered free from their vehicle.

A uniformed police officer approached them. 'This way, sir,' he said, and the two officers followed him along the alleyway. At the end lay the body of someone covered by a large sheet.

The uniformed officer stopped near the body. 'His name's William Hockney, sir.'

'Hockney?' Comby said, lifting the corner of the covering. 'Private Detective.'

'Yes, sir. There's an office in Redcar.'

'Robbery?' Comby said, studying the dead man's features.

'Doesn't appear so, sir. We found a wallet with credit cards and money on the body.'

'Did you know him, guv?' Hardman asked.

'A little,' Comby said, placing the sheet back over the body. 'Hockney was a policeman himself way back. What's his office address? he said to the PC.

He handed Comby a business card, who glanced at it briefly before popping it into his top pocket. 'Right, Mick,' he said, looking at Hardman. Sunny Redcar it is.'

Comby and Hardman pulled up on Redcar High Street and looked at the window above a charity shop, which had the name *Erimus Detective Agency* emblazoned across it.

Comby took the card from his pocket and glanced up at the office. 'This is the place,' he said, hauling himself from the car as Hardman followed him. The two men slowly climbed the stairs, stopped to check the name on the door and gathered their breath before entering.

A young woman in her late twenties sat behind a desk casually flicking through a magazine. She glanced up briefly at the two officers who had stopped before her, and Comby coughed.

The woman put aside her magazine. 'Mr Hockney's not in yet. And before you ask, I've no idea when he will be.'

Comby pulled out his credentials. 'Inspector Comby and Detective Sergeant Hardman.'

She picked the magazine up again. 'And?'

'When was the last time you saw Mr Hockney alive?' Hardman asked.

The woman looked up and dropped her magazine on the floor as Comby glared at his junior officer.

Hardman shrugged. 'It got her attention, guv.'

'Alive?' she said. 'What do you mean alive?'

Comby edged closer. 'We're sorry to be the bearer of bad news, but we've found a body in Middlesbrough, Miss …?'

'Kim. Kimberly Weatherly. I'm Mr Hockney's secretary.'

Comby shook his head at Hardman. 'We have reason to believe that the body is your employer, Miss Weatherly. I'm sorry.'

'Dead? How?'

'It appears he was stabbed.' Comby stepped closer. 'We will need official identification. Do you know if Mr Hockney has anyone who could do that?'

'I'll do it. Bill hasn't any close family, I'm …' She reached into her handbag, pulled out a tissue, and blew her nose.

'I see,' Comby said. 'Can I ask what cases Mr Hockney was working on?'

She stood. 'Yes, of course. I'll get the files.'

Comby and Hardman emerged from the building and stepped into the street.

'Bloody hell, Mick. Your people skills need a bit of attention.'

'Well.' He sneered. 'The snotty cow was looking at us like something you find on the bottom of a shoe. It grabbed her attention. Didn't it?'

Comby marched towards their car. 'Oh, it did that all right.'

# CHAPTER TWO

**March 2016** - Phillip Davison trudged from his bedroom into the kitchen of his dingy, depressing bedsit, closely followed by his dog, Baggage. He opened the cupboard, took out the last two slices of bread, and popped them in the toaster.

He frowned at the dog, who wagged his tail and cocked his head to one side. 'Well, Baggage,' Phillip said. 'We've hit rock bottom.' He scraped the last traces of butter from the tub and discarded the carton.

He patted the dog on the head. 'Are you hungry, boy? Of course you are. You're always hungry.'

Opening the cupboard again, he pulled out a tin of dog food. 'This is the last one, Bagsy.' He held out the tin for the dog to see as if he would understand. The dog, wagging his tail furiously, spun around in a circle a couple of times. Phillip smiled. 'Pavlov would have loved you. Who needs a bell?' He opened the tin and added the last handful of broken biscuits to half of the meat. Patting the dog on the head again, he frowned. 'I've had to mix some bits and pieces to eke it out. It's austere times we're living in, boy.'

Phillip placed the bowl on the floor and watched as the dog devoured it. He sparsely buttered his toast and tramped into the living room with the satisfied Baggage following closely behind. The front door rattled, the post dropping on the carpet with an apologetic plop. Baggage raced towards it and made a token gesture of barking. Phillip followed the dog and picked up the mostly brown envelopes. He eyed the letters. 'Bill, bill,' he muttered, discarding them one by one onto the hall table, then stopping at a white one, he read the letterhead. *J & D Worthey & Co.*

*Solicitors,* written in bold type across the top.

He opened the letter and read the contents. 'Baggage,' he said, grinning. 'Our luck may be changing.' The dog cocked his head to one side and wagged his tail faster. 'We've come into money. Steak from now on, my boy.' Phillip squatted and rubbed the dog's head, then, standing again, jumped into the air and clicked his heels together.

Samuel Davison, Sam to his friends, sleepily opened his eyes and glanced around the room. He was lying in the middle of a king-size bed. To his right lay a blonde-haired woman, the bed sheet barely covering her nudity, while to his left lay an attractive brunette. He sat up, trying to fathom where he was, his brain still muddled by the previous night's alcohol intake. On the other side of the room was a second king-size bed occupied by two equally naked women. Further to the right of this was a single bed with a redhead within it. Sam crept from the bed, not wanting to disturb his sleeping companions. He was naked and acutely aware of this searched amongst the array of clothing strewn across the floor. Locating his trunks, shirt and jeans, he quickly dressed and tottered towards the bathroom, moving unsteadily, having not sobered up from the night before. He ran the tap and filled a glass with water, downing it in one before filling it again and drinking it.

'Hi, handsome,' said a soft Welsh voice. Sam spun around to view the blonde whom he had woken up next to, standing naked in the doorway.

He refilled his glass. 'Hi, gorgeous. I've got a raging thirst.'

'Are you leaving?' She sashayed closer to him.

'I thought I'd better. I've something on this morning, and I'm afraid last night's a bit of a blur.'

She glided closer and nodded her head backwards. 'Oh, I can fill you in on that. We had a bit of a party. You were impressive, taking on all five of us.'

'Five! That's some going even by my standards.'

She leaned against the wall. 'Listen. If you fancy me and you getting together again, I'm here for the next couple of nights?'

Sam looked her up and down. 'I'm sorry … I've forgotten your name.'

'Amanda.' She went back to the bedroom and returned moments later with a card bearing her name and mobile number.

Sam glanced at it. 'Thanks. I'll give you a ring.'

He couldn't help but stare at the woman. Her blonde hair and makeup, although looking the worse for wear, did nothing to detract from her sexiness. The woman's beautifully shaped breasts and hourglass figure and her perfectly coiffured pubic area made for an appealing sight. She closed the door to the bathroom and ambled forward, stopping a foot from him. She smiled and licked her lips. 'How about something on account? Before the others wake?'

'Well, I—'

She stopped his protests with a finger to his lips and held up a condom between the fingers and thumb of her other hand. 'Shall I?' she said, expertly tearing open the foil. Her eyes lowered to the burgeoning bulge in his jeans.

'Why not,' Sam said.

Sam found himself outside the Thistle Hotel on Corporation Road fifteen minutes later. He took out his mobile phone and called his friend Emily. 'Where are you, Em?'

'At the flat. Why?'

'I need a lift.'

'Where're you?' she said.

'Outside the Thistle Hotel.'

'In town?'

'Yeah.'

'You copped off with one of those Welsh hairdressers, didn't you?'

'Em, you wouldn't believe me if I told you.'

'Why?'

'I'll tell you when you pick me up.'

Sam waited for a little over ten minutes when a battered, red Ford Fiesta pulled up next to him. He opened the passenger door and jumped in beside Emily.

Emily stared at him, breaking into a broad smile. 'Well?'

Sam smiled back. 'Very.'

Emily made a face. 'Come on, spill the beans,'

'I didn't get off with only one of them,' he said, rummaging through the glove box and pulling out a bag of crisps.

Emily held up two fingers. 'Two?' Sam shook his head. 'Three ... four? she said. 'You're kidding? Aren't you? All five?' Sam nodded and picked up an open can of coke next to Emily.

'Sam,' she said, 'you're a sexual athlete, man.'

He slurped the drink and leaned back in his seat. 'I know.'

'How the hell did you manage that?'

'I'm not that sure. I was shit-faced if you remember.'

Emily rolled her eyes. 'Oh, god, yeah. The way you were knocking back those shots it's a wonder you're still standing or sitting at the moment.'

'I remember going back to their room and someone suggesting we play strip poker. Twenty minutes later, I had them all down to their briefs. Apart from the redhead. She wasn't wearing any. There's something incredibly sexy about a woman who goes commando. And then one thing led to another, I suppose.'

Emily banged her seat playfully. 'I hate that saying. One thing led to another. People say that and miss out all the tasty bits. I want to hear the good bits. Not the edited highlights.'

'Well,' he said. 'If I remember right. Brunette number one stuck the lips on me first and then Blondie. And well, then they all piled in, mob-handed like.'

'And you shagged all five?'

'Pretty much. I won't lie and say it was my best performance ever, but what can you expect with five of them? I had to spread myself pretty thin.'

'Sam. You're like the Linford Christie of sex.'

'Linford Christie was a sprinter. I like to think I'm more of a Mo Farah.'

'Or,' she said. 'Daley Thomson, the decathlete.'

'I'm not sure we did all the ten events. Six or seven, maybe.'

Emily pouted. 'Couldn't you have saved one for me? I mean. Five is pure gluttony?'

'I know what you're saying. If I'm honest,' he said, gazing into space. 'It was the sexual equivalent of an all-you-can-eat buffet. I'm going to stick to one or two in future.' He tapped Emily's hand. 'I'm pretty sure they were all straight, anyway. I don't think you'd have had much luck.'

Emily scoffed. 'Give over. There's always one or two bi-curious. That little blonde was a bit tasty. I could teach her a thing or two. I like it when they play hard to get. I mean, I've had loads of married lasses over the years. Once I get them into bed, they're like putty in my hands.' Emily showed Sam her hands in case he'd forgotten what they looked like.

'I thought you were seeing Mad Stella?'

'Leave off,' she said, rolling her eyes. 'I'm giving her a wide berth. She's so intense. Not to mention her sex toy obsession. Don't get me wrong. I like the odd one, but she's mental about them. Not only that, but she buys everything oversized. I think it might have something to do with her being a midwife.'

Sam laughed. 'I'm not even going to try and understand what you mean by that remark, but I'm sure Freud would have a field day.'

Emily closed her eyes and shook her head. 'Some of the things she whips out. Christ, I didn't know they did them that big. She definitely has issues in that department. The sight of them, and I'm reaching for the aspirin. So, in answer to your question, Mad Stella is history.'

'I could never understand lezzies. With your dildos and strap-ons. I mean, if you want a knob,' Sam said, 'why not go for the real thing? I could give you the number of someone if you like.'

Emily rolled her eyes again and smiled. 'Lezzies. That's so un-PC. It's not that part of a man we don't like. It's what's hanging off it.'

Sam put his hand in his jeans pocket. 'Fair point. Have you any money on you? I'm starving.'

'Eighty pence.'

Sam huffed. 'And I've got £1.20. That might be enough for a bacon butty.'

'There's nothing back in the flat,' she said. 'I used the last of the milk and bread this morning. In fact, Old Mother Hubbard was around earlier and left in disgust, muttering something about it being worse than her house.'

'She always was a moaning cow. That Old Mother Hubbard,' Sam said.

They pulled up outside their flat and went in. Sam ignored the post on the floor, and Emily, who followed him inside, gathered it up, flicking through its contents.

Sam strolled into the kitchen and started opening cupboards as Emily held up an envelope. 'Hey, Sam! There's a letter from a solicitor here.'

Sam blew out his cheeks. 'Christ. You're right about there being nothing in the cupboards. What are we going to eat for the rest of the day?'

Emily studied the letter. 'I might give Mam a ring and see if I can't blag our lunch.'

'Isn't your dad still mad at you?' Sam wandered back through into the hall. 'In denial about your sexuality?'

'Yeah, but he's away working this weekend. He still can't accept I'm gay. He thinks I haven't met the right bloke yet.'

'What about your mam?'

'She's okay with it. She said to me I must be gay if I'm living with you and still not interested in men. She now realises I'm a fully paid-up member of the Sapphic society,' she said and framed her face with her hands.

Sam paused his search for something edible. 'I'm not sure if your mam was paying me a compliment or not.'

Emily laughed. 'Definitely a compliment. I think my mam fancies you. It's Sam this and Sam that. And how's that lovely Sam doing.'

Sam raised his eyebrows. 'How old's your mam again?'

'Don't even think about it, Sam,' she said, pointing a finger at him. 'That would be so gross.'

'I once shagged Micky Chivers's mam,' Sam said. 'Don't repeat that to anyone, though. Especially Micky Chivers. He has a bit of a temper.'

'Holy Mary?' Sam nodded. 'The churchgoer?' Sam winked 'But she's so prim and proper,' Emily said.

He closed his eyes, nodding to himself. 'Well, behind that veneer of respectability, she wasn't. She collared me one long, hot summer's day in the potting shed. It was my first blowjob if I remember. She was quite adept.'

'What were you doing in the potting shed?'

'Putting the lawn mower away,' Sam said. 'I'd been cutting the grass for her. Trying to earn a bit of cash to go to a concert. Can't remember who I was going to see.'

'How old were you when Lady Chatterley pounced then?'

'Fifteen.'

Emily deliberately dropped her jaw open. 'Fifteen! She'd get arrested these days.'

'One minute, she was telling me the best soil to grow rhododendrons in, and the next—'

'Don't … One thing led to another.'

Sam winked again. 'It most definitely did. Acid soil. In case you were wondering.'

She held out the envelope. 'I wasn't. Do you want this letter?'

'From solicitors, you said. I'm not sure about that. It can't be good news, can it?' Sam carefully inspected the envelope.

'Well, don't open it,' Emily said. 'Just wait for the bailiffs or police to turn up.'

He turned the letter over and studied it. 'How have they got my address anyway? I'm not on the electoral roll?'

Emily held out her arms. 'Search me. They're apparently keen though.'

Sam folded his arms. 'You see, this is why I'm not on Facebook or Instagram. It's too easy to track a person down. Anonymity is such a rare commodity these days.'

Emily theatrically held up a finger. 'Hey. It could be from the Child Support Agency. You must have knocked out some nippers in your time.'

'Nah. The CSA would send it in a brown envelope. My mate, Vic, gets them all the time.'

'Vic?' she said. 'He's the one with four kids by four different women?'

Sam grinned. 'That's the one. Vic's celibate now. He said he can hear the CSA sharpening their pencil when he looks at a woman.'

Emily plucked the letter from Sam's hand. 'Why doesn't he just get the snip?'

Sam grabbed the envelope back. 'Bit late now. That particular horse has bolted.'

Emily clapped her hands together. 'Open it then. Maybe it's the manager of the British Olympic sex team. Looking to recruit you.'

Sam frowned at her and, tearing open the envelope, read it.

Emily playfully stamped her foot. 'Well? What does it say?'

'It says my uncle has died.'

She placed a hand on his shoulder. 'Oh, I'm sorry. Were you close?'

'I've never met him. It says I'm one of the beneficiaries in his will.'

Emily snatched the letter from Sam. 'You're kidding. My God, Sam, you could be minted.'

Sam put his arms around Emily's waist and picked her off the floor. 'I know, Cinders. You will go to the ball.'

'When you say ball, Sam,' Emily said. You mean a fabulous slap-up meal at Al Fino's, followed by a night of clubbing, boozing and debauchery?'

Sam smiled and raised his eyebrows. 'Isn't boozing already covered in the debauchery?'

Emily winked and tapped the side of her nose. 'Maybe, or maybe not.'

Sam placed her back on the floor and waved his hands around his head. 'Well, whatever it is, Emily Simpson, hang on to my coat tail. It's going to be a wild ride.'

Albert Jackson sat at his antique desk, meticulously opening his morning post. He held in his hand an ornate silver-plated letter opener, which he used precisely. He slipped its point into the corner of the envelope and carefully ripped open the top of each one.

The room was large, with a high ceiling, inside an old Victorian house. It was immaculately tidy, obsessively so, with not a single item out of place. Most of the walls had floor-to-ceiling shelving crammed full of videos and DVDs, all perfectly arranged in alphanumeric order. Every piece of furniture and cushion was deliberately and precisely placed as if someone had taken out a tape measure for added accuracy.

He picked up the last letter, a white one, and repeated the opening process again. Then, discarding the envelope, he dropped it into a waste bin next to him. He studied the letter and, having read and digested its contents, placed it meticulously on top of his other correspondence, slightly straightening the pile about a quarter of an inch. He stood, pushed the chair under the desk, and headed off into the kitchen for a well-deserved cup of green tea.

# CHAPTER THREE

**2016** – Sam climbed the stairs to the solicitor's office and stopped close to a desk where a young woman sat deep in conversation on the phone. She smiled at him and continued her call. He stood patiently, looking around at the black-and-white paintings of old parts of Middlesbrough that adorned the wall.

The woman ended her conversation and switched her attention to him. 'Good morning,' she said.

Sam leant on the counter, pulled the crumpled letter from his back pocket and handed it to her. 'I've got an appointment with Mr Boothby, gorgeous.'

The woman smiled, took the letter from him, and read it. 'If you'd like to come with me, Mr Davison,' she said, and Sam followed her into a waiting room. 'If you'd wait here, Mr Boothby won't be long.'

Sam thanked her, sat, and looked around the room at the other two occupants. A slim man, approximately the same age as himself, he guessed, and a smaller, somewhat conservatively dressed man. This man wore clothes way beyond his age, more suited to a man in his sixties – he had on a dickie-bow and a tweed jacket. Sam couldn't remember the last time he'd seen anyone under sixty or outside of a function wearing one, and despite the man's attire, he looked in his late thirties. The other two nodded at him, Sam smiled back, picked up a magazine lying close by and waited.

Charles Boothby sat in his office, busily signing letters. There was a tap on the door, and his secretary entered. 'The three gentlemen have arrived, Mr Boothby. Should I show them in?'

He glanced up from his paperwork. 'Good. Bring them all through together, will you?'

She nodded, left the office, and headed back into the waiting room where the three men sat silently. She smiled pleasantly. 'Samuel Davison, Phillip Davison and Albert Jackson. If you'd like to follow me, gentlemen, Mr Boothby will see you now.' The three of them glanced at each other and followed the secretary as she showed them into the solicitor's office.

Boothby stood and offered his hand. 'Good day, gentlemen,' he said, shaking hands with them in turn and then indicating for them to sit. The three complied and sat on the chairs arranged in front of his desk.

'Could you organise some drinks for us,' he said to his secretary, 'and hold all my calls until after this meeting.'

She nodded at her employer. 'Tea or coffee, gentlemen?'

'Tea,' Sam and Phillip said in unison.

'What type of tea is it?' Albert asked.

She frowned. 'Tetley, Mr Jackson.'

Albert rubbed his chin, reached into his jacket pocket, and pulled out a small jar with tea inside it. From another pocket, he took out a stainless steel perforated egg-shaped article. 'Can you put one spoonful of the tea inside this?' he said, handing her the oval object. 'Place it in recently, but not boiling water, and allow it to infuse for six minutes precisely.'

'Yes,' she said, furrowing her brow, before taking the items from him.

Sam, Phillip, and the solicitor stared at Albert, who smiled back at them. 'You can't beat good tea,' Albert said.

Boothby clasped his hands together. 'Well, gentlemen.' He glanced at each of them in turn. 'I've got a Samuel and Phillip Davison.' The two nodded, and he continued. 'And an Albert Jackson.' Albert nodded too. 'You're probably wondering what this is all about.'

'Money, and lots of it,' Sam said. Phillip, who stifled a smile, glanced across at Sam as Albert looked on and rolled his eyes.

'Quite.' Boothby smiled. 'I'm the executor of your late uncle's estate. William Hockney, did any of you know him?'

Sam and Phillip shook their heads.

'I met him once when I was a child,' Albert said. 'He bought me a red London bus for my birthday.'

'Wow,' Sam said. 'He must have been really wealthy. Those buses aren't cheap.'

Albert rolled his eyes again. 'A toy one,' he said and fixed his attention back on Boothby. 'I believe he was the black sheep of the family.'

'I can't help you with that,' Boothby said. 'I can tell you what I do know. Your uncle was murdered in August of this year and his killer has never been found, despite the police mounting a largescale investigation.'

Sam held his hands up and stared wide-eyed. 'I didn't do it,' he said as Phillip stifled another smile.

'No one's suggesting you did, Mr Davison.'

'I'm only joking,' Sam said. 'I've got an alibi anyway. For any day you care to mention,' he said, theatrically winking at the solicitor.

'I don't think the murder of someone is the least bit amusing,' Albert said.

'I never said it was,' Sam said. 'All I want to know is how much is coming my way?'

Albert's mouth dropped open as Phillip smiled and shook his head.

Sam held out his hands and glanced between the others. 'It's the reason we're here, isn't it?'

Boothby nodded. 'It is indeed, Mr Davison. I was trying to fill you in on the circumstances of his death.'

'Have we missed his funeral?' Albert asked. 'I would have liked to have gone.'

'I'm afraid so. Your uncle was cremated last month, and it took up until now to locate you three. Your late uncle died intestate, and you're his nearest relatives.'

Phillip looked across at Albert while addressing Boothby. 'As the gentleman was saying.' He nodded towards Sam. 'Without wishing to sound mercenary, Mr Boothby, it is the inheritance we're here for. I didn't know my uncle, so I can hardly grieve for him, can I?'

Boothby nodded again. 'Your uncle ran a private detective agency in Redcar. He retired from the police after having worked in Cleveland Constabulary as a detective inspector for some years. He had a decent reputation, I believe.'

Sam sat up and moved nearer the solicitor. 'This Detective Agency. Was it a large one?'

'Not really. He ran it himself, and a young lady looked after the office for him.' Boothby looked down at the paperwork in front of him. 'Cutting to the chase, gentlemen, your uncle's assets, after funeral costs and other expenses, come to a little over £24,000.'

Sam sat back in his chair. 'I can cancel the Ferrari then.'

'Looks that way,' Phillip said, smiling.

'What about the detective agency?' Albert asked.

'Yes,' Sam said. 'Hasn't that any value?'

Boothby smiled. 'Not really.'

'Isn't his office worth anything?' Phillip said.

'I'm afraid not. The agency and the flat that goes with it are heavily mortgaged.'

'Could we rent it out?' Phillip said.

'I suppose so,' Boothby said, 'but, you would only be paying the mortgage though. Should they realise somewhere near the asking price, the current estimate of the premises would only be enough to cover the repayment to the bank.'

Albert brushed a piece of dirt from the corner of Boothby's desk. 'How did he manage to run this agency if it made no money?' Albert said.

'That's a good point,' Boothby said, pulling a piece of paper from a file on his desk. 'The business was healthy and the turnover excellent.' He looked at the three cousins above his glasses. 'Your uncle had several contracts with companies in the area. Some quite lucrative.'

'So, where's the money?' Sam said.

'Your uncle had expensive hobbies, shall we say.' Boothby sighed. 'From what I've heard, he liked to gamble and was quite a one with the ladies.'

Sam winked at Albert and Phillip. 'Sounds like my type of bloke.'

'Couldn't we sell it as a going concern then?' Phillip said.

'Possibly. I'm not sure how easy it would be to get a buyer, though.'

Albert straightened the bits of paper on Boothby's desk. The annoying sight of them scattered about carelessly had captured his attention since he'd entered. 'We could run it ourselves,' he said.

Sam and Phillip stared at him as Albert continued his fastidious tidying of Boothby's desk. He picked up a pen and pencil before placing them neatly with some others inside a receptacle on Boothby's desk. Albert stopped, realising the other three were staring at him. 'Sorry,' he said, lowering his eyes. 'It's a bit of a habit of mine. I like things tidy.'

Sam smiled at Albert. 'You can come around to my flat if you like,' Sam said. 'It's a shithole.' Albert rolled his eyes and ignored him.

Boothby nodded slowly. 'Yes. I suppose you could run it. The business probably wouldn't be large enough to keep you three employed. I'm not sure what occupations you have at present.'

'I'm between jobs,' Phillip said. 'To be honest, any job at the moment would come in handy. I'm interested in running it until something more permanent crops up.'

'I'm interested too,' Albert said. 'I'm comfortable, financially, but I'd be keen. It would give me something to do. My—'

Sam edged forward again, staring at Albert. 'Hold on, cowboy, I'm interested too. I'll be honest. I haven't got a pot to piss in.'

'It may be worth you three considering it,' Boothby said. 'I'll give you the address, and you can have a look at the property. I'll get Kim to meet you there.'

'Who's Kim?' Phillip said.

'Kim is the young lady who worked for your uncle. She has the keys and knows far more about the business than me. She currently lives in the flat that goes with the property.'

'I'm not trying to rush you or anything,' Sam said. 'But when will we get our share of the money?'

'There are some bits and pieces to sign, but I don't see why we can't get the money to you in a couple of days.'

'Great,' Sam said. 'The baby will get its new shoes.'

Albert frowned at Sam. 'Baby?'

'A figure of speech, mate. I haven't actually got a baby. Well, none that I know of,' he said, winking at his cousin.

Sam bounded out of the solicitors, jumped into Emily's waiting car, opened the glove box, and looked inside, frowning deeply at the empty compartment. 'No snacks?'

'Never mind that,' Emily said. 'Are we rich?'

'You must have snacks.' Sam playfully banged the dashboard. 'Oh, Emily, life's not worth living without them. Anyway, what do you mean, we?'

'I'm sure you wouldn't begrudge your oldest mate a few quid.'

'You're not my oldest friend,' he said. 'Tommo is. He's two years older than you.'

'Oldest female.' She pulled a packet of crisps from her side of the car and held them up in front of Sam. 'Worcester sauce … Your favourite flavour.' Sam made a grab for them, but Emily pulled them away and out of reach.

'Oh, Em, stop teasing.'

She showed Sam the packet again. 'Fifty-fifty.'

Sam lifted his nose and turned his head away. 'Fifty-fifty for a packet of crisps.'

Emily pulled open the bag and waved it under his nose. She raised her eyebrows. 'Sixty-forty.'

'Nah.' Sam continued to look away from her.

Emily pulled out a large crisp and held it aloft. 'Oh my God! Look at the size of this one.'

'Seventy-thirty,' Sam said as Emily handed the packet to him, and Sam eagerly started eating.

'You're so generous, Sam. Only taking thirty per cent.'

'Yeah, right,' Sam sputtered through his crisp-filled mouth.

'Well?' She shook his arm. 'How much are you getting?'

'Eight-grand.'

Emily laughed and nudged Sam. 'You can cancel the Lamborghini then.'

'That's what I said in there,' Sam said. 'Only it was a Ferrari.'

Emily knitted her brow. 'Still, it's a windfall. Eight thousand buys an awful lot of alcohol,' she said.

'It sure does. I'm going to become a detective as well.'

Emily spun to face him. 'Just like that?' she said, and Sam nodded. 'Somehow,' she continued narrowing her eyes, 'I can't see you as a Sam Spade type.' She started the engine up and put it in gear. 'Although,' she said, nudging him. 'You have got the right first name.'

'Apparently ...' Sam popped the last crisp into his mouth. '... My uncle ran his own detective agency, and I'm going to run it with my two cousins.'

'Cousins?' She put the car back in neutral.

'Yes. There are three of us. We each got a share of the £24,000, and we've decided to continue to run the business. The office is mortgaged to the hilt, and we probably couldn't sell it as a going concern. So, it makes sense.'

Emily burst out laughing. 'Of course, it does,' Emily said. 'Doing something you've never done before with two people you've just met sounds like a winner. What could possibly go wrong?' She raised her eyes and shook her head.

'Oh,' he said, adopting a serious face. 'My uncle was murdered.'

Emily's jaw dropped open. 'Murdered? Who by?'

'By whom,' Sam said, and Emily rolled her eyes. 'The police don't know,' Sam said.

'There's your first case,' Emily said, nudging him again. 'The murdered uncle.' She waved her hands about and then fixed Sam with an icy stare.

'No way.' Sam poured the last few crumbs of crisps into his mouth. 'There's no money in it.'

Emily put the car in gear again. 'Where to now, blue eyes?' she said, attempting to impersonate Humphrey Bogart.

'Tommo's. I'm meeting my two partners there.'

'Tommo's it is.'

# CHAPTER FOUR

Phillip and Albert sat in The Sidewinder public house. Phillip, a pint of beer in front of him, and Albert, nursing a fresh orange.

'So, Albert. Tell me a little about yourself.'

'I'm thirty-eight and live alone in a huge Victorian house in Nunthorpe.'

'The house is yours?'

'My late mother and father left it to me.'

Phillip took a sip of his pint. 'If you don't need the money, why are you doing this?'

'I'm a little …' He paused for a moment. 'Introvert. My counsellor thinks it would help me if I ventured out and met more people.'

'What about the OCD?' Phillip asked.

Albert gasped. 'How did you know?'

'I worked with someone who had it. Drove me around the twist.'

Albert smiled and took a sip of his orange. 'I know. It has that effect on people. What about you? What do you do?'

'I'm unemployed at the moment. I live in a dingy bedsit on Marton Road with my mongrel dog, Baggage.'

'Baggage?'

'Yes. I had nowhere to live when I lost my job at my girlfriend's father's firm, so I moved into a bedsit. I found Baggage outside my flat one day, half-starved. He was probably thrown out after Christmas, and I took him in. Dogs need a bit of looking after, so, Baggage seemed appropriate.'

'How did you lose your job?' Albert asked.

'I broke up with my girlfriend, and her dad sacked me.'

'That's terrible. Couldn't you have taken him to an industrial tribunal for wrongful dismissal?'

'Unfortunately not. Long story. Maybe another time.'

Albert nodded, realising a change of subject was in order. 'What about Samuel?'

Phillip laughed. 'He seems okay. A bit of a character.'

Albert rolled his eyes and looked upwards. 'I'm not sure. He's a little flippant for my taste.'

'He's all right. He reminds me of myself. When I was fifteen, that is.'

Albert chuckled. 'I know what you mean.'

The door burst open, and Sam and Emily strode in. Sam made his way over to Albert and Phillip. 'Emily,' Sam said, 'this is Phillip and Albert, my cousins. This is Emily, you two.' Emily shook hands with the pair.

'What about a drink?' Sam said.

Phillip raised his still three-quarters full pint. 'I'm all right.'

'So am I,' Albert said.

'Em?' Sam said.

'I'll have half a lager,' she said.

'Lager it is.' Sam held out his hand. Phillip smiled, and Albert rolled his eyes as Emily pulled a note from her pocket and handed it to Sam, like someone who'd been doing this sort of thing all her life.

The three cousins sat in the corner of the small pub, discussing the detective agency, while Emily talked with Maria, one of the barmaids. Tommo had arrived half an hour after Emily and Sam to relieve Maria, and they chatted until the three cousins joined them at the bar.

'All sorted?' Tommo asked.

'Yes,' Sam said. 'Phillip's phoned Kim – she works at the detective agency – to arrange a meeting, and we're going to Redcar to meet up with her.'

'How are you getting there?' Emily said.

Sam put his arm around her shoulder. 'Well ... We were hoping ...'

'You're a cheeky sod, Sam Davison.'

'I'll get you an ice cream,' Sam said. 'A lemon top. I know how much you like lemon tops.'

'With sprinkles,' she said, feigning excitement.

'Of course.'

'And raspberry sauce?' she said, clapping her hands together.

'Absolutely,' Sam said.

Emily sighed. 'Sam. It may have escaped your attention, but cars need petrol, and petrol costs money.'

'We'll pay you,' Albert said. 'We wouldn't want you to do it for nothing.'

'If we all chip in a tenner,' Phillip said. 'Would that be okay?'

'A tenner each is a little too much,' she said.

Albert straightened the beer mats on the bar. 'Nonsense. You should be duly recompensed.' He reached into his pocket and took out a small purse and the others watched as he extracted a note from it. The bill had been folded carefully into a little square. Albert unfolded it and handed it to Emily. Phillip gave her a second note, and all eyes turned to look at Sam.

'Can you wait until I get my inheritance?' he said, patting his pockets. 'I'm a little impecunious.'

Emily rolled her eyes. 'I'm keeping a note of what you owe me, Davison.'

'What about a drink to celebrate?' Phillip said. 'To seal the deal?'

Albert ventured into his purse again, pulling out a second folded twenty-pound note. 'I'd like to buy you all a drink.'

Sam tapped one of the pumps. 'Mine's a pint.'

'I'll have the same,' Phillip said.

'Emily?' Albert said.

'Coke.' She glanced at Sam. 'I'm driving.'

'I'll have another orange, barman,' Albert said. 'One for yourself, my good man,' he said, handing Tommo the now unfolded note.

'Tommo,' he said. 'Call me Tommo.'

Emily's car pulled up outside the detective agency late afternoon, and she and the three cousins got out and headed inside. They went up a flight of stairs and into a small office. They could hear someone moving about in the next room, so the four ventured inside.

'Hello,' Phillip shouted.

Kim came through to reception from the kitchen. 'Hi, you three must be Bill's nephews?'

Sam stepped forward. 'Yes.' He offered his hand and smiled, turning up his male charm to the maximum. Emily looked at Sam and shook her head as Albert and Phillip introduced themselves.

'This is Emily,' Sam said. 'A friend of mine.' He nudged Emily with his shoulder.

'I'm Kim. I worked for your uncle.' She lowered her head. 'I'm sorry about what happened to him,' she said, reaching into her pocket and taking out a tissue.

'Don't worry,' Sam said. 'We didn't know him.'

Emily glared at Sam.

'You'll have to fill us in about him,' Phillip said. 'Only Albert ever met him, and that was when he was a kid.'

Sam wandered into the middle of the room and performed a slow pirouette. 'Yeah. He bought Albert a London bus. A big red one.'

'Wow!' Emily said. 'Was he rich?'

Sam looked across at her. 'We've done that one,' he said, and Emily stuck her tongue out at him.

'So, this is it?' Phillip said.

Kim frowned. 'It's not much. Bill was a—'

Sam winked. 'A bit of a lad.'

Kim smiled. 'He certainly was.'

'How did you two meet?' Albert asked. 'If it's not impertinent.'

'Bill was very kind to me. I was living in a hostel when we met, and he gave me a bit of work. We just hit it off. He took me on full-time about three years ago.'

Sam looked across at Kim and raised his eyebrows. 'You and Uncle Bill weren't …'

'No.' She glared at Sam. 'He was like a dad to me,' she said, dabbing her eyes with a tissue.

Emily walked across and put her arm around her. 'Maybe we can find out who did it?' Emily said, mouthing *dickhead* at Sam.

'Do you think you can?' Kim said.

The three men looked at each other.

'We'll try,' Phillip said. 'We'll definitely try.'

Emily waited patiently while Kim showed the cousins around the office, explaining the agency's current contracts and other outstanding work. Although they were not really sure if the business would support the four of them, they asked Kim if she would be prepared to stay on, and she readily agreed. Albert offered to go unpaid, wanting to help and not really needing the money.

# CHAPTER FIVE

Sam exited the bank, walked over to Emily's car, and got in beside her. He reached into his inside pocket and held out an envelope.

Emily snatched it from him. 'What's this?'

Sam opened the glove box. 'Your share.'

She nudged Sam gently. 'My share? I was only kidding about that.'

'I know you were, but I owe you a lot. I've probably borrowed more than that from you over the years.'

She took out the wad of notes. 'How much is here?'

Sam took a bite of a Twix he'd found. '£2,400, spraying bits of the chocolate bar about. 'That's what we agreed. Thirty per cent.'

'I can't take all this,' she said, staring at the money. 'It's your inheritance.'

'Yes, you can. I'd only piss it up against a wall anyway.' Sam took another bite. 'Put it towards a new car.'

Emily kissed him on the cheek. 'Thanks, Sam.'

'Easy tiger,' he said. 'People will talk.'

Emily started the car up. 'Where are we off to?'

'Can you swing by Tommo's?' Sam said. 'I've got some money for him, too.'

'More of your inheritance?'

'Indeed. It's payback time. C'est la vie. Easy come, easy go.'

Tommo stood leaning over the bar, reading the paper. It was quiet today. Typically, Wednesdays were quiet, but today, it was even quieter. He put it down to the fact that it was near the end of the month and before most people's payday. He turned a page of the paper, looking up when the only customer in the bar stood, waved at him, and left before Tommo resumed reading his paper.

Emily and Sam entered, and Tommo looked up again as they walked over and stopped at the bar. Sam glanced around the empty room. 'It's packed in here.'

Tommo sighed heavily. 'It's dead. You're only the fourth or fifth I've had in today.' He moved from behind the bar and kissed Emily.

'I'll have a pint,' Emily said. 'It might help to keep you solvent.'

Tommo shook his head. 'Don't joke, Em. I've had a few rough months.'

Sam pulled out an envelope. 'Well, let me brighten your day.'

Tommo frowned. 'What's this? You've not got a job as a bailiff, have you?'

Emily put her hand on Tommo's arm. 'Things aren't that bad, are they?'

'Not quite.' Opening the envelope, Tommo pulled out a handful of notes and held them aloft. 'What's this?' He looked at Emily, who shrugged.

'It's for you,' Sam said. 'From my legacy.'

'How much is here?'

'One thousand four hundred.' Sam smiled. 'I must have bummed that much from you over the years. Like I said to Emily, I'd only piss it up against the wall.'

'Sam, I don't know what to say.'

'Don't say anything. Just get us a pint, will you? I'm spitting feathers.'

Tommo pulled two tankards from above the bar and began filling the glasses with beer. 'Sure thing, mate.' He rested one of the pints on the bar. 'What are you planning to do with the rest? Give it to some other charity cases?'

Sam put his arm around Emily's shoulder. 'Didn't I say? My mate Emily and I are going to hit the town.'

Emily looked at Sam. 'Tonight?' she said. 'It'll be dead. Why don't we go for a nice meal and save ourselves for tomorrow?'

Sam rolled his eyes. 'Oh, Em. You're no fun.'

Tommo placed the second pint on the bar. 'In any case, haven't you got work on for the detective agency?'

'It's a bit slow at the moment,' Sam said, picking up his drink. 'We do it on a rota system. When a customer comes in, the next in line takes that case. Phillip's working at that new distribution warehouse on Portrack Lane. Someone's nicking stuff, and he's been employed by the owners to find out who it is.'

'What about Albert?' Tommo asked.

Sam smiled. 'Albert? You and he have become quite the bosom

pals.'

'Yeah, well, I like him. He's a little unusual, but I like him.'

Sam sipped his pint and shrugged. 'Takes all sorts, I suppose.'

Tommo smiled and nodded. 'I'm taking him shopping tomorrow. I'm going to see if I can drag him into the twenty-first century.'

Sam took another mouthful and placed his drink down. 'Have you ever considered working for the Samaritans?'

Emily playfully punched Sam. 'Leave him alone. I like Albert too. He's sweet.'

Sam gently nudged her. 'Oh, he's sweet, all right. Sweet. And nutty as a fruitcake.'

The next day, Albert awoke at precisely 07.35. After showering twice and brushing his teeth three times, he headed downstairs to prepare his breakfast – a rather meagre one, consisting of a medium-sized egg sitting atop a slice of wholemeal granary bread, lightly buttered, having been toasted for precisely eighty seconds. He had prepared himself a small cup of Darjeeling. The tea was placed inside his perforated stainless steel, oval-shaped device, which he then popped into the recently, but not boiling, water. After consuming the food and imbibing his beverage, Albert washed up the dishes, wiping them with a paper cloth, which he then discarded before placing the clean dishes in the dishwasher to be re-washed.

He sat in his favourite chair, staring at the vast shelving in the front sitting room of his house, which was stacked and overflowing with books, videos, and DVDs. The alarm on his wristwatch beeped, reminding him of Tommo's imminent arrival. Tommo had offered to take him into town and help him pick out some more modern and up-to-date clothes. Tommo described Albert's dress sense as: *'Something my great-uncle might wear if he didn't give a shit about his appearance.'* Albert smiled at that. For some reason he found hard to understand, he liked Tommo. He glanced at his watch, realising Tommo was already late. Albert tutted. He knew his timepiece was accurate – it was radio-controlled and received a signal twice a day. This was not the way to start the day. Punctuality was important to him, fitting snugly between good table manners and politeness on his importance league table. The bell on his front door chimed, and Albert stood, straightening his bow tie and sleeveless cardigan before heading for the door.

Tommo stood there – his chubby face bedecked with a smile stretching the entirety of it. 'Morning, Albi, how are you?'

'Very well. You're a little late, though.'

'Late?' Tommo glanced at his wrist. 'My watch says I'm on time.'

Albert pointed to his watch. 'Well, mine is radio—'

Tommo brushed past him and into the hall. 'This all yours then?'

'Yes, it was my late parent's house. They left it to me.'
'No siblings then?'
'No, I'm an only child.'
'Ah, an only child is a lonely child,' Tommo said as he headed on into the front room.
Albert furrowed his brow. 'Pardon?'
Tommo continued through into the lounge. 'Something my dear old mother used to say. An only child is a lonely child.'
'Are you an only child?'
'I wasn't, but I am now. I had a brother who got himself killed.'
'I'm sorry.'
Tommo shook his head. 'Don't be. He was a tosser. Always sponging money off Mam and Dad for drink and drugs. He never worked a day in his life. Then, one day, he nicked a car and drove along the parkway at the speed at which Lewis Hamilton typically operates. His journey abruptly stopped when he left the carriageway and had an altercation with a tree.' Tommo headed through into the kitchen. 'Man meets tree. Tree wins,' he boomed, holding his hands out wide for effect.
'And he died?'
Tommo opened one of the cupboards. 'Albert,' he said, 'hitting a tree at 140mph isn't going to end happily, my friend. There's no lotion for that.' He winked at Albert and smiled. 'What about a nice cup of tea?' he continued.
'Of course. How rude of me.'
Tommo held out his hands. 'Point me in the direction of the teabags, and I'll make us a brew.'
Albert frowned. 'I haven't any tea bags. I only use tea.'
'Tea? How quaint. I can't remember the last time I had a cuppa made with proper tea.'
Albert beamed. 'I've got Earl Grey, Darjeeling, Assam, Keemun, Yunnan, and Lapsang Souchong. Several types of green tea and a selection of herbal ones ... If you'd prefer?'
'Wow, Albi. You've cornered the market on teas. I'll have a Darjeeling. I much prefer the Indian blends to the Chinese, if I'm honest.'
Albert grinned. 'Really? It's my favourite, too.'
'Any biscuits?'
Albert opened a cupboard. 'Let me see. I've got Kit Kats, Breakaways, Penguins, and Trios. I'm a bit of a chocoholic. I've also got plain biscuits if you'd prefer.'
'Don't be daft,' Tommo said and guffawed. 'If it hasn't got chocolate on it, it isn't a biscuit in my eyes.'
Albert pointed to several packets in the cupboard. 'Right, which one would you prefer?'
'I'll have one of each, I think.'

'Ah …,' Albert said.

'What's the matter?'

'You see … I usually open one packet at a time. When I've finished that pack, I open a new one, and so on. I'm …' Albert paused. 'A little funny about it. My therapist says I have OCD.'

'Loved them.'

Albert frowned. 'Who?'

'OCD … They were great back in the eighties. What was that big hit they had? Enola Gay … Nah nah nah nah nah nah nah, loved that song.'

'I'm not sure you understand. I've got obsessive—'

'I know, Albert.' Tommo smiled. 'I was yanking your chain. OMD had a hit with Enola Gay. It was a sort of joke ... You know, humour?'

Albert chuckled. 'Oh, I see.'

Tommo moved towards the open cupboard. 'Anyway, putting aside your idiosyncrasies, let me at those bickies.'

Albert looked on in horror as Tommo embarked on what he could only describe as a *ransacking of his cupboards*. He felt lightheaded, watching helplessly as Tommo ripped several packets open. His heart rate quickened, and as Tommo threw the emancipated biscuits onto a plate, Albert promptly fainted.

Albert could hear voices as he came around.

'Is he okay?' Sam said.

'I think he's fainted, that's all,' Tommo said.

'Fainted?'

'Yeah, he got all worked up about me opening more than one packet of biscuits, and he passed out.'

Sam shook his head. 'Opening biscuits? Are you kidding me?'

'He has OCD.'

'They were great them. What was that hit they had?'

Tommo rolled his eyes. 'I've done that gag. It was me that cracked it first.'

'I wondered who I'd got it off.'

'He's waking up,' Tommo said. 'Albi, you all right, mate?'

Albert opened his eyes. 'Yes. I'm sorry about that. I'm not sure—'

Sam pulled him into a sitting position. 'You need a little help with that OCD of yours. I mean, getting all worked up over biscuits.'

Albert swung his legs around and planted them on the floor. 'I've started to see a therapist twice a week. To cure me of it.'

Tommo looked at Sam. 'I bet he charges an arm and a leg, too?'

'She,' Albert said. 'Miss Waltham.'

Sam nudged Albert. 'What's she like, this therapist?' he said as his womanising antenna began to twitch. Tommo rolled his eyes.

Albert smiled. 'She's beautiful.'

Sam raised his eyebrows. 'How old is she?'

Tommo glared at Sam. 'For Christ's sake, Sam, stop thinking about your libido for a moment, will you?'

Sam held up his hands. 'I'm only asking.'

'How much do these sessions put you back then?' Tommo asked.

'Sixty pounds an hour.'

Crumbs from the Kit Kat Tommo had stuffed in his mouth shot out, almost reaching terminal velocity in the process. 'Sixty quid!'

Sam sighed. 'Well, this is all very fascinating lads, but I need to get into town.'

Tommo helped Albert to his feet. 'Oh, I forgot to say. We're giving Sam a lift.'

Albert rubbed the bump on the back of his head. 'I must have knocked my head when I passed out.'

Tommo glowered at Sam. 'Ah. Sorry about that, mate. We dropped you when we were carrying you in here. Are you sure you feel okay?'

'Fine. Shall we go?'

Sam and Tommo sat in the car, watching for ten minutes while Albert went through his regular routine of locking up the house. This consisted of checking that he had locked the front door several times before going around to the back. He returned moments later and proceeded to try the front door again, rattling the handle to confirm it was locked. After disappearing for a few more minutes, he returned once more and tried the door again.

Sam shook his head slowly. 'What's he doing now?'

'He's checking the windows.'

'The time it's taking him, you could have dropped me off and then come back.'

Tommo looked at Sam. 'He can't help it, you know.'

Sam huffed. 'I know he can't, but how can you plan anything if he always does this? What's he doing now?'

'He's going back inside,' Tommo said.

'Oh, for Christ's sake,' Sam said, banging his head on the dashboard. He grunted and opened the passenger door. 'Albi! Will you move your arse?'

Albert turned around, with the key to the door paused near the lock. 'I think I may have left the gas on,' he said.

Sam pointed at the car. 'Albert, get in this car right this minute, or I'll take a bloody axe to that door, and you'll have nothing to lock.'

Albert trudged towards the car with his head down and got into the back. 'I'm pretty sure I've left the bathroom window open as well. What if I'm burgled?'

'Albert,' Tommo said. 'You've checked the doors and windows

several times. They're all locked.'

'I like to be sure, that's all. I'd never forgive myself if I were burgled. Could I perhaps do one last check?' he said, reaching for the door handle.

Sam banged his head on the dashboard again.

Tommo started up the engine. 'Albert, belt up and breathe deeply because we're going.' He put the car in gear and moved off. Albert stared forlornly out of the car window at his house as the car drove away.

# CHAPTER SIX

Tommo stood behind the bar with Maria, busily restocking the shelves, when Emily and Sam staggered in. Tommo looked up and rolled his eyes, realising how drunk the pair of them were.

Sam reached the bar and leant on it. 'Now then. Pint, big fella.'

Tommo shook his head at his friend as Sam attempted to plant his elbows on the counter, slipping off several times before finally succeeding. 'Haven't you had sufficient?' Tommo said.

Sam adopted a stern face. 'No. I've had just enough.'

Emily laughed, putting her arm around Sam and allowing her chin to rest on his shoulder. 'Oh, come on, Tommo,' she said. 'Don't be mean.'

Tommo began pulling the drinks. 'Look at the state of you two. It's a wonder you can still stand.'

Emily put her hands on Tommo's cheek and kissed him on the lips. 'Isn't he cute?' she slurred. 'He's like a big, cuddly bear.'

Maria placed an arm around her boss. 'He is. That's why we love him so much.'

Sam handed a note to Tommo. 'Get yourself and Maria one,' he said, picked up his pint and climbed unsteadily onto a stool, perching precariously on its edge.

Tommo rolled his eyes, and Emily affectionately rubbed his cheeks. 'So where have you two been?' Tommo said. 'Have you actually got any of your inheritance left? Or have you blown the lot in one drunken night?'

Sam slipped off his stool but managed to stay upright – his drink sloshing over the sides of the glass. 'Where haven't we been?'

'Well, make this your last,' Tommo said. 'I'm closing in five minutes.'

'Why can't you find yourself a nice girl, Tommo?' Emily said. 'I think you're fantastic.'

'I don't know,' Tommo said. 'No self-respecting woman wants me.'

She leant forward and waved him closer with her hand. 'If I weren't gay, I'd shag you.' She grinned and took a swig from her pint. 'Yeah. Shag you good and proper,' she said as Maria looked on and giggled.

'Cheers,' Tommo said. 'I appreciate that.'

'Yeah,' she continued. 'I'd plough you into the mattress.'

Maria giggled again. 'Too much information, Em.'

'I'm just saying, is all.' She put her pint down. 'I don't really want this,' she said to Sam, who was now asleep. 'I said,' she shouted, her raised voice causing Sam to spill more of his drink.

'What?' he said, struggling to keep his eyes open.

'I said I don't want this drink. I think I've had enough.'

Sam put his half-full glass on the bar. 'Well, Madam, should we go for something to eat? I need sustenance.'

Emily clapped her hands together. 'Kebab.'

Sam theatrically bowed in front of her. 'Kebab it is, your ladyship.' He held up a finger. 'With extra garlic sauce?'

'Oh, yes,' Emily said, pouting at him.

Emily leant across the bar and puckered her lips. 'Big kiss, Tommo.' Tommo bent down and kissed her. Maria came from behind the bar and hugged Emily and the tottering Sam before the two of them staggered out of the pub.

Tommo picked up the remainder of Sam's pint. 'Waste not, want not.'

Maria grabbed Emily's. 'I'll have the lager.'

Tommo, downing the drink in one, let out a loud burp. 'What a bonny state those two will be in come the morning.'

Emily and Sam staggered hand in hand from the taxi and Sam took the key from his pocket and promptly dropped it. 'Bollocks!' he said. Bending to pick it back up, he staggered and grabbed hold of the fence to stop himself from falling over.

Emily pushed Sam aside. 'Let me,' she said, pulling up the sleeves of her jacket. 'You're far too drunk. This needs a woman's touch.' She dropped to her knees and carefully picked up the key, holding it aloft. 'Piece of cake.' Clumsily getting back to her feet, she inserted it slowly into the keyhole while Sam leaned against the wall for support.

Sam plopped onto the sofa next to Emily, who was flicking through the television channels, hardly stopping on any of the stations for more than a second or two. 'There's nothing on. All these channels, and there's nothing on.'

Sam yawned. 'Well, turn it off. Who wants to watch shit anyway?'

Emily got up and switched the television off, flopping back down next to Sam. 'It was a good night,' she said, pushing Sam affectionately.

Sam nudged her back, a little harder. 'It was.'

'Oi!' she said. 'Who are you nudging?'

Sam stuck his tongue out at her. 'What are you going to do about it, blondie? You're only about this big.' He formed a small gap between his index finger and thumb in front of her. 'You're a tiddler.' Sam laughed at his own joke.

'I'm stronger than you think,' she said. 'Arm wrestle. I want an arm wrestle. I'll show you what I'm made of.'

'You're no good at arm wrestling. I always win.'

Emily got up, moved to the other side of the coffee table, and knelt down. 'Left hand.'

Sam knelt across the table from Emily and put his left hand in hers. 'Say when.' Emily was already pushing with both her hands.

Sam struggled at first but then slowly started to push her hands down. Sensing she was about to lose, Emily leaned across and kissed Sam on the lips. Sam, taken by surprise, allowed Emily to recover some of her lost ground. They carried on kissing until Sam eventually pulled away. 'Well?' he said.

Emily stared at him. 'Well, indeed,' she whispered before allowing their lips to meet again in a passionate union.

Emily opened her eyes, gradually allowing her senses to acclimatise. She looked around at the unfamiliar bed and, glancing to her right, spotted the naked body of Sam lying next to her, face down. Emily brought her hand up to her mouth as the realisation of the previous night's events gradually filtered into her consciousness. Quickly getting out of bed, she stopped, catching her breath as Sam shifted his position. Satisfied he wasn't waking up, Emily gathered her clothes from the previous night and raced to her bedroom.

After grabbing a towel and some fresh clothing, she showered, changing into a pair of jogging bottoms and a t-shirt before heading back to her room. She sat on the edge of her bed, not knowing what to think when her mind drifted back to the night before. She blushed as the images of her and Sam and what they had got up to bludgeoned their way into her thoughts.

'Christ,' she said softly. What had possessed her? She was gay, for God's sake. Why would she sleep with Sam? She raised her hands to her face, desperately trying to push the memories away. She heard Sam moving about in his bedroom and listened to him as he headed along the hall. She sat motionless, staring at the wall, as music from the kitchen drifted into her earshot.

She sat like this for five minutes before standing and summoning her courage. She decided to face Sam and headed to the kitchen.

Sam stood next to the oven, whistling along to a tune playing on the radio. Emily strode into the room, stopping near the table.

Sam glanced back over his shoulder, pushing the sausage and bacon around the pan. 'Hi, Em. Fancy a spot of breakfast?'

'No, I'm fine.' She paused and took a deep breath. 'Sam. About last night?'

He turned to face her, holding a sausage on the end of his fork. 'Are you sure? I've got best back bacon and those thick sausages you love.'

Unsure if he was trying to be funny, Emily paused again but let it pass. 'Last night?' she tried again.

He cracked an egg into the frying pan. 'Last night? What about last night?'

'Sam!' she shouted. He turned around, startled, dropping a tomato from his hand. The two of them watched it as it bounced along the floor, coming to rest next to the pedal bin. 'For God's sake,' she said. 'Forget about your stomach for a minute.'

He turned off the gas ring and sat at the table. 'What about last night?'

'What about last night?' she repeated. 'Sam. We had sex. We had sex … I'm gay. We had sex, and you're carrying on as if nothing's happened.'

'Ah, that,' Sam said. 'I was sort of hoping you wouldn't mention it.'

'How the bloody hell can I not mention it? It's not the kind of thing you can brush under a carpet, you know.' She stood, pacing around the room. 'I'm gay, me. I've always been gay. I've had dozens of women. Affairs, relationships, one-night stands, but in all those years, I have never, repeat never, had sex with a man.'

'Not even a grope or anything?'

She glared at him. 'No. Not even a snog. I've known since … forever that I'm gay.'

'Can't we just put it down to experience?'

'Experience.' She threw her hands in the air. 'It's not like going on a bleeding roller coaster or swimming with dolphins.'

'Em, listen. We were hammered. It happened. You're gay, and we both made a drink-fuelled error of judgement. This just reinforces your sexuality. Now you know for sure that you don't enjoy sex with men.'

'I … well … I never said …' She stopped mid-sentence.

Sam rose to his feet and ambled towards the cooker. 'Wait a minute. Do you mean you did enjoy it?'

'I don't know … I'm confused … I've never been with a man … I'm not sure what to think. God,' she said, slumping onto a chair and putting her head on the table, 'my headaches.'

He smiled at her. 'Would you like to do it again? Just to be sure?'

Emily slowly raised her head and glowered at him. 'You bastard,' she said, picked up a mug from the table and launched it at him. Sam ducked, and the mug shattered against the far wall.

'Easy, tiger. I was only joking.'

'I'm not laughing, you twat.' She stood. 'This isn't about you. To you, it's just another notch on the bedpost. Another shag.' She stormed out of the kitchen, burst into her bedroom and slammed the door shut behind her.

Sam picked up a sausage and devoured it, washing it down with a gulp of tea before heading after her.

'Em,' he said, tapping on the door. 'I'm sorry. I didn't mean to be insensitive. Can't we talk about it?' He could hear her moving about inside, and between the banging about, he could clearly hear Emily crying. Shit, he thought. What the hell was she crying for? She never cried, not properly. He'd seen her eyes glisten with tears over some chick flick, but even when she'd split up with partners, he'd never seen her cry. That was one of the things he liked about her. She was tough. Tougher than a lot of his male friends. It was like having a best friend, only with huge tits. His mind drifted back to the previous night and the sight of Emily's breasts. It was the first time he'd seen them in all their glory, unfettered. He remembered how impressive they looked. Sam gave his head a metaphorical shake. Get a grip, Sam, he thought as his higher reasoning drew a mental sword and commenced battle with his libido.

'Em. Emily. Open the door. I'm sorry. Don't go all girly on me. I promise I won't make silly jokes. I actually ...' his voice trailed off into a whisper.

'Piss off,' she shouted as something inside her room crashed to the floor.

'Look,' Sam said. 'Can we talk about it? You know me. I'm a Neanderthal. I can be sensitive if I really try.'

'Sensitive, my arse,' she said. 'It was just another shag to you. Just another woman you've managed to bed. I hate you. You, you ... dickhead!'

Sam sighed and headed back to the kitchen for another sausage. He turned as Emily's bedroom door opened, and she emerged, pulling a small suitcase behind her.

'Where are you going?' he said, with the sausage paused in mid-air. Sam hurried from the kitchen and joined her at the door.

She paused on the threshold. 'I need some space. I'm going to Mam's.'

'You can't leave me on my own,' he said, gently pulling her arm. Sam's words were muffled by the sausage he'd crammed into his mouth. 'I'm useless, and I've made way too many sausages.'

For a moment, she almost relented. Her mood lifted slightly at the sight of the comical figure in front of her. She was tempted to put her hand on Sam's cheek but resisted the urge and turned towards the door again.

Sam lowered his head. 'Don't go. Can't we just put this whole silly incident behind us? Let's just imagine it never happened.'

She paused, turning her head to face him halfway down the path. 'I can't, Sam. It did happen.' She stared at him. 'Didn't it mean anything to you?'

'Not really,' he found himself saying but not quite understanding why he'd said it. 'Besides, who's going to clean the toilet, and there's a tonne of washing.' Sam closed his eyes, realising the enormity of his words and instantly regretting saying them. Why was he saying such things? It was as if someone else had spoken them.

'Aahh,' she screamed, flung open the gate, almost crashing into Tommo, who was making his way along the footpath.

'Hi, Em,' Tommo said, smiling.

'Bloody men,' she said, pushing the startled Tommo aside. 'You can all f-off.' She threw up the boot of her car, tossed in the suitcase, and slammed it shut. Emily glared back at Sam, got in the driver's seat, and roared off.

'What's up with Madam?' Tommo said as he followed Sam back inside and through to the kitchen. Tommo sniffed. 'Is that breakfast I can smell?'

Sam groaned. 'Help yourself, I'm going for a shower.' His appetite was now gone, having thumbed a lift and disappeared down the road along with Emily.

Sam showered and dressed, his mood darkening as he realised Emily wasn't coming back. Not today, anyway. He made his way into the Kitchen, where Tommo sat at the table, finishing off the last remnants of the breakfast.

'Wow,' Tommo said. 'That was fantastic. It filled a hole nicely. I do like a good fry-up.'

'Where the hell do you put it all?' Sam said.

Tommo patted his ample stomach. 'In here, mate. I'm surprised you two are not still in bed.'

Sam narrowed his eyes and sat at the table. 'What do you mean by that?'

'Well, you two were in a bonny state last night. I thought you'd be nursing a hangover.'

Sam sighed loudly. 'A little. Hangovers are the least of my problems.'

'Now then, my fellow,' Tommo said in a fake posh voice. 'What's the problem with Emily then?'

Sam sighed again. He pushed away a plate with a half-eaten sausage and looked across at Tommo, who raised his eyebrows. Sam paused. How was he going to put this, he thought as Tommo's eyes bored into him. Bollocks, just come out and say it. 'Me and Em ...We ...' he said and gulped. 'Slept together last night.'

Tommo's mouth dropped open. 'When you say slept together...you mean?'

'Yes, Tommo. We had sex. We shagged. We did it. I screwed her, and she screwed me.'

'I don't believe you.' Tommo looked upwards. 'Not content with shagging every heterosexual woman on Teesside, now you're working your way through the lesbian population.'

Sam half-smiled.

Tommo got up from his seat and ambled across to the sink, filling it with hot, soapy water. 'So how did this happen?'

Sam shrugged, and Tommo put on a tight-fitting pair of pink rubber gloves, stretching their fingers before allowing them to snap back with a loud crack. 'Now then, Mr Davison,' he said, in a mock German accent. 'It's time for your prostate examination,' he said, wiggling his fingers.

Sam smiled again, his mood lifting a little. Tommo always had that effect on him. 'It just happened,' Sam said. 'We were very drunk, as you know. It started as an arm wrestle, and then ... well ...'

'Don't you dare say one thing led to another? Christ, Sam. Don't ever write your memoirs. You'll struggle to fill a chapter.' Tommo began washing up, humming merrily.

'A gentleman never tells,' Sam said.

'Divulges,' Tommo said. 'It's a much better word,' he said, rinsing a soapy plate under the tap before depositing it on the draining board.

'You don't clean toilets, do you?' Sam asked.

Tommo grunted. 'Not yours, I don't. I shared a flat with you for six months, or have you forgotten, because I haven't? I still need counselling. I don't know how Emily puts up with your personal habits.' Tommo pulled a face. 'You certainly have issues in that department.' Tommo narrowed his eyes and peered outside. 'Oh, look,' he said. 'A Robin Redbreast. I love those birds.' He chuckled. 'Aggressive little buggers they are. Fight like hell with each other. Pound for pound, they're probably the hardest birds around, although bluetits would run them a close second. Imagine that. In the red corner, little Robin Redbreast, and in the blue ...'

Sam got up from his seat. 'Much as I'm enjoying this ornithological discussion, I'm going for a pint.'

Tommo finished the last pot, pulled off the gloves and laid them on the drainer. 'You know, Howard Thompson,' he said to himself, 'you'd make someone a cracking husband.' He followed Sam towards the front door. 'Do we have to go to a pub?' he said as Sam pulled on his coat. 'I spend most of my life inside one. You won't find any answers at the bottom of your glass, you know.'

Sam bounded outside. 'Maybe not, but it's always worth looking.'

They reached the Red Lion ten minutes later, and Sam headed straight for the bar. He glanced around the room, half filled with people, and sighed loudly.

Tommo joined him. 'What's up now? I've never heard anyone sigh so much.'

'Do you ever get the feeling you've taken a wrong turn in life?'

'No. I'm pretty happy. Although the love of a real woman wouldn't go amiss.'

'No luck with your cousin's mate?' Sam said.

'Helen? No. She just doesn't get me. She thinks I'm a slob. If she'd only give me a chance, I could show her I'm a modern, sensitive man.'

Sam blew out hard. 'I'm looking around this room, and there are at least seven women in here I've been to bed with. *Seven.* It's not even that full. Is this all my life is, Tommo? Stumbling from one sexual conquest to another.'

'What can I get you?' a female voice said.

Sam turned to view the barmaid and glanced at Tommo. 'Make that eight.'

'Two pints, Kirsty,' Tommo said.

The barmaid moved further along the bar to pull the drinks.

'I didn't know you and Kirsty …' Tommo whispered.

'Yes,' Sam said. 'And her mother.'

'You know, Sam,' Tommo said, furrowing his brow, 'the Boro's not a huge place. You will run out of women, eventually.'

Sam looked at the drink the barmaid had placed in front of him and ran his fingers around the rim.

'You all right, Sam?' the barmaid asked.

'Never better, Kirsty. Never better.' Sam slowly began banging his head on the counter.

Tommo put his hand on Sam's shoulder. 'What you need is to settle down with one of them. You need to find the right woman,' Tommo said as Kirsty shook her head and sidled along the bar.

'I have,' Sam said, looking directly at Tommo. 'We had sex last night.'

Tommo frowned and shook his head. 'That's never going to work, is it?'

'But she's the one,' Sam said. 'I've always thought it.' He lowered his eyes. 'I just used to push my feelings aside because she's gay. I always thought she was unattainable.'

'And now you don't?'

Sam shrugged. 'I'm not sure what I think.'

Tommo blew out his cheeks. 'A proper dilemma. I've never come across something like this.'

Sam dropped his head down again. 'It's like wanting something but knowing that you can never have it,' Sam said. 'That's fine, you accept that, but the barrier that stood between us has been torn down. What do I do, Tommo?'

'Tell her. Let her know how you feel.'

'I can't.'

'Why not? Emily may feel the same.'

'What if she doesn't? It would crush me.' Sam took a long swig from his pint and plonked his glass down. 'She'd probably move out for good. Oh, Christ, Tommo. What have I done?'

Tommo frowned. 'I've never seen you like this since …'

Sam shook his head. 'Don't. I've never thought about Lisa for weeks.'

'What are you doing the rest of the day?' Tommo said, sensing a change of subject was in order.

Sam puffed out his cheeks. 'I'm meeting a client at the agency this afternoon. I was sort of hoping Emily would drop me off. I suppose I'll have to get a taxi now.'

'I'll take you,' Tommo said. 'I'm not back in the bar until seven.'

Sam picked up his friend's pint. 'I'd better have this then if you're driving.'

Tommo snatched it back. 'Bugger off. I'm allowed one.'

# CHAPTER SEVEN

Anne Jacobs entered Hockney & Associates Detective Agency. She headed up the stairs stopping at the reception desk where Kim sat sifting through paperwork.

She held out a card to Kim and smiled. 'I believe I'm expected. Anne Jacobs.'

'If you'd like to take a seat, Miss Jacobs, I'll tell Mr Davison you're here.'

Kim knocked on the door to the office and entered. Sam sat, staring vacantly out of the window, while Tommo, seated at Albert's desk, flicked through a magazine.

'Anne Jacobs to see you, Sam.' Sam continued to stare outside.

'Sam,' she repeated.

He turned to face her. 'Sorry, Kim, I was miles away.' Tommo glanced up from his reading.

'Miss Jacobs,' Kim said.

Sam stood. 'Show her in.'

'Do you want me to go?' Tommo asked.

'No. It's probably some lost cat job.'

The door reopened, and Kim walked through, accompanied by Anne Jacobs. She was tall, perhaps five feet ten, without the vertiginous heels she had on. Slim, attractive, with an archetypal hourglass figure, her long hair was tied back elegantly with a bright red lace ribbon.

Sam offered his hand. 'Miss Jacobs?'

She reached across the desk and shook it. 'Mr Davison?'

'Yes.' Sam nodded towards Tommo. 'This is one of my associates,

Mr Thompson. Can I get you a drink?'

'No, I'm fine,' she said and eased into the seat Sam had indicated.

'So,' Sam said, 'what can I do for you?'

'Straight to the point. I like that. I need a gentleman locating.'

'Oh yes,' Sam said. 'Your husband?'

'No, no, nothing like that. I'm not married. The gentleman in question owes me a bit of money. I'm looking to find this man so I can recover what I'm owed.'

'I see,' he said, pretending to make notes on his pad. In reality, he was doodling Emily in bold capitals. 'What's his name?'

'Sidney Stankovich.'

'Sounds foreign?'

'Polish, I believe,' Jacobs said.

'And that's it?'

'That's it. If you locate Stankovich, I'd like you to tell me his whereabouts so I can pursue my claim.'

'We charge £150 a day, plus expenses.'

'If you can find Mr Stankovich, I'll pay you £5,000.'

Sam raised his eyebrows. 'He must owe you a lot of money?'

'Find him within a week, and I'll double it.' She took a card from her handbag and slid it across the desk. 'He's a local businessman, so, I'd start there.'

Sam rose from his seat. 'I'll see what I can do.' They shook hands, and then she sashayed from the room.

'You all right?' Tommo asked. 'Normally, when an attractive woman is anywhere in your vicinity, you're all over her. No flirting or suggestive remarks this time.'

'That name, Stankovich,' Sam said, rubbing his chin. 'It sounds familiar.' He leant back in his chair, deep in thought. Then, he jumped to his feet and hurried through to Kim's office. 'Kim,' he said, 'have you ever heard of someone called Sidney Stankovich?'

'Stankovich, yeah. He owns a nightclub in Middlesbrough. *Abandon*. Your uncle knew him.'

'My uncle knew him?'

'Bill was working for Stankovich, trying to find an Eagle.'

Sam frowned. 'A bird?'

'No. A statue made of some precious metal. Hold on, I'll have a look in Bill's notebook.' She opened the drawer and flicked through the pages of a book. '*The Romanov Eagle*. It was made for the Tsar of Russia. Worth a mint, apparently.'

'And did he find it?'

'No. Bill thought it was a wild goose chase, but Stankovich was paying him well, so he persisted.'

'The woman that was just here, Miss Jacob's, have you seen her before?'

'Never.' She flicked through the book again. 'There's a note here,' she said, showing it to Sam. Below Eagle, Hockney had written three names.

Sam studied the book. His uncle had written Anne Jacobs, Rupert Green and Sidney Stankovich. There was a question mark next to the names. Below this, he'd written EAGLE.

'Rupert Green?' Sam said.

Kim tapped her chin with a finger. 'I remember him. An enormous fat bloke, with a funny-looking guy, called Sleen.'

'Sleen?'

'Yes. Your uncle was working for him, too.'

'Doing what?'

'I don't know.' Kim shrugged. 'Bill used to keep most of his business to himself. To be honest, I wasn't all that interested in what he was doing.'

'You don't have a number for this Green?' Sam said.

'It may be in one of Bill's diaries.'

'Thanks,' Sam said and returned to his office.

Tommo tossed the magazine he'd been reading on Phillip's desk. 'I'm going to have to go. Do you want a lift?'

'No thanks, mate. I'm going to do a bit here. I'll jump in a taxi later.'

'Are you in the pub tonight?'

Sam opened a drawer, sifting through it. 'Maybe.'

Tommo had been gone about an hour when Kim popped her head through the door. 'I'm off home,' she said. 'I'll see you tomorrow.'

Sam stood. 'Kim. Where do you keep the information on the cases Bill was working on?'

'Most of it's in a filing cabinet in reception. I think bits and pieces are in the drawers inside your desk. Bill wasn't the most organised.'

'Any other stuff. Letters, that sort of thing?'

'I've opened the correspondence that looked like bills, but there are a couple of personal ones on my desk. I meant to give them to you or one of the others. I didn't think it was my place to open them.'

'Thanks,' Sam said. 'I'll see you tomorrow.'

Sam collected the letters from Kim's desk and returned to his own. There were three. He opened the first. It was a letter from a friend of Bill's who lived in Australia. Clearly, they'd been friends for some years, judging by its tone. Sam put it aside, making a mental note to get in touch with the letter-writer and give him the sad news. The second was junk mail, disguised as a personal letter, which he threw in the bin. Sam picked up the third, a printed label with the address of the Detective agency stuck on the front of the envelope. He tore it open and pulled out a card. A key dropped onto his desk. Who sends a postcard in an envelope? Sam thought. And what was the key for? The postcard looked old. It had a picture of a tulip field on the front, and on the reverse, it said, OUR LADY NO 346. Strange, he thought. What did that mean? There was something else. On the corner of the postcard was a red fingerprint, and as he studied the card, it dawned on Sam that it could be blood. Opening the drawer, he placed it inside, along with the key. He would speak with Kim tomorrow, he mused. Maybe she could shed some light on it. Sam pulled out his mobile and checked to see if Emily had been in touch. She hadn't. He sighed to himself and headed off to get a taxi.

**2015** – Bill Hockney pulled the car up outside the house, checked the address in his notebook, straightened the regimental tie he was wearing – the one he'd obtained especially for the occasion, picked up his leather bag and climbed out. Walking up the path to the house, he stopped outside, knocked on the door, and waited for someone to answer.

Hockney was sitting in the small conservatory looking out into the garden when a man entered carrying two cups. He placed one next to Hockney and sat opposite him with the other.
Hockney nodded outside. 'Beautiful garden you have, Mr Brady. Very colourful.'
'Thanks. It's my wife's domain, though. I can't take any credit for it. Except sitting in it on a sunny day.'
Hockney turned to face Brady. He picked up his tea and took a sip.
Brady put down his cup. 'So how can I help you, Mr Hockney? You mentioned a relation of mine.'
'Call me Bill.' Hockney said, placing his own cup down. 'Like I told you on the phone. I'm writing about the history of the Yorkshire Rifles. It's a subject close to my heart. Both my father and I were in them.' He pointed to the crest on his tie.
'This regiment,' Brady said. 'It's the one my Great-Uncle Arthur was in?'
'Yes, it is. At the moment, I'm covering their history from 1943 to 1945.'
'The Second World War?'
Hockney took another sip of tea. 'That's right. Have you heard of Market Garden?' Brady shook his head. 'Market Garden was an operation thought up by General Montgomery,' Hockney continued. 'A bold idea to drop troops behind the German lines and seize some strategic bridges, thereby giving the allies a great opportunity to shorten the war.'

'Now you mention it, it does ring a bell. Didn't they make a film of it?'

'Yes, they did. It was called *A Bridge Too Far*. Unfortunately, the plan failed.'

'Was my uncle involved in this?'

'No,' Hockney said. 'After its failure, the allies had to make their way across Holland the traditional way – village by village, town by town. This is where the Yorkshire Rifles came in. Your uncle was involved in this fighting.'

'Didn't he die in Holland?'

'He did.' Hockney took a piece of paper from his leather bag and handed it to Brady. 'This is a photocopy of the official records. Your uncle was killed when a shell from a Tiger tank hit a house that he and some of his Platoon were sheltering in.'

Brady took the paper from Hockney. 'Terrible.'

'Brave lads,' Hockney said.

'So, you're looking for any bits and pieces relating to that time?'

'That's right.' Hockney sat up straight and adjusted his tie. 'Histories are much better when they include real stories. Names and faces, etc.'

'I may be able to help there.' Brady stood up. 'My sister was doing one of those family trees a while back, and she put some things in a box.'

'I'm grateful for this, Mr Brady. Some people don't like to discuss these things.'

'I don't mind. A guy a while back asked about my uncle,' he said as he headed into the hall.

'Oh, yes?' Hockney said.

Brady ducked into the cupboard under the stairs. 'Yes. I didn't like him at all. He was creepy. Here we are,' Brady said, holding an old box. He backed out of the small space.

'Creepy?'

'He offered me money for information. There was something I didn't like about him.'

Hockney raised his eyebrows. 'Money?'

Brady stopped with the box in his hands. 'Yes. Why would you offer money to a complete stranger? I didn't want paying or anything.'

'Of course not,' Hockney said. 'What did he want?'

'He said he would buy any of Arthur's things. Said he was a collector.'

'How odd?' Hockney said.

'That's what I thought.' He put the box on the table and removed the lid.

'I have heard of shady characters worming their way into people's houses,' Hockney said. 'Conning people out of medals and such like. Bloody vultures.'

'Indeed,' Brady said. He held a finger up. 'Williamson. That was his name. I only remember because my wife's maiden name is Williams.'

'Williamson?' Hockney rubbed his chin. 'I'll have to watch out for him, in case any of the other people I have to see run into him.'

'Hector. His first name was Hector.'

'Hector Williamson,' Hockney said.

Brady emptied the contents of the box onto the table, scattering the assorted bits about.

Hockney picked up one of the documents. 'Would I be able to photocopy these?'

'Not a problem,' Brady said, smiling. 'I've got one in my office next door. I work from home, you see.'

'Super,' Hockney said.

Hockney shook hands with Brady at the door's threshold, thanked him for his help, and got into his car with his leather bag tucked under his arm. He fished inside his jacket pocket and pulled out a postcard, its corners crumpled with age. Written on the back in capitals, *OUR LADY 346*. He had noticed it on the floor when Brady had gone to photocopy the documents. It must have fallen from the box, Hockney reasoned. He looked back across at the house and shook his head. Hockney smiled to himself, pulled an envelope from his folder, and deposited the postcard inside it. Folding the envelope in half, he slipped it into his pocket.

# CHAPTER EIGHT

Tommo was in his bar serving a customer when Albert ambled in, dressed in a pair of stylish jeans, lilac shirt, dark-blue velvet blazer and finished off with a pair of oxblood brogues.
Albert reached the counter, and Tommo smiled. 'Smart,' Tommo said.

Maria stepped from behind the bar and, stopping next to Albert, ran her hand the length of his arm. 'Wow, you scrub up well, Albert. I love velvet.'

'Put him down,' Tommo said. 'What can I get you, Albi?'

'I don't know. I don't drink much. I usually have a small port at New Year's. Just to see it in.'

'God, you're a party animal. What about a pint of one of my fine ales?'

'I'm not sure.'

Tommo pulled a small amount into a short glass and handed it to Albert. He took a sip and pulled a face.

'Don't you like it?' Maria asked.

'It's a little bitter,' Albert said.

Tommo leant across the bar. 'The thing is, Albert, real ale drinking is about acquiring a taste. Everyone dislikes it the first time. Try this one,' he said, pulling another sample before placing it on the counter.

Albert tentatively tried it, his face not as contorted as before. 'That's a little better.'

Tommo nodded, putting another sample into a glass. 'IPA. India Pale Ale. We've narrowed it down a little. Try this one,' he said handing him another drink. 'This one's a little fruitier.'

Albert tasted the third drink, looked up at Tommo and smiled. 'I quite like this one,' he said, and Tommo pulled him a full pint.

'So,' Maria said. 'Where did you get those threads?'

'Tommo kindly helped me out. We went shopping the other day, and I bought these along with some others. My clothes were a little dated if I'm honest.'

'Well, who'd have thought that Tommo was such a fashionista,' Maria said as she stroked Albert's arm again.

Albert was on his third pint of IPA when Sam wandered in. He waited for Sam to reach the bar and then threw his arm around him. 'Here he is, my partner.'

Sam looked at Tommo, who smiled and shrugged.

Albert patted Sam on his back. 'Let me buy you a pint, Sam.'

'Yeah, all right,' Sam said.

'Tommo, my good man. Get Sam one, will you? I'll have another, too. One for yourself and the lovely Maria as well. I'm in the chair.' He hiccupped.

'You want to go easy,' Tommo said. 'You're not used to drinking.'

'Nonsense.' He chuckled. 'To think I've missed out on all this fun. Where have you been all my life?' he said to his glass of beer as Tommo shook his head.

'Wait until you get your first hangover,' Sam said. 'You won't be so cocky then.'

'Where's that delightful and attractive female friend of yours?' Albert asked. 'Emily, isn't it?'

'So, Albert,' Tommo said. 'We're on for Saturday? You haven't forgotten about it, have you?'

Albert took a large swig of his drink. 'Yes, we're still on. Wouldn't miss it for the world ...' He frowned. 'What is it we're doing again?'

'Going to the match.'

'Of course,' Albert said. 'We're going to a game,' he said, patting Sam on his back again.

Sam smiled. 'Football? Somehow, I can't see you at a football match.'

'I'm taking Albert to the club shop first,' Tommo said. 'Get him kitted out with a top and scarf.'

Sam stepped back to view Albert fully. 'Good luck with that. You look smart, by the way, Albert.'

'Why don't you ever wear velvet,' Maria said to Sam. 'It's such a sexy fabric. The girls would love it.'

Tommo rolled his eyes. 'I don't think Sam needs any help in that department.'

Albert winked at Sam. 'A bit of a ladies' man are you? What's your secret?'

Sam exaggeratingly winked back at him. 'If I told you, it wouldn't be a secret.'

Albert tapped the side of his nose with a finger. 'Ah, I see. Trade secret, eh?'

Sam had a couple more before leaving the others. Albert had become increasingly inebriated during the evening, departing with Maria before midnight. Maria had promised Tommo that she would take him home in a taxi, and Tommo watched the unsteady Albert totter off, his arm draped around Maria's shoulders.

Albert woke, the persistent ringing of his front doorbell rousing him. He looked to the left and then to the right of him. Maria was on one side, and another woman, he couldn't remember her name, was on the other. He tried to bring it to mind, but the effort made his head ache more. Albert slid along the bed, not wanting to wake his two sleeping companions, and got out. He stood and, wobbling, grabbed onto the dresser for support. He took deep breaths as the doorbell sounded again. Albert gingerly descended the stairs, pulling on a monogrammed bathrobe and a pair of leather mules on his way. He opened the door to Tommo, who was smiling at him.

'Bloody hell,' Tommo said, looking Albert up and down. 'It's Hugh Hefner. Look at the state of you.' Tommo stepped inside carrying a plastic bag in his right hand as Albert turned and slowly headed into the kitchen, his gait adopting that of an elderly man. 'Well, at least you got home all right,' Tommo said. Albert waved his hand to get Tommo to lower his voice. 'You do the crime,' Tommo said. 'You have to do the time.' He held up a carrier. 'Hangover cure.' Tommo searched through the cupboards and, locating some paracetamols, handed them to Albert along with a glass of water. 'Take these,' Tommo said.

Albert slumped in a chair. 'I feel dreadful. I think I'm dying.'

'You're not. What you need is some food inside of you.'

Albert closed his eyes, the thought of eating utterly repulsive. 'Something greasy, like sausage and bacon,' continued Tommo, opening his carrier.

Albert stood and made a run for the downstairs toilet. Tommo smiled, put the kettle on, and paused when he heard footsteps on the stairs. He leaned back against a cupboard, interested to see who it was, as Maria and her friend Tina entered.

Tommo's jaw dropped open. 'Oh my God.' He stared at the pair of them. Maria's shocking pink hair had taken on a *dragged through a hedge backwards* look, and Tina's wasn't much better either. They both wore a large shirt, just about covering their briefs. 'What the hell happened here?' Tommo said. 'It's like I've stumbled into an orgy.'

'We went clubbing last night,' Maria said. 'God, Albert's an animal.' She looked at Tina, who nodded back at her.

'Clubbing?' Tommo said. 'I thought you were putting him in a taxi?'

'He wanted to go on somewhere else after we left the pub,' Maria said. 'So, we went clubbing.'

Tommo pointed towards the toilet. 'Have you seen the state he's in? He thinks he's dying.'

'That'll be the tequila slammers he was knocking back,' Tina said.

Tommo nodded his head upwards. 'You didn't ... did you?'

'No,' Maria said. 'He passed out as soon as we got him into bed.'

Tommo smiled and shook his head. 'You do know he's probably still a virgin.'

'No way,' Tina said. 'He's nearly forty.'

'Any breakfast going?' Maria asked. 'I'm starving.'

'You're opening the pub today,' Tommo said. 'You haven't forgotten that, have you?'

'I know, I know,' she said, getting up from her seat. 'I'll be all right once I get some food inside me.'

Tommo shook his head again. 'I'm not a bloody café.'

Maria sauntered across to him and kissed him on the cheek. 'Come on, Tommo. I love your breakfasts. You're a fabulous cook.'

Tina joined her friend and took hold of his arm. 'Yeah, Tommo. Show us your big fat sausage.'

Tommo rolled his eyes as Tina and Maria burst out laughing.

'Okay,' Tommo said. 'But you two owe me big-time.'

**2015** – Hockney pulled up outside a building above the ground-floor solicitors and looked up at an office. There was a sign in the window that read, *H. Williamson & Partner.* He got out and headed up the stairs. At the top was a black door with a sign like the one in the window, so Hockney tried the door. It was locked. He knocked rather optimistically and turned as the door behind him opened.

A man came out. 'There's no one in,' the man said.

'You don't know when he'll be back?' Hockney asked.

'Never.' The man closed his own door and locked it. 'He's dead.'

'Dead?'

'Yes. His body was fished out of the Tees. Police think it was suicide.'

'Right,' Hockney said. 'Did you know him well?'

'Not really. We were only on nodding terms.'

'What about his partner?' Hockney tapped the sign on the door. 'Is he about?'

The man slowly shook his head. 'I've never seen a partner.'

'Did he have any family, do you know?'

The man headed for the stairs and stopped at the top. 'Can't help you there.' He paused. 'Although, you could try The Lobster. I think he used to drink quite a lot in there. Someone might be able to help you.' The man disappeared down the stairs, and Hockney took one last look at the door and then left.

Hockney waited at the bar of The Lobster as the barman finished serving a customer and turned his attention to Hockney. 'What can I get you?' he asked Hockney.

'Pint of beer,' Hockney said. The barman pushed a glass under the tap and began pulling the pint. 'I'm looking for someone called Hector Williamson,' Hockney said, handing the barman a note. 'Take one for yourself.'

'Cheers,' the barman said. 'Hector Williamson … How well did you know him?'

'Know?'

'Yeah.' The barman raised his eyebrows. 'I'm sorry, but Hector died. It was an accident, although the police believe it was suicide.'

'Oh, I didn't know him at all. He did some work for a friend of mine, and I was hoping to put some more his way.'

'Archie's your best bet.' He nodded towards a man sitting in the corner reading a paper. 'They were drinking buddies.'

'Thanks.' Hockney picked up his pint and headed over to where the barman had indicated. He reached the man. 'Archie?'

'Who's asking?' the man said, hardly lifting his head.

'Bill Hockney.' Hockney offered his hand. 'I was looking for a friend of yours. Hector Williamson.'

'Hector?' Archie put aside his paper but ignored Hockney's outstretched hand.

'Sad news,' Hockney said. 'Tragic accident.'

'What makes you think it was an accident?' Archie said.

'That's what the barman told me.'

Archie leant in closer. 'Hector was murdered,' he whispered.

'Murdered?' Hockney feigned surprise. 'Who by?'

'No one knows.'

Hockney pointed at a seat next to Archie. 'Okay, if I …'

Archie nodded. 'He was working on a case,' Archie said. 'He told me about it, you see. He was trying to find a valuable statue or something. Hector thought it was a wild goose chase, though.'

'And you believe he was murdered because of it?'

'Last time I saw him,' Archie said, 'he was worried about something. He didn't say what, but I could tell.'

'Have you spoken to the police?' Hockney asked.

Archie scoffed. 'The police aren't interested. The coppers think it was suicide.'

'And you're certain it wasn't?'

'I am. I knew Hector well, and believe me, he wouldn't commit suicide.'

'But, how can you be sure?' Hockney asked.

'I can't.' He leant closer again. 'What was Hector doing in Middlesbrough at that time of the night?' he said as if the question was self-explanatory.

Hockney took a large drink from his pint. 'But the police must have a reason for thinking it was suicide.'

Archie laughed. 'Suicide, my arse. They said Hector had money problems. Hector always had money problems. It doesn't mean he killed himself. I've got money problems, and I'm not reaching for the razor. Hector had this saying, "Don't worry about what you owe, let them worry that wants it off you".'

'Shame,' Hockney said. 'Whether it was suicide or not.'

Archie narrowed his eyes. 'What did you want with him anyway?'

'I had some work for him, that's all.' Hockney finished his drink and nodded at Archie. 'Sorry again,' he said, put down his empty glass, and then left.

# CHAPTER NINE

Sam arrived at the office early, even before Kim. He put the kettle on, made himself a cup of tea, sat at his desk, and continued sifting through his uncle's paperwork. He'd been doing this for around half an hour when Kim arrived. She briefly popped her head into the office before taking a seat at her desk. Phillip appeared shortly after, accompanied by Baggage.

Kim moved from behind her desk, squatted next to the dog, and patted his head. 'Aw, who's this?'

'Baggage,' Phillip said.

'Baggage? What sort of name's that?'

'I found him on the streets and took him in. You know how much dogs need looking after? So, I thought Baggage would be a great name.'

'Fancy calling you that,' Kim said, kissing the dog on the head and rubbing his ears. 'He's a handsome chap.'

'I've had to bring him in today. My neighbour usually watches him, but she's away this week.'

'I'll look after him,' Kim said. 'Have you brought his drinking bowl?'

Phillip pulled a face. 'I didn't think.'

Kim cuddled Baggage. 'How silly is your dad?' she said as Baggage's tail wagged quickly. 'I'll find something for him.'

'Thanks,' Phillip said, heading into the office. He took off his coat and hung it up. 'Morning, Sam.'

Sam glanced up. 'Are you still working at the distribution depot?'

Phillip sat. 'No. I finished that. It was two guys stealing all the stuff. They were getting away with thousands. The owner was over the moon.'

'Well,' Sam said getting to his feet. 'I've been looking through some of Uncle Bill's post. What do you make of this?' He passed Phillip the postcard and the key.

'It's a postcard and quite an old one by the look of it. What's the key for?'

'It was inside an envelope. It came in the mail.' Sam frowned. 'Why would you send a postcard to yourself? I've no idea what the key opens. I've tried it all over the office, but I can't find anything that it fits.'

'How do you know he posted it to himself?'

Baggage wandered into the room and stopped to look at the pair of them.

Sam held up the envelope with the label and pulled out printed labels from his desk drawer, showing them to Phillip. 'I found these in the drawer of Bill's desk. For some reason, it looks like he posted it to himself.'

'Someone else could have posted it. Maybe Bill gave them one of the envelopes.'

'Possibly.' Baggage nudged Sam's hand. 'What do you think, Bagsy?' Baggage cocked his head to one side and wagged his tail slowly as if he were deep in thought.

'It's no good asking Baggage,' Phillip said. 'I don't think there's any Bloodhound in him. A bit of Labrador, Alsatian, maybe even Boxer, but definitely no Bloodhound.'

'Can you see the blood on the back?' Sam said. 'Bill was stabbed to death in Middlesbrough. Remember?'

'Yeah. It's possibly blood. But it still doesn't prove conclusively that he posted it. Now, if we could get it tested …'

'True, but if Bill didn't post it, though, why would someone send it inside an envelope without a covering letter? Surely there would be a note?'

'Maybe Bill knew about it and might have been expecting it. It's probably just another case he was working on.'

Sam sat. "I'm still not convinced.'

'Should we involve the police?' Phillip said. 'It may be evidence.'

'You're joking,' Sam said, holding the envelope up to the light. 'We're a detective agency and Bill was our uncle. I think we should solve this case.'

'It's not a lot to go on.'

'Maybe,' Sam said. 'But we're just starting.'

Baggage, satisfied nothing exciting was happening, headed back towards reception and Kim.

**2015** – Hockney entered the small bistro and stopped at a wooden sign with, *please wait to be seated*, written across it. A waiter instantly moved over to him from behind a desk.

'Good afternoon,' the waiter said.

'I'm meeting someone here. Mr Stankovich.'

'Ah, yes. If you'd like to come this way,' the waiter said, and Hockney followed him across the restaurant.

Stankovich rose from his seat and offered his hand. 'Bill,' he said smiling. 'Take a seat. How about a drink?'

Hockney looked at the waiter. 'Whisky and ice, please.' The waiter jotted down his drink order, nodded politely, and left them to it.

The two men chatted pleasantly about nothing in particular while eating their starters.

Mid-way through their main course, Stankovich leant forward towards Hockney. 'Any progress on the Eagle?'

'A little,' Hockney said.

Stankovich raised his eyebrows. 'Oh, yes?'

'I managed to speak to a relation of Arthur Parchester. He allowed me to look through some of Parchester's bits and pieces.'

'You've got a lead on where the Eagle is?'

Hockney smiled. 'Life's never that simple.'

Stankovich laughed. 'I didn't think it would be.'

'There are a few other names to check out. Mates from Parchester's regiment. People he was close to.'

'And you think ...?'

'Possibly one of these men helped Parchester to get the statue across to England. Maybe they would know what happened to it when it reached these shores.'

'Have you a name?' Stankovich said.

'I haven't narrowed it down yet. I'll keep you informed.'

'Great. Anything else?'

'Parchester's relation mentioned Hector Williamson. He was a private detective like me. He said Williamson was trying to buy Parchester's belongings from him.'

Stankovich pushed his food around the plate. 'Yes?'

'I thought you might know something about him. He's dead, you see.' Hockney sipped his drink and stared at Stankovich.

Stankovich met Hockney's gaze. 'Really? Dead, you say?'

'Possibly murdered.'

'Murdered?' Stankovich sipped his drink.

'The police fished him from the Tees.'

'I hope you don't think I had anything to do with it?' Stankovich said.

'Not at all. But you did say there are other interested parties. Maybe they did.'

'Possibly.' Stankovich drained his glass and motioned to the waiter, who nodded and headed to the bar. 'I'm paying you a lot of money to find this Eagle, Bill. You can't expect to make that amount of money without a risk being attached. It's very valuable. Some people may be prepared ... well, let's just say, to go to any lengths.'

'No. I suppose not,' Hockney pushed the remnants of his lunch aside and stood.

'No dessert?' Stankovich asked.

'Watching my waistline. I'll keep you informed.' Hockney emptied his glass and left.

'You do that,' Stankovich said to himself.

As Hockney walked towards the door, Stankovich watched him leave. He put his hand into his pocket, took out his mobile and made a call. 'Follow Hockney,' he said into the phone. 'He's cleverer than I thought. He knows about Hector Williamson, so don't let him out of your sight. I want to know everywhere he goes and everyone he meets.'

Phillip and Sam had been sifting through the mountains of paperwork all morning, their desks strewn with letters and paper, some of which went back years.

Sam sighed. 'This is impossible. We're not even sure of what we're looking for.'

'What were you saying about this statue?' Phillip said.

'A bloke called Stankovich employed Bill to find it. Apparently, it's worth a mint. That's what Kim told me.'

'Maybe Bill found it? Maybe that's why he was murdered?'

Sam pondered. 'Possible, I suppose.'

'Did you say you were looking for some information on someone called Green?'

'Yes, why?'

Phillip tossed a small address book across to Sam, who quickly flicked through the pages, stopping about halfway through. The name Rupert Green and a telephone number next to it were written and underlined. Underneath this, the name Anne Jacobs and her number.

'Anne Jacobs,' Sam said to himself.

'Who?' Phillip said.

Sam tapped the book. 'Underneath Rupert Green is the name, Anne Jacobs.' Phillip shrugged, and Sam continued. 'Anne Jacobs was here yesterday. She wants me to find Stankovich.'

Phillip grabbed the notebook back and stared at the names. 'Bill was working for this Stankovich, and this woman wants you to locate him. There has to be a connection.'

Sam picked up a pen and rattled the end between his teeth. 'Yes, but what has this Green got to do with it as well? Why would Bill write both their names on the same page unless they were linked?'

Phillip nodded, slowly. 'We need to talk with this Green and find out what he knows. He might have info on how Bill was killed.'

'What do we say though?'

'We could make up some story about looking into Bill's cases,' Phillip said. 'Maybe hint that we're trying to find out who killed him.'

'Good idea,' Sam said, leaning back in his chair.

Kim walked in, followed by Baggage. 'Have you brought any food for him?' she said and patted the dog on the head.

'No,' Phillip said. 'I generally feed him at teatime.'

Kim frowned. 'He looks hungry to me.'

Phillip smiled. 'He always looks hungry.'

'I'm going to the shops, and I thought I might take him with me. Have you got his lead?'

Phillip picked it up, and Baggage, seeing it, padded across and took hold of it in his mouth before returning to Kim and dropping the lead at her feet.

'Kim,' Sam said. 'Have you seen this key before?' He handed it to her.

She examined it before returning it to him, shaking her head. 'No.'

'What about this postcard?' Sam said, holding it up.

'No. I haven't seen that either. Why?'

'It was in Bill's post,' Phillip said. 'Have a look on the back.'

Sam turned it around, and Kim studied it. 'Our Lady, 346. What does that mean?'

Sam shrugged. 'No idea.'

Kim dropped to her knees and rubbed Baggage's ears. 'Aren't you clever?' she said, clipping the lead on the dog's collar. She looked between them. 'Do you two want anything while I'm out?'

Sam pulled a note from his pocket. 'Can you get me a sandwich, please? I didn't have any breakfast.'

'I'm all right,' Phillip said.

Kim paused at the door. 'I remember Bill asking me to email him a picture of the Virgin Mary when he was away.'

Phillip and Sam glanced at each other and then at Kim. 'The Virgin Mary?' they said in unison.

'Our Lady is another name for The Virgin Mary, isn't it?'

'You're right,' Sam said. 'Where did you email it to?'

'He was staying at a place in Cumbria. I don't remember where exactly.'

'What was he doing there?' Sam said.

She shrugged. 'Something about a case. I'm not sure what.' Kim turned and headed off.

'What do you think?' Sam said.

Phillip was still staring at the door. 'I don't know,' he said. 'Why was Bill in Cumbria?'

Sam looked down at the papers again. 'We'll have to keep delving.'
Phillip nodded towards the door. 'She's attractive. Kim, I mean.'
'She is.' Sam looked up. 'Haven't you got a girlfriend then?'
Phillip closed his eyes and shook his head. 'No.'
Sam smiled and leaned back in his chair. 'I get the feeling there's a story?'
Phillip turned and looked directly at Sam. 'This time six months ago, I was living in one of those beautiful apartments in Stockton near the riverside. I had a well-paid job working for my girlfriend's dad. Nice car and all the trappings.'
'And?'
Phillip briefly looked upwards. 'And now I don't.'
Sam raised his eyebrows and put his feet on the desk. 'What happened? Come on. You can't tell me half a story.'
'She caught me in bed with her sister, Mandy.'
Sam blew out his cheeks. 'Ouch. That'll do it.'
'Karen, my girlfriend, went to work one morning when I was still in bed. The next thing I knew, someone was getting in next to me. I thought it was Karen. Well, before I realised it wasn't, she was on top of me. I should have pushed her off, but when you're that far gone …'
'Tell me about it. This sister, did she have the hots for you or something?'
'Mandy made it clear she fancied me, but I was having none of it. She looked like trouble if you know what I mean. I tried to keep her at arm's length.'
'I certainly do. I've met plenty like her in my lifetime. They don't know what they want, but they know how to get it.'
'That was Mandy in a nutshell,' Phillip said. 'When Karen told her dad about it, he fired me, took back the company car and threw me out of the flat.'
'Couldn't you have had him for unfair dismissal?' Sam said.
'He'd thought of that.' Phillip groaned. 'He made it look like I'd been stealing cash from the company and told me he'd go to the police if I made a fuss.'
'The twat.'
'So,' Phillip said, 'for the last few months, I've been living in a dingy bedsit with Baggage, eking out my savings.'
'Which is why you're keen to work here?'
'Exactly. Karen's dad put some rumours out about me as well. So, getting another job on Teesside was proving difficult.'
Sam rocked back in his chair. 'Lucky this came along then.'
Phillip nodded. 'What about you? Haven't you anyone?'
Sam sighed. 'No. I've tended to play the field.'
'You don't sound happy about it.'

Sam frowned. 'To be honest, I'm tired of that style of life. Every pub and every restaurant I go into, I seem to run into a woman I've slept with. I can't go on like that all my life. I'm thirty-five, for God's sake.'

'So, you're planning to settle down then?'

Sam rocked forward on his chair, planting his feet on the floor. 'Maybe, when I find the right woman.'

'There must be someone who you've really liked?'

'There was. There is.' He sighed. 'My sexual conquests are book-ended by the only two women I've ever …'

'Loved?' Phillip said.

Sam screwed up his face. 'Not sure about love.'

'Have they got names?' Phillip asked.

'Lisa. A long time ago.'

'And the other?'

Sam raised his eyebrows. 'Keep this to yourself. Emily.'

'Emily's … Isn't she?'

Sam rubbed his eyes. 'A lesbian. I don't do things easily.'

'Tricky. Does she know how you feel?'

'Not exactly.' Sam rolled his eyes. 'We slept together.'

Phillip leant back in his chair. 'Wow.'

'Now she won't speak to me. We were drunk, and it just happened. She went back to her mam's.' Sam waved an arm. 'Anyway, enough about me. What about you and Kim?'

'Me and Kim?'

'It's obvious she fancies you and that you fancy her.'

'Is it?'

Sam tapped the side of his nose with his finger. 'Take it from me. I know.'

Albert entered. 'Morning chaps,' he said, taking off his coat before sitting at his immaculately tidy desk. Despite this, he proceeded to straighten the few pieces of paper on top of it, then removed a red pen, which was mixed with some blue ones, and placed it in its rightful home with the other red pens. Phillip and Sam watched, and Albert continued to move this and that an inch or two. Satisfied, he smiled to himself.

'I see your therapy's paying off?' Sam said.

'What have you two been up to then?' Albert said, ignoring Sam's jibe.

'We may have a lead on a case Bill was working on,' Phillip said.

'It might have something to do with his murder,' Sam said.

Albert stared intently at the pair. 'Really?'

There was a knock on the outer office door, and Phillip got up to see who it was. 'Can I help you, gentlemen?' he said to the two men standing outside.

'Detective Inspector Comby, and this is my colleague, Detective

Sergeant Hardman.' He pointed to his partner as they presented their identifications to Phillip.

'You are?' Comby asked.

'Phillip Davison.' The two policemen wandered past him into the main office, and Phillip followed behind them.

'We're investigating the murder of William Hockney,' Comby said. 'We were hoping to speak with Miss Weatherly.'

'She's out,' Sam said, eyeing the officers.

'You are?' Comby asked.

'Sam Davison. Bill was our uncle.'

'I can't remember seeing you at his funeral,' Hardman said.

Albert straightened his paperwork, again. 'We didn't really know him.'

Comby looked at Albert. 'And you are?'

'Albert—'

'What's this about?' Sam said. 'Have you found out who murdered him?'

Hardman sauntered across to Sam's desk. 'We're still investigating.'

'We have a few leads to follow up,' Comby said. 'We were going to ask Miss Weatherly if she could give us any more information.'

'We were discussing that,' Albert said.

Sam deliberately pushed his cup from his desk and watched it smash on the floor. Phillip looked over at Sam, who looked across at Albert and placed a finger to his lips. Albert nodded his understanding.

Comby moved nearer to Albert. 'Oh yes?' he said, ignoring Sam, who was now picking up the pieces of broken china.

Albert shuffled in his chair. 'Err, well … I meant—'

Phillip coughed. 'What Albert means, Inspector, is, we were wondering if any progress had been made.'

Comby picked up a black pen from Albert's black pen holder and fingered the implement before placing it into the blue pen dispenser. 'I see. You haven't any information you would like to share with us?' He picked up a piece of paper and glanced at the letter.

'No,' Sam said. 'We'd tell you if we had.'

Comby put the paper back on the edge of the desk as Albert's eyes shifted nervously between the pens and the offending piece of paper. He snatched the paper up and put it back with his other paperwork before straightening the pile a quarter of an inch. Comby narrowed his eyes at Albert, who, oblivious to his audience, removed the black pen and placed it back with similar-coloured ones. He looked up, as everyone in the room stared at him. 'It's a little habit of mine,' Albert said, brushing some dust from the corner of his desk.

Comby looked first at Sam and then Phillip. 'You boys aren't thinking of running your own investigation, are you?'

'Of course not,' Phillip said.

Comby nodded slowly. 'Good.'

Albert removed a duster and began to polish his desk, cleaning the top of it as the two policemen looked at Albert again.

The Inspector took a card from his pocket and placed it in front of Albert. 'If you come by any information, please get in touch,' he said. Albert picked it up and put it inside a small plastic tray with other cards within it.

'We will,' Sam said.

Comby looked over at Hardman and then nodded towards the door. On their way out, Hardman glanced across at Albert as Albert nonchalantly polished the handles on his drawers.

The two policemen descended the stairs and marched outside. Hardman turned to his superior. 'What do you reckon, guv?'

'I think the little guy was going to tell us something. They may be holding out on us.'

'Weird little bugger,' Hardman said. 'All that tidying and cleaning. He's not right in the head.'

'Yes,' Comby said. 'We may have to pay him a visit at his home when the other two are not around and see what he knows.'

Hardman opened his notepad. 'I only got his first name—'

Comby stroked his chin. 'Albert? They must have the business registered. Find out his full name and where he lives.'

'Will do, guv,' he said, following Comby across the road and into the café.

## CHAPTER TEN

**2015** – Hockney glanced in his rear-view mirror at the car behind him, having been followed since he'd left the meeting with Stankovich. He wasn't sure if it was one of Stankovich's men, but he suspected it was, which meant Stankovich didn't trust him. Spotting his opportunity, when the lights turned red on a set of temporary traffic lights, Hockney accelerated, weaving his way past parked cars and turned into a side street. The car following was blocked by vehicles heading in the opposite direction, stopping its progress. Hockney sped on, putting distance between himself and the pursuer, turning down one street after another before pulling up inside an alleyway out of sight. He got out and headed off for his liaison.

Hockney entered the hotel, took out his mobile, and texted, 'I'm in reception.' A few seconds passed before he received a reply: 'Room 27'. Looking up at the sign above one of the corridors, he followed the directions to the room, tapped on the door, and waited. The door opened slightly as the occupant inside viewed him before opening it fully. Anne Jacobs beckoned him inside, and Hockney entered, closing the door behind them.

Hockney lay in bed next to Miss Jacobs – her face still flushed red from their sexual encounter. He propped himself on a pillow and looked at her as their breathing slowly returned to normal.
She slid onto her side, propping herself on her elbow. 'What have you found out?'

'Parchester had pals in his regiment. One of his friends is interesting.'

'Interesting?' She pushed herself closer, allowing her breasts to wrestle free from the constraints of the cotton sheet. 'In what way?'

'He came from Brotton, which isn't too far from where Parchester lived. They may even have known each other before being called up.'

'I see. Have we a name?'

Hockney smiled. 'I may have to keep that to myself until I know more.'

'Don't you trust me?' she said, moving her face closer to him – her long blonde wavy locks cascading across her face. Her full lips, devoid of the bright red lipstick she'd been wearing when he'd arrived, now only inches from his. She brushed her hair away, pushing it dismissively over the top of her head with her hand. 'I thought we had a rapport.'

'In my game,' he said. 'It doesn't do to trust anyone. Trust is earned and shouldn't be expected.'

She laughed. 'Quite right, too.' Pressing her lips to his, she slipped her hand beneath the sheets towards his groin. 'Looks like you're ready to go again.'

'Whenever you are,' Hockney said.

Hockney exited the hotel and made his way on foot back towards where he'd left his car, but then remembered the champagne he'd consumed in Miss Jacobs' room. He stepped onto the high street and flagged a passing taxi, giving the driver directions back to his office. Sitting back in the seat, he pondered. Miss Jacobs was intriguing, he thought. She was obviously playing him. They had discussed the possibility of finding the Eagle and sharing the money between them if he did. He had to admit it was tempting. Offering him money was one thing but seducing him to get the statue was altogether different. Maybe she did genuinely find him attractive. Smiling to himself he realised that even if that were true, could he actually trust her. Stankovich was troubling, too. He would have to play his cards close to his chest with them both. Keep Stankovich dangling for as long as possible while enjoying himself with the lovely Miss Jacobs. The only other mystery was the fat man, Green. He'd already been in touch asking for an update on his search for the Eagle, and Hockney needed to know a little more about him and his companion, Sleen. He rubbed his chin, deep in thought. There was just a little bit too much for him to do on his own. Reluctantly, he decided to enlist some help – another pair of legs would come in useful.

He leant forward and placed his hand on the driver's shoulder. 'Change of plan, mate. Can you drop me off at *The King William* in Dormanstown?'

The driver sucked in air. 'Are you sure? You need an armed guard to go in there.'

'I'll be okay. I know the landlord.'

Hockney entered the sparsely populated pub as the barman behind the counter, lifted his head from his paper to view Hockney with a mixture of friendliness and suspicion.

The barman put aside his paper. 'What can I get you, mate?'

Hockney leant on the bar and nodded towards the pumps. 'Pint of Smiths and a double Bells.'

The barman collected the drinks and placed them on the counter as Hockney handed him a crisp twenty-pound note. 'Keep the change.' Picking up the glasses, he headed away from the bar and over to a middle-aged, grey-haired, unshaven man sitting at a table reading a paper.

The man didn't move as Hockney approached. 'Bill,' he said, not even bothering to look up at Hockney.

Hockney nodded towards the betting slips on the table. 'How are the horses treating you, Rocco?'

The man folded his newspaper and put it aside. 'Lots of luck, just the wrong type.'

'I've got some work for you,' Hockney said. 'Make that ten-pence Round Robin you're picking out into a ten-pound Yankee.'

'Dodgy, is it?' Rocco said.

Hockney sat opposite, pushing the whisky across to Rocco. 'Not really. I need a bit of information about someone.'

'Oh yeah?'

'I want you to follow him and see who he meets, where he goes, that sort of thing.'

Rocco raised his eyebrows. 'How much?'

Hockney put his hand inside his jacket pocket and pulled out his wallet. He took five twenty-pound notes from it and slid them across to Rocco. 'A ton now and the same when you've got something to tell me.'

Rocco moved to pick them up, and Hockney grabbed his arm. 'I want this keeping between us, Rocco. Understand?'

'You know me, Bill, I'm the soul of discretion.'

Hockney slid the pint across the table towards Rocco., reached into his jacket pocket again and took out a pen, writing the name *Rupert Green* on a betting slip. 'He's staying at that posh country hotel near Yarm. Wainston Hall.' He tossed the pen onto the table. 'Keep the pen. It might change your luck.'

Rocco picked it up, fingering it as he smiled. 'Thanks.' He looked up at Hockney. 'Still in the offices at Redcar?'

'I am,' Hockney said as he stood. 'End of the week?'

'End of the week, Bill,' Rocco said, depositing the notes and pen into his pocket. 'Scouts honour.'

Hockney jumped in another taxi and headed for his meeting with Rupert Green. He travelled up the A66 towards Middlesbrough before turning onto the A19 south. The driver took the exit for Crathorne and, heading for Yarm, pulled into Wainston Hall Country House Hotel, stopping outside the entrance. Hockney paid the driver and set off inside. He reached the reception and introduced himself before being shown into a small sitting room where Rupert Green was already seated at a table.

Green smiled. 'Bill, have a seat.'

He shook Green's hand and sat opposite. 'I could get used to this,' he said, looking around the opulent room.

'It's very nice,' Green said. 'I've stayed here on a couple of occasions when I've had business in the area.'

The waiter who had shown Hockney to his seat had remained next to the two men.

Green nodded towards the waiter. 'Drink?'

'Whisky with ice.' The waiter nodded and left.

Green sat back in his chair, resting his hands on his ample stomach. 'Well, Bill. What have you found out?'

'Parchester,' Hockney said, looking to elicit some response. Green nodded. Hockney raised his eyebrows. 'You obviously know of him?'

Green smiled. 'Yes, I'm aware of Mr Parchester.'

The waiter returned, placing a drink next to Hockney. 'Cards on the table,' Hockney said, picking up the glass. 'You know Stankovich quite well.'

Green took a sip from his glass. 'I do. He and I collaborated for a while. He's a distant relation of mine.'

'And Anne Jacobs?'

Green chuckled. 'My, you have been busy. Tell me, have you slept with her yet? I only ask because she's quite manipulative in that department.'

Hockney smiled inwardly. Years of perfecting his poker face in the police force allowed him to remain unfazed. 'You sound as though you're talking through experience.'

'Good God, no. Wrong sex, old boy. On the other hand, Stankovich has …' He allowed the words to reverberate.

Hockney drained his glass and placed it back down. 'Can I be candid?' He looked directly at Green, who nodded. 'I'm not bothered about these petty rivalries,' Hockney said. 'I'm only interested in making a living for myself.'

'Of course you are. What has Stankovich offered you?'

'Half a million.'

Green raised his eyebrows a little. 'I'm not interested in getting involved in a Dutch auction. I'm only interested in obtaining the Eagle.'

Hockney sat back in his chair and smiled. 'Isn't that what Stankovich and Miss Jacobs are after?'

'Ah, my dear friend, their pursuit is purely about greed. They want the Eagle for its worth. I want the Eagle for its beauty.'

'So?' The waiter placed another drink next to Hockney. 'What are you offering?'

'I will match what Stankovich offered.'

'Why wouldn't I sell it to Stankovich if I find it? You're both offering the same, and he made the offer first.'

Green smiled. 'My dear fellow, because Stankovich does not intend to pay you.'

'If that's true …' Hockney narrowed his eyes. 'Why should I trust you?'

'As I've said. I'm not bothered about the money. I want the Eagle for my collection. If it came up for sale tomorrow, I would buy it. Whatever the cost. Find the Eagle, and *I will* give you the money. You have my word.'

'What about Miss Jacobs?'

Green held up a finger and wagged it slowly. 'I wouldn't trust her either.' He lifted his glass to his lips and sipped before placing it back down. 'What does she know?'

'She initially employed me to find Stankovich but then asked me about the Eagle.'

'Hah!' Green said. 'A smokescreen. She and Stankovich are …' He paused for a moment. 'What's that lovely modern-day parlance? An item. I would be extremely careful of Miss Jacobs.'

'Why would they both employ me?'

Green chuckled. 'My dear fellow, one should cast one's net far and wide when out fishing.'

'I see.'

'What have you found out?' Green said.

'I've done some checking into Parchester's regiment. At the moment, I'm looking into the possibility that someone else smuggled the Eagle from Holland across to England for him.'

Green nodded. 'I see. Do you have a name?'

'Not yet. As you can imagine, this was a long time ago.'

'Yes, I understand that, but it's an excellent start.' Hockney drained his second glass. 'Another?' Green asked.

Hockney stood. 'No thanks.'

'When do you expect to know more?'

'A week, maybe.'

Green smiled. 'Good.'

'I may need a little more money. For expenses.'

'Absolutely.' Green turned and waved over to Sleen, who had silently appeared in the doorway. Green whispered something into Sleen's ear, and he disappeared. 'Sleen has gone to get you some money. Can I offer you a lift home?'

'No, that's fine. I'll take a taxi.'

Green smiled again. 'I can see that you don't trust me either.'

'I don't trust anyone.'

Sleen arrived back, pulled an envelope from his inside pocket and handed it to Green. 'There's £2,000 in here,' Green said. 'Let me know if you need more,' he said handing Hockney the envelope.

Hockney deposited it into his jacket pocket. 'Thank you,' he said, offering his hand to Green who shook it firmly.

'One week,' Green said. Hockney nodded and then left.

Hockney waited outside the hotel for the taxi to arrive and was deep in thought when the bright red car pulled up. A man got out of the passenger seat and approached him.

'Get in,' he said, thrusting the barrel of the gun into Hockney's side, his accent thick Eastern European. Hockney complied, getting into the rear seat behind the driver, and looked across at the gunman, whose eyes were obscured by the dark sunglasses he wore – his face a collection of small scars and his nose bent to one side. He reminded Hockney of a retired boxer with a record of his fight career writ large across his features.

'What's this about?' Hockney said.

'Shut up,' the man said. 'Keep your mouth closed, and I won't have to smash that face of yours.'

# CHAPTER ELEVEN

Phillip and Sam were sitting quietly in the office when Tommo marched in, closely followed by Albert. They looked up from their desks and stared at Albert. He was wearing a coat with a Middlesbrough crest on the front, and beneath this, he had on a Middlesbrough top. On his head was a Boro bobble hat, and around his neck, a scarf.

Albert grinned and sat behind his desk, putting his plastic carrier on top. 'We've been shopping. Tommo's going to take me to a match.'

Phillip slowly shook his head. 'You're a marketing man's dream, Albert.'

Sam rocked back in his chair, placing his hands behind his head. 'Who are you supporting, then?'

Albert beamed. 'The Boro.'

'Ignore him,' Tommo said. 'He's yanking your chain,'

'We've been busy while you two have been shopping,' Sam said.

Tommo slumped into a chair. 'Oh yeah?'

Sam winked at Tommo. 'We think we might have a lead on Bill's murder. Who needs the police?'

Albert put his hand in his bag and pulled out a Boro bedside clock. 'Look what I've got.'

'What the hell do you want a Boro clock for?' Phillip asked.

Albert held it up for everyone to see. 'To tell the time. I'm going to put it next to my bed.'

Sam rolled his eyes. 'You haven't got a duvet cover and matching pillowcases as well, have you?'

Tommo laughed, looking up at the ceiling. 'No. I managed to drag him out before he bought one of those.'

Sam closed his eyes and shook his head. 'You need to get that OCD under control. I thought you were getting better. You'll end up in the poor house.'

Tommo stared wide-eyed at Sam. 'There's a poor house?'

Albert paused before continuing to empty the contents of the bag. 'I'm going to see my counsellor tomorrow. Miss Waltham's pleased with my progress.'

Sam sat forward and banged his hand on the desk. 'Anyway, like I said. 'We may have a lead on Bill's murder.'

Albert, now holding a Middlesbrough tankard in his hand, looked over. 'You have?'

Phillip held up a book. 'We found a notebook of Bill's with a list of names. Underneath these, he'd written *Eagle*.'

'Who's on this list?' Albert asked.

'Sidney Stankovich, Rupert Green and Anne Jacobs,' Sam said.

Albert put his hand back into the bag and looked at Sam. 'You've met Miss Jacobs?'

'Yes, the other day. Tommo met her as well.' Tommo nodded.

'These other people,' Albert said, arranging his Middlesbrough merchandise neatly on his desk. 'How are they related?'

'Kim told me that Bill was employed by Stankovich to locate a statue of an Eagle,' Sam said. 'Apparently, it's worth a lot of money.'

Tommo rubbed his beard. 'Did Bill find this Eagle?'

'We don't know,' Sam said. 'But if he did, why has Miss Jacobs employed me to find Stankovich?'

Albert opened the diary on the top of his desk and studied one of the pages. 'I thought I knew the name,' he said. 'Rupert Green phoned me yesterday and asked me to meet him tomorrow. He said he may have some work.'

'Where does he want to meet?' Sam asked.

'Wainston Hall, near Yarm.'

Tommo sat back in his chair and held out his hands. 'Well, I think it's pretty obvious. Either Stankovich has the Eagle, or none of them has it.'

'I did some checking on Stankovich,' Sam said. 'He's out of the country. On business.'

Albert took off his bobble hat. 'Maybe Bill found it and wouldn't give it up. That might be why he was murdered?'

Sam looked across at Phillip. 'Yes. That's what we thought.'

'We'll be rich if we find it,' Phillip said. 'It's worth a fortune.'

Tommo rubbed his hands together. 'What's our plan?'

'You're not even in this detective agency,' Sam said.

Tommo smashed his right fist into the palm of his left hand, grimacing as he did so. 'I'll be your muscle. I mean, look at you three. You'll run a mile if there's any trouble.'

'He has a point,' Phillip said.

Albert picked up his alarm clock, adjusting the time to match the clock on the office wall. 'I vote Tommo's in.'

'Okay, big fella,' Sam said. 'You can look after Albert when he meets up with Rupert Green, to make sure he doesn't come to any harm.'

Albert pulled a Middlesbrough pencil case from his bag, pausing with it mid-air. 'Wait a minute, I'm not overly keen on meeting Green. He may be the one who killed Bill.'

'Killed Bill,' Tommo said. 'Great title for a film.'

Sam ignored Tommo and looked at Albert. 'You'll have to meet up with Green if we want to crack this case. He might have some valuable information.'

'He's expecting to meet you,' Phillip said.

Albert paused with his Middlesbrough mug in his hand. His eyes were drawn towards Baggage, who padded his way into the office, wandered over to Albert and sniffed at his leg. Albert recoiled. 'Oh, my God. It's a dog.'

'It's only Baggage,' Phillip said. 'He won't bite.'

Albert shrunk back further as Baggage neared. 'I've got a phobia of dogs. I've had it since I was a child.'

Sam rolled his eyes. 'Now there's a surprise.'

Baggage walked over to Tommo, who rubbed his ears. 'He's a big softy.'

Kim entered carrying a plastic bag. 'Bloody hell,' she said. 'It's a full house.'

'Kim,' Sam said. 'You told me yesterday that Bill met with someone called Rupert Green?'

'Yes, he did,' she said. 'A big, fat bloke. He had a funny sidekick with him. A little fella with goggle eyes.'

'And you don't know what job Bill was doing for him?' Sam said.

Kim dropped to her knees as Baggage padded over and sat next to her. 'I have no idea.' She rubbed Baggage's ears, kissing him on the head. 'Who's a lovely boy?'

Sam looked around at the others. 'So, it could have been about the Eagle.'

Kim stood, staring at the four of them in turn. 'Right. Who wants a cuppa?'

'I'll have one,' Phillip and Sam said in unison.

'I'll have to go,' Tommo said. 'Don't forget we're going to the match tomorrow, Albert. I'll nip down later and get you your ticket.'

'Albert can borrow mine,' Sam said. 'I'm not in the mood for football. I've more important matters.'

Albert grinned. 'Thanks, Sam.'

'I'll drop it off at Tommo's in the morning.'

Albert stood and followed Kim as she left. 'Kim,' he said. 'Can you make me a cup of—'

'I know, Albert,' Kim said. 'Your special tea.'

'You will brew it for—'

'Yes, Albert. I'll bloody time it.'

'Why don't you lend her your clock!' Sam shouted.

Albert returned and picked up his new Middlesbrough mug before racing after Kim. 'Kim? Can you make it in my new mug? You will need to wash it thoroughly first,' he continued as Phillip and Sam shook their heads.

'Albert!' Kim said. 'If you don't get out of here, I'll set Baggage on you.'

Albert came scurrying back, sat at his desk, and continued to empty the contents of the bag.

**The Next Morning** – Albert sat in a chair in the office of Miss Waltham, his therapist, staring casually outside, watching a man mow the lawn in front of the building. The smell of newly mown grass drifted up through the room's open window, transporting him back to his school days. Not a happy time, he mused. His attention was drawn away from this, and he turned to face the door as Miss Waltham entered – mid-forties, with long brown hair tied up sternly in a bun. She wore a grey, nondescript skirt and matching jacket over a cream blouse – her minimal makeup gave an air of someone who was trying to appear plain but not unattractive. She sat opposite Albert and smiled. Albert beamed back. The way a schoolboy might look at the object of his affection across a classroom.

Miss Waltham popped on a pair of glasses and looked at him. 'Sorry about that. Where were we?'

'I was telling you about the case we're working on.'

'That's right. Your uncle. The one who was murdered.'

Albert lowered his eyebrows. 'Uncle Bill. Sam thinks he's found a clue.'

Miss Waltham peered over her glasses. 'Sam is the one who's a bit of a ladies' man?'

'Yes. Tommo said he's had more sexual conquests than Soft Mick.'

She frowned. 'Who's Soft Mick?'

'I'm not sure, but Tommo's mentioned him a few times.'

'How are you coping at the moment? Now that you're getting out and about more.'

Albert smiled. 'Well, I've managed to get my morning showers down to two now.'

Miss Waltham flicked through her file, searching her notes. 'Well done. And it was—'

'Seven,' Albert said.

'My God. Your water bill must have been enormous.'

Albert laughed. He liked Miss Waltham. She was charming and not at all like the stern Mr Billings, his previous therapist. He gazed at her lovingly as she pushed her glasses back up the bridge of her nose.

'That's a vast improvement,' she said. 'We need to keep working on that. What about other aspects of your OCD?'

'I'm not as bad when locking the house up. It used to take me an hour.'

'And now?'

Albert smiled again. 'About half that.'

'Are you still using the technique we discussed last time?'

'Yes,' he said. 'Every time I feel the urge to repeat things, I close my eyes and count to five. I get some funny looks from people, though.'

She smiled. 'That's unimportant. It's vital that you continue to make progress. Tell me more about the people you've got to know since you've ventured into the wide world?'

'They're lovely. Tommo's my favourite. We're going to a football match later today. It'll be my first time.'

'Splendid. And which team will you be supporting?'

'The Boro. Tommo said *you should support your local team.* I was born in Middlesbrough, so they should be my team. He's quite vehement on that. He hates glory supporters.'

Miss Waltham looked up from her notes. 'Glory supporters?'

'People who support a team because they're already successful. The team, not the person. Tommo hates people like that. He calls them …' Albert shifted in his seat and lowered his voice to a whisper. 'A bunch of twats.'

'My, he sounds like a colourful chap.'

'He is. Oh,' Albert said, 'I had my first drink last week. Well, my first real drink.'

'Really?'

Albert blushed. 'I'm embarrassed to say I got rather drunk.' He considered mentioning the two women he'd woken up with but thought better of it.

'How did it make you feel, drinking? How did it affect your OCD?'

'That's the funny thing. After I'd had a couple of drinks, I forgot about it. It suddenly seemed unimportant, and I didn't feel anxious at all.'

Miss Waltham took off her glasses and put one of the arms in her mouth, tapping it between her teeth before putting them back on. 'Well, that tells me the root cause of your OCD is inhibitions. Alcohol is a well-known disinhibitor. I can't condone excessive drinking, though, as we don't want to remove one problem and replace it with another. Maybe the odd glass of wine wouldn't hurt.'

'I haven't tried wine. I'm an IPA man.'

'Beer?'

Albert sat up straight. 'Tommo says *real men are beer drinkers*.'

'Did he really? What's he like, this Tommo?'

'Huge. Like a big Bear.'

Miss Waltham rubbed the length of her pen between her index finger and thumb. 'Really.'

'That's what Emily calls him.'

'Who's Emily? Tommo's girlfriend?'

'No.' Albert said. 'Emily lives with Sam.'

'Sam's girlfriend?'

'Erm, no. Emily's …' Albert paused, lowering his voice again. 'Emily's a lesbian.'

'Really. What interesting people you know.'

'She's moved back in with her mum at the moment. I think Sam and Emily have had some disagreement.'

Miss Waltham nodded. 'What about your relationships with the opposite sex? Any movement on that front?'

Albert blushed again. 'I've got my eye on someone.'

'Oh, and has she a name, this potential paramour? I'd like to hear about her.'

'I'd rather not say … until …'

'I understand.' She patted him on his knee. 'Maybe another time. When it's progressed a little.' She glanced at the clock on the wall. 'Well, it appears our time's up.'

Albert looked at the clock. 'It's flown by,' he said and got to his feet. 'Before I forget.' Albert opened his carrier bag. 'I've got you these,' he said, handing Miss Waltham an expensive-looking box of chocolates.

'Oh, Albert. My favourite. Thank you so much.'

'Same time next week … Vanessa?'

Miss Waltham closed her notebook and picked up another book. 'Yes. I'll put it in my diary.'

Albert stood smiling and then left. With the heady smell of Miss Waltham's perfume filling his nostrils, he bounded downstairs and outside to the waiting Tommo.

Miss Waltham stared at the two of them from her upstairs office window. She removed her glasses, putting the end of one of the arms in her mouth again. 'A big bear indeed.'

Tommo turned the car into the grounds of Wainston Hall, located a parking space and pulled into it. He looked across at Albert, who'd hardly spoken during the journey. 'You all right, Albi?'

Albert smiled. '… Yes. I was thinking about Miss Waltham and my session this morning.'

'Your therapist?'

'Indeed. You're a man of the world, Tommo. How does one go about …?'

'You fancy her?' Tommo said.

'Well … yes.'

Tommo put a hand on Albert's shoulder. 'Albert, I'm not sure that's going to work. That sort of thing is frowned upon. Patients and their therapists.'

Albert's smile evaporated. 'Oh.'

'Listen. Maybe when you've got your OCD thoroughly beaten, you could ask her out.'

'Yes, I see. That's another reason for me to overcome my problem.'

Tommo tapped Albert on the knee. 'It certainly is. More pressing matters, old boy.' Tommo said, adopting a cultured voice.

'Mr Green?' Albert said.

'Are you okay with this?'

'I'm not sure. Green could be the one who killed Uncle Bill. Maybe he'll kill me.'

'Don't be daft, Albert. He's never even met you. Why would he want to kill you?'

Albert frowned. 'I don't know. I'm foolish, aren't I?'

'I'll be there with you outside the dining room. Any problems, shout for me, and I'll come running. I'll smash a few heads,' he said, pounding a fist into the palm of his left hand.

Albert put his hand inside his blazer pocket and pulled out a hip flask.

'What the hell's that?' Tommo asked.

'It was my dad's. I thought a little Dutch courage wouldn't go amiss.'

Tommo took the hip flask from him and opened it. He sniffed at the top, frowning quizzically at the strange smell. 'What is it?' he said, handing it back to Albert.

Albert took a swig. 'Port.'

'Port?'

'It's all I had in the house.'

Tommo shook his head and smiled. 'Okay, Keith Richards. Fill your boots.'

Albert took another large swig and then returned the hip flask to his pocket.

'Ready?' Tommo asked. Albert nodded, and the two of them got out of the car and headed inside.

Phillip sat outside a coffee shop on Linthorpe Road, flicking through a newspaper as Baggage lay at his feet. Phillip looked up as Baggage stood and began wagging his tail. Kim headed towards them, and Phillip stood grinning at her.

She reached the pair, squatted and allowed Baggage to lick her face. 'Hello, Bagsy,' she said, rubbing his ears.

'You made it then?' Phillip said.

'I said I'd be here, and I keep my promises,' she said as she sat beside him.

Phillip made a gesture with his hand. 'Drink?'

'Medium latte for me, and a small skinny latte for Baggage.'

Phillip frowned. 'Baggage?'

'Yes. I got him one the other day, and he liked it.' She opened her bag and took out a small carrier. 'I've even brought him a bowl.'

'You're mad.'

'Run along, now,' she said ushering him away. 'I'll look after Bagsy. Won't I, son.' She patted the dog's head. Baggage looked first at Phillip and then at Kim as if confirming what she'd said. Phillip shrugged at the pair of them and headed into the coffee shop.

As Baggage lapped at the bowl, Kim and Phillip sat at the table, watching him finish his drink. Kim patted the dog on the head again.

Phillip smiled at her. 'You love dogs, don't you?'

'I do. I've always had a dog. My last one, Sandy, had to be put down a year ago. I haven't had another since. My ex-boyfriend, Tony, wasn't keen on them, though.'

'What happened to him? You didn't get him put down, did you?'

Kim laughed. 'I like that. Maybe I should've had him neutered as well.'

'Oh dear. It sounds like he upset you.'

Kim sighed. 'Long story short. My boyfriend was seeing someone else behind my back. The girlfriend he had managed to keep from me.'

'I see.'

'Yep, the two-timing rat.' She patted Baggage again, and the dog looked up at her with foam surrounding his mouth.

'And you didn't suspect?'

'He told me he worked away. In fact, he was playing away.'

'What did you do?' Phillip said.

'I threw him out, along with all his possessions. I made a mess of Redcar high street.'

'Good on you.'

Kim looked at Phillip. 'What about you? Nobody in your life?'

'There was, but not anymore.'

'There's a story there. I can tell.'

'Well … it's just we…I mean.' Phillip struggled to find the right words.

'She didn't do the dirty on you, did she?'

Phillip thought for a moment and genuinely wanted to tell her the truth. After all, a relationship built on lies is not a relationship at all. Come clean, be honest. That was the best thing to do, he thought. 'Yes, and with my best mate.'

'Oh, you poor thing,' Kim said, putting her hand on his arm.

'I came home early one day, and there they were.'

'How awful. I hope you turfed the cow out?'

'It was her flat, and I worked for her dad. He'd bought it for her. So, I left and moved into a bedsit.'

'What about your job?'

'She got her dad to sack me.'

'The bitch,' Kim said. 'I hope I run into her. I'll break her nose.'

Phillip put his hand on hers. 'It's all history. I'm over it now.'

Sam slipped up to the pair of them unnoticed. 'Now then, you two.'

Kim smiled at him. 'Hi. Phillip and I are having coffee. Why don't you join us?'

Baggage nudged Sam's leg with his nose, and Sam reached down and patted the dog's head. Satisfied, Baggage lay back under the table. 'I'm on my way to Tommo's pub. Otherwise, I would.'

Phillip picked up his cup and took a sip. 'You do know he's not there. He's gone with Albert to meet that Green bloke. Then the pair of them are going to the match.'

'I know. I'm lending Albert my season ticket, remember.' Phillip nodded, and Sam nudged him. 'You two look cosy, mind.'

Kim looked at Sam. 'I was telling Phillip about my two-timing former boyfriend. Phillip was telling me about his awful ex-girlfriend. We're kindred spirits.'

Sam glanced at Phillip. 'Really? You'll have to tell me all about her.'

'I will.' Phillip glared at Sam, nodding at the preoccupied Kim stroking Baggage.

Kim looked at her watch and gave it a shake. 'What time is it?'

'12.45,' Phillip said. 'Why?'

'Sorry, Phillip, I'll have to go. I'm meeting a friend in town. I didn't realise it was that late. This bloody watch is always stopping.'

'Maybe we could do this again?' Phillip asked.

Kim smiled. 'We might even make it a meal if you like?'

Phillip nodded. 'I'd like that.'

'I'll give you a ring,' she said, bending to kiss Baggage.

Sam raised his eyebrows at Kim. 'This friend you're meeting. What's she like?'

Kim stood and shuffled her feet. 'Erm, not really your type.'

Sam winked at Phillip. 'Not my type. They're all my type.'

'She might be gay,' Phillip said.

Kim kissed Phillip on the cheeks, patted Baggage and then she was gone.

Sam's eyes followed Kim until she was out of sight before turning to face Phillip. 'Being gay's not a barrier these days.' He laughed. 'Anyway. I think you and I need to have a little chat over a pint. About that terrible ex of yours.'

Phillip put his hands up to his face, pulling them down to his chin. 'Yes. Lead on.'

## CHAPTER TWELVE

Tommo sat on a stool at the bar with a beer in his hand, some distance away but close enough to keep an eye on Albert. Albert had been shown into the dining room by a member of staff, and Tommo had decided to act like a punter and wait for his return. He sat nonchalantly while maintaining his vigilance in case anything kicked off.

Albert sat alone at a table, escorted there moments earlier by a waiter, and cradled his pint of beer, trying desperately to appear calm. It wasn't easy, and his heart, already beating vigorously, would gallop when anyone entered the room. Albert glanced at the door for the umpteenth time as a portly, balding man approached the table where Albert sat. Albert rose from his seat and stepped forward, offering his hand to the man, who, oblivious to Albert, walked casually past.

'Mr Jackson?' said a voice from behind him.

Albert spun around to be confronted by a large individual twice the size of the other man. His enormous belly, sticking out in front of him, came close to colliding with Albert. The man held out a fat, sweaty hand, and Albert reluctantly took hold of it. 'Yes,' Albert said, surreptitiously wiping his hand on his trousers.

'Rupert Green.' He nodded towards Albert's beer. 'I see you've already got a drink. Would you like a look at the menu?' Green lumbered awkwardly into the inadequate chair, which groaned alarmingly beneath his considerable weight.

'Yes, thanks,' Albert said and sat back down.

The two of them ordered their meal, chatting pleasantly about nothing in particular until the waiter returned, placed a plate in front of each of them, nodded politely, and left. The men continued the conversation while they ate, and eventually, after finishing their pudding, Albert pushed the empty plate away and dabbed gently at his mouth with his napkin.

Green sat back, allowing his hands to rest on his ample stomach. 'I do like to get the meal out of the way before talking shop,' he said. He smiled at Albert. 'Can I get down to brass tacks, Mr Jackson?'

Albert sat upright. His head a little light from the port and two pints he'd drank. 'Please do.'

'I'd like you to find something for me. A statue of an Eagle.'

'An Eagle? Albert said, feigning ignorance.

'Yes. Cards on the table, Mr Jackson. I did ask your uncle some time ago to locate this Eagle for me.'

'How did you know he was my uncle?'

'I always check people out thoroughly.' Green picked up the wine bottle, holding it aloft. 'Are you sure you wouldn't like a glass of this excellent wine?'

'Perhaps a small one.'

'I know, for example, that you and two other gentlemen have taken over the running of your uncle's agency.'

Albert tasted the wine. 'My cousins.'

Green nodded at the glass in Albert's hand. 'What do you think?'

'Lovely,' he lied. It tasted okay, but it was no IPA, as far as Albert was concerned.

Green looked directly at Albert. 'Your uncle was, I believe, working on a lead. Bill was investigating a soldier who fought in the Second World War. Arthur Parchester.'

Albert took a notebook from his pocket and jotted down the name. 'Arthur Parchester.'

'Have you come across that name before?'

'No. We've been going through our uncle's paperwork. I don't think we've seen anything relating to that name.'

'I see,' Green said, narrowing his eyes. 'From what your uncle discovered, Parchester smuggled the Eagle across from Holland in 1944. Possibly inside a statue of The Virgin Mary.'

Albert continued making notes. 'This happened a long time ago, Mr Green. What makes you think you have any hope of finding it? You must recognise that. It's entirely possible the Eagle has been discovered already.'

'Impossible,' Green boomed, causing nearby diners to look in his direction. 'I'm a collector of antiques, and I specialise in statues in particular. If it had been found, I would know about it.'

'This Arthur Parchester,' Albert said, consulting his notes. 'Surely he's dead?'

'He is. Parchester died in Holland in 1944. However, his descendants are still alive. I believe your uncle spoke with a member of his family.'

'I see. Have you his name?'

Green laughed. 'Mr Jackson, surely you don't want me to do your job for you?'

'No, of course not,' Albert said.

'The Eagle has considerable value.' Green sipped his drink. 'I'm offering you and your colleagues a substantial finders' fee. £250,000.' Green sat back, resting his drink on his stomach.

Albert dropped his pencil onto the table, watching it roll and fall off the edge. He bent and picked it back up. 'How much?'

'You heard me correctly, Mr Jackson.'

'Well, I'll have to consult with my associates and discuss our plan of action.'

'I must warn you,' Green said, lowering his voice. 'Other individuals are equally as determined as me in their pursuit of this Eagle. You will have to be very careful.'

Albert glanced around. 'You're aware that my uncle was murdered?'

'I am. My sincerest condolences.'

'I didn't really know Bill,' Albert said. 'I'll see what we can do, Mr Green.' Albert stood and offered his hand.

Green shook it firmly. 'Good luck, Mr Jackson. Please keep me informed.' Sleen appeared at Green's side and handed an envelope to his employer. 'I've organised some expenses for you,' Green said, holding out the envelope. 'This is my business card. Let me know when you have any information.'

'I will.' Albert nodded at both Green and his associate and left.

Sam sat at a table in The Sidewinder as Phillip joined him, carrying two beers. Phillip popped a pint in front of Sam and sat opposite. 'You did say the stout?'

Sam nodded. 'So?' he said, holding out his arms.

Phillip took a swig from his glass. 'What?'

'Your ex-girlfriend? The one who cheated on you. I'm interested to hear about her.'

Phillip groaned. 'It just came out. Kim was telling me how her ex-boyfriend did the dirty on her, and I found myself …'

Sam sat back in his chair, a smile on his face. 'Lying?'

'Not lying as such. Kim sort of assumed that's what happened. What would you have done?'

'I would have lied, like you. The thing is, though, my aim would have been to get Kim into bed. If I'm reading this right, you've something a little more long-term in mind.'

'Yes, I really like her. What can I do? Should I come clean?'

'I wouldn't, but then I'd insist that black is white until a woman produces irrefutable evidence to the contrary. Photographs or videos usually suffice. Although I would still argue the point.'

'I'm not you, Sam.'

'She will find out.' Sam smiled. 'They always do, and if I could give you one piece of advice? Enjoy the ride until she does. Literally.'

Phillip shook his head a little. 'She might not find out. She doesn't know my ex.'

'True, but Teesside's not a big area. I don't really go in for girlfriends, so it's rarely been a problem for me.' Sam tapped his chin with a finger. 'On the odd occasions I've had brief relationships, I would throw caution to the wind and hope for the best.'

'How can you do that? Go from one woman to another?'

'It's not the kill. It's the thrill of the chase. I just pick them up with the aim of bedding them as soon as possible. If I do, and they're good in bed, I might go back for seconds. Or thirds, on rare occasions.'

'That's so mercenary.'

'I know.' Sam took a swig of his drink. 'But it's who I am. I stopped trying to fathom myself out years ago. However, mercenary implies a payment of some sort. I never charge them for my services. I do it gratis.'

'What about Lisa?'

Sam sighed. 'She was different. Lisa was a female version of me. I was besotted by her and much younger then, more naïve. Turns out she was playing the field behind my back, and I'd been blind to it.'

'Maybe that's why you're like you are?'

'Maybe,' Sam said. 'Like I said. I don't really give it too much thought.'

'You were saying the other day that you're sick of that life?'

'Moment of weakness.' Sam swatted away the comment. 'Forget about what I said.'

Phillip closed his eyes and shook his head. 'I wish I'd told her the truth now.'

'If you had, she might not be interested in you. What happened with her ex might colour how she views you. She's apparently interested now, and you've got your secret weapon, too.' Sam stroked Baggage, who, snoozing under the table, lifted his head slightly and then went back to sleep.

Phillip's mouth dropped open. 'I can't do that. That's so—'

'Mercenary.'

'Yes.'

Sam laughed. 'A dick has no conscience. There are seven billion people on the planet. If you removed all the ones conceived outside of relationships, the world wouldn't have a population crisis. All around the globe, right now, people are getting down and dirty behind their partner's back, using every trick in the book to achieve that goal. It's not love that makes the world go around. It's sex.'

'That's not me. That's not who I am. I'm—'

'That's your trouble,' Sam said, 'You allow feelings to dictate. Excuse the pun.'

'You must feel some sympathy for the women you sleep with? The women who're looking for something more than a quick shag? The ones looking for something a little more substantial?'

Sam blew out his cheeks. 'Sometimes, but they're all adults. I don't force them to do something they don't want to. Actually ...' He winked at Phillip. 'A lot of them enjoy the experience.'

'What about the ones that want more?'

Sam shrugged. 'I can't help that. Life's full of disappointment, I'm afraid. They'll get over it.'

'I'm not buying that,' Phillip said.

'Okay,' Sam said, frowning. 'Sometimes I feel a bit of guilt when I treat them badly, of course, when I don't return their calls. When I stand them up or when they catch me with another woman. I'm not totally heartless. It's just, I can't seem to turn other women down.'

'Have there been many of those?' Phillip said, raising his eyebrows. 'Women who caught you out?'

'Quite a few over the years.' Sam laughed. 'I've lost count of the number of scenes I've been involved in. The names I've been called. Not to mention the pints I've had thrown at me.'

Phillip shook his head. 'And still, you go on.'

Sam winked. 'Over time, I've learned how to spot the most volatile women. I generally give them a wide berth now. I've got a sixth sense.'

'So how do you pick them? Your unsuspecting victims?'

'I tend to look for out-of-towners these days – people only visiting. That way, they won't expect anything other than sex. Women aren't that different from men in that respect. If they think they can get away with it, a lot do.'

'I should be taking notes. I could write a book.'

'I could write several.' Sam smiled and then rubbed his chin. 'Sometimes they fall into your lap.' Sam lifted his head in thought. 'I was up at the magistrate's court one day on a drunk and disorderly charge. One of the magistrates was a middle-aged woman. She looked quite prim and proper, but I could see her eyeing me up in court. Long story short. I ended up back at her place on the night.'

'You're kidding,' Phillip said.

'Nope. Teachers, policewomen, cleaners, lawyers, bank clerks, you name it. One minute, you're out and about, minding your own business ... the next, you're in bed with them. Or in the back of a car with them.

Or in a disabled toilet in Marks and Spencer with them, or up against a wall down a back alley with them.'

'What about Emily?'

Sam closed his eyes and brought his hands up to his face, slowly pulling them down. 'Christ, Phillip, you had to mention her.'

'Still not speaking?'

Sam dropped his eyes down. 'Forget about Emily. Emily's ...'

'The one?' Phillip said.

'If I were you,' Sam said, sidestepping Phillip's comment. 'I'd keep quiet about your ex and hope that Kim never finds out. If she does, deny it. Say your ex is a lying cow and that you would never do anything like that – preferably while holding Baggage in your lap.'

Baggage lifted his head on hearing his name. Satisfied that nothing significant was happening, he went back to sleep.

Sam stood and snatched up the empty glasses. 'I'll get us another, shall I?'

Tommo and Albert entered the pub – Albert decked out in all his Boro regalia.

Gene looked up. 'Morning, you two,' he said in his usual camp timbre. 'Off to the footie, boys?'

Tommo positioned himself behind the bar, picking up a pint glass. 'Morning, Gene, Albert's attire gave it away, did it? What'll it be, Albert?' Tommo said.

Albert pressed his back up against the wall, closing his eyes as Baggage stood in front of him, sniffing at Albert inquisitively. Albert opened one eye and looked at the animal, unable to breathe. The dog, satisfied he wasn't getting a pat from this strange individual, headed over towards Tommo for a stroke. 'A pint of IPA, please,' Albert said, allowing himself to breathe again.

Phillip joined Albert at the bar. 'He won't harm you, Albert. He's soft as a brush.'

'Hey,' said a customer to Tommo. 'I thought you said dogs weren't allowed in your pub?'

Tommo popped a pint on the bar in front of Albert. 'That's right, Charlie.'

'Well, what about that, there?' he said, pointing at Baggage. 'That's a dog, isn't it?'

'That's Baggage,' Tommo said. 'Baggage isn't a dog. He's almost human. He comes here for a stroke, and then he'll sit happily in the corner. Isn't that right, boy?' Tommo rubbed the dog's ears. Satisfied with the world's state, Baggage trotted back over to the other side of the room and slumped under a table.

'Why can't I bring my dog in?'

'Because your mutt is always yapping. It growls at anyone who comes within six feet of it, and when it's not doing that, it'll sit on the floor with its head between its legs, licking its balls.' Tommo popped the second pint onto the bar.

'Fair point,' conceded Charlie.

Phillip offered a twenty-pound note to Gene. 'I'll get these. One for you and Tommo.'

'Oh, cheers, handsome.' Gene winked, took the money and gave him his change.

Tommo strolled from behind the bar and walked over to the table, where Baggage lay underneath as the others followed him. Tommo sat at the table. 'Where's Sam?'

Phillip fished inside his pocket. 'He had to go somewhere. Something about seeing a man about a dog, but he left this.' Phillip pulled out a season ticket and passed it across to Tommo.

Tommo handed it to Albert. 'Guard this with your life, Albert.'

Albert took it from him, his face lighting up like a child on Christmas morning. 'Wow,' he said, sitting down next to Tommo.

Tommo looked at Phillip and winked. 'A woman.'

'A woman?' Phillip said,'

'Man about a dog,' Tommo said. 'It's Sam's code for meeting a woman. Anyway, forget about lover boy. You can fill him in later.'

Phillip sat at the table with the other two. 'What happened this afternoon? How did the meeting with Mr Green go?'

Tommo patted Albert on the shoulder. 'Albert will tell you.'

Albert, who was still staring lovingly at the ticket, put it inside his jacket and sat back about to begin as Baggage appeared from under the table and popped his head between Albert's legs. Albert stiffened and gasped. 'Nice doggie,' he whispered.

'Even Bagsy is interested,' Tommo said.

'Give him a pat,' Phillip said, 'and he'll leave you alone.'

Albert did this, and Baggage, now seemingly happy, lay back down. Albert let out a huge sigh and began. Albert told Phillip about the meeting with Green, telling him how Green had said that Uncle Bill had been employed to find the Eagle and that Green had offered them £250,000 to locate it.

Phillip sat back in his chair. 'Wow, £250,000.'

'He mentioned someone called …' Albert opened his notebook. 'Parchester.'

Phillip digested the name. 'Parchester … I've heard that name before. I think there might have been something with that name on it in Bill's paperwork.'

'Really?' Albert said. 'I told Green that I hadn't heard of the name.'

Phillip nodded. 'That's not a bad thing. We'll keep our cards close to our chest until we know more. Green may have had something to do with Bill's death after all.'

Albert took a large gulp of his pint. 'Yes, I see what you mean.'

Tommo stood. 'You ready, Albert?'

'I am.' He opened his carrier bag and took out a Boro scarf. 'We're off to the match.'

'I know,' Phillip said, smiling. 'Good luck. I'll probably head over to the office and see if I can find any info on this Parchester.'

Tommo and Albert stood, and Baggage got to his feet, stretched, and looked up at the pair. Tommo rubbed the dog's ears. 'See you later, Bagsy.'

Albert tentatively patted Baggage on the head. 'Good doggie.'

Miss Jacobs and Sam lay in bed together, the pair still panting from their exertions. She looked to her left at Sam, smiling at him. 'You're quite good at that.'

Sam put his hands behind his head on the pillow. 'I've had no complaints.'

'Confidence. I love it. Are all the women you seduce as satisfied as me?'

Sam looked at her. 'I didn't seduce you. You seduced me.'

'So …' She licked her lips. 'Did you enjoy it?'

Sam sat up a little and picked up his glass from the bedside table. 'The champagne's really nice.'

Jacobs laughed. 'You're a rascal. Maybe I could have another attempt at impressing you?'

'Feel free, I've got all afternoon.' Miss Jacobs took the glass from his hand, placed it down and kissed him passionately.

Kim entered the coffee shop and spotted Emily. She waved across at her. Smiling, Emily returned the wave as Kim collected her Latte, headed over to join her, and sat opposite.

'Hi,' Kim said.

'How are you?' Emily said.

'Very well. You?'

'Fine.'

'So, what have you been up to?' Kim asked.

'Work, mostly. I'm staying at Mam's.'

Kim stirred her coffee. 'I heard.'

'Sam mentioned it, did he?'

'In passing. Sam's been moping around lately. When I asked him what was wrong, he came out and told me.'

Emily rolled her eyes. 'Didn't he try and seduce you?'

'No,' Kim said. 'He'd have failed if he had. I've met his sort before.

Jack the lad types don't interest me anymore. He's attractive enough, but I'm looking for someone a little more reliable.'

Emily chuckled. 'I know what you mean. Did Sam tell you anything else?'

'Like what?'

'Why I left?'

'No.' She frowned. 'He said you two had a disagreement about something but didn't go into details?'

Emily lowered her eyes. 'I see.'

'Well, you'd better tell me. You obviously have a reason for asking me to meet you?'

'It was nothing. I was just trying to find out how Sam is, that's all. I was worried he wasn't coping – living on his own.'

Kim smiled and took a sip of her coffee. 'Really?' Kim said, putting down her cup.

Emily took a huge breath. 'We slept together.'

Kim picked up her cup and took another sip of her coffee. 'I thought as much.'

'You knew?'

'Yeah, sort of. I figured it must be something serious for two good friends to fall out, and sex does it every time.'

Emily smiled. 'I like you, Kim.'

'I had to come and find out what you wanted. When you phoned and asked if I fancied a coffee, I thought Emily needed to get something off her chest. Or maybe she fancies me.'

Emily stared at Kim. 'But you're not gay,' Emily said.

'True. But I thought maybe you were trying your luck.'

Emily planted her elbows on the table, looking into Kim's eyes. 'And would you be interested?'

Kim smiled at Emily, maintaining eye contact. 'I'm straight.'

'Not even bi-curious?'

Kim laughed. 'Been there, done that.'

'Really?'

Kim laughed again. 'Long time ago. Someone I worked with. A drunken escapade.'

'And ...? Did you enjoy it?'

'It was ... interesting. I won't say I didn't enjoy it, but it's not for me. Even with someone as pretty as you.'

Emily feigned annoyance and playfully banged her hand on the table. 'Damn!'

'You and Sam are like two peas in a pod. You're like a female version of him and are good together.'

'That's what everyone says. Sam said I'm like his best mate with big tits.'

Kim looked directly at Emily. 'You like him, don't you?' Kim said.

'Yes. Sam's my best mate. We've been friends for years.'

'No, Emily,' Kim said and took another drink. 'I mean, you really like him.'

Emily shrugged. 'I suppose.'

'Complicated.'

Emily frowned. 'What do you think I should do?'

Kim took hold of Emily's hand and gently squeezed it. 'Speak with him. It won't go away, and you can't avoid each other forever.'

Emily sat up straight, forcing a smile. 'I will, maybe later. What about you?'

'Me?' Kim said.

'No one in your life?'

'I've got my eye on someone,' Kim said and took a sip of coffee. 'I just need to see if he comes up to scratch first.'

'Sleep with him, you mean?'

Kim laughed. 'No. I've had enough of men who mess me about. Before I fall in deep, I want to be sure he's the real deal.'

'Does he have a name?'

'Phillip.'

Emily nodded. 'Phillip. Phillip's cute.'

'We'll see,' Kim said. 'So, there's no time like the present.'

'For what?'

'Ring Sam.'

'Oh, I'm …'

Kim smiled at Emily. 'The elephant in the room doesn't get any smaller. It just keeps blowing its trunk.'

'I can't anyway. My mobile's knackered.'

'Use mine.' Kim located Sam's number and pushed the phone across to Emily. Emily picked it up and paused briefly before pressing the dial button. The phone rang for a few seconds and then went to answerphone. Emily was lost for words, the phone beeping for her to leave a message. She slid the phone back across the table to Kim, who looked at her and threw up her hands. Emily shook her head, and Kim rang off.

Sam made his way along the corridor from room number 21 and Miss Jacobs. He took out his phone and checked it. He looked at the screen, which informed him there was a message. He retrieved the message and listened. There was silence for a few seconds, and then it ended. He searched for missed calls and located the number of the last caller – a mobile number that he didn't recognise. So he rang it.

'Hi,' said a female voice on the other end.

'Who's this?' Sam asked.

'Kim.'

'It's Sam. I'm returning your call.'

'I know. Your name is stored on my phone.' Emily came out of the toilets, and Kim put her hand on the phone. 'It's Sam,' she mouthed.

Emily shook her head and held up her hands.

'Sorry about that,' Kim said. 'I must have dialled you by mistake.'

'No problem. Is Phillip with you?'

'No,' she said. 'I'm in town doing a bit of shopping.'

'I'll try the office. See you later.'

Kim looked at Emily, who was staring at the floor, deep in thought. 'Are you okay?' Kim said.

'Yes, fine. I've just realised that I said I'd meet someone.'

'Oh, okay,' Kim said.

'Sorry about that,' Emily forced a smile.

Kim smiled. 'No problem.'

'Thanks for the talk. I'll see you later.' Emily hugged Kim a little too tightly, kissed her affectionately, and then headed off. Kim looked on, trying to figure out what had just happened.

# CHAPTER THIRTEEN

**2015** – Hockney was driven out into the countryside. The driver pulled off the main road and headed up a farm track towards a dilapidated building, but the car came to a stop outside a farmhouse. The man next to Hockney nudged him in the ribs with his gun, indicating for him to get out. Hockney did, and headed towards the building, encouraged forward by the man and his constant pushing in the back. He entered the gloom of the building and glanced about as a figure in the corner of the room remained in the shadows.

'Mr Hockney,' he said before stepping nearer. His accent a thick, Eastern European.

'Mr…?' Hockney said.

'My name is unimportant.' He pointed to a chair located to the left of Hockney. 'Have a seat.' Hockney sat.

'The Eagle,' the man said.

'What about it?'

'Have you located it yet?'

'I'm not even sure it exists,' Hockney said. 'I'm beginning to believe it's just a legend.'

The man lit a cigarette and drew on it. 'Oh, I can assure you that it does.' The smoke drifted towards Hockney. Its aroma was unusual.

'Turkish,' the man said, showing Hockney the cigarette. 'In case you were wondering.'

'I wasn't.'

The man perched on the edge of a table. 'Sidney Stankovich?'

'What about him?'

'He's employed you to find the Eagle. Yes?'

'Yes.' Hockney couldn't see the point of lying.

'Rupert Green?' He wandered closer to Hockney. 'He has, too?'

'Yes.'

'Let's not forget, Anne Jacobs,' the man said.

'Yes,' Hockney said. 'All three have asked me to locate the Eagle.'

'I want the Eagle,' the man said, his voice heavy with threat. 'If you find it, I want you to bring it to me.'

'That's a big if.'

The man drew a few more times on his cigarette and then stubbed it out. 'What have you found out so far?'

'Not a great deal. I think it's a wild goose chase.'

'If you believe that, why are you working for the others?'

Hockney shrugged. 'They're paying me well. I have bills that need paying.'

The man pulled out another cigarette, lit it, and drew deeply from it. 'Not to mention your gambling interests. Why did you go to see Parchester's relation?'

'I thought he might have information.'

'And did he?'

Hockney smiled. 'He didn't have a letter or anything telling us where to find it. If that's what you think.'

'I believe that you're holding out on us,' the man said. He glared at Hockney. 'That's not an intelligent thing to do.' He nodded at the armed man who pushed the gun into Hockney's side. 'Hector Williamson tried to be clever, Mr Hockney,' he continued. 'I don't need to remind you how that ended.'

Hockney glanced at the gunman and then looked back towards the smoking man. 'I thought he might have letters or papers relating to when his uncle was in Holland. I told him I was writing a book on the regiment his uncle had been in. There was nothing of note.'

'Are you sure?' he said as his accomplice nudged Hockney again.

'Absolutely.'

'I don't care if you keep the others hanging on, but when you find any more information, I want to know. Do this, and you can continue to plan for old age. Don't … well, let's just say, the Tees is a big river.' Hockney nodded, catching sight of the man's ring on his finger. The design he recognised instantly. Two Eagles back-to-back. One carrying a sceptre, the other an orb. The symbol of The Romanovs.

The man stood in the doorway, watching the car containing Hockney trundle along the farm track and out of sight.

He took out his mobile and dialled a number. 'I've just had a word with our friend Hockney. I think he'll play ball with us from now on. I lied and told him we killed Williamson. It may focus his mind a little and make him less likely to do anything stupid.'

'Good, Alexei,' said a voice on the other end. 'Keep me informed. I want that Eagle.'

Hockney was driven back to Redcar and sat in silence for the duration of the journey until the car pulled up at the far end of the high street, and Hockney got out. The man with the gun took out a card and handed it to Hockney. It was blank, except for a printed mobile number. He glowered at Hockney, put up his window, and drove off. Hockney mentally noted the licence plate before jotting it down in his notebook. He wandered back to the office, briefly stopping at Kim's flat to check on her. She was out but had left a note pinned to the door informing him that Rocco had called asking Hockney to ring back. Hockney took down the paper on which Kim had written Rocco's number, unlocked his office door and made himself a cup of tea. With a drink in hand, he positioned himself behind his desk and rang the number.

'Hockney.'
'Rocco. You've got some information?'
'That Green bloke is staying at Wainston Hall.'
'I know? Has he had any visitors?'
'He's got someone working for him. A guy called—'
'Sleen,' Hockney said.
'What's the use of employing me if you know all about him?'
'Go on,' Hockney said.
'He met with a woman at a pub in Crathorne.'
'Have you a name?'
'No. But I've got photos.'
'Can you bring them over?' Hockney asked.
Rocco groaned. 'Can't you drive across? I lost my licence two months ago. I took a risk driving over to Yarm.'
'I've been drinking,' Hockney said. 'Phone Fast-Eddie and tell him there's fifty quid in it for him. I'll pay him when he gets here.'
'Okay. Do you want me to keep following the fat bloke?'
'No. I think I know who the woman is. When I see the photos, it'll confirm it.'

Hockney sat back in his chair and rubbed his chin. He picked up his tea and took a large swig. He couldn't fathom what was going on here. Miss Jacobs was, according to Green, in tight with Stankovich. Yet he felt sure the photos Rocco had obtained were of her. Why was she meeting with Green if she was working with Stankovich? It was clear to him she was either planning to double-cross one, or both of them. Who had sent the goons to scare him as well? They sounded Russian. Was that Green, Stankovich or Jacobs? He remembered the licence number of the car and telephoned an ex-police colleague.

'Bill,' Robards said. 'Long time no hear.'

'How's police work?' Hockney asked.

'Same as. Long hours, not enough pay.'

'And the family?'

'Fine. Listen, Bill. I'm a bit rushed at the moment. You obviously need a favour.'

'I need a licence checking out.' Hockney read out the number. The other man repeated it back to him.

'I'm out of the office at the moment, but I'll run it through the computer when I get back. It'll cost you, though. Double malt.'

'I think my expenses can run to that. Do you still drink in the Central?'

'No. There's a little micro pub I like to go to on Baker Street. *The Sidewinder.*'

'Tomorrow?' Hockney said.

'About six?' Robards said.

'See you then.'

Robards dialled a number.

'Hi, Geoff,' Miss Jacobs said.

You'll never guess who's just rang me?'

'Who?'

'Bill Hockney.'

'What for?' Jacobs said.

'He wants a licence number checking. It could be a coincidence, or maybe he knows about us?'

'How can he? We've been discreet.'

'I'm meeting him tomorrow,' Robards said.

'Let me know how that goes?'

'I will. Are we meeting up later?'

'Not tonight,' she said. 'I've something on. Tomorrow, perhaps.'

'Okay. I'll ring you tomorrow.'

Hockney finished his tea and waited for Fast-Eddie to turn up. He did so half an hour later and handed Hockney a brown envelope as Hockney gave him fifty pounds in return. They chatted briefly before Hockney returned to his office. He viewed the photos, which indeed showed Miss Jacobs sitting at a table with Green. They appeared comfortable in each other's company, at least to Hockney. After replacing the pictures in the envelope, Hockney moved across to a filing cabinet in one of the corners of his office and pulled it to one side revealing the bare floorboards beneath. Levering one of the boards up, Hockney placed the envelope containing the photos inside, along with all the other stuff he had managed to obtain on the case. He replaced the board and the cabinet. Satisfied no one would suspect what lay beneath, he headed off out.

**The Next Day** – Hockney sat in the corner of the Sidewinder pub and observed the four other people in there. A couple sat in the opposite corner to him, a man sat at the bar and behind the bar stood a giant barman. He was about six feet four tall and physically imposing. He looked like someone you'd see wearing a rugby shirt on the pitch at Twickenham during the Six Nations. Although neatly trimmed, his full beard gave the man an ursine appearance. Hockney couldn't imagine trouble breaking out in this pub with him behind the bar, and good luck to anyone who tried, he thought. He turned his head as the door to the pub creaked open, and Detective Inspector Geoff Robards walked in.

Hockney pushed a full pint across the table to where Robards now sat. 'Now then,' Hockney said.

'Cheers,' Robards said, took a large swig and placed the half-full glass down.

Hockney smiled. 'Tough day?'

'Yes.' He checked his notebook. 'That licence number. It's a hire car. I phoned the company it was hired from, and they gave me a name. James Kirkland.'

Hockney shook his head. 'I don't know him.'

'He lives in Belmont, near Durham. A bit of previous,' he said, tearing the page from his book and handing it to Hockney.

'Cheers, I appreciate this.'

'There's a problem though. Kirkland's in prison. Doing four years for GBH.'

'Somebody's used his name then?'

'I'd say so.' He finished his pint. 'I know the prisons are a mess, but I don't think they're allowing inmates out to hire cars.'

'Interesting.'

'What are you working on?' Robards said.

'Nothing, really. The car was parked outside my office a few times. You know me, always suspicious. Probably nothing.' Hockney put the paper inside his jacket pocket. 'Another?' he said, pointing at Robards empty glass.

'I'd love one.'

'A chaser?' Hockney asked.

'Tommo!' Robards shouted to the barman. 'Have you any of that Irish malt left?'

Tommo looked across at the pair. 'Enough for a couple of doubles.'

Hockney got up, walked to the bar, and placed the empty glasses down. 'Two pints and two doubles, please.'

Tommo pulled the pints and, while they were settling, poured the whiskies. 'Eighteen pounds, please.'

Hockney handed him a twenty. 'Keep the change.'

Tommo topped up the two pints and placed them on the bar. 'Cheers.'

Hockney collected the drinks, returned to his table, and handed Robards a pint and one of the shorts.

Robards lifted the whisky. 'Old times, Bill.'

'Old times,' Hockney said.

Hockney woke early the next day, and after showering and dressing, he grabbed a quick breakfast, then travelled in a taxi and collected his car from where he'd left it the previous day. After driving back to the office, he spoke briefly with Kim, informing her he would be away for a couple of days on some business. He hadn't told her where he was going, not wanting to put her at any unnecessary risk. After collecting some clothing and other items he would need for his overnight stay, he set off, arriving late afternoon in Whitehaven on the Cumbrian west coast. He booked into a hotel in the centre, phoned and arranged a meeting with a gentleman called Stephen Jones at his home just outside of town. He quickly showered and dressed – not forgetting to put on his regimental tie – and set off for his meeting.

Hockney arrived outside the picturesque semi, its well-maintained lawn and borders attractively framing the building. He got out and headed up the drive to the house with his leather folder tucked under his arm. The door opened before he reached it.

'Mr Hockney?' a man said.

'Yes. Mr Jones?'

'Stephen. Mr Jones sounds a little formal for my liking.' The two men shook hands.

'Call me Bill.' Jones ushered Hockney inside, who waited in the hall, allowing Jones to pass him and lead him into a room to their right.

'Take a seat, Bill. I'll rustle up some drinks. Is tea okay?'

Hockney placed his leather folder on a table close by. 'Tea's fine. Milk, no sugar, please.'

Jones returned holding a tray with the drinks. He placed it on the table between them. 'So?' he said filling the two cups. 'You were inquiring about my uncle?'

'Yes,' Hockney said and took a sip of tea. 'I'm writing a book.' He pointed to his tie. 'My father and I were both in a regiment called The Yorkshire Rifles. Your uncle was in the same regiment during the war.'

'Did your father know him?' Jones said.

'No.' Hockney took another drink of tea. 'My dad was in the regiment after the war. I spoke to the family of a gentleman called Arthur Parchester. Parchester and your uncle were pals.'

'I see.'

Hockney removed some of the photocopied letters he'd obtained about Parchester. 'These are copies of the letters the Parchester family had. Arthur Parchester was killed along with your uncle in Holland.' Handing the pieces of paper to Jones, Hockney allowed him to read through the documents, remaining silent throughout.

Jones sighed. 'It's incredibly sad when you consider they never came back. I'm not sure how I can help, though.'

'I'm trying to give a human angle to my book and not just mention names, dates, etc.'

'I see. So, you're looking for information about my uncle's background. Photos, stuff like that?'

'That's it exactly. Because your Uncle William and Arthur Parchester were good mates, it adds a personal touch to the story.'

'I don't think we have anything like you got from the Parchester family. When my mum had to go into a care home, I emptied her house. I can't remember there being much. Maybe a few photos.'

'When did your mam pass away?' Hockney said.

'She's not dead. She's in a nursing home close by. She was only a girl when William was killed. About ten or eleven, I think.'

'Would it be possible to talk with her?'

'You could try, but Mum's got dementia, I'm afraid. Some days are better than others. I'm not sure if she would remember.'

Hockney nodded. 'I had a family member who had dementia.' He frowned. 'Quite often, they remember things from years ago rather than the recent stuff.'

'We could go tomorrow if you want?' Jones said.

'That would be great. If I could get some insight into what William was like, and what he did before the war. I do think these lads deserve to be remembered.'

'Absolutely. I'll have a dig through the loft and see if I can find any photos.'

Hockney drained his cup. 'Fantastic.'

'One pm?' Jones said.

'One's fine.' Hockney stood. 'Thank you for your time, Stephen.'

'You're welcome,' he said as he showed Hockney out.

Hockney got into his car and drove away, heading back into Whitehaven. He pulled into the hotel's car park, turned off the engine and took out his phone.

'Morning, Bill,' Kim said.

'I need you to do me a favour.'

'Go ahead.'

'Can you get me a photo of The Virgin Mary?'

'Where am I going to find someone called Mary who's still a virgin?' Kim said.

'Hilarious, Kim. The religious icon.'

'I do know who The Virgin Mary is. I did go to St Bede's. I'm a good Catholic girl, me.'

'Can you fax it up to me?'

Kim laughed. 'Fax. How dated is that? I can email it.'

'I haven't got an email,' Hockney said.

'If you had a modern phone, I could send it directly to you instead. You've got that ancient thing you carry around.'

'Well, I haven't. So, what do you suggest?'

'Where is it you're staying?'

'A hotel,' Hockney said.

'Have you the hotel's email?'

'I can get it.'

'Text the email address,' she said, talking slowly as if to a young child. 'You can text, Billy?'

'You're getting far too big for your boots, young lady. I'll text you the email shortly.'

'You love me really,' she said.

He smiled. 'Mmm.' And rang off. What a different person Kim had become since their first meeting. Hockney sat back and smiled to himself. Kim was the closest thing to family he had. He would have to make a will when he returned. Kim should have the little money he had if anything happened to him. In any case, he didn't have anyone else to leave it to.

Hockney went inside and stopped at the reception. A young lady behind the desk finished her phone call. She hung up and turned her attention to him. 'Good morning, sir. Can I help you?'

'I was wondering if I could have something emailed to the hotel from my office. It's a photograph.'

'Not a problem, sir.' She handed Hockney a card with the hotel's details on it. Hockney took out his phone and texted the hotel's email address.

Kim texted him back. 'Two minutes', it said.

Hockney looked at the receptionist. 'She'll be emailing it shortly.'

'If you'd like to take a seat. I'll let you know when we've received it.'

Hockney nodded, strolled over to the other side of the foyer, sat in an armchair, and waited.

Hockney entered his hotel room, placing his leather folder on the bed and an envelope containing the photo Kim had emailed. He eased off his jacket and threw it over the back of a seat. He sat on the edge of the bed, kicked off his shoes and loosened his tie. Hockney sighed, picked up the bottle of scotch from the bedside cabinet, and poured himself a generous whisky. Sitting back against the headboard, he drank deeply.

# CHAPTER FOURTEEN

Phillip sat at his desk back at the office, sifting through Hockney's notebooks while Baggage, who'd been fed and watered, lay snoozing on an old blanket Kim had brought in for him. Occasionally he would let out a yelp and move his legs as if chasing something in his canine dream. Phillip's phone sounded, and Baggage opened an eye. Then, as if realising dogs don't use phones, he went back to sleep.

'Hello,' Phillip said.

'Are you at the office?' Sam asked.

'Yeah. Why?'

'I've met with Miss Jacobs.'

'This meeting, it didn't take place in bed, did it?'

Sam laughed. 'Might have.'

'Sam. I'm not sure if sleeping with clients is an appropriate thing to do.'

'I thought I might be able to get some information out of her. Besides, she seduced me. Champagne and everything.'

Phillip sighed. 'What a wonderful life you lead. However, you could have rebuffed her advances. I mean, it would have been the ethical thing to do.'

'You're joking. It's been a week since my last shag. I'm only human.'

'A week! Lucky you.'

'What are you doing at the minute?' Sam asked.

'I'm looking through Uncle Bill's things. Albert met with Green, and he mentioned someone called Parchester. Apparently, Bill was investigating him.'

'Parchester? There's one of Bill's books in my desk drawer. Have a look in there.'

'I will. Did you manage to get any info from Miss Jacobs? Between the—'

'She didn't confess to Bill's murder if that's what you mean. I'm good, but I'm not that good.'

'Are you planning further meetings?' Phillip said.

'I hope so. She's the real deal.'

'Oh yeah. In what way?'

'Knows every trick in the book, and some, if you understand what I mean?'

Phillip shook his head. 'Not really. How old is she?'

'Late forties, I think. Looked after herself, though. Fit as hell.'

Phillip stood and made his way over to Sam's desk. 'It's hard work, this detective malarkey.'

'It certainly was,' Sam said. 'Hard, I mean.'

Phillip rolled his eyes. 'Are you coming back here?'

'I thought I might head over to Tommo's. What about you?'

'I'll finish off here and probably head home.'

'Is Kim there?'

'No,' Phillip said.

'She rang me earlier.' Sam said.

'Rang you? Why?'

'She said she'd misdialled.'

'Oh, right.'

'Don't worry, Phillip, I've got scruples. I'm not about to step on your toes. But if you want my two-pennyworth, I'd get in there before someone else does. She's a good-looking lass.'

'Thanks for the advice. I'll see you tomorrow, maybe?'

'Maybe,' Sam said.

Phillip thought for a moment. Why would Kim ring Sam? Did she fancy him? He had no chance if she did, even with his secret weapon of Baggage. Phillip looked down at the dog. 'What do I do, Baggage?' The dog raised his head a little.

Kim entered. 'Who are you talking to?'

'Baggage.'

The dog jumped up and bounded across to Kim. 'Hello, Bagsy,' she said, hugging him. 'Who's a good boy? Look what I've got for you.' Baggage wagged his tail expectantly, performing several pirouettes for good measure. Kim took out a sizeable bone-shaped chew, which she gave him. Baggage took it from her and returned to his blanket with his prize.

Kim headed towards the kitchen. 'Cup of tea?' she said over her shoulder.

'I'd love one.' Phillip got up from his seat and followed her. 'I was talking to Sam.'

'Oh yeah?'

Phillip stood at the threshold of the kitchen doorway. 'He said you called him.'

Kim paused, waiting for the kettle to finish boiling. 'I called him?'

'Yes,' Phillip said, folding his arms.

She placed two cups on the work surface and popped a tea bag in each. 'I didn't call him.' She poured the boiled water from the kettle into the cups. 'Emily did.'

'Emily?'

'Listen, Phillip, I'm betraying a confidence here, so I don't want you telling Sam. You promise?'

'Scouts honour,' he said, holding up two fingers, scout-like.

'Were you ever a scout?' Kim asked.

'Yes. I've got a knot-making badge and everything.'

'Mmm,' Kim said. 'I met Emily in town for a cup of coffee. She was asking about Sam.'

Phillip took the cup from her and rubbed his chin. 'Right.'

'You know something,' Kim said.

'Know what?'

Kim eyed him suspiciously. 'What has Sam said? About him and Emily?'

'Nothing.'

'I don't believe you. You're hiding something.'

Phillip smiled. 'I'm not.'

'Spill the beans.'

'There's nothing to tell. Honest.'

Kim sipped her tea. 'Emily likes Sam,' Kim said.

Phillip scoffed. 'I know that. They're mates.'

'No,' she said. 'There's more to it than that. I can tell. We need Sam and Emily back together.'

'What do you mean back together? They were never together, to begin with. Emily's gay, for God's sake.'

Kim waved a hand. 'Minor details.'

Phillip remembered Miss Jacobs. 'Minor details? What about …' He stopped mid-sentence.

'What about what?'

'Nothing.'

'Come on, spit it out,' Kim said.

'Nothing,' Phillip said. Kim looked at him expectantly. 'Nothing, nothing,' he said.

'Okay. What are you doing for tea tomorrow?'

'Me, nothing,' he said.

'What about if I cook us something? It won't be Delia Smith standard, but I can do a decent Spag Bol.'

'I'd love that,' Phillip said.

'Okay then. Half seven?'

'Half-seven it is.'

Kim smiled. 'Good. I'll look forward to it.'

Kim left, and Phillip looked down at Baggage, who was chomping happily on his chew. 'What do you think of that, Bagsy?' Who, too preoccupied with his chew and not in the least interested in human relationships, ignored him.

Phillip stood and walked across to Sam's desk, searching through one of the drawers. Finding a notebook, he returned to his own desk and flicked through its pages. Stopping, he put it down, picking up his mobile,

'Sam. It's Phillip.'

'Yeah, mate.'

'Kim was in town today, and she met Emily.'

Sam stopped at the end of Baker Street. 'Emily?'

'She was asking about you.'

'What did she say?'

'Kim was a bit cagey, but that phone call you got from Kim …'

'Yes?'

'It was actually Emily,' Phillip said.

Sam leant against a shop window. 'Right. Maybe I should ring her?'

'It might be better if you went around to her mam's.' The phone went silent for a moment. 'Are you still there?' Phillip said.

'I might wait until tomorrow.'

'It's your call. I just thought you ought to know.'

'Thanks, Phillip. Appreciate it.'

Sam sat in the corner of The Sidewinder, looking at photos on his mobile. He glanced towards the door as Tommo and Albert entered.

Tommo walked across and put an arm on Sam's shoulder. 'You missed a great match.'

'We were brilliant,' Albert said. 'Should've won by more. Thanks for loaning me your ticket,' he said, reluctantly handing it back to Sam.

'Glad you had a good time,' Sam said.

Albert pulled out his little purse. 'I'll get the drinks in,' he said, heading for the bar.

Tommo caught a glimpse of the screen of Sam's phone. A picture of a smiling Emily looked back. 'You all right, mate?'

Sam turned off his phone. 'Yeah. Look, I'm going to head off home.'

'What's up?'

Sam stood. 'Nothing. A bit of a headache, that's all. I'll see you tomorrow.'

Tommo frowned. 'Okay, mate. I'll see you tomorrow.' He watched as his friend disappeared out of the door.

Albert returned moments later, placing three pints on the table. 'Where's Sam gone?'

'He's not feeling too well. We'll have to share his pint.'

'I think we can manage that,' Albert said, grinning.

Sam returned home to his flat, briefly switching on the television before turning it off. He took out his mobile and, finding Emily's number, dialled. The phone sounded for several rings before going to answerphone. Sam hung up, pulling his arm back he resisted the urge to launch the phone at the wall. He trudged into the kitchen and took out a bottle of lager from the fridge. Standing, he swigged from it, while he waited for his microwave chicken curry for one to warm up.

Sam sat on the settee in the lounge of his flat, flicking through the photos on his phone – there were hundreds. He stopped only when one of Emily popped up. He smiled at a selfie he'd taken of himself and Emily in Whitby the previous year. He drained his bottle of lager and placed it on the coffee table next to him, along with the other nine empties. That was the last one, he thought. He cursed himself for not getting some more. He would have to start on the vodka next.

Sam rang Emily's number for the fifth time. Again, it went to answerphone.

'Why won't you talk to me, Em? I'm dying here, and you couldn't give a shit,' he slurred, the half bottle of vodka and beers he'd consumed sitting in front of him. He began to write a text to her but then deleted the message, like the other three he'd removed. He turned off his phone, lay on the settee and pulled a coat hanging on the back over himself. He closed his eyes and thought of Emily as sleep scooped him up into a drink-filled, inebriated darkness and deposited him temporarily into a drunken man's oblivion.

He woke at three in the morning. Having taken a couple of paracetamol for a headache, he was sure would arrive, downing half a carton of orange juice and a pint of water, he visited the toilet before heading to his bed, but as he passed Emily's bedroom, he stopped and pushed open the door. Then, undressing, Sam slipped into her bed, pulled one of the pillows close to his body and sniffed it. Emily's perfume filled his nostrils and he closed his eyes as sleep washed over him like gentle waves lapping at the shore of lake tranquillity.

## CHAPTER FIFTEEN

Emily sat in the café, periodically picking up her mobile and checking the time. Deb was late, but then she was always late. It was one of her more annoying features. She looked at the empty coffee cup and crumb-filled plate in front of her, picked up the last remnants of her caramel shortcake slice with her index finger and thumb and popped them into her mouth. She could feel the staff behind the counter watching her. The café in the Hill Street Centre was busy at this time of day, and she sensed that the workforce was waiting to pounce the moment she moved. If Deb didn't arrive soon, she would have to buy another coffee, she thought. Emily took out her purse just as Deb came into view. She waved at Emily, and through a series of familiar and, at times, comical mimes, the two of them managed to communicate to each other that Emily wanted another coffee with a caramel slice.

Deb sat opposite Emily, placing the coffee and cake on the table opposite her. The two of them kissed and embraced as close friends do before sitting back in their seats.

'You okay?' Emily said.

'Fine, Em. You?'

Emily placed her hands around the cup, pulling it close to herself. 'I'm all right. How's your mam?'

Deb smiled and sat back in her chair. 'She's fine. My dad's fine, the dog's fine, so is the cat and the goldfish.'

'You haven't got a goldfish,' Emily said, sticking her tongue out at her friend.

Deb sighed. 'Emily. The only time I see you these days is when we have an occasional Saturday out. And rarely for a cup of coffee. When this occurs, you usually have something you want to tell me. So, let's forget all the extraneous crap and cut to the chase.'

'Extraneous. What sort of word is extraneous?'

'I'm trying to increase my word power. I've bought myself a book, called appropriately—'

'How to increase your word power?' Emily said.

'Yes. Have you read it?'

Emily rolled her eyes. 'Just a lucky guess.'

Deb sat back in her seat and stirred her coffee. Emily picked up her spoon and did the same. Then, she picked up the caramel slice and took a small bite as crumbs cascaded onto the table.

'These caramel slices are incredibly friable,' Emily said.

'Friable?'

'It means—'

'I know what it means, but surely incredibly friable is tautology,' Deb said, lowering her eyes. 'Something is either friable or not.'

Emily took a second bite. 'There can be degrees of friability. Some things can be crumblier than others.'

Deb, putting a hand on either side of her face, leant forward towards her friend. 'Much as I love this word fight at the okay café,' she said, adopting a posh voice. 'We really need to get down to brass tacks.'

Emily placed the remainder of the cake down, pushing the plate away. 'I'm living at my mam's at the moment. I've been there about three weeks.'

'Is that it? You've finally got sick of picking up Sam's shitty boxers. Hardly front-page news, my dear.'

'Trunks,' she said, stirring her coffee again. 'Sam wears trunks, not boxers.'

Deb ignored Emily. 'Have they done this place out?' she said, and took a large bite of Emily's cake.

'Sam and I …' Emily paused, searching hopelessly for the appropriate words. 'Slept together.'

Deb almost choked on the cake. Coughing and spluttering, she picked up her coffee and took a large swig from it. 'You shagged Sam?'

Emily glared at her friend. 'A little louder, Deb. I don't think they heard you in Marks and Spencer.'

'You shagged Sam?' she whispered.

'Yes.'

Deb downed the last of her coffee. 'Well, bugger me. Wait a minute.' Opening her handbag, she pulled out a small notebook. 'Yes, I thought so. I've written it here, see.' She waved the book under Emily's nose. 'In December 2001, Emily told me she was gay. It's here in black and white, darling. You said you were gay, and now, Emily, you've gone all hetero. Not with any guy, mind. With Sam, who's had more women than Soft Mick.'

Emily smiled at her friend. 'Soft Mick hasn't had that many. He exaggerates a lot.'

Deb pouted. 'Oh, tautology again. So, what's Sam doing? Has he run out of straight women? Has he decided to mop up anything with a pulse?'

'It just happened. We'd had a lot to drink and …'

'Don't you dare say one thing led to another, Missy? I want details. Was it good, did you enjoy it?'

Emily looked around. 'I …'

Deb sniggered. 'Oh, my God, you did. Tell me, Emily.' Straightening her face, she glanced left and right. 'Is he a big chap?'

Emily rolled her eyes. 'I knew I should have told Helen instead of you.'

'Helen? She's far too prudish for this revelation. No, you were right to tell me, darling. I am your best friend.'

'Too prudish? Now, who's being tautological?'

Deb leant forward towards Emily. 'Do you remember Mary, who worked at the Co-op? Well, she told me that Sam's hung like a Derby winner. That's the only reason I asked.'

Emily snorted. 'Yeah. You've had the hots for Sam for years.'

Deb rolled her eyes. 'Hots. I'm not fourteen, you know.'

'Well, if you must know … I'm not that sure.'

'How can you not be sure?'

'It's the first time I've seen one up close and personal.'

Deb adopted a pervy grin. 'Really? So, you never had a grope of one when you were young and not quite sure of your sexuality?'

'Never. And besides, after Mad Stella and her toys, everything else seems, well … small.' Deb pushed out her bottom lip, and Emily sighed. 'About this big,' she said, holding her hands apart.

'Corr!' Deb said.

Emily put her hands over her eyes, slowly pulling them down her face. 'There's something else …' Emily emptied her coffee. 'My period's late, and I'm usually as regular as clockwork.'

Deb burst out laughing, bending at the waist and putting her hand to her mouth to compose herself. 'This is priceless. The first time you have sex with a man, and you're already up the duff.'

Emily crossed her arms and sat upright, turning her head away. 'I'm glad you're enjoying yourself.'

'This is better than Jeremy Kyle.'

Emily glared. 'Oh, I'm going if you're just going to laugh about it.'

Deb straightened her face. 'Sorry. Listen, you're probably not pregnant. The odds are in your favour. You're almost certainly worrying about nothing. Have you done a test?'

'No.' She lowered her eyes. 'I'm not sure what to do.'

Deb took hold of Emily's hand. 'Let's go to Boots, get a pregnancy test and then you'll know.'

Tears appeared in Emily's eyes. 'What will I do if I am? What would I say to Sam?'

Deb frowned. 'Come on, one step at a time.' She looked at her friend, trying to remember if she'd ever seen her cry before.

Deb and Emily stood in the cubicle of the ladies' toilet in Marks and Spencer as Emily stared into space, the pregnancy test in her hand. 'What do I have to do?' Emily said.

'Give me strength,' Deb said. 'You piss on it.'

Emily held out her hand. 'Will you hold it for me? Look at my hand it's shaking. I'm frightened I might miss.'

Deb rolled her eyes. 'Friendship, who needs it?' She grabbed the tester from Emily. 'Sit down then.'

'I'm not sitting on a public toilet,' Emily said. 'You don't know who's been in here.'

'Put some paper on the seat. That's what I do.'

Emily wrinkled her nose. 'The paper might not stop the germs.'

Deb puffed out her cheeks. 'Oh, for God's sake.'

'Can't I hover?'

'You can fucking fly for all I care. Just piss on it, will you? Christ. If this ever gets out, I'll never forgive you.'

Emily gave a lopsided grin. 'I'm not sure I can go.'

'Are you kidding me? You've had two coffees. You must want to go.'

'I don't think I can,' Emily said. 'It must be nerves.'

Deb glared at her friend and grabbed the handle of the cistern. 'I'll flush the toilet. It might give you the urge.' Deb looked upwards. 'I've got better things I could be doing than this.'

Emily gave a puppy-dog look. 'Sorry.'

Deb and Emily emerged from the toilet – Deb having spent a full five minutes washing her hands.

Emily turned to look at her. 'I'm so sorry.'

'Hover, you said. Hover. At one point, I think you managed to get some in the toilet.'

'I was nervous, that's all.'

'Anyway, more pressing matters. You'll have to tell Sam.'

Emily dropped her head down and threw out her arms. 'Well, that's it, isn't it? My life is over.'

'Stop being melodramatic. You're pregnant. You haven't lost a limb. We'd better head for your flat.'

'I don't think he'll be there. He's usually at Tommo's.'

Deb rubbed her hands together. 'Well, we'd better go there then. I fancy a pint anyway.'

Tommo had managed to set the bar up quickly. He'd put three new barrels on and restocked the fridges – putting the older bottles at the front, something he quite often forgot to do, leaving him with out-of-date drinks sitting at the back. The man who delivered the pies had turned up on time this week, a rarity. Tommo smiled to himself, sat on the stool behind the bar, pulled a half of beer, toasted himself for good measure, and downed it in one. Sam had been in earlier and had helped a little but had seemed unusually preoccupied. Tommo had put it down to the fact that Emily hadn't answered or returned any of Sam's calls. He knew his mate well, though. Sam had tried to put on an air of nonchalance, but he cared deeply for Emily, and although Sam would never like to admit it, Tommo could see the toll it was taking on his morose friend. Tommo pushed thoughts of his friend aside, made himself a tea and sipped it while flicking through a newspaper. The door creaked open, and Emily and Deb entered.

Tommo walked from behind the bar and hugged Emily. 'Hi, Em.' Tommo, a master at reading people – honed over years of working behind bars – sensed something as Emily clung to their embrace a little longer than necessary.

Her shoulders drooped. 'Hi, Tommo. Sam not in?'

'No, you've missed him. He said he had some errands to run.'

Emily frowned. 'Oh.'

Tommo held out his hand towards Deb, smiling. 'And who's this delightful creature?'

Deb pouted. 'Yeah, all right, Tommo. Cut the flannel,' she said, half-heartedly hugging him.

Tommo returned to the other side of the bar. 'Can I get you ladies a drink?'

Deb surveyed the beers. She had an appetite for most things alcoholic but a particular liking for real ales, a legacy from a past boyfriend. 'What's that one like?' she said, pointing to one of the pumps.

'Dirty Twat? Very nice.'

Deb nodded. 'Yeah, that's the one. I'll try a little of that, please. Great name.'

Tommo pulled a little of the beer into a small glass and handed it to Deb. She sniffed it and took a drink, allowing the liquid to slosh around her mouth before downing the rest. 'Oh, I like that.'

Tommo raised an eyebrow. 'Half?'

She screwed up her face. 'Half? What's one of those?'

Tommo scrutinised Emily, her sullen face looking at the floor. 'What about you, Em? Can I tempt you with one of my fine ales?'

Emily lifted her head and scowled. 'No. I'll have a bloody double brandy and coke.'

Tommo pulled the pint as Deb nudged Emily in the ribs. Emily frowned at her friend, who was shaking her head, then, staring quizzically at first and realising what Deb was hinting at – when she patted her stomach – sighed loudly.

'On second thoughts,' Emily said. 'I'll have an orange juice.' She gave a sideways glance at Deb, who nodded approvingly.

Tommo – who had picked up a short glass and placed it under the optic – turned around abruptly, frowning at Emily. 'You had me going for a moment there. Orange Juice? It's got vitamin C in it, you know. It's considered quite healthy.'

Emily glared at him. 'I'm serious.'

Tommo looked across at Deb, who nodded back at him. 'Fresh or cordial?'

Emily looked up towards the ceiling and groaned.

'Fresh,' Deb said.

Tommo took a carton of orange and poured some into a glass, dropping a few ice cubes into the drink. Handing it to Emily, he topped up Deb's now settled pint. 'Well, wonders will never cease,' he said as he placed the now full glass on the bar, paused for a moment, stroking his chin with his right hand, and stared at the two drinks. 'Wait a minute,' he said, pointing at Emily. 'You're pregnant.'

Deb looked across at Emily, who had her face in her hands. 'You've got to hand it to him,' Deb said. 'He's bloody good.'

Tommo beamed. 'Is she?'

Emily nodded, and Tommo burst out laughing as Deb placed a hand over her mouth. 'Sorry, Em,' she said.

Tommo grabbed a pint glass from under the counter. 'It's Sam's, isn't it? I think I'll have a drink myself.'

Emily folded her arms. 'You know, you two could be a little more understanding. This is my life here.'

'I'm sorry,' he said. 'You and Sam as parents.' He burst out laughing again. 'I couldn't imagine two more irresponsible people.'

Deb tried to stifle her laughter, shaking her head at the doubled-up Tommo, but his outburst made it impossible. She finally cracked, and the pair collapsed into a fit of giggles.

'I'm going,' Emily said, glaring at the pair. 'You two can eff off!'

'Em,' Deb said. 'Don't be like that. At least drink your orange juice. You're drinking for two now, remember?'

Emily headed for the door. 'Piss off.'

Tommo raced from behind the bar, intercepting Emily near the threshold. 'Let's calm down. Does Sam know?'

Emily pushed Tommo in the chest with two hands. 'No. Why do you think I'm here, you fat get!'

Tommo put his massive arms around Emily, swallowing her up in his embrace. 'He's probably gone back to the flat. We'll go around there and see him. I'm sorry. I didn't mean to upset you.'

Emily sobbed into his chest. 'I'm sorry I called you fat.'

Tommo pulled a face at Deb and patted Emily on the back. 'I forgive you.' He winked at Deb.

'We've time for another pint, haven't we?' Deb said.

'Yeah,' Tommo said. 'I'll phone Gene and get him to come in early, and then we'll all head over there.'

Emily, still buried in his ample frame, hugged him tighter. 'Thanks, Tommo.' Tommo looked across at Deb, who had a hand over her mouth to stifle her laughter.

Sam stood outside Emily's mam's house and glanced through the glass in the door. He paused before knocking, took an enormous breath, and then tapped gently on the door. He half hoped no one would answer, not really knowing what to say to Emily, but he had made an effort and if no one was in, at least he could tell anyone who asked that he'd tried. His conscience would be clear, and it was up to Emily now. She was the one who was stubborn. He was about to turn and go when someone came to the door. Sam gulped, summoning his courage, and waited. The door swung open, and Emily's mother stood there. She wore an apron and had flour on her hands and one of her cheeks. Early-fifties, with long blonde hair tied back casually in a half-hearted attempt at a bun, she was attractive in a mumsy sort of way, he thought, her likeness to Emily apparent.

She smiled at him. 'Sam. Come in.'

He followed her through into the kitchen, where she washed her hands under the tap and motioned for him to sit down.

'I'm looking for Emily, Mrs Simpson.'

She brushed her hair away from her face and took off her apron. 'She's not in, I'm afraid. I think she was meeting one of her friends in town.'

Sam frowned. 'Oh.'

'I'll make us a cuppa, shall I?'

'Err … No. You look like you've got your hands full at the moment.'

She picked up the kettle and filled it. 'Oh, don't worry about that. I'm due a break, anyway.'

Sam sat at the table. 'Do you know what time she'll be back, Mrs Simpson?'

She turned and put the kettle on. 'Alison. Call me Alison. Mrs Simpson sounds so formal.' Sitting down next to him, she patted him on the knee. 'Emily didn't say, but she'll probably be hours. We'll have a nice cup of tea, and you can tell me all about it.'

Sam's libido pricked up its ears as explicit images elbowed their way into Sam's mind. 'Has Emily said anything about me?'

'Not really. She mentioned you'd had a little argument.' She stood and walked over to the oven. 'Are you hungry, Sam? I've made some fadgies. They're still quite warm. Would you like one of my fadgies, or maybe two?'

Sam's jaw dropped open. Was he being seduced, or was she only playing with him? He wasn't sure. His mind whirred with possible scenarios. What if her husband came home, Sam thought. Or Emily? Her husband sometimes worked away at weekends. He remembered Emily telling him that. But if Emily returned and found them? His mind desperately tried to reach a resolution. Decline the fadgies, make his excuses, and leave, he thought. That's the safest thing to do. The honourable thing.

'I'd love one,' he said.

He was both relieved and disappointed when the aforementioned fadgies turned out to be just that. Emily's mam popped a couple in front of him, and he watched her slowly butter them – the butter melting into the warm bread. She went to the fridge and returned with some cooked ham, which she delicately placed inside. Then, she slowly sliced a large tomato and popped it on top. Sam had never before been turned on by the sight of someone making sandwiches, but he certainly was now.

'There you are handsome,' she said, pushing the plate across to Sam – her tongue briefly appearing at the side of her mouth, slowly traversing the length of her lips before disappearing again.

He took a bite from one and watched her move towards the oven. Bending down, she checked on its contents inside as Sam surveyed her pert bottom.'

'If you want anything else, Sam.' She looked back over her shoulder at him. 'There's plenty more. You only have to ask.'

Sam couldn't see any panty outline through her jeans. Maybe she was wearing a thong or even going commando. His libido hectored him, now appearing as a bulge in his jeans. 'No, I'm fine for the moment.'

'So?' She returned to her seat and looked him in the eyes. 'What did you and Emily fall out over?'

'Oh, nothing.' He glanced at the baggy shirt she was wearing. The second button on it had been unfastened. By accident or design, he couldn't decide, but he could now see the top of her breasts and the lacy white bra beneath. Sam finished his second sandwich and watched Emily's mother remove another tray of buns from the oven. Her hair, her eyes, her aroma, everything captivated him. His resolve was weakening by the minute. A voice sounded in his head. Don't *you fucking dare,*

*Sam. It's Emily's mam.* While another, even louder, bellowed, *Do it!* Sam rose from his seat, trying to disguise his erection. 'I should go.'

She eased closer. As her hand disappeared inside the top of her blouse, flapping it to cool herself. 'Are you sure?' she purred. Sam's mind's eye conjured up a vision of the two of them on the kitchen table, her blouse ripped open, their jeans around their ankles.

'Yes ... I've got to be somewhere ... somewhere important. I've just remembered.' He jumped to his feet and raced towards the door like someone who'd just heard the three-minute warning. 'Tell Emily I called, will you?' he said, racing past umpteen imaginary scalded cats and out of the house.

Emily's mam leant back against the kitchen table. 'You've still got it, babe,' she said, re-buttoning her shirt and smiling.

Tommo, Deb, and Emily sat waiting in the bar for Gene, who arrived ten minutes later. Gene Milligan had worked in Tommo's bar since it opened two years ago. Late-forties, bald – his hair had vanished years earlier along with his slim waistline, which was now poured over the top of his too-tight jeans – his liking for late-night cocktails and doner kebabs, writ large across his waistline.

Gene pulled off his coat. 'Phew,' he said in his imitable camp timbre. 'I came as quick as I could.'

Deb extravagantly winked at him. 'Who was the lucky man?'

'Good one, Deb. Gorgeous as ever,' he said and flamboyantly kissed her on the cheeks. 'Em,' he said, 'You look positively radiant, darling. You're not keeping something from us, are you?'

Emily's eyes filled up, and turning, she raced for the door. 'What the hell did I say, Tommo?' Gene said.

Tommo patted him on the shoulder. 'Don't worry. She's in a funny mood.'

Deb headed after Emily as Tommo stopped at the threshold. 'Maria will be in later. She had a hair appointment or something.'

Gene pouted and rolled his eyes. 'What colour's the soft mare going for this time?'

'Who knows?' Tommo said, then followed Deb and Emily outside.

Sam lay on the settee watching the television when he heard a knock on the front door. He sighed. He did not feel in the mood for company, so he ignored it. Someone knocked, much louder this time. The sort of *I'm not going away anytime soon* knock, so Sam hauled himself to his feet and trudged towards the door. He opened it. Tommo, Emily, and Deb stood outside.

'Can I come in?' Emily said.

Sam stepped aside. 'Of course. It is your home. You do still live here, don't you?'

Emily forced a smile. 'Thanks.'

The three entered, Sam leading the others into the living room. The empty bottles of lager and the half-full bottle of vodka were still on the coffee table. 'Sorry about the mess,' he said, quickly gathering up some of the bottles.

Tommo took Deb's arm. 'We'll go and make a cup of tea,' he said, reluctantly pulling the grinning Deb from the room and closing the door behind them.

Sam forced a smile. 'Nice to see you,' he said, and Emily fell sobbing into his arms.

Deb stood with her ear near the kitchen door as Tommo held out a cup of tea for her. He winked at him as she took the drink. 'Wonder what's happening?' she said.

Tommo sat at the table. 'We'll find out soon enough.' He rubbed his beard thoughtfully. 'Have you ever thought about having children, Deb?'

She sat opposite him. 'Sometimes. It goes with being a woman, feeling broody, but it only takes the smell of a shitty nappy or the scream of one of them to bring me to my senses, though.'

'I've always fancied having a son. Sebastian.'

Deb sneered. 'Sebastian. Why the bloody hell would you call him Sebastian?'

'I like the name,' Tommo said as he hid behind his mug. 'What's wrong with Sebastian?'

'It sounds like a posh get's name. I prefer Gregory.'

'Gregory? I don't like that at all. There was a lad at our school called Gregory. He wore round specs and always had snot hanging from his nose.'

Deb wrinkled her nose. 'Tommo, that's disgusting.'

'It's true. Ask Sam.'

'Anyway,' Deb said, 'before you can have a son you'll need a woman.'

'Cheers, Deb. Depress me, why don't you.'

'Sorry, Tommo,' She patted him on the arm playfully. 'Rules are rules.'

'What about you?' he said.

She pouted. 'You're not my type, mate.'

Tommo blushed. 'No … I meant, haven't you got anyone at the moment?'

'No. Not since Andy.'

Tommo swigged his tea. 'Andy. What happened there?'

Deb picked up a carving knife. 'Andy was a wanker. If I ever run into him again, he'll be sorry.' She swished the blade through the air. 'I'd put an end to his philandering ways.'

Tommo chuckled. 'Hell, hath no fury.'

'Bloody right.' They both turned as the door opened.

Emily and Sam entered holding hands and glanced at Deb, the knife still hanging in mid-air.

Sam nodded towards the knife. 'What's going on here?'

'Nothing,' she said, placing the knife back on the table. 'I was telling Tommo about Andy.'

Emily nodded and smiled to herself. 'Mm, Andy.'

Sam beamed. 'We're going to be parents.'

'We know,' Tommo said.

'Don't let the social services find out,' Deb said. 'They'll intervene.'

'Cheeky cow,' Emily said.

Sam put his arm around Emily's shoulder. 'Yeah. She'll make a fantastic mother.'

Emily stared lovingly at Sam. 'And I think Sam will make an excellent dad.' Sam kissed her on the cheek.

Tommo got up from his seat. 'Where are they?' he said, walking towards the door laughing. 'Where have you hidden the real Sam and Emily?'

Sam rolled his eyes. 'Tommo, you're hysterical.'

'Should we have a drink to celebrate?' Deb said.

Emily shook her head. 'I can't have alcohol, but I'll have a soft drink, though.'

Sam waved at Tommo. 'You come with me. We'll go to the shop for some bubbly.'

'Champagne?' he said, following Sam out of the room.

'Well, maybe Prosecco,' Sam said.

Emily and Deb waited for the door to shut behind the two of them, and Deb closed the kitchen door. 'He took it well then?' Deb said.

'Sam's over the moon.'

Deb smiled at her friend. 'I know I joked about it, but I'm really pleased for you. If you're sure that it's what you want.'

'Never more so,' she said, and her friend hugged her tightly. Emily laughed. 'You should try it.'

'I'd need a man first,' Deb said.

'What about Tommo?'

'Tommo?' Deb frowned. 'Tommo's nice, but I don't think he's really boyfriend material.'

Emily sat at the table. 'Why not?'

'Well, he's not my type for one.'

'He owns a pub, and you love beer.' Emily raised her eyebrows. 'Some women might call him a catch.'

Deb sat opposite her friend. 'Well, not me. Anyway, it's only a micropub. I mean, look at the size of Tommo. He's like a front-row-forward.'

'He's kind and considerate.'

'Emily,' Deb said, 'I like my men fit. Muscles to die for. Andy's abs were fantastic. You could bounce a cricket ball on them. And when he was naked and in the shower with me, my God, I used to orgasm looking at him.' She huffed. 'I couldn't fit in the shower with Tommo.'

'But Andy did the dirty on you.'

'I know he did, but what a body.' She closed her eyes and smiled.

Emily patted Deb on the shoulder. 'All I'm saying is, don't rule him out.'

'Stop trying to play the matchmaker,' Deb said. 'You just want a foursome.'

'Oh, well. You can't blame a girl for trying.'

'What about your mam and dad?' Deb said.

'Sam and I are going over there later today.'

Deb rolled her eyes. 'Sam and I? Can I come? I'd love to see—'

'Sorry, Deb,' Emily said, shaking her head. 'Parents only,' she said, affectionately patting her friend's cheek.

## CHAPTER SIXTEEN

**2015** – Hockney and Mr Jones pulled up outside *Seaview Nursing Home*, got out of their respective cars and headed inside.

Hockney looked around at the attractive building set in beautiful grounds. 'It looks lovely,' Hockney said as Jones approached.

Jones briefly stopped and surveyed the surroundings. 'It's one of the better homes.' He headed inside and past reception, nodded politely at the woman behind the desk, who returned his nod, and the two men continued along a corridor. They reached a room, and the door to it opened. An elderly lady was sitting in a chair, facing the television.

Jones sat next to her and took hold of her hand. 'Hello, Mum. How are you?'

She studied Jones without a hint of recognition – staring at her son, searching her memories for a name to fit the face. 'Are we going home, Jim?' she said.

'I'm Stephen, Mum. I've brought a friend with me. This is Bill. He's travelled from Teesside.'

She glanced at Hockney. 'Stephen?'

Hockney moved forward. 'Hello, Mrs Jones.'

'Agnes,' Jones said.

Hockney held out his hand and smiled. 'Agnes.'

She frowned. 'You're not Billy. Billy's dead.'

'Not Uncle Billy, Mum. This is Bill. A friend of mine. He's come to ask you about Billy.'

Hockney sat beside her. 'Can I show you some photos, Agnes?'

The old lady looked up at him and smiled as Hockney removed the photocopied pieces of paper from his leather folder and handed one to her. She stared at the photo of a young man dressed in a soldier's uniform holding the hand of a young girl.

'It's our Billy and me. Doesn't he look handsome in his uniform?'

Hockney took out his notebook. 'He does.'

'All the girls fancied him,' she said. 'He could've had his pick of them.'

Jones smiled. 'How old were you when the photo was taken, Mum?'

'About eight or nine.' A smile appeared on her face. 'Billy would give me sweets.' She looked at the two men. 'From his allowance. He called me his little angel.'

'What about your mam and dad?' Hockney said. 'What were they like?'

The smile fell from her face, and she frowned deeply. 'Mam was never the same after Billy died.'

Hockney passed her another photo. 'Do you remember this chap?'

She laughed. 'That's Arthur. Billy's best pal. Arthur …' she said, searching her memory for his name. 'Arthur Parchester.'

Hockney made notes. 'What was Arthur like?'

She giggled and her face lit up. 'Arthur was funny. He would do voices from the radio, and he could play the ukulele like George Formby.'

A care assistant entered carrying a tray with a teapot and some biscuits on it. 'I thought you might like a drink.'

'Thanks,' Jones said.

The care assistant smiled at the old woman. 'How are you, Agnes?'

The old lady lifted her head and stared back. 'Have you seen our mam?'

'She hasn't come in yet.' She stroked Agnes on her arm. 'I'll let you know when she does.'

Agnes, suitably placated, looked at the photos again. 'Billy was a good footballer. Dad said he could have played for The Boro if …' She looked away, trying to remember her train of thought.

Jones poured the tea for Hockney and himself into the teacups. He opened a plastic beaker on the tray and filled it two-thirds with tea, topping it up with a generous amount of milk. He added two sugars to it and pressed the lid back on.

'Here's your tea,' Jones said, handing his mother the beaker.

'What did Billy do before the war?' Hockney asked.

'He was training to become a carpenter. Dad got him a job as an apprentice at old man Cowen's.'

'Old man Cowen's?' Jones said.

'Yes. You remember, Jim. He had that workshop on the high street in town.'

Hockney looked inquisitively at Jones. 'Jim was my dad. She

sometimes gets us confused.' Hockney nodded. 'I remember,' Jones said, turning back to his mother.

The three continued to chat, Hockney and Jones interjecting now and again with questions about Billy and his life before the war broke out as the old woman recounted her childhood and the characters from it. Once the tea was finished, Jones placed the empty cups back on the tray and stood. 'I'll pop these into the kitchen,' he said, picking up the tray. He turned towards the door and glanced at Hockney. 'You'll be all right for a minute?'

Hockney put his hand on the old lady's arm. 'Fine. We'll be fine.'

Jones left, and Hockney glanced over his left shoulder, watching him exit. He put his hand inside his folder, pulled out the photocopy he'd received from Kim and gave it to the old lady, without saying a word.

She smiled. 'It's Our Lady,' she said. 'It was our Billy's.'

'Do you remember it?'

'I do. A young soldier brought it around one day. He said Billy had sent it.'

Hockney glanced towards the door. 'Do you remember what happened to it?'

'Dad put it in the corner of the washhouse, under an old blanket.'

'Where was this?'

'At our house.' She studied Hockney. 'Mam got upset when she saw it again after Billy died. She said it reminded her of him too much, and Dad got rid of it.'

'Can you remember where?'

The old lady furrowed her brow, deep in thought as Jones came back into the room. Hockney surreptitiously took the piece of paper from the old lady and returned it to the folder.

'How are we doing?' Jones asked.

Hockney smiled. 'Fine. Your mam was telling me about the house she lived in.'

'In Saltburn?'

Hockney looked at the old lady. 'I'm not sure.'

'It was Saltburn where you lived wasn't it, Mum?' Jones said. 'Near the station?'

Agnes looked at Jones. 'He gave it to a church.'

Jones looked across at Hockney and shrugged. 'Gave what?'

She looked at the two men. 'Our Lady.'

Jones frowned. 'I think it's time for us to go,' Jones said. 'She sounds a little tired.'

Hockney nodded and took hold of the old lady's hand, patting it gently. 'It's been lovely meeting you, Agnes.'

The two men stood, and Hockney moved towards the door, while

Jones hugged and kissed his mother. He joined Hockney at the threshold and turned to wave. 'See you later, Mum.'

The old lady looked up at him. '346,' she said. 'It had the number 346 on the bottom.'

Jones turned to Hockney, shook his head a little, and smiled at him as the two men made their way towards the exit.

Jones stopped at reception to speak to the care assistant who'd brought them the tea before joining Hockney outside. 'Mum was a little more lucid today,' Jones said. 'Some days …'

Hockney's eyes glistened. 'She reminds me of my mother.'

'Was she in care?'

'In the end. We kept her at home for as long as possible, but when they become a worry, you have to put them somewhere safe.'

'Did she have dementia?'

Hockney lowered his eyes. 'She did. Much worse than your Mum. In the end, she didn't recognise any of us. It's strange when the memories go as if they take the person with them. Maybe that's all any of us are. A collection of memories.'

'I know what you mean. I hope it was some help?'

Hockney smiled, offering his hand to Jones. 'It was,' he said as Jones shook it warmly.

Jones put a hand inside his jacket pocket and pulled out an envelope, handing it to Hockney. 'Before I forget. I managed to find a few photos of Billy.'

Taking them from Jones, Hockney placed them in his leather folder. 'Thanks, you've been extremely helpful.'

'If I can be of any further help,' Jones said. Hockney nodded and strode across to his car.

'Don't forget to send me a copy of that book,' Jones said.

Hockney stopped at the passenger door and forced a smile. 'I won't.' he said and got into his vehicle.

# CHAPTER SEVENTEEN

Phillip stood outside Kim's flat, straightened his shirt a little and brushed some imaginary bits of dust from his trousers. He took the piece of gum from his mouth and wrapped it inside the paper he'd been saving. Taking a deep breath and gripping the bottle of wine in his left hand, he knocked. What if his breath smelt, he thought. Bringing his right hand up to his mouth, he breathed on it while trying to decipher if it did. Certain it didn't, he stood up straight and waited.

Kim opened the door and stepped forward to kiss him on the cheek. 'You smell lovely.'

'I thought I'd better have a bath. I didn't want to stink your flat out.'

'Where's Bagsy?' she said, glancing outside.

'I left him with my neighbour.'

Kim beckoned him inside. 'You could have brought him, you know. I've got a bowl ready.'

'I'll have to take a doggie bag for him.' He followed Kim into the kitchen.

'Is he okay with your neighbours?'

'Yeah. Mrs Cavendish spoils Baggage rotten.'

Kim nodded at the bottle in Phillip's hand. 'Oh, wine. I was just thinking I could do with a glass.'

'I brought white, not red.'

Kim smiled, pointing to a chair. 'I'm not a fan of red. It tends to give me a headache.'

'Me too.'

'It shouldn't be too long,' she said. 'What about a glass now?'

'Of course.' He held out the bottle.

Kim took the wine from him, poured two large glasses, and handed one to Phillip.

'Cheers,' he said, and the pair clinked their glasses together.

Kim sat opposite. 'So? Sam and Emily?'

'Sam and Emily?'

'Yes. *Sam and Emily.*'

Phillip put his glass on the table and sat back in his chair. 'They slept together.'

Kim rolled her eyes. 'Tell me something I don't know.'

'You knew? How?'

'Emily told me.'

'When?'

Kim sat back in her chair and took a sip of wine, smiling at Phillip. 'We met for coffee.'

He picked his wine back up. 'Right.'

'She asked me if I'd meet her in town. I was curious. I thought maybe she fancied me and was trying to get me into bed.'

Phillip choked on his wine. 'Really?' he said, wiping the wine, which had escaped from his mouth, off his chin with a napkin. 'And …?'

'It turned out she just wanted to ask about Sam. Shame, really, because she's attractive.' Phillip stared open-mouthed at her. 'I'm only kidding,' Kim said and got up from her seat. 'Been there, done that.' She winked at him as she walked away.

'What, with another woman?'

Kim poured the spaghetti into a colander. 'Years ago.'

'You're a dark horse.'

She winked at him, again. 'Come on. I bet you have some little secrets, too.'

'Yeah. I've slept with a woman as well.'

Kim laughed, sharing the drained spaghetti between two plates. She spooned on the sauce and handed one to Phillip. 'Parmesan?'

'I'm not really keen on it. Who was this woman?'

Kim sat. 'Someone I worked with, no one special. We were staying in a hotel.'

'In the same bed?'

'Yeah. Girls do it all the time. Sleep in the same bed, I mean. We're not as hung-up as men.'

'And it … happened?'

'It did.' She wiped some of the sauce slowly from her lips.

'Did you—'

'I didn't *not* enjoy it, but it's not for me.'

'What was she like, this other woman? Just so I can get it straight in my head, like.'

Kim smiled. 'Is this turning you on?'

'I'm only human,' Phillip said.

'Well, before you get too carried away with your libido, let's get back to Sam and Emily.'

'That's all I know. Well apart from …'

'Apart from?' Kim said narrowing her eyes at him.

'He likes Emily.' Kim nodded and encouraged Phillip to continue. 'I mean, really likes her.'

'Loves?' Kim said.

'Well, I'm not sure if it's love. Besides, there's Miss Jacobs.'

'Miss Jacobs?' Kim frowned. 'The woman who he's working for?'

Phillip twirled the spaghetti around his fork. 'Yep.'

'Sam didn't …?'

'He did.'

'The twat.'

'Why? It's not like he and Emily are a couple. It may be unprofessional of him, sleeping with a client, but—'

'But nothing. Emily loves him.'

'Really? She said that?'

'Yes indeed. Well, not in so many words. There was something else. Something Emily wasn't telling me.'

'What?'

'I think she's pregnant.'

Phillip dropped his fork onto the plate. 'Did she say she was?'

'No. I sensed it.'

'Bit of a leap, Kim.'

'I know. I just have this feeling. Call it women's intuition.'

'Does that even exist?'

Kim adopted a serious face. 'Oh, yes.'

'I bet she's not.' He lifted his fork back up and carried on eating. 'They wouldn't be that stupid.'

Kim forked a mouthful of food into her mouth. Slowly wiping the tomato sauce from around her lips with her finger. 'Are you willing to bet?'

'A fiver?'

Kim laughed. 'A fiver. What sort of bet is that? Uncle Bill would be turning in his grave.'

'All right. What do you want to bet?'

'If I'm right.' She raised her eyebrows. 'You have to decorate my spare room.'

'And if you're wrong?' Phillip said.

'You get to decorate me.' Phillip's fork dropped from his hand and bounced once before clanging to the floor.

Emily and Sam walked into Emily's mam's house. 'Mam, where are you?' Emily shouted.

'I'm in here,' a voice said. Sam followed Emily through into the kitchen.

Emily's mam smiled. 'Sam. Twice in one day.'

'What do you mean?' Emily said, frowning at Sam.

'Sam was here earlier looking for you.'

Emily looked at Sam. 'You didn't say.'

'I forgot.'

'You two made up then?' her mam said.

Emily looked out into the garden. 'Where's Dad?'

'He's away on a driving job. He had an emergency call from work. Why?'

'We've got something to tell you?' Emily said.

Her mam smiled. 'This sounds interesting. You're not pregnant, are you?' She laughed.

'Yes.'

'Stop messing about.'

'I'm not. I'm pregnant, and Sam's the dad.'

Emily's mam sat on a chair close by, allowing the words to slowly sink in. 'But … how?'

Emily glanced upwards. 'The usual way, Mam.'

'But I thought you're—'

'Gay,' Emily said. 'It's a little complicated, but you're going to be a granny.'

She smiled and stood, hugging her daughter tightly. 'Oh, Emily, that's wonderful. You're definitely keeping it?'

'Yes,' Sam said as Emily's mam pulled him into the hug.

'Well done young man,' she said patting him on the cheek. 'Wait until your dad hears. He'll be over the moon that his little girl is going to be a mum.' She cupped Emily's face and looked between them both. 'What about you two?'

Emily looked across at Sam, who nodded. 'We're going to give it a go. No promises, though.'

She grabbed Sam again, hugging him tightly. 'Come here, gorgeous.'

Sam could feel her breasts pressing into him. Her perfume filled his nostrils, returning him to earlier in the day. His libido stirring, Sam forcefully pushed the thought away, trying desperately to remember Boro's Carling Cup-winning team to subdue his mounting erection.

'This baby's going to be gorgeous,' Emily's mam said and pinched Sam's cheek. 'Well done, handsome. I'll put the kettle on and make a nice cuppa. You can tell me all about it.'

'Joseph Job!' Sam blurted out.

'Joseph Job?' Emily said.

The two women looked at him, and a frown appeared on their faces. 'Sorry,' he said. 'Just something I was trying to remember earlier.'

Phillip knocked on his neighbour's door, a muffled bark coming from within. The door opened, and Mrs Cavendish stood there with Baggage. 'It's your dad, Baggage,' she said as Baggage nuzzled his leg, looking for his expected stroke. Phillip obliged, rubbing his ears.

'I got you these,' Phillip said. 'For looking after Bagsy.' He handed the old lady a box of chocolates.

'You shouldn't be so daft. I love having Baggage here. He's great company, aren't you, boy.' She rubbed Baggage's head affectionately.

Phillip opened the door to his flat as Baggage shot inside, returning seconds later with his lead in his mouth.

'A bloody walk, now?' Baggage's tail wagged frantically.

'Guess where I've been tonight?' he said, fastening on the dog's lead, and rubbing Baggage's head. 'With the lovely Kim.' Baggage cocked his head to one side as if digesting the words. His tail wagging faster still.

## CHAPTER EIGHTEEN

Baggage padded his way across the garden towards the hole in the fence. He lifted his nose as a hundred different aromas filled his nostrils. One caught his attention – the scent of another dog. He padded through into the field, stopping now and again to sniff the air. The flutter of a bird to his right made him turn sharply, and he stared at the Magpie, picking at some carrion on the floor. The dog's right leg hung in mid-air, ready to pounce as the bird, unaware it was being watched, went about its business. Baggage crept closer. He was only twenty feet from it now, and unable to hold his nerve any longer, he made a dart for it. The bird, reacting quickly, took flight, and as Baggage jumped high, he snapped at fresh air – the Magpie's speed and agility lifting it clear of his attacker. He composed himself again, and looking around the field, he spotted the bitch some distance away, studying him. He bounded after her, darting off through the thick grass. He chased and then stopped. The bitch mirrored his move before running off again. He resumed his pursuit, and they carried on like this for several minutes – the gap between them gradually closing. She stopped with Baggage no more than ten feet from her now. He walked towards her, the pair performing a merry dance, pirouetting around each other and occasionally stopping for Baggage to sniff at his prize. He paused as a voice drifted across the field towards him. He listened, intently. His head slightly cocked at an angle, trying to decipher the direction of the sound as the bitch eyed him inquisitively.

'*Baggage!*' it said in long, drawn-out syllables. The voice echoed through the open space. 'Baggage. Where are you, boy? I've got something for you.

Baggage turned and moved towards the voice as the bitch looked on incredulously. He stopped and glanced back at the other dog before bouncing off again.

Kim held out her arms. 'There you are,' she said as Baggage ran to her, wagging his tail excitedly. She ruffled his ears as he licked her face. 'Look what I've got for you, boy,' she said, holding out a massive bone-shaped chew. He pirouetted, took the present from her and headed back towards the house with his prize, followed closely by Kim.

Phillip looked at the sleeping dog. 'I wonder what he's dreaming about. Look at his legs twitching.'

'Probably a *Lady Dog*,' Sam said.

'You would say that.'

Sam shook his fist. 'Go on Baggage. Give her a good seeing too.'

Kim entered carrying two cups. 'Give who a good seeing too?'

'Nothing,' Phillip said.

'I've made you two a cup of tea.' She placed the drinks on their desks.

Sam nodded towards the dog. 'Actually, we were wondering what Baggage was dreaming about.'

Kim knelt next to the dog, stroking his head. 'Bones, probably.' Baggage opened a sleepy eye, before falling back asleep. 'He looks tired,' Kim said to Phillip.

Phillip picked up his mug. 'I took him for a long walk this morning. I think I've worn him out.'

'Hasn't Albert showed up yet?' Sam asked.

Kim stood. 'No. I think he's with his therapist.'

Sam stood and rubbed his chin. 'I had something to tell the three of you. I suppose I can tell Albert later.'

Kim winked at Phillip. 'Tell us what?'

'I'm,' he began. 'Well … when I say me, I mean Emily and I—'

'She's pregnant,' Kim said.

Sam furrowed his brow. 'How'd you know?'

Kim smiled at Phillip. 'Women's intuition.'

'I know it's a little strange, Emily being gay and that, but we've decided to give it a go.'

Kim walked across to Sam and hugged him. 'Oh, that's great news. Isn't it great, Phillip?'

Phillip stood and offered his hand. 'Yes, it is. Well done, son.'

Kim turned and strolled towards the door. 'I'd better get going.' She stopped at the threshold to glance back at Phillip.

Sam frowned. 'Going? You've only just arrived.'

'I've got to go and get some paper and paint for my spare room. Phillip's going to decorate it for me. Isn't that right, Phillip?'

'I guess so,' Phillip said as Kim sashayed out of the room.
'What's got into her?' Sam said.
'We had a bet. Kim guessed Emily was pregnant, and we had a little wager.'
'Oh, yeah. Who won?'
'Who'd you think? I'm decorating her spare bedroom, thanks to you.'
Sam laughed. 'What would you have won?'
Phillip sighed. 'What do you think?'
'Ah. Sorry about that. If only I'd worn a condom.'
Phillip looked towards the door Kim had left by. 'If only.'

Albert sat opposite Miss Waltham, who looked up from her notes. 'This case you're working on. It sounds dangerous.'
'I thought that, but Tommo said he'll look after me.'
'This Tommo sounds really nice.' She peered over the top of her glasses and smiled.
'He is.'
'And you think your uncle's death has something to do with this Eagle?' Miss Waltham said.
'That's what Sam and Phillip think.'
Miss Waltham looked over the top of her glasses again. 'Phillip is the one who likes the secretary—'
'Kim.'

**2015** – Hockney arrived back in Redcar in the early afternoon, slowly ascended the steps to his office and trudged in. Kim, who was talking with someone on the phone, waved pleasantly at him. Hockney made a gesture with his hand of someone drinking. Kim nodded that she wanted one as she continued to talk, and Hockney headed into the kitchen.
He returned with two cups of tea moments later, handing one to Kim. 'How'd your trip go?' she said, taking the cup from him.
'Good. Any calls?' Hockney sipped his drink.
'A couple.' She consulted her notepad. 'Mr Stankovich wants to talk with you. Sounded urgent. And Geoff Robards phoned. He was asking where you were. Typical copper. Every conversation's like an interrogation.'
'Goes with the job. Did you tell him?'
Kim raised her eyebrows. 'Bill, you know me, I'm the soul of discretion. I said you were away, and I had no idea where.'
'Good girl.' He gave her a peck on the cheek. 'Any post?'
'Lots and lots of brown envelopes.'
'File them in the round filing cabinet, will you?' he said, nodding at the metal bin close to her desk before turning and heading for his office.
'You'll have to pay them eventually,' she shouted after him.

Hockney sat at his desk, opened his leather folder, removed the contents, and scattered them across the top. He took hold of the envelope Jones had given him and pulled out the photos, flicking through them one by one. He stopped at a young-looking William Jones smiling at the camera. He was wearing a bib and brace set of overalls and held what looked like a saw in his hand. Hockney scrutinised the photo. It had apparently been taken while he was working somewhere. It wasn't William Jones fascinating him, though, nor what he was doing. It was where he was. William Jones stood outside a church. A large window could be seen behind him, and gravestones lay to his right, but what church was it? There weren't any clues in the photo. Hockney picked up the telephone, located Jones's number and called.

'Hello,' Jones said.

'It's Bill Hockney.'

'Hi, Bill.'

'I've been looking through those photos you loaned me, and I thought I might include a couple in my book. There's one in particular of William before the war, standing outside a church. I thought I could use that one to show that these brave young lads had lives before they went off to fight.'

'I know the one.'

'Have you any idea where it was taken?' Hockney said.

'No, I'm sorry, I don't. Mum might, but she's been a little unwell.'

'Oh, I'm sorry to hear that. Don't worry about it. Let me know how she is.'

'I will,' Jones said.

Hockney hung up, stood, and walked across the room. Pulling the filing cabinet away from the wall, he deposited the photos beneath the floorboards. Putting his hand back inside the hole, Hockney pulled out a plastic bag and glanced inside at the velvet roll. Replacing the floorboards and cabinet, he placed the roll on his desk and headed through to reception.

'I'm off out to get a sandwich,' Hockney said. 'Do you want anything?'

'I fancy a bag of chips,' she said. 'Bugger the diet.'

'Diet? There's not a picking on you.'

'Tony said I was overweight.'

Hockney walked over to Kim and kissed her on the cheek. 'Tony's a wanker. You're well shot of him. I'll swing for him if I ever run into that tosser.'

'Thanks.'

'Anything with them, gorgeous?' he said, walking down the stairs.

'Curry sauce,' Kim shouted.

Hockney and Kim sat eating their chips – the table a mass of paper and condiments. He picked up a piece of white buttered bread and made himself a chip butty.

'How did things go in Whitehaven?' Kim said.

'Pretty well. I got some useful information.'

'You will be careful, Bill?' she said. 'Some of your clients don't look the sort to be messing with.'

'Don't you worry about me.' He squeezed her hand. 'I'm a wily old dog.'

'About the bills.'

Hockney sighed. 'How much are they?'

'Well. There's the phone and electric, and this month's mortgage is due.'

Hockney reached into his jacket pocket. 'How much?'

Kim lowered her eyes. 'About a grand.'

He pulled out an envelope and passed it across the table to her. 'There's fifteen hundred there. The other five hundred is for you.'

'No,' Kim said. 'I couldn't.'

'Of course you can. Buy yourself something nice. It'll only end up on the back of some useless nag.'

'Are you sure?' she said.

'Yes, I'm sure. The clients I'm working for are generous, and I'm going to string them out a bit longer.'

'This statue they're paying you to find. Do you think you'll find it?'

Hockney laughed. 'I'm not even sure it exists. If I do find it, you and I won't have to worry about bills anymore. We'll leave cold and damp Redcar and set up a detective agency somewhere warm. Bermuda or Jamaica.'

'Oh, I like the sound of that.'

'Don't hold your breath, though,' he said. 'I think it's a wild goose chase. I've got something else for you.' He headed for his office, returned moments later, placed the velvet roll on the table, undid the tie, and opened it. Kim looked at a beautiful pearl necklace.

'Wow,' she said. 'It's gorgeous. Where did you get it from?'

He ran his fingers across the pearls. 'It was my mam's. It's the only thing I've never sold over the years. It's been in and out of hock plenty, though.' He lifted it up and held it out. 'I want you to have it.'

'I couldn't.'

'Why not? It hardly suits me, and I haven't anyone else to leave it to.'

'It's too much, Bill.' She kissed him on his cheek and studied the pearls.

He put his hand to her face. 'You're like a daughter to me, and I can't think of a better recipient.'

She hugged him. 'Thanks, but I couldn't.'

Hockney smiled. 'Have a think about it. I'll keep it safe until you change your mind.'

'I might not.'

He wrapped it back up. 'I'll leave it to you in my will.'

'Yes, do that,' she said, 'but hopefully, I'll have a long wait.'

Hockney wrapped his arms around Kim, hugged her tightly, and kissed her head.

Phillip walked towards the kitchen next to Kim's office. She was sitting on a chair staring out of the window, and he watched her from the threshold of the room. Kim was oblivious to him and looked sad, her brow a deep furrow. She reached into her bag and took out a tissue.

'You okay?' he said as Kim turned away from him to blow her nose.

'I was thinking of Bill. One of the last times we talked was in here.' She shook her head. 'He told me we would move somewhere warm if he ever found the Eagle. Jamaica or Bermuda.'

Phillip walked across, sat beside her and placed an arm around her shoulder as Kim pushed her head into his chest.

'I miss him,' she said and blew her nose again.

'We're trying to find out who killed him. Sam and I think we may have some leads.'

'It won't bring him back, though.'

'No,' Phillip said. 'It won't.'

Baggage padded into the room and made his way over to Kim, placing his head on her thigh. He stared up at her with his huge, saucer-like eyes as if sensing her sadness.

Kim smiled at the dog, cupping his chin with her left hand while rubbing his head with her right. 'Are you hungry, boy?' Baggage's tail wagged excitedly. 'Well, I'd better get you fed.' She planted a kiss on his face, stood and walked across to the sink, pulling a can of dog food from out of the cupboard beneath.

'I wish you'd give me as much attention as him,' Phillip whispered.

Kim turned around. 'Sorry? Missed that.'

'Nothing.' He turned to leave and headed for the door.

'Try wagging your tail a bit more,' Kim whispered.

Phillip stopped at the door. 'Pardon.'

'I was talking to Baggage.'

Phillip smiled at her and then left.

'Your dad,' she said, stroking the dog while he ate, 'needs to be a bit less backward at coming forward.' Baggage looked up at Kim as if digesting what she was saying before resuming his eating.

# CHAPTER NINETEEN

Sam and Phillip sat at their desks in the office when the silence was broken by the sound of Baggage padding across the floor, a ball hanging loosely from his mouth. He stopped, dropped it next to Phillip's chair, and stared up at him, his tail wagging furiously.

'I haven't got time to throw your ball, Bagsy. I'm snowed under. Maybe later.' He rubbed the dog's ear, and Baggage, as if understanding, picked up his ball and trotted over to Sam.

'What's the matter, son?' Sam said as Baggage dropped the ball into his lap. 'Phillip not playing?'

Sam bounced it to the other side of the room, and Baggage ran across to retrieve it. Returning with the ball in his mouth, he dropped it next to Sam.

Phillip glanced up from his paperwork. 'He'll have you doing that all day.'

'I don't mind. There's not much on at the moment. I'm waiting for that big job worth millions to walk through the door.'

'An office is hardly the place to throw balls.' Phillip looked at Sam. 'Shouldn't you be picking out a pram or something?'

'Emily's mam and dad are buying one for us.' Sam grinned and bounced the ball across the room again.

Phillip jumped up. 'I think I'll make a cuppa.'

Sam sat back in his chair, balancing on its two back legs. 'Milk, no sugar, mate.'

Phillip headed out of the office to reception and smiled at Kim, who was flicking through a magazine.

'Cup of tea, Kim?'

She put down the magazine and smiled. 'Oh, I'd love one.'

Phillip made the teas and carried the three cups through to reception. He handed Kim hers, looking down at the paperwork on her desk. 'Much on?'

'Bit quiet,' Kim said. 'We're doing okay, though. The business, I mean. I was just doing the monthly accounts.'

'Good.' He took a thoughtful sip of his tea. 'I may end up doing this forever. I see you've bought the paper and paint,' he said, nodding at the items stacked up in the corner.

'I did.' She grinned. 'I just need a big strapping lad to do it for me.'

A man entered the reception. 'Did someone mention me?' he said.

Phillip turned around and looked at him.

The man offered his hand. 'You all right?' he said, nodding at Phillip.

Phillip shook it. 'Phillip Davison. You are?'

Kim sighed. 'This is Tony,' Kim said. 'My ex.'

He turned his attention to her. 'How are you, babe?'

'What do you want?' Kim said.

'Darling. Don't be like that.'

'I'm not your darling. What do you want, Tony?'

Phillip looked across at Kim. 'I'll leave you to it.'

Kim smiled at Phillip. 'It won't take long.'

Phillip smiled back and collected the teas, heading back to his office.

Tony edged closer to Kim. 'Why the hostility?'

'Why do you think? You're a two-timing bastard.'

'It's over with Jen.'

Kim stared out of the window. 'So? Who cares?'

'Listen, babe. I was stupid. I made a horrendous mistake.' Moving closer, he took hold of her arm, and Kim pulled it free.

'That's no concern of mine.'

'I was sorry to hear about Bill.'

'No you weren't,' she said, turning to face him. 'You hated Bill.'

'I wouldn't say that. I know me and Bill never really hit it off, but I didn't want him dead.'

'Yeah, well. He is.'

'What about a cup of coffee.' He nodded towards the door. 'One of your favourite cakes, too. On me.'

Kim picked up her mug. 'I've got tea.'

Tony sat on the edge of Kim's desk. 'What about a drink later, then?'

'Tony, I've moved on.' She glanced towards Phillip's office as Tony followed her stare.

'I see.' He shrugged. 'Maybe another time?'

She turned to look out of the window again. 'Mmm.'

He headed for the door and stopped near the top of the stairs. 'See you soon, darling.'

She turned to watch him leave. 'Not if I see you first,' Kim whispered.

Tony made his way downstairs and out of the building. He took out his mobile phone and dialled. 'I've been to the agency.'

'And?' said the voice on the other end.

'Early days, but it went better than I thought. She didn't throw anything at me.'

'We need to find out what they know. Do you think she'll play ball?'

'Doddle,' Tony said. 'Kim's like putty in my hands. Always was. There may be a fly in the ointment, though.'

'Oh, yeah?'

'She could have a thing going with one of the blokes that own the agency.'

'Which one?'

'Phillip Davison,' Tony said.

'Leave it with me. I'll see what I can dig up on him. Maybe he has a skeleton or two hidden away.'

Deep in thought, Phillip sat back at his desk while Sam continued to throw the ball for the now panting Baggage.

'Sam!' Phillip said. 'For Christ's sake. I'm trying to concentrate here, mate.'

The ball bounced and wedged behind a filing cabinet in the corner, and Baggage ran over to it, trying to decipher where it had gone. His head tilted at an angle as if deep in thought.

Sam looked at Phillip. 'What's up?'

'Nothing.'

'What's up? You went to make tea, all smiles. And you return all sullen. You and Kim haven't had a tiff, have you?'

'No. It's just …'

'Come on. Spit it out.' Sam rocked back on the rear two legs of his chair. He picked up his tea and took a deliberately loud slurp. 'Tell Aunty Sam.'

Phillip nodded towards reception. 'Kim's ex is in there.'

'I see. What's he like?'

Phillip sneered. 'Babe this and darling that.'

'Christ! You've got it bad. You and Kim haven't even bumped hips yet, and you're like this.'

'What if—?' Phillip glanced towards reception.

'What if?' Sam said, putting his hands behind his head. 'You'll have to fight for her. Don't let some nobhead get the better of you. Her ex-boyfriend hasn't got your secret weapon, either.' Sam nodded at Baggage, still trying to decipher where his ball had gone. Baggage padded across to Sam, looking up at him, hoping he would provide an answer.

'What's up, boy? Lost your ball?' Baggage wagged his tail, moved across to the filing cabinet, and barked apologetically.

Sam got up from his seat and walked over. 'Go and speak to her,' he said to Phillip. Sam looked behind the filing cabinet and could see the ball wedged between it and the wall. He bent down and tried to get his hand to it as Baggage licked his face in a pre-emptive thank-you for his efforts.

'Hold on, Bagsy,' Sam said. 'I haven't got it yet.' The dog licked his ear. 'Christ! This is like spending a night with Claire Yearly. You're nearly as passionate as her.' Sam stood, accepting defeat.

'Who's Claire Yearly?' Phillip asked.

'The worst kisser I've ever encountered,' Sam said. He raised his eyebrows. 'Not bad in the sack, though.' He looked at the ball. 'I can't get to it. Not while Baggage is molesting me anyway.'

Phillip sighed. 'Move the filing cabinet.'

Sam tried. The weight of it thwarted his efforts. 'It's too heavy.'

'If you shifted a few of the newspapers on top, that might help.'

Baggage barked as if confirming what Phillip had said. Sam began removing the papers from the top, placing them on the floor next to his desk. He picked up a large handful, raising his eyebrows at Phillip. 'He must have been collecting these racing papers for years.' Finally, he deposited the last few on the ground.

Sam rubbed his hands together. 'Right, Bagsy. This is it.' Grabbing hold of the cabinet, he began to pull as Baggage wagged his tail expectantly and performed a fast double pirouette for good measure.

Sam pulled it away from the wall, and the liberated ball dropped at his feet. Baggage gathered it up and made for his bed with a hop and a skip.

Sam looked at the dog. 'You're not going to help me put it back then?' Baggage ignored him as he juggled the ball in his mouth.

Sam took hold of the cabinet again and prepared to push it back when he noticed that one of the floorboards was loose. With his interest piqued, Sam pulled the cabinet further away from the wall.

'Hey, Phillip,' he said. 'There's a loose floorboard here. It looks as if it's been levered up at some time.'

Phillip got up from his desk and joined Sam. Baggage released the ball from his mouth and padded over, looking first at the floor and then up at Sam and Phillip.

Sam got on his knees and removed the piece of board. Putting a hand inside, he pulled out a leather folder and a plastic carrier bag. He took them across to his desk and, opening the folder, removed several pieces of paperwork. Scanning them, one item caught his attention – a document he recognised.

Sam quickly read it. 'There's a will,' he said to Phillip, who joined him. 'Uncle Bill left everything to Kim, look.' He handed it to Phillip.

Phillip viewed it. 'It hasn't been signed or witnessed, but it looks like Bill wanted it to go to Kim.'

Sam nodded. 'Looks that way.' Sam snatched the will from Phillip and shouted Kim.

'Yes?' Kim popped her head through the door, trying to avoid looking directly at Phillip.

Sam held out the will, and Kim trod over to him. She studied its contents, smiled to herself, and handed it back to Sam. 'Bill never signed it.'

Phillip put a hand on Kim's arm. 'But it's clear he wanted you to have his stuff.'

'It's not legally binding,' she said. 'What good is a detective agency to me anyway?'

Sam opened the carrier bag and pulled out a velvet roll. 'There's this as well,' he said and handed it to Kim.

Kim's eyes welled up with tears as she took it from him, placed the roll on the table and opened it. Inside, the pearl necklace gleamed.

'Wow,' Sam said. 'Are they real?'

'Yes,' Kim said. 'They were Bill's mam's. He wanted me to have them a while ago. I wouldn't take them, though. He said he'd leave them to me when he died. I didn't think …'

Phillip took hold of the sobbing Kim as she buried her face into his chest.

# CHAPTER TWENTY

**2015** – Hockney sat at his desk, opened his leather folder and took out the photo of William Jones standing outside the church. He smiled to himself. Even if his parents had given the statue to a church, there was nothing to suppose it was the church in the photo. Stankovich believed the Eagle was hidden inside the statue of the Virgin Mary, but Hockney was sceptical. The Eagle probably lay buried somewhere in Holland. But what if it had been smuggled across the channel? Surely, someone would have found it by now. However, Green was convinced it hadn't been discovered. Hockney opened a drawer, took out a small address book, flicked through its pages and stopped at the name Richard Wallwick. Beneath this was Middlesbrough archives and a telephone number. He dialled the number.

'Hello,' said a female voice. 'Middlesbrough archives.'

'Can I speak to Richard Wallwick, please?' Hockney said.

'Can I ask who's calling?'

'Bill Hockney.'

'One moment, Mr Hockney.' Hockney waited.

'Richard Wallwick,' a voice said.

'Hi, Richard. I don't know if you remember me, Bill Hockney?'

'Ah, yes. Detective Inspector.'

'Retired, actually. I now run a small detective agency.'

'How exciting. What can I do for you, Bill?'

'I'm looking for some information. I was wondering if you know of anyone who could identify a church for me. From a photograph?'

'How intriguing,' Wallwick said. 'Is this a case you're working on?'

'No. It's a little more prosaic than that. I'm writing a book about an army regiment. The Yorkshire Rifles.'

'That sounds interesting.'

'My father and grandfather were in them. I'm covering the history of the regiment during World War Two, and I've come across a photo of someone who served during that time. It's a bit of background information I need.'

'And this photo of the church you want identifying?'

'It shows a young man before the war. It appears he was doing some work at this church, and I'm hoping to use this picture in my book. It's just me being thorough, Richard.'

'I'd love a copy of this book when you finish it.'

'I'll make sure you get one,' Hockney said.

'Now then. Who do I know who could help? I may have to ask a few of my colleagues and get back to you.'

'That's fine.'

'If you give me your number, I'll see what I can do.'

Hockney gave Wallwick his phone number, thanked him, and rang off.

He opened the contacts on his phone and rang Stankovich.

'Bill, how are you?'

'Good. My secretary said you needed to talk to me,'

'I was wondering how your search is progressing?' Stankovich said.

'I've discovered that the statue of the Virgin Mary made its way back here.'

'Fantastic,' Stankovich said. 'Have you a location?'

'It's not as easy as that. It ended up at the parents' house of a friend of Arthur Parchester.'

'A fellow soldier?'

'He was in the same regiment. After he was killed, though, his parents gave it away.'

'Who to?' Stankovich said.

'That's the problem. William Jones – that's the name of Parchester's friend – has a sister who's still alive but in a care home. She suffers from dementia and wasn't of much help to me.'

'Is this why you went to Whitehaven?'

Hockney smiled to himself. 'I wondered if you knew.'

'Bill,' Stankovich said, 'the Eagle is worth a great deal. I wouldn't want you to get silly ideas about your role in this venture.'

'We have an agreement, Mr Stankovich. I wouldn't dream of reneging on that.'

'Good, good. What's your next move?'

'I'm not sure. Other than locating every Virgin Mary statue in the area.'

'Keep looking,' Stankovich said. 'It has to be out there,'

'I will. It will cost, though.'

'Not a problem. I'll have one of my men bring some money over. Cash, I suppose?'

'Cash is king, Mr Stankovich.'

'Indeed. What about the fat man?'

'He doesn't know what I've told you.'

'Can we keep it that way?' Stankovich said.

'Certainly.'

'Keep in touch, Bill.'

Hockney dialled another number.

'Ah, Bill,' Green said. 'I was wondering when you would ring?'

'I've got a bit of news. The statue of The Virgin Mary was smuggled across to England after the war by a friend of Parchesters. It made its way to this man's parents' house.'

'Excellent. And from there?'

'It appears his parents gave the statue to a church after the death of this soldier. The trail goes cold from there.'

'So, it could be inside a church somewhere?' Green said.

'It could, but there are a lot of churches in the area.'

'But at least we've narrowed it down somewhat.'

'I can keep looking if you want, Mr Green?'

'Please do. We've got this close.'

'I'll need further funds.'

'Not a problem. I'll send my man across with some.'

'Cash,' Hockney said.

'Naturally.'

Hockney sat back in his chair and smiled. He opened a drawer in his desk and took out a bottle of whisky and a glass, pouring himself a large measure. His mobile sounded. 'Anne,' he said. 'I was about to ring you.'

'I've saved you the bother. How's your treasure hunting going?'

Hockney took a sip of his drink. 'I have a bit of news on that.'

'Oh, yes.'

'Can we meet?' Hockney said.

'I'll book a room and put a bottle of bubbly on ice.'

'Where and when?'

'The usual. One o'clock?'

'One is fine.'

Hockney lay in bed next to Anne Jacobs as she propped herself on her elbow and looked at him. 'So?' she said, rubbing his chest with her right hand. 'The statue?'

He smiled. 'First things first. What's your connection with Green?'

'Green?'

'I know you met him.'

She licked her lips. 'You're better than I thought. Did you have us followed?'

Hockney laughed. 'I'm an ex-copper. You learn to distrust everyone you meet.'

'He wants us to work together on finding the statue,' she said. 'He thinks two heads are better than one.'

'And are they?'

She sat up. 'I haven't said I'm working with Green.'

'You do know that Green's paying me to find the statue?'

'It was mentioned.'

'And you're paying me.'

'Look, Bill, cards on the table. The statue's worth a fortune. There's enough for everyone. Green desperately wants the statue for himself, but I'm prepared to share it.'

'With Green?' Hockney said.

'I don't much care if it's with Green or someone else.'

'Me?' He looked directly at her.

'Why not?' She leaned in close to him. 'We have a rapport, don't we?'

'Maybe.'

She smiled at him. 'Find the statue, and we'll share the money from its sale. You could set yourself up somewhere nice. Somewhere sunny.'

'I'll give it some thought,' he said.

'Well, while you're thinking about it, I still have the rest of the afternoon free.' She leant forward and kissed him on the lips.

Hockney exited the hotel and jumped into a waiting taxi. He had deliberately left his car back in Redcar, suspecting he would be followed if he had used it. Stankovich was apparently keeping tabs on him, and Hockney suspected Stankovich wasn't the only one. Miss Jacob's proposal was attractive, but he was confident he couldn't trust her either. If the Eagle was in England, and Hockney still wasn't sure it was, why share it with anyone else?

Hockney sat with Kim in Valentino's Trattoria as the waiter placed their lunches in front of them. 'Can I get you anything else?' he asked.

Hockney shook his head. 'No thanks.' Hockney's phone rang. He reached into his pocket to retrieve it. 'Bill Hockney.'

'Bill. It's Richard Wallwick.'

'Oh, hi, Richard. Any news?'

'Yes,' Wallwick said. 'The chap you need to speak to is a Reverend Stephen Honister. He's the minister of All Saints Church in Saltburn.' Hockney wrote down his name. 'He's a bit of an anorak where places of worship are concerned. I believe he's even written a couple of books on the subject.' Wallwick laughed. 'I met him once. Very nice man. I'm sure he can help.'

'I appreciate this,' Hockney said. 'Next time I'm through there, I owe you a couple of pints.'

'Sounds good. Don't forget about my copy of your book.'

'You're first on my list.' Wallwick gave Hockney the number of the Reverend before they hung up.

Kim looked at Hockney. 'Who was that?' She put a little pasta in her mouth.

'A case I'm working on.'

'The one with the statue?'

'Yes. Bloody waste of time if you ask me, but they won't take no for an answer. As long as they keep paying, I'll keep looking. Some people have more money than sense.'

'I suppose,' Kim said.

'What about watching something on telly after we've eaten? Maybe a bottle of wine?'

'I'd rather go to the pictures?' Kim said. 'There's a film I've wanted to see for ages.'

Hockney rolled his eyes. 'Not a chick-flick?'

'Might be.'

'Yeah, okay,' Hockney said. 'But I'm taking my hip flask.'

Hockney was up early and went for a stroll along Redcar seafront before collecting a newspaper on the way back. He took out his mobile and searched for the Reverend's number that Wallwick had given him. The phone sounded a couple of times before someone answered.

'Reverend Stephen Honister,' a voice said.

'Hello, Reverend. You don't know me, but I was given your number by Richard Wallwick from The Middlesbrough Archive. My name's Bill Hockney.'

'Ah, yes. Richard said someone would be ringing me about a picture?'

'That's right. I have a pre-war photo of a young man standing outside a church somewhere. I believe it's local, and I'm trying to find out which church it is.'

'I have a service at eleven, but I'm free after twelve. Why don't you pop along with the photo, and I'll take a look?'

'That's very kind of you. Twelve it is.' Hockney rang off and headed back to his flat for some breakfast.

Hockney stopped the car outside All Saints Church in Saltburn. He picked up his leather folder and headed up the walkway, passing along the side of the church. Stopping at a gate to the vicarage and composing himself, he marched towards the door. He looked about for a bell and, unable to find one, lifted the heavy knocker – the ironwork resounding against the wood. Footsteps approached the door from inside, and the massive piece of wood swung open.

Hockney smiled at the man. 'Stephen Honister?'

'Yes, Bill Hockney?' The two men shook each other's hands warmly. Honister beckoned Hockney inside.

'Have you come far?' Honister asked. 'Richard didn't say where you lived.'

'Not far,' Hockney said as he sat where Honister had indicated. 'Redcar.'

'Not far at all. Can I tempt you with a drink, Bill? I always treat myself to one or two after Sunday service. It's always a little nerve-racking. I never quite know how it will sound.'

'Have you a whisky?'

'An excellent one, as it happens,' Honister said. 'A friend of mine travels up to Scotland regularly and frequently brings a decent malt back for me. This one,' he said, holding up the bottle, 'is formidable.'

Honister quarter-filled two glasses and handed one to Hockney, positioning himself in a chair opposite. 'So? You have a photo?'

Hockney opened his folder, pulled out a picture, and passed it on to Honister. 'I have.'

The Reverend put on his reading glasses and viewed the snap. 'I'm pretty sure that's All Saints Church in Skelton.' He stood and moved across to the bookcase. Locating a book, he sat back down, flicking casually through the pages. 'Here,' he said and passed the book to Hockney.

'Yes,' Hockney said. 'It looks the same.'

'Who is the young man in the photo?'

'William Jones. He was a soldier in the Second World War and was in the Yorkshire Rifles. I'm writing a history of them and trying to show these brave lads had a life before war broke out.'

'What happened to him?'

'He was killed in Holland in 1944. I met his sister and nephew, and they gave me the photo.'

Honister took a sip of his drink. 'Well, now you know where it was taken.'

'I do. Thank you very much.'

'You can keep that book,' Honister said. 'I've quite a few left. I was a little ambitious when I ordered them.'

'I must pay you for it.'

'I won't hear of it. I'm glad to be of help to the fallen.' He smiled at Hockney as the pair clinked their glasses together.

## CHAPTER TWENTY-ONE

Phillip returned to the office, and Sam looked up from his desk. 'Is she okay?' Sam said.

Phillip slumped in his seat. 'Yeah. I think finding the necklace brought back bad memories. She's gone to her flat for a lie-down.'

'And you're leaving her on her own? This is your big chance. Women are vulnerable when they're emotional.'

'Christ, Sam. You're so mercenary.'

'I know. But you don't want Kim's toe-rag ex to muscle in, do you? You shouldn't leave her on her own. That's all I'm saying. Take it from someone who knows.'

'She's not on her own. Baggage is with her.'

Sam raised his eyebrows and tossed back his head. 'Oh, well. That's all right, then.'

'What was in the paperwork you found?' Phillip asked. 'Anything interesting?'

'Yes. There are all sorts. Look at these.' He passed a handful of photos to Phillip.

Phillip studied the pictures. Slowly perusing each one in turn before looking up at Sam. 'Who are these?'

'The woman is Anne Jacobs.'

Phillip raised his eyebrows. 'The woman you …?'

Sam smiled broadly. 'That's the lady herself.'

'And the fat man? Green?'

'Not sure if it's Green,' Sam said. 'I haven't met him, but from Albert's description, it could be.'

Phillip nodded.

Sam picked up more pictures. 'It also seems like Bill was writing a book about an army regiment. There is lots of information about the Yorkshire rifles.'

Phillip frowned. 'Yorkshire rifles?'

'Yes. There are photos of soldiers from the regiment. And another of a bloke stood outside a church. It looks ancient.' Sam handed another set of pictures to Phillip, who flicked through them before returning the photos to Sam.

'Why would he hide this stuff under the floorboards?' Phillips said. 'It has to be important?'

Sam rocked back in his chair. 'But how important? Oh, and there's this.' He tossed Phillip a book.

Phillip held it up. 'East Cleveland places of worship, by Reverend Stephen Honister. I bet this is a great read.'

Sam nodded towards the book. 'There's a page marker inside.'

Phillip opened it. 'All Saints Church, Skelton. What's the significance of that?'

'I don't know but Bill wouldn't have hidden these things unless they were important.'

Phillip held out his hand. 'Let me have another look at the photo of the man outside the church. Could this be the same church?' Phillip said, handing the photo and book back to Sam to look at.

'Maybe. It's hard to tell.'

'And this photo of a soldier,' Phillip said. 'Isn't it the same man outside the church?'

Sam scrutinised the photos. 'Yes. I think it is.'

'Anything else in the paperwork?'

Sam picked up a collection of documents. 'A business card for Oliver Brady marketing solutions. A card for a bed and breakfast place in Whitehaven. On the back, it's got a name written on it, Stephen Jones. Sam put his feet onto the desk and rocked back in his chair. Do you remember Kim telling us she emailed something across to Bill in Cumbria?'

Phillip nodded. 'The Virgin Mary picture?'

Sam raised his eyebrows. 'Whitehaven's in Cumbria.'

'We'll have to ask Kim if she remembers Bill travelling over there.'

Albert walked in. 'Morning, Phillip, morning, Sam.' He removed his coat and hung it up.

'We've found some more stuff,' Phillip said.

Albert stopped at his desk. 'Stuff?'

Sam handed Albert the photos. 'Do you recognise this bloke?'

Albert studied the photos. 'It's Rupert Green.'

'The woman with him is Miss Jacobs,' Phillip said.

Albert sat at his desk. 'So, they know each other.'

Phillip stood. 'Apparently. I'll let Sam fill you in on the rest. I'm nipping through to Kim's.'

Phillip tapped on Kim's door and listened as the faint barking of Baggage could be heard from inside. The door opened, and a bleary-eyed Kim beckoned him in.

Phillip smiled. 'How are you feeling?' he said, stroking Baggage as they both followed Kim into the kitchen.

'A lot better. It was the shock of seeing the necklace again.'

Phillip tentatively put his arms around her. 'Good.'

She hugged him back and kissed him on the cheek. 'Thanks.' Their eyes met and locked on each other.

'We found some stuff of Bill's. Paperwork and photos.'

'Oh, yeah?' She moved away from him to fill the kettle. 'Cuppa?'

'I'd love one,' Phillip said. 'Can you remember Bill ever going to a place called Whitehaven?'

'In Cumbria?' she said, popping a tea bag in each of the two cups.

'Yes.'

'He stayed there for a couple of days. I told you that. I think it was to do with a case he was working on.'

'The Eagle?' Phillip said

'I think so. Bill got me to email him a photo of the Virgin Mary to the hotel he was staying at.'

'Have you got the photo?'

Kim shrugged. 'It was a random one from the Internet. He just wanted any photo.'

'Bit strange, don't you think?'

Kim smiled. 'Bill used to do a lot of strange things. I didn't get involved in that side of the business.'

Phillip rubbed his chin. 'So, you don't know why he asked you to email this photo?'

'Nope. Anytime I asked about cases, Bill would say it was better I didn't know.' She handed Phillip his cup of tea. 'Baggage!' The dog padded his way back into the kitchen. 'Look what I've got for my favourite boy,' she said, holding out a bone-shaped chew, which he took from her and headed back to the living room with his prize.

'You spoil that dog.'

'I've no one else to spoil.' She put her cup on the worktop and stepped over to him, took his cup, and deposited it next to hers. 'For Christ's sake, Phillip. Bloody kiss me.'

Phillip strolled back into the office, followed by Baggage. Albert stiffened as the dog made its way across to him, and he tentatively patted Baggage's head, letting out a huge sigh as Baggage, seemingly satisfied with his pat, walked over to Sam.

Sam rubbed the dog's ears. 'I don't know why you're so frightened of Baggage. He's as soft as a brush.'

'I can't help it,' Albert said. Rubbing some hand cleanser into his hands, he sniffed them. 'I find dogs a little scary, that's all.'

Phillip sat at his desk. A huge smile filled his face.

Sam met his stare and winked. 'You were quite some time. Everything all right?'

'Brilliant.'

'I've filled Albert in on what we found. Did Kim know anything?'

'She remembers emailing Bill a random photo of The Virgin Mary when he was in Whitehaven, but she doesn't know why he wanted it though.'

Sam held up the card. 'Was he staying at the B&B?'

'No. He was staying at a hotel in the town.'

'I think someone should go up to Whitehaven,' Albert said. 'Maybe the people who own this bed and breakfast know something?'

Sam rocked back in his chair. 'Good idea. What about you, Albert?'

Albert frowned. 'I'm not a great traveller. I get car sick on long journeys.'

Sam rolled his eyes. 'Really. I find that hard to believe.'

'I'll go,' Phillip said.

Albert stared wide-eyed at Phillip. 'You shouldn't go alone,' Albert said. 'Bill was murdered, remember.'

Sam nodded. 'He's right. I'll come with you.'

'That's settled then,' Phillip said.

Sam took out his phone. 'I'd better ring Emily.'

'Will she be okay on her own?' Phillip asked.

'Yes. She's got her mam and dad to help her out. Duty calls, and I've never been to Whitehaven.'

Phillip raised his eyebrows. 'Maybe I should phone ahead and warn them you're coming.'

# CHAPTER TWENTY-TWO

Sam and Phillip headed along the road. And passed a signpost up ahead informing them they were only three miles from Whitehaven.

Phillip pulled over to the side of the road. 'Where's this B&B?'

Sam fished in his pocket and pulled out the card. 'Stepney Street.'

Phillip programmed the sat-nav and drove off again.

'How are we going to approach this?' Sam asked. 'We don't know anything about this bloke.'

Phillip rubbed his chin. 'I've been giving it some thought while you were pushing out the Zs. Why don't we say we're trying to finish Bill's book? About the Yorkshire Rifles.'

'Not a bad idea. Play it dumb and see what they say. What about getting something to eat first, though?'

'We'll find a pub and have dinner before we head over,' Phillip said as he turned off the main road.

'It's getting late,' Sam said. 'Why don't we stay the night and go to the B&B in the morning? We've got a change of clothing. A good night's sleep will do us a world of good.'

'What about if I phone the B&B and see if they have any rooms?'

Sam frowned. 'I'm not sure about that. We don't know why Bill went there or even if he went there. Just because he had the card doesn't mean he stayed. It could be a wild goose chase.'

Phillip yawned. 'What about if we stay at the hotel Bill stayed in, and I'll ring the B&B tonight to arrange to meet in the morning. I'm absolutely knackered. A good night's sleep will sort us out.'

'Sounds like a plan,' Sam said.

Sam and Phillip sat at a table in a pub, the remnants of their dinner in front of them.

Sam let out a satisfied burp. 'That was great.' He nodded behind Phillip. 'We're being watched,' he said as two middle-aged women – a blonde and a brunette – looked in their direction.

'We haven't travelled here so you can get your leg over.'

'I'm only saying.' Sam nodded again. 'Here they come.' Phillip rolled his eyes.

'You two aren't from around here?' the blonde said.

Sam leant back in his chair. 'No. From the big city. Well, Middlesbrough.' He pointed at the two empty chairs next to him, and the women sat.

'Never been to Middlesbrough. Have we, Vicki?' The blonde said.

The brunette shook her head in answer. 'I'm Katherine, Kat to my friends. This is Vicki.'

'Sam, and this is Phillip.' Sam said, pointing at Phillip.

'So, what's Middlesbrough like?' Kat asked.

Sam smiled. 'Wonderful. I live there.'

Kat giggled. 'I'll have to visit sometime. What are you boys doing here anyway?'

Sam edged closer. 'We're trying to find out who murdered our uncle.'

'You're pulling our leg.' Kat said as she glanced at Vicki.

'Honest,' Sam said, crossing his heart. 'Isn't that right, Phillip?'

Phillip sighed again. 'Yes. We run a detective agency.'

'Wow,' Kat said. 'How exciting. I love all that Phillip Marlowe stuff.'

Sam looked around furtively. 'We think there might be a clue to his killer. Right here in Whitehaven.'

Phillip glared at Sam. 'No offence, ladies, but we need to get going,' Phillip said.

'Oh, what a shame,' Kat said. 'I'd love to hear more.'

'If you're in here later?' Sam said as Phillip pulled him by the arm, pushing him towards the door. 'Eight o'clock.'

'What did you say that for?' Phillip asked.

'We're staying the night. There's nothing wrong with a bit of company. They may be able to give us some helpful information.'

'Yeah, like what you're like in bed.'

'She's a looker, that Kat.' Sam raised his eyebrows. 'I love older women. All that experience.'

'Sam.' Phillip huffed. 'We've come here trying to find out why Bill was here. Not so you can get fixed up.'

'I'm only human.'

'What about Emily?'

'Christ!' Sam said. 'What are you, my conscience? I've already got one of those.'

Phillip marched off. 'Let's find our hotel, shall we? Get some sleep and go to the B&B tomorrow.'

Sam sighed. 'It's just one long day of fun with you.'

Phillip finished hanging his clothes in his bedroom when there was a knock on the door. He opened it to a grinning Sam standing outside. 'Are we going down to the bar?' Sam said, as he stepped through the doorway.

'Yes,' Phillip said, 'but I'm not drinking a lot. I'm absolutely knackered.'

Sam rolled his eyes. 'Albert would've been more fun than you.'

'Have you phoned Emily?' Phillip said. 'You remember Emily? The woman who's carrying your child?'

'Yes, yes, I phoned. She's fine. Everything's fine.'

'Good. Let's go then.'

Phillip and Sam sat at a table in the hotel dining room, and a young waitress stopped at the table. 'Are you ready to order?' she said.

Sam smiled at her. 'I'll have the chicken tikka.'

'Rice or chips?'

Sam winked. 'Both. I can do that, can't I?'

The waitress smiled at him. 'You can. You can have whatever you want.'

Phillip rolled his eyes. 'I'll have the beef and ale pie,' he said, and the waitress jotted down their order.

'Drinks?' she asked.

Sam turned his charm knob a little higher. 'Two pints of beer, gorgeous.'

The waitress smiled again at Sam, took the menus from them, and headed off.

Sam looked across at Phillip. 'What?'

'Don't you ever get tired of that? All the flirting.'

'No. I've been doing it for so long that I can't stop myself. There's no harm in it.'

'As long as your flirting doesn't become horizontal. We haven't got time for that malarkey.'

'Loosen up a bit, Phillip,' Sam said. 'Kim's not here. What happens in Whitehaven stays in Whitehaven. I won't tell.'

'Focus on the case. Your sex life can wait. I phoned the B&B earlier.'

'Oh, yeah?' Sam eyed the waitress, who'd returned with two glasses of beer. 'Thanks, darling,' Sam said.

Phillip ignored the two of them. 'I spoke to a woman. Her husband wasn't in.'

'Mrs Jones?' Sam said as he watched the waitress disappear.

'Yes. I told her I wanted to speak about my uncle. I said he was a friend of her husbands.'

'And?' Sam said.

'She seemed nice. I've arranged a meeting at eleven in the morning. I didn't tell her anything.'

'Eleven.' Sam said, still watching the waitress.

'Sam! Are you listening?'

'Yes, I'm listening. I heard every word. We're meeting him tomorrow at eleven. At the B&B.'

Sam heard the tap on his bedroom door, opened it wide, and saw the waitress from earlier standing outside.

'Hello, gorgeous,' he said and beckoned her inside.

'I can't be very long,' she whispered. 'I'll be missed if I am.' She wrapped her arms around his neck and kissed him.

'I can do quickies,' he said and returned her kiss passionately while deftly allowing his hands to slide onto her backside. The waitress responded, pulling Sam's shirt free from his trousers. He felt for the zip on her skirt and expertly pulled it down, allowing it to drop to the floor. She stepped from within it, and the pair of them fell onto the bed, tugging wildly at each other's clothing. The waitress straddled Sam, pushed his trunks to his knees, and pulled the material of her briefs to one side, allowing him access, but stopped. A loud wailing noise filled the air.

Sam sat up. 'What the hell's that?'

'Shit! It's the fire alarm.' She jumped off him.

'Fire alarm? Christ, I didn't know I was that good.'

'I'll have to go. My boyfriend will wonder where I am.' Her skirt was already pulled back up, and her underwear straightened.

Sam slid to the side of the bed, pulling his trunks up over his still erect penis.

'Sorry,' she said, kissed him on the cheek and headed for the door.

'What do I do?' Sam said.

'We have to meet outside in the car park,' she said, and the door banged shut behind her. Sam pulled on his trousers and put on his shirt. His erection now a distant memory. Grabbing his keys, he exited his room and followed the snake of people heading outside.

The guests and some of the staff stood in the car park, shivering in the chill night air. Sam looked around but couldn't see Phillip and glanced across at the waitress standing with a man.

An older man in a suit came outside and held up his hands. 'Don't worry, it's a false alarm. If you'd all like to return to your rooms, I apologise for the inconvenience.' The customers filed back inside. Sam glanced at his watch and stopped outside Phillip's room. He paused about to knock, but dropping his hand down, he headed meekly back to his bed.

Sam, bleary-eyed, walked into the dining room and joined Phillip, already seated at a table.

Phillip looked up. 'Morning,' he said. 'You look rough.'

'I feel rough. What happened to you last night?'

'Me?' Phillip said. 'What do you mean?'

'Didn't you hear the fire alarm?'

'Fire alarm? No. I had a great night's sleep. That's the comfiest bed I've ever slept in.'

'Good for you,' Sam said. 'Some of us were stood in the car park at two o'clock this morning while you were sleeping soundly.'

'So? Was there a fire?' Phillip said and took a bite of his toast.

'Does it look as if there was?' Sam snatched the menu from its holder. 'Bloody false alarm.'

'Didn't you sleep well?' Phillip said.

'No, I didn't. I hardly got a wink after it. Disappointing night all round.'

'Well,' Phillip said, 'get your breakfast, we'll check out and head across to the B&B.' He grinned at Sam.

Phillip pulled the car up outside the B&B and checked the address on the card again. Satisfied that it was the right place, he turned off the engine and looked across at Sam. 'This is it.'

Sam got out of the car. 'I'll let you do the talking,' he said, heading up the drive with Phillip.

Mr Jones showed Phillip and Sam through into a lounge, pointing to a couple of armchairs. 'Have a seat, boys. I'll go and rustle up some drinks.' He returned a few moments later carrying a tray with a teapot and a plate of assorted biscuits. 'You say you're Bill's nephews. How is he?'

Sam looked across at Phillip. 'I'm afraid he's dead, Mr Jones.'

'Dead?' He shook his head. 'How, I mean…When?'

'Earlier this year,' Phillip said. 'Uncle Bill was murdered.'

'Good God. Who by?'

Sam picked up a biscuit. 'The police haven't found that out.'

'Yes,' Phillip said. 'He was stabbed in Middlesbrough. Can I ask you how well you knew Bill?'

'Not well at all. Bill came to see me about a book he was writing. A member of my family was in a regiment that fought in the Second World War.'

Phillip picked up his tea. 'The Yorkshire Rifles?'

'That's right. Bill was looking for background information about my uncle. I let him borrow some family photos. He took copies and posted them back to me.'

'Was there one of a man standing outside a church?' Phillip asked.

'Yes. I believe there was.'

'We know the ones,' Sam said.

'Are you continuing his book?'

'No,' Phillip said. 'We're trying to discover who murdered him. This is just following up on leads. We found some information belonging to Bill, and your card was with it. Bill ran a detective agency, and we've taken it over.

'I see. I'm afraid I can't help you further.'

Phillip nodded. 'No, that's fine, Mr Jones. It was a long shot, anyway. Bill was working on a couple of cases, and we're checking up on them.'

'It's sad to hear about his death,' Mr Jones said. 'He seemed like a nice bloke.'

Phillip started the engine, checked his mirrors and headed off.

'I thought we were going to pretend we're continuing Bill's book,' Sam said.

'It just came out.'

'Do you think Bill was actually writing a book about the regiment?'

'I'm not sure,' Phillip said. 'Jones seemed genuine enough.'

'That's what I thought,' Sam said. 'Back home, I suppose?'

'Yes, back to the Boro.'

## CHAPTER TWENTY-THREE

**2015** – Hockney travelled to Skelton in a taxi, indulging in the usual small talk along the way before getting dropped off on the high street. He took out a small map of the village he'd printed off and headed for All Saints church. The bright sunny day and the stroll warmed him up considerably. Hockney took off his coat and marched on, eventually reaching the end of a path leading up to the church. He paused, glanced around and took out the photograph from his pocket. He studied it and then the church and, deciding it was the same place, walked up the footpath towards the door.

'Can I help you?' a voice said.

Hockney turned to face an elderly man in overalls. 'I was hoping to have a look inside.'

'Out of luck, I'm afraid. The church is shut. It no longer holds services.'

'Right.' Hockney moved closer to the man.

'It's been shut for years. You can visit, but you have to make an appointment.'

'I see,' Hockney said. 'Do you work here?'

'I keep the grounds tidy to stay active.'

'I'm writing a book,' Hockney said.

'About churches?' the old man said, leaning against his rake.

'Not exactly.' Hockney walked towards him and held out the photograph.

The man took out his spectacles and studied it. 'That's an old one. Looks pre-war.'

'It is. The man in the photo was in the army during the war. The Yorkshire Rifles.'

'Oh, yes. I've heard of them.'

Hockney took back the photo and put it in his pocket. 'I'm looking for some background information.'

'Stan Wilkinson,' the gardener said. 'He's the man you need to talk to. He knows everything about this church.'

'How do I get in touch with him?'

'You can't at the moment. Stan's in Australia visiting his family. He won't be back until next month.'

'I see.' Hockney turned to face the church. 'Do you mind if I take a few snaps?'

'No, you go ahead.'

He offered his hand to the gardener. 'Bill. Bill Hockney.'

'Ernie Thompson,' he said, shaking it firmly and smiling. 'I was about to stop for a brew. Do you fancy one, Bill?'

Hockney smiled. 'I'd love one.' Hockney followed the gardener around the back of the church and into a garden shed.

The two of them chatted pleasantly for an hour. Hockney was happy to let the elderly man regale him with stories, occasionally interjecting with a question or two. Ernie clearly loved talking, and Hockney, using his years of experience in the police force, allowed him to do that. After finishing the tea and biscuits, Hockney got up. 'Have you a number for Mr Wilkinson?'

The old man paused for a moment, tapping his lips with his index finger. 'Is it just a look around you're after?'

'Yes, and maybe take a photo or two.'

Ernie stood and wandered across to an old chest of drawers. He opened the top one and pulled out a key. 'I'll have to stay with you while you look around. But you seem like an honest gent.'

'I promise I won't nick anything. I was in the police for twenty-five years.'

'Uniform?' he asked, beckoning Hockney to follow him.

'Both. I was a Detective Inspector when I retired.'

The two men reached the front door of the church and stopped. Ernie placed the key into the lock and turned it. 'Don't mention this to a soul,' he whispered. 'I'll get shot if Stan finds out. He treats this church as if it's his own.'

'Scouts honour.'

Ernie pushed open the massive door, and the two of them stepped into the building. The gardener turned on the lights, and Hockney looked around the beautiful church. Two rows of pews led to the altar at the far end. It smelt old – a mixture of dampness and wood. An enormous stained-glass window gleamed, sunshine cascading through it, leaving multicoloured shadows on the floor. The two men walked forward, Hockney glancing left and right.

Ernie looked at Hockney. 'It's a beautiful little church. Stan likes to keep it immaculate.'

Hockney walked forward. 'It is.' He stopped when he spotted it – a statue of The Virgin Mary sited to the left, near the font. His heart rate quickened, and hairs on the back of his head rose a little.

'There's something serene about churches,' Ernie said. 'Where life begins and ends.'

'Indeed,' Hockney said. Stopping close to the statue, he stole a look. It was larger than he had imagined. Could it be the one? He hardly dared hope. Hockney took out his mobile and began taking photographs, snapping various bits of the church as he moved around.

'I'll leave you to take your photographs,' Ernie said. 'I'll be outside.'

'I won't be long,' Hockney said, edging closer to the statue, stopping within touching distance. He turned as Ernie walked back along the aisle and closed the door behind him with a resounding thud. He waited for a second or two and then leapt into action. Grasping the statue, Hockney lifted it. The weight of it was a surprise, and he viewed its base. There, on the bottom, now faded with age but still visible, the number 346. He replaced the statue and, with a broad smile on his face, made his way out.

'All finished?' Ernie asked.

'I am. Thanks very much.'

Ernie locked the church door, and the two headed back to his garden shed. 'Another cuppa?' Ernie said, depositing the key back inside the drawer.

'Yes, please,' Hockney said.

Hockney took out his mobile phone and searched through the contacts. He called Rocco.

'Yes, Bill,' Rocco said.

'How's your luck?'

'Shite.'

'Could you do with some folding stuff?'

'Is it legal?' Rocco asked.

'If it were, I wouldn't be asking you to do it.'

'How much?'

'A grand.'

The phone went quiet for a moment. 'A grand … You've got my attention, Bill.'

'I need something getting for me. Do you know Skelton?'

'I know it,' Rocco said.

## CHAPTER TWENTY-FOUR

Tony entered the pub and spotted Inspector Robards standing at the far end of the bar, so he headed over.

'I've got you a pint,' Robards said.

'Cheers,' Tony said.

'Your ex-girlfriend, Kim.'

'I'm listening,' Tony whispered.

'I've been doing a little checking up on her current squeeze, Phillip Davison. He used to work for his girlfriend's father. Had a good job and lovely flat by all accounts.'

Tony took a large swig of his drink. 'What happened?'

Robards picked up his scotch. 'She caught him in bed with her sister. You can imagine how that went down?'

'I can, Geoff.'

'Maybe Kim doesn't know this. Perhaps she'd be interested?'

Tony grinned. 'I think she would.'

'Anything on what the detective agency is up to?' Robards said.

'Two of them travelled up to Whitehaven the other week and visited someone called Jones. He owns a B&B there.'

'What did they go there for?'

'I'm not sure. I think they're just fishing. Following in dear Bill's footsteps.'

Robards lowered his voice a little as some people passed nearby. 'Comby thinks the cousins know something about Hockney's murder. He doesn't know what, though.'

'Does Comby know anything?'

'He's a fat fool. Couldn't discover his arse with both his hands. You must get in tight with Kim again and find out what they know.'

'You think Hockney knew the whereabouts of the statue?' Tony said.

'I'm sure of it, but Rocco's gone to ground, so we'll have to try a different approach. Ask Brendon to go around to Albert Jackson's. Comby thinks he's the weak link in this case. If anyone spills the beans, it'll be him.'

'Maybe it would be better if I went?' Tony said. 'Brendon can be a bit headstrong.'

Robards smiled. 'No. He might recognise you from the Detective Agency. Maybe Jackson would benefit from some arm twisting.'

'Okay. I'll need some more cash while we're on.'

'See what's on the box tonight.' He pushed a newspaper towards him. 'Keep in touch.'

Tony watched Robards leave, opened the paper, and pulled the brown envelope from within. He slipped it into his jacket pocket, drained his pint, and headed off.

**2015** – Hockney pulled off the trunk road, coming to rest in an empty car park next to a large field. He turned off his engine and waited. A taxi appeared, stopping on the main road. Rocco got out before hurrying to Hockney's car and climbing in.

Hockney handed him a wad of notes. 'Half now. Half when you do the job.'

'Skelton, you said?' Rocco fanned the money and then pocketed it.

'Yes. There's a church – All Saints. I need you to go there. Behind the back of the church is the gardener's hut. Inside the hut, you'll find a chest of drawers. In the top drawer is a key.' Hockney fumbled in his pocket for a piece of paper and handed it to Rocco.

'What's the key for?'

'Get the key and get me a copy of it. There's a place on the high street that'll do it. Then, return the original and bring me the copy. I'll give you the other five hundred when you do.'

'Don't I get to know what the key opens?'

Hockney smiled. 'It's better you don't.'

'I'll ring when I have the key.' Rocco grasped the door handle, and Hockney took hold of his arm. 'Wear gloves, Rocco, and don't get caught.'

'I've done this sort of thing before, Bill. I'll be in touch.'

Hockney watched Rocco leave the car park and disappear from sight. He waited another five minutes before starting the engine and heading off.

Rocco had walked a small distance before flagging a taxi down. He jumped in and headed for his local, arriving minutes later. He paid the cab fare and got out, but a second car pulled up next to him as the taxi drove away.

Brendon showed Rocco the revolver he was cradling in his lap. 'Get in,' Brendon said, and Rocco did as he was told. Tony sat in the back next to him, holding another gun loosely in his hand, staring menacingly at Rocco.

'What's this about?' Rocco said as the vehicle moved off.

Tony nudged him in the ribs with the weapon. 'Shut the fuck up.'

The car made its way out of Dormanstown and back along the Trunk road before turning left at some lights. It carried on until it reached a roundabout, turning left for Warrenby. The car pulled into a deserted car park, coming to a stop outside a derelict building. Tony nudged Rocco again, who took the hint and got out. Brendon led the way, followed by Rocco and Tony. They entered, making their way along a corridor and into a darkened room.

'Evening, Rocco,' a voice said.

Rocco strained to see who it was in the darkness, but as his eyes adjusted, he recognised that Inspector Geoff Robards had spoken.

'Inspector Robards. What's all this about?'

'Hockney.'

'What about him?' Brendon punched Rocco in the stomach, and Rocco, winded, doubled up.

'Should we start again?' Robards said.

Rocco stood straight, glanced across at Brendon and moved a little away. 'I've seen him from time to time,' Rocco said, eyeing the two men now stood either side of him.

'Search him,' Robards said.

The two men rifled through Rocco's pockets, placing several items on a table in front of Robards. Robards picked up the wad of notes and fanned them. 'I suppose you're going to tell me you won this on the horses.'

'A Yankee.' Brendon motioned towards him, and Rocco stole himself for another strike. Tony grabbed hold of his arm, and Brendon landed a second, much harder blow. Rocco crumpled to his knees, gasping for breath as the two men stood him back up.

'I know you met with Hockney at your local, Rocco. I know he gave you some money. You were spotted in Corals making sizeable bets. I'll give you one last chance before I walk out of here and leave you with my two friends. I'll come back when they've kicked the shit out of that attitude of yours.'

'Please.' Rocco held out a hand as Brendon slid closer. 'He asked me to follow a woman, and I took some photos, that's all.'

'The woman?'

'I don't know. She met with a fat bloke at a posh place near Yarm.'
'And that's it?'
'That's it, Inspector. Honest.'
'What's this?' Robards held out a piece of paper. 'All Saints Church?'
'It's my sister's son, Oliver and his wife. They're having a christening in a couple of weeks. That's the church.'
'Are you sure? You're not leaving anything out?'
'I swear.' The two men took hold of his arms. 'Please don't hit me again.'

Robards surveyed their captive for a moment, picking up the items his men had taken from Rocco, including the money, and handed them back to him. 'I want you to do me a favour. If Hockney gets back in touch with you, I want you to phone me immediately. Have you got that?'

'Absolutely.' Rocco took his things from Robards.

'One more thing,' Robards said, taking hold of Rocco's arm. 'Don't tell Hockney about this.' Robards smiled. 'Unless you'd like to be floating face down in the Tees.'

'No.'

'Take him back to where you found him.' Brendon nodded towards the door, and Rocco, Tony and Brendon left.

Robards took out his mobile and phoned. 'It's Geoff. Hockney had you followed.'

'Where?' Jacobs said.

'When you visited Green.'

'I see,' she said.

'Why didn't you tell me about this?'

'It was nothing. Green and I have a history. He was trying to discover if I had any info on the Eagle, that's all.'

'Are you sure?' Robards said.

'Yes, I'm sure. Green's not the problem, it's Stankovich.'

'Leave Stankovich to me,' Robards said.

'Why don't you pop across here?' Jacobs purred. 'I could do with some company. I'll order a bottle of bubbly if you like?'

'I'll be ten minutes.'

Hockney left his office and headed downstairs. He stopped at the door and glanced outside into the road at a car parked on the other side of the high street. Rocco had phoned earlier and informed him he had managed to obtain the key. They had arranged a meeting in Middlesbrough, but Hockney was confident he was being watched. He slipped further back inside the building and assessed his options. He headed back upstairs and went inside, locating the spare key to Kim's flat. Kim was out in town, so he wouldn't have to answer any of her awkward questions or assuage her fears. He opened the door to the fire escape and peeked out. The position of the staircase was such that anyone across the road couldn't get a clear view of the door. He crept outside and closed the door behind him, tiptoeing down the stairs into the yard below. The fence to the adjoining property had a couple of missing boards. Hockney pulled off a third, the nails holding it quickly yielding, and he squeezed through. Moving across the neighbouring yard, he repeated the process, removing enough boards from the fence separating the properties to allow him to get through to the next. He reached the last of the premises, this time making his way to the side door of the final building. He unbolted the gate and opened it a small amount, looking outside. The side street was empty. He took out his mobile and, searching through his contacts, dialled.

'Jimmy. It's Bill Hockney, are you busy?'

'No,' said a man on the other end.

'How would you like to earn fifty quid?'

'I'm listening.'

Hockney waited inside the yard of the last building until a car pulled up outside. Watching a man get out of the car and walk towards the high street, Hockney crept outside and slipped into the back of the vehicle. Lying in the footwell behind the front seats, he waited. The man returned shortly after.

'You okay, Bill?' Jimmy said.

'Never better.'

The car pulled away. 'Irate husband?'

'Something like that.'

The car travelled along the seafront, turning right at the small lake and continuing on. It reached a crossroads before turning right onto The Trunk Road. The driver increased his speed and headed towards Middlesbrough.

Jimmy glanced through the rear-view mirror. 'I don't think we're being followed.'

Hockney got up off the floor and sat on the back seat. 'Good.' He took out his wallet and removed five ten-pound notes, dropping them on the passenger seat in front.

'Where do you want me to drop you off?'

Hockney looked out of the window at the fading sunlight. 'Anywhere in the town.'

The car pulled up on Albert Road. Hockney thanked Jimmy and got out. The vehicle screeched its way off as Hockney slipped into a shop doorway out of sight. He took out his phone.

'Rocco, where are you?'

'I'm setting off now. Half hour tops.'

'Let me know when you're there,' Hockney said.
'Will do.'
Tony removed the gun from Rocco's side as Robards stepped forward. 'Good lad, Rocco. Tony and Brendon, here ...' He put his hand on Brendon's shoulder. 'Will follow you into the pub. Don't try anything stupid.'
'I wouldn't, Inspector. Honestly.'
Robards patted Rocco on the face. 'Good.' He held out his hand. 'Give me the mobile.' He passed it across to Robards as Rocco's shoulders drooped.
'Where did he tell you to meet?' Robards asked.
'The Talbot,' Rocco said.
'Is that still open? I thought they'd knocked it down.'
'It's still open.'
'And you've no idea why he asked to meet there?'
'Like I said, Hockney wanted me to get something for him.'
'If you're lying—'
'Honestly. That's all he told me,' he said as Brendon and Tony moved either side of him.
Robards looked at his men. 'You two,' he said, nodding at Rocco. 'Don't let him out of your sight. If he tries anything, slit his throat.'

The two men followed Rocco through the streets to The Talbot public house. Rocco went inside and Brendon followed close behind, while Tony waited outside down an alley. Tony took out Rocco's phone and texted Hockney.
'I'm here.'

Rocco sat in the corner of the pub, cradling a pint as Brendon stood at the bar about twenty feet away, observing him. Each time the door opened and someone entered, the two men would turn to look. Brendon looked away from Rocco as an argument erupted in one of the corners. Rocco seized his opportunity. Pulling up one of the legs of his trousers, he reached down and pulled out a mobile phone. He manoeuvred the handset below the table but out of sight of Brendon and began to text, stopping briefly when Brendon looked at him. Seeing Rocco was still there, Brendon turned to view the two men in the corner, whose argument had now escalated into a pushing match – their companions trying to keep the two combatants apart. Rocco finished his text, pressed send, and secreted the mobile back into his sock. He took out the key ring from his jacket pocket and carefully slid the new key he'd had cut for Hockney off it. He looked across at Brendon, who by now was wholly engrossed in the fight taking place. Two burly bouncers burst through the doors, wading into the battle, and Rocco took his chance as the battling men scattered a table of drinks across the floor. People jostled for the position, some to escape the melee and others to gain a better view. He bolted for the toilets, bursting into the first cubicle. Lifting the cistern lid, he dropped the key inside. He pushed down the seat and hoisted himself up, opened the window above it and pushed the top half of his body through it. Turning adroitly, he pulled the rest of himself through and dropped into the yard outside. He jumped on some empty barrels and leapt at the top of the wall. Then, expertly pulling himself over, he fell onto the floor outside. He could see Tony standing at the end of the alley, some distance away, and Rocco, backing along its length, melted into the night.

Brendon turned and viewed Rocco's now vacant chair. He raced for the toilets, but they were empty. Running back into the bar and out through the door, he glanced about. Tony, sensing something was wrong, joined him. 'What's up? Where the hell is Rocco?'

Brendon threw his hands up. 'He's legged it. He got out the toilet window.'

'Jesus, Brendon.' They sprinted along the alley, stopping at the far end. He was gone. Brendon took out his mobile and rang.

'This better be good?' Robards said.

'He's gone. There was a fight in the pub, and he somehow managed to slip out.'

'Stay there. I'm on my way.'

Hockney had hidden out of sight after receiving the text from Rocco telling him not to go to the pub. He waited in the darkness of a doorway for his mobile to ring.

'Rocco? What happened?'

'Robards collared me outside my flat and took my mobile. Luckily they didn't find the one you gave me. This is too heavy for me, Bill. I'm going to ground.'

'What about the key?'

'I told Robards I was meeting you so that you could give me something. He knows nothing about the key. I've hidden it in one of the cisterns in the Talbot's toilets.'

'Good lad. What about your money?'

'Keep it safe. And Bill,' Rocco said, 'watch yourself. That Robards is dangerous.'

'You look after yourself. I'll be fine.'

Hockney waited until it was almost closing time before making his way across to the Talbot. He stopped outside and checked in both directions before entering. Moving straight through the bar into the toilets, he checked the cistern of the first cubicle, and there, in the bottom, he spotted the key. He dried it on some paper towels and turned towards the door, colliding with Brendon, who was coming in. Hockney reacted quickly, smashing into Brendon, who was reaching inside his coat. Brendon, winded by the blow, dropped to the floor. Hockney brought his foot down hard between Brendon's legs, and he let out a massive groan and doubled up. Hockney exited through the door, moving swiftly through the bar and outside where he spotted Tony. Hockney, momentarily nonplussed, paused as Tony lunged forward with a knife in his hand. The blade pierced Hockney's side, and Hockney swung a fist, catching Tony on the side of his head, the blow causing him to stumble and fall backwards. Hockney kicked out, finding the younger man square on the jaw and seizing the moment, fled, turned a corner and stumbled on.

# CHAPTER TWENTY-FIVE

Rupert Green sat reading in his room in Wainston Hall. There was a knock at the door, and placing his newspaper on a nearby table, he looked up. 'Come in,' he said.

Sleen stepped inside. 'You wanted to see me, Mr Green?'

'Yes. I've been having a think and I'm a little bit concerned.' He poured himself a brandy from a decanter before continuing. 'Our friend Albert Jackson. There doesn't appear to be a lot happening concerning the Eagle.'

'Would you like me to have a word?'

'Yes, I would. Just remind Mr Jackson that my patience is not endless. Impress on him the urgency. We don't want any of the others finding it first.'

'I'll go now.'

Green took a sip of his drink and leaned back in his chair. 'Use an unmarked car. We don't want anything linking us in case he decides to inform the Police.'

'Very good, sir.'

Tommo stood behind the bar as Deb wandered over to him. 'Another two beers and an orange for the mum-to-be.'

Tommo looked across at Emily and Sam, who were seated at a table in the corner. 'I still can't see those two as parents,' he said, pulling the pints.

Deb shook her head. 'Sam will never stay faithful. He's probably racked up a few already.'

Tommo frowned. 'That's a bit harsh, Deb. He'd have mentioned it to me if he had.'

She pushed a note across the bar and scoffed. 'Like you'd say anything.'

'I'd tell you,' Tommo said, topping up the pints. He filled a glass with orange juice, popped in a few ice cubes and placed it near the other drinks before picking up the note and handing Deb her change.

Deb took a swig of one of the beers. 'Are you working tonight?'

'No. I'm off this evening.' He smiled. 'Perks of being the boss. Why?'

'Nothing. I'm at a bit of a loose end, that's all. Emily's no fun now that she's not drinking. Not to mention the tears.'

'Tears?'

Deb rolled her eyes. 'Hormones. I'd never seen her cry until the other week. Now, she never stops.' She picked up the three glasses, nodding at Emily and Sam. 'I would have come in for a chat. We could have ripped those two to bits.'

'You should come to mine,' Tommo said. 'I'm a dab hand in the kitchen. I could rustle something up for us.'

Deb looked towards the floor. 'I'm not sure. I'll take a rain check on that. One of my other friends might come out. I do like my nights out.'

Tommo shook his head. 'No. That's fine. I'm sure you've got lots of things to do on a Saturday night. I'd better get on with changing this barrel,' he said and darted for the cellar.

'Another time,' she shouted after him.

Deb returned to the table and sat opposite Emily and Sam. Sam stood. 'Right, Em. I'll see you in The Lion about four?' he said, bending to kiss her. 'Deb, you'll have to drink both those pints.'

'I think I can manage,' she said. Deb looked back towards the cellar door and then focused on Emily. 'What are you two doing at four?'

'Sam and I are having a spot of tea, old girl.'

'Lucky you.' Deb placed her hand around her pint. 'Tommo invited me to his place tonight. For something to eat.'

Emily spat out her orange juice. 'Really. Are you going?'

'I sort of turned him down.'

Emily frowned. 'Why?'

'I've told you. Tommo's not my type.'

Emily pushed out her bottom lip. 'Poor Tommo. I bet he's heartbroken.'

'Give over. A big bruiser like him won't be bothered. He'll be used to knockbacks.'

'Don't let his size fool you.' She leaned in close to her friend. 'You've probably crushed him. He's a great, big softy at heart.'

The door to the cellar opened, and Tommo came back out carrying some bottles. He glanced across at Deb before taking his place behind the bar.

Emily pushed out her bottom lip again. 'Poor Tommo.'

Deb stood and downed half of her ale. 'I'm going to the toilet. Are we going soon?'

'As soon as you're ready.' She lifted her glass. 'If I drink much more of this stuff, I'll be turning orange.'

Deb downed the remainder of her drink and put down the glass. 'Try another soft drink.' She walked towards the toilet, passing Tommo behind the bar. Their eyes briefly met, and a half smile exchanged between the pair as she entered the cubicle.

Deb came back out of the toilet and stopped at the bar. Tommo leaned across it, talking to Albert's therapist, Miss Waltham. She waited, and then Tommo turned to face her.

'Another?' he said.

Miss Waltham looked Deb up and down. 'No. We're going,' Deb said and stared back at Miss Waltham.

Tommo nodded and forced a smile. 'See you later.'

Deb returned to the table, and Emily stood. 'Are we off, then?' Emily said as Deb continued to stare back at the bar. Miss Waltham was now leaning in close to Tommo, and he let out a loud laugh. Emily put a hand on her friend's arm. 'Are we going?'

'Who's that woman?' Deb said.

'Which woman?'

'The one at the bar with Tommo.'

Emily looked across. 'I don't know. Never seen her before.'

Deb sat and picked up the second pint. 'I think I'll have this drink.'

'I thought you said you'd had enough.'

Deb frowned. 'Look at her. She's all over him.'

'So? What are you bothered about?'

'I'm not. I'm Just saying.'

'I'll find out for you,' Emily said.

Deb glanced at Emily and then stared back at the bar. 'What?'

'The woman talking with Tommo.'

Deb shrugged. 'If you like.'

Emily walked across to the bar, stood next to Miss Waltham and smiled at her.

Tommo turned to face her. 'Oh, hi, Em. This is Miss Waltham. Albert's therapist.'

'Vanessa,' she said, tapping Tommo's hand. 'Call me Vanessa.'

'Vanessa. This is Emily.'

Miss Waltham turned to face Emily. 'Albert's mentioned you.'

'Ooh. What's he been saying?'

'Only good things. Albert's very fond of you.'

'What can I get you, Em?' Tommo said.

'Nothing. We're going, that's all.' She smiled at Miss Waltham. 'I love Albert, he's a proper character.'

'He is that,' Miss Waltham said.

'Nice to meet you, Vanessa. We'll see you later, Tommo,' she said as Emily and Tommo pecked each other on the cheek before heading back to Deb.

Deb nodded towards the bar. 'Well?'

Emily smiled. 'It's Albert's therapist.'

'Therapist?'

'For his OCD. *Vanessa*,' Emily said, slowly enunciating her name.

Deb snorted. 'Vanessa?' She glanced towards the bar as Miss Waltham let out a laugh, her hand resting on Tommo's arm.

Emily put her hands on either side of her face and leant forward towards Deb. 'You're jealous.'

'What.'

'You're bloody jealous.'

'Don't be stupid. Why on earth would I be jealous?' Emily continued to stare at her friend, and a huge grin filled her face. 'I'm not,' Deb said, 'I was interested in who she was, that's all.'

Emily laughed. 'Mmm. Not convinced, Deb. Maybe you should have taken up his offer of dinner at his place. Maybe *Vanessa* will.'

Deb stood. 'Let's go.'

'What about the rest of your drink?'

Deb picked up the glass and threw the drink into her mouth, emptying her glass in seconds. 'What drink?' she said and let out a loud burp.

Emily stood, and the two women walked towards the door. Emily waved at Tommo, who blew her a kiss.

Deb stopped. 'Hold on a second,' she said, walking across to the bar as Emily watched. 'That thing we spoke about earlier?' Deb said as Tommo looked at her. 'The meal at yours,' she continued, and Tommo nodded. 'You're on. I'll be there at eight.' Deb turned promptly and headed for the door.

'Eight,' Tommo said as his eyes followed the exiting Deb.

Emily smiled at her friend, who joined her outside. Deb threw out her hands. 'What?' she said and marched up the road, closely followed by the now grinning friend.

Comby sat in his car's front passenger seat, finishing off the remainder of his BLT. Hardman pulled open the door and flopped down heavily next to him.

'Jesus, Mick. You're going to bugger the suspension on this car.'

'I've phoned Albert Jackson,' Hardman said.

'And?'

'He sounded a little shocked.'

Comby nodded. 'Good. He definitely knows more than he's letting on. What time did you say we were going around?'

Hardman started up the car. 'Six.'

'Six? That's a little late.'

'I thought it would give him time to sweat. And we have to interview the solicitor on the Falstaff case, guv.'

'Oh, yes, I forgot about that. First things first, though. Let's get some grub.'

'You've just had a sandwich, haven't you?'

'It was rubbish. I threw half of it away.' Comby growled. 'BLT my arse. I couldn't find the bacon.'

Sam leant against the bar of *The Blast Furnace,* glanced at his watch, drained his pint, and turned, bumping into Anna Forbes.

'Hi, handsome,' she said.

'Anna.'

She slid closer to him. 'Where are you off in such a hurry?'

'I have to be somewhere,' he said, his exit now barred by her.

She pushed a hand through her hair. 'You don't have to rush off, do you?'

'Well—'

'What about buying me a drink?' She moved her mouth close to his ear. 'You and I could nip around to my house after if you fancy?'

Sam took a step backwards. The sight of Anna's breasts, wonderfully displayed in her low-cut top, roused his slumbering libido. 'I'd love to, but I'm sort of with someone now.'

'So what? It's never stopped you in the past.' She edged closer. 'I won't tell. Soul of discretion, I am.'

Sam pulled his jacket from the back of a stool, strategically placing it in front of his loins. 'It's serious.'

Anna burst out laughing. 'Serious? You've never been serious about a woman in your life.'

'I'm going to be a dad.'

Anna tutted. 'You haven't let some daft lass catch you out with that, have you?'

'What do you mean?'

'Claiming she was on the pill or something. Anyway ...' She ran her fingers through her hair again. 'I thought you always wore a rubber.'

'I do. It wasn't like that. It just happened.'

Anna theatrically rolled her eyes. 'So, who's this fabulous woman?'

Sam gulped. 'Emily.'

'Emily Simpson?' Sam nodded. 'But she's gay.'

'I know that,' Sam said. 'I do live with her.'

Anna pulled a face. 'Oh, my God. You haven't been doing that thing with a turkey baster, have you?'

Sam frowned. 'What thing?'

'You know. The man puts his jiz in the turkey baster, and then the woman inseminates herself.

'I'm bloody sure we haven't,' Sam said, pulling on his jacket. 'We don't even own a turkey baster.' Sam's eyes widened. 'And I hate Turkey. We did it the conventional way. The way people normally do it.'

Anna looked upwards. 'But she's gay. Take it from me.' She raised her eyebrows. 'I've had first-hand experience of Miss Emily Simpson.'

'No way?' Sam said. 'You and Em?' He briefly closed his eyes. 'God, I wish I'd been there to watch. When was this? She never mentioned it.'

Anna opened her handbag and took out her lipstick, liberally applying the bright red cosmetic. 'It was when Paul and I were having one of our breaks. I was an emotional wreck at the time, near Christmas. I was a little drunk if I remember.'

'So now you're blaming the drink.'

'I was easy prey. Emily's quite persuasive, you know. And well … It just happened. I was mortified the next morning and begged her not to say anything.'

Sam leant against the bar. 'What was it like?'

'Come back to mine, and I'll tell you all about it. It'll put some lead in that jumbo pencil of yours.'

'I can't, Anna. I can't.'

'Why not?' she whispered. 'He's clearly interested,' she said, nodding towards the burgeoning bulge in his jeans. Sam pulled off his coat again and placed it in front of himself. '*He's* got a mind of his own,' Sam said. 'But I'm the one calling the shots. He answers to me. Not the other way around.'

'Come on, Sam. A dick has no conscience. Isn't that your mantra?'

'Not today, it isn't.'

Anna took out her perfume and sprayed a little around her neck. 'Remember that thing I do with my tongue?'

Sam sniffed as her perfume filled his nostrils. 'Yeah,' he said as his libido started to disrobe.

'I'm even better at it now.'

Sam closed his eyes, trying to remember all the managers Middlesbrough had since the war.

She leaned in close, and her lips brushed Sam's ear. 'Emily need never know. You won't even have to work very hard. I'm horny as hell. Ready to go, so to speak.'

'This is not fair. I'm trying to stay faithful.'

Anna allowed her hand to rest on his bum. 'Love and war, Samuel. Love and war.'

Tommo entered and raced across to where Sam and Anna stood, pushing himself between them. 'Put him down, Anna,' he said, pulling Sam by the arm. 'He's spoken for.'

Anna pouted. 'Lucky you,' she said, and Tommo pushed Sam towards the door.

Sam glanced back at Anna, who had stuck her tongue out at him. The length of the lizard-like appendage, impressively long. 'Thank God you were there,' Sam said. 'I was about to break. I'm only flesh and blood.'

'It's only been a few weeks. Can't you stay faithful that long?'

'It feels like years,' Sam slumped onto a wall. 'I'm not sure I can keep it up.'

'Of course you can,' Tommo looked upwards. 'You want to live in my world. Months, sometimes years, pass between my sexual encounters. Luckily, I spotted you through the window. What would have happened if Emily had come in?'

'She's shopping with Deb. I'm meeting her in The Lion soon.'

'Even so,' Tommo said.

Sam grabbed Tommo's arm. 'Anna said she's even better with her tongue.'

Tommo stopped, and his jaw dropped open. 'What the …'

'Yeah,' Sam said. 'God, I need a shag.'

'What about you and Emily? She's not off limits because she's pregnant.'

'I know. It's just—'

Tommo started walking again. 'You'd have only regretted it if I hadn't saved you.'

Sam raced after him. 'We were drunk when we did it. She's not drinking now, so it's a little tricky.

'Just ask her.'

'No wonder you never get your leg over.' Sam scoffed. 'Just ask her?' He rolled his eyes. 'You have to seduce a woman and make her feel special. Not say. Em, fancy a cuppa. Yeah, I'd love one, Sam. Anyway, Emily, what about a shag? That'll work.'

'Yeah, well. You'd know.'

Sam followed Tommo into the Sidewinder. 'Aren't you supposed to be meeting Emily?' Tommo said, nodding towards the door.

Sam saluted. 'On my way now, sir,' he said, turned and left.

'And make sure you're not waylaid,' Tommo shouted.

Emily entered the Red Lion carrying several bags and sat at a table as Sam joined her from the bar. She lifted the shopping and plonked it on the seat beside her. 'My bloody feet are killing me.'

'What do you want to drink?' Sam asked.

'I know what I'd like. A bloody double brandy and coke, but this little person in here wouldn't be happy.' She gently patted her belly.

'Orange?'

'Make sure it's fresh, though. I need my vitamin C.'

Sam walked to the bar and waited patiently until a woman moved along to serve him. She smiled. 'Now then, gorgeous. Pint?'

'Yes, thanks. And a glass of fresh orange for Madam, over there.'

The barmaid pulled the pint and placed it in front of Sam. 'Ice with the orange?'

Sam took out his phone and studied it. 'Thanks.'

'£4.30, please.' She placed the glass of orange down next to the beer.

Sam pulled out a fiver and handed it to her. 'Keep the change.'

The barmaid waved Sam closer, lowering her voice. 'Is Emily pregnant?'

'Yes,' he said, putting his phone away and looking at her.

'So, the rumours are true?'

Sam raised his eyebrows. 'What rumours?'

'You and Emily.' She raised her eyebrows a little.

'Oh, that. Yeah.'

'You must be good, Sam. Turning gay lasses straight.'

'Well, you had your chance.' He picked up the glasses. 'Last Christmas.'

'Sorry, pretty boy,' the barmaid said. 'I like someone a little more reliable.'

Sam placed the drinks on the table, sat opposite Emily, and picked up the menu. 'Are we going to eat?' he said, 'I'm starving.'

'I'll have the tuna salad,' Emily said.

'Tuna? I don't think I've ever seen you eat tuna.'

'Well, there's a first time for everything.' Emily leaned across the table to kiss Sam on the cheek.

Sam smiled back at her. It was the first show of affection she'd shown him since their fateful night. Sam's libido nudged him in the ribs. 'Em,' he whispered. 'You know us two?'

Emily picked up her phone from the table and studied the screen. 'Yes. What about us?'

'Well ... You know, since the night?'

She started texting. 'What night?'

Sam put his hand on her arm. 'Can we leave the phones alone for a moment?'

'Yeah, sure. I'll turn it off. I've finished what I was doing, anyway.' Emily put her phone away.

Sam glanced around the room. 'The night we ...'

Emily nodded towards Sam's mobile on the table. 'Your phone.'

'My phone?'

'Turn it off. If we're going to have a serious talk, I don't want interruptions.'

'Yeah, sure.' Sam fumbled with his handset and turned it off, placing it back on the table.

Emily picked it up. 'Is this a new phone?'

'Em,' he said, grabbing it from her and putting it back down. 'Forget about the friggin' phone.'

Emily leant in closer. 'The night when we did it.'

'Yes.'

Emily held out her arms. 'What about it?'

'Well …' He looked around the room again and lowered his voice further. 'We haven't done it since.'

'Haven't we?' Emily said. 'I was pretty sure we had.'

Sam sat back and folded his arms. 'You're not taking this seriously.'

'Sorry.' She placed a hand on his cheek and smiled. 'I was only kidding.'

'I'll be honest. I'm gagging for it, Em. I'm like a smackhead waiting for his next hit.' He took hold of her hands. 'It's been purgatory.'

'Why don't you just knock one out?' Emily said.

'I did. I have. That's no substitution for the real thing. Christ, Emily Simpson … You have a lot to learn about men. We do that every day. Even when we're in relationships. Even when we're getting regular sex, we still wank!' Sam glanced around the room, realising he'd spoken a little loud.

Emily frowned. 'Really?'

'Of course. It only takes a well-turned ankle to have us running for the bathroom with a box of Kleenex. We do it to relax. To help us sleep. To destress us … For just about anything.'

Emily shook her head. 'I don't know how you live with those things.'

'Well, we do.'

'So, what you are saying is you'd like us to have sex?'

'In a nutshell. Yes.' Sam adopted his best puppy dog eyes.

'Aw, look at you,' she said, pinching his cheek. 'How can I refuse that face?' She kissed him. 'Why didn't you just ask?'

Sam threw out his hands. 'Ask?'

'Yeah. That's what I'd have done.'

'I'll never disparage Tommo again.'

Emily narrowed her eyes. 'You haven't been discussing our sex life with Tommo, have you?'

'Only in passing.'

Emily carefully brushed away a stray bit of hair that had fallen across Sam's eyes. 'Mmm. What about tonight?'

'Yeah?' Sam said and grinned.

'First things first,' Emily said. 'Lunch.'

Sam stood. 'Tuna salad.' He bent, kissed Emily, and then glanced around the room, acutely aware that at least three sets of female eyes, seated at different tables, were watching his every move.

Albert sat in the front room, wondering what to do. The police had phoned and said they were coming around at six to speak with him about Bill's death, but what could he tell them? He didn't know anything. He tried calling Tommo, but after ringing a few times, it went to the answer phone. Should he try Sam? Or perhaps Phillip? He straightened the cushions on the chaise longue as his heart beat rapidly. Why was this? And what was he nervous about? What would his therapist recommend? He closed his eyes and counted to ten as the front doorbell sounded. Albert looked at his watch. It was too early for the police – they had told him six. Maybe it was Tommo or one of the other boys. Albert leapt to his feet and bounded into the hall, stopping briefly to wipe a small smudge on the hall mirror. He grabbed the handle and opened the door.

Brendon stood outside. 'Albert Jackson?'

'Yes,' Albert said, studying the man – the scar above his right eye a worrying sight.

Brendon pulled a gun from his coat pocket and pointed it at Albert. 'Can I have a word?'

Albert backed into the hall, the man motioning with the gun for him to move further inside. Albert headed through into the lounge, closely followed by the gunman. 'The statue, Mr Jackson,' he said, indicating that Albert should sit down.

Albert sat, almost missing the edge of the chair. 'What statue?'

'I do hope you're not going to be difficult. It would be awful to mess up such a lovely house.'

'I've no idea where it is,' Albert said.

'Why did your two friends travel up to Whitehaven?' he said, sitting opposite Albert.

'Holiday?'

'Now listen to me, Jackson!' Brendon said, swatting a cushion next to him aside. The cushion bounced along the floor before coming to rest against the sideboard. 'One more smart-arse remark like that, and I'll smash your face in.'

Albert gulped and sat back in his seat. He had never felt so frightened in his life. He glanced at the cushion on the floor and inwardly groaned, its present location, almost as alarming as being held at gunpoint. 'I'll just pick that cushion up,' he said and got up from the chair.

'Forget the cushion,' Brendon shouted. 'Sit back down and tell me everything you know.'

Albert did as he was told, and his eyes flicked between the cushion and the man. Steeling himself, he tried to ignore it as the front doorbell sounded again.

Brendon jumped up. 'Who's this?'

'I don't know.'

'Are you expecting anyone?'

'No. I mean, yes. The police are coming at six.'

'Police?' Brendon moved towards the window and glanced outside. 'It's Sleen. Let him in and bring him through to this room. Don't say anything about me. Have you got that?'

'Yes.'

'And Jackson, no funny business or …' Brendon said as he held out the gun.

# CHAPTER TWENTY-SIX

Sam and Emily sat in the pub and had finished eating when Tommo bounded in. 'Sorry to interrupt you two lovebirds, but I need to borrow Sam for an hour.'

'As long as he's home by eight,' Emily said.

'Cross my heart,' he said, pulling Sam to his feet. Sam kissed Emily on the cheek before Tommo tugged him towards the door and outside.

Sam pulled his arm free from Tommo. 'What the hell's up with you?' He followed Tommo across the road, struggling to keep pace with him.

'Bit of an emergency.' They reached his vehicle, and Tommo got in.

Sam climbed into the passenger seat. 'What?'

'Somethings up with Albert. He phoned me, mumbling about two men.'

'It's not going to get violent, is it?' Sam said. 'I'm a lover, not a fighter.'

Tommo shook his head. 'If there's any skull cracking to do, I'll do it.'

Sam opened the glove box. 'What else did he say?'

Tommo slammed it shut. 'Nothing. Albert was just rambling. He sounded as if he was in shock.'

'This will be a wild goose chase. I just know it. Someone's probably opened a packet of bourbons before he'd finished the Mint Viscounts.'

'No,' Tommo said. 'It sounded more serious than that.' He started up the engine, and the vehicle screeched away.

Sam and Tommo sped across to Albert's. They parked outside and headed along the driveway towards the house. Tommo held his finger up to his mouth to indicate silence, and Sam nodded his understanding.

They stopped at the front door, the house eerily silent and in darkness.

'There are no lights on,' Tommo whispered.

'What do we do?'

Tommo fished in his pocket and held up a key. 'I've got this.'

'He gave you a key?'

'Yes. Albert trusts me.'

Sam took hold of Tommo's arm. 'Shouldn't we have brought a weapon?'

Tommo looked at Sam wide-eyed. 'Like a pump-action shotgun?'

Sam rolled his eyes. 'I was thinking more of a baseball bat or something similar.'

'You leave any rough stuff to me.' Slowly, he turned the key in the lock. 'This is Nunthorpe, not Chicago.'

They entered through the now-open door, and Tommo crept inside with Sam close behind. They made their way into the front room, allowing time for their eyes to adjust to the darkness. Tommo could see a figure seated in a chair on the far side of the room.

'Albert?' he whispered. The figure didn't stir. He crept closer as Sam matched his movement stride for stride. Tommo reached the person sitting in the chair and nudged his arm. Albert looked towards Tommo. 'Sam, get the light switch,' Tommo said.

Sam turned and clumsily edged back towards the door, stumbling over something. 'Shit,' he said.

'For Christ's sake, Sam,' Tommo said through gritted teeth. 'Can you make any more noise?'

Sam got to his feet and turned on the light. 'Bloody hell,' Sam said, realising the thing he'd fallen over was the body of a man – a large knife protruding from its chest. 'It's a body,' Sam said, gazing at a gun lying on the floor near to the corpse.

Tommo stared briefly across at the dead man and turned his attention back to his friend. 'Albert, what happened?'

Albert looked vacantly past Tommo at the body and brought a hand up to his mouth. 'There's another over there,' Albert said, pointing behind the settee.

Sam tiptoed his way over and tentatively looked over the top of it. 'There is, too,' Sam said as he stared at Tommo and then at Albert.

'It's Sleen,' Albert said. 'He works for Mr Green.'

Tommo leant closer towards Albert. 'What happened?'

'I'm not sure. The other man forced his way in,' Albert said, pointing at the man Sam had tripped over. 'He had a gun. Then Sleen arrived. He told me to bring Sleen inside but say nothing. I did as I was told, and then they started fighting. I must have passed out. When I woke up, they were both dead.'

'What are we going to do?' Sam said. 'Should I phone the police?'

Tommo rubbed his chin. 'No. How are we going to explain this to them?'

'We can't leave the bodies here,' Sam said. 'They start to smell after a while. That's what I've heard.'

'This is no time for levity, Sam,' Tommo said.

The front doorbell sounded, and Sam raced towards the window. 'Who the hell's this?'

Albert looked at Tommo. 'The police are coming. They phoned before the men turned up. That Inspector Comby and his Sergeant. They said they'd be here around six.'

Sam threw his hands in the air. 'Brilliant. We're banged to rights.'

Tommo raced over to the window and, nudging Sam aside, lifted the curtain. He peered outside into the gloom. 'It's Phillip. I phoned him earlier.'

Sam slumped onto the settee. 'Great, Tommo. Why not implicate everyone you know?'

Phillip stared, speechless, at the bodies as Baggage looked up at his owner. Phillip glanced at Sam, who shrugged and then back at Tommo. 'What the hell …?' Phillip said.

'They barged in on Albert,' Tommo said. 'Got into a fight and stabbed each other to death.'

Phillip shook his head. 'The police aren't going to believe that. Albert, are you sure you didn't have anything to do with this?'

Tommo rolled his eyes. 'Albert wouldn't hurt a fly.'

'I don't know,' Sam said. 'Someone moving his cushions might push him over the edge.'

Tommo glared at Sam. 'This is not a joking matter. We have to get rid of these bodies before the coppers arrive.'

'You've phoned the police?' Phillip said.

'No,' Tommo said. 'They called earlier and said they wanted to speak to Albert.'

Sam pushed between Tommo and Phillip. 'Slow down, cowboy,' Sam said. 'What do you mean get rid of the bodies?'

Tommo held out his hands. 'If the police find them here, Albert won't stand a chance.'

Sam threw up his arms. 'You can't get rid of bodies. It's against the law.'

Tommo placed a hand on Sam's shoulder. 'I know that. We'll move them until the police have gone, and then—'

Phillip pushed past Sam. 'How can we get rid of two bodies?'

Tommo sighed. 'I don't know. Let's get them into the garage for now.'

Sam dropped onto a settee. 'I don't believe this. I'm on a promise tonight, and I've somehow ended up in a plot of a Tarantino movie.'

Tommo and Phillip stared at him. 'Well, I am,' Sam said. 'I'm going to be a dad as well. Now you're asking me to play Burke and Hare. My poor child will grow up with me in cell block H.'

Sam, Phillip and Tommo lifted the two bodies into the garage as Baggage sat looking on. He padded across to where one of the men had lain and sniffed at the blood. Albert sat staring vacantly into space as the dog wandered over to him, wagging his tail.

The three men returned, and Phillip stared down at the patch of red Baggage had sniffed. 'What about the blood?' Phillip said as Sam and Tommo joined him.

Tommo bent down, grabbing the edge of the rug. He pulled up the corner and looked beneath. 'We'll have to move this. It hasn't soaked through to the carpet. Give me a hand with it.'

Phillip and Tommo rolled up the carpet and carried it through into the garage, dropping it over the bodies.

Sam looked at a large patch on the floor. 'What about the other blood stain?'

Tommo and Phillip looked at each other. 'What about if we move the settee?' Phillip said.

'It won't look right,' Sam said. 'Who has a sofa at a stupid angle like that?'

'Well, all right,' Tommo said. 'We'll leave a big patch of blood on the floor and hope the police don't notice.'

'Have you got any better ideas, Sam?' Phillip asked.

'Funnily enough, no,' Sam said. 'I haven't had much experience cleaning murder scenes. A bit of a gap in my knowledge, old boy.'

Tommo grunted loudly. 'You're not frigging helping, Sam.' Tommo grabbed one end of the sofa and pulled it across the stain. 'There. What's wrong with that?' he said as Sam rolled his eyes and slumped onto the settee.

Tommo turned his attention to Albert, who hadn't moved an inch. 'Albert?' he said, squatting next to him. 'What time did the police say they were coming again?'

Albert turned to face his friend. 'Six.'

'We need you to focus. Can you do that? The three of us will hide in the garage,' he said as Albert nodded.

The doorbell sounded, and Phillip hurried over to the window and surreptitiously glanced out. 'It's them,' he whispered.

Albert stood with panic writ large across his features as Tommo took hold of his face between his two huge paws. 'Albert. We're counting on you.' Albert nodded and watched as Sam, Phillip, and Tommo headed into the garage, followed by Baggage. The doorbell sounded again, and Albert trudged out of the lounge and into the hall. He sucked in a huge breath, walked towards the door and opened it. Comby and Hardman stood outside.

'Good evening, Mr Jackson,' Comby said. 'Can we come in?'

'Please do.' Albert moved to one side, allowing the officers to enter. He led them through the hall and into the front room. Albert pointed to the settee covering the stain, and the two officers sat. Comby shifted his seating slightly on the sofa so that he was directly opposite Albert. Albert sat in an armchair, watching the two policemen shuffling about as they attempted to adopt an appropriate and comfortable position. The two officers looked at each other, frowning.

'Everything okay?' Albert said.

Comby looked at Albert. 'Yes.' Hardman continued to stare around the room. 'We wanted to talk about your uncle,' Comby continued. 'We haven't been able to make a lot of progress in—'

'Why's this settee at such a funny angle?' Hardman said.

'Fen Shui,' Albert said.

Hardman frowned. 'Feng Shui?'

'It's vital for one's well-being.'

Comby glanced sideways at his partner. 'I see.'

'You mentioned my uncle,' Albert said, displaying a calmness he didn't feel.

'Yes.' Comby focused his attention back on Albert. 'We were wondering if you had any useful information.'

'What sort of information?'

'Cases your uncle was working on. Anything that would help us to discover who killed him.'

Hardman dragged his eyes away from the strange surroundings he found himself in and stared at Albert. 'Only the other day in the office,' Hardman said, 'you sounded as if you knew something.'

'I'm not sure I follow.'

'What my colleague's getting at, Mr Jackson,' Comby said, 'is it appeared you had something you wanted to tell the two of us.'

'I'm not sure why you had that impression.'

Comby stroked his chin. 'And your friends?'

'The same. None of us has a clue.' Albert's eyes darted to his right as Baggage walked in. The dog, making his way over to the two officers, sat at their feet.

Comby patted the dog on the head. 'Hello. Who's this handsome-looking fellow?'

'Baggage.'

Hardman rubbed the dog's head. 'Baggage. What sort of name is that?'

Albert giggled. 'I know. I'm looking after him for a friend.'

Baggage, seemingly satisfied with his pats, moved across to Albert.

With a little jump, he leapt onto Albert's lap. Albert stiffened, his former confidence rapidly diminishing. He forced himself to stroke the dog's head. 'Good boy,' he said.

'So,' Comby said. 'About your uncle.'

Baggage licked his face, and Albert tried not to recoil too much. 'We don't know anything. Good dog,' he said as he shuddered.

Hardman sat back on the settee and resumed his shuffling about. 'What about the Eagle?'

Albert fought the urge to jump up and run to the bathroom to wash his face. 'Eagle?'

'Your uncle was looking for it,' Hardman said.

Comby reached into his inside pocket and took out his notebook. 'Your uncle's secretary, Kimberly Weatherly, mentioned it to us when we initially interviewed her.'

Albert let out a sigh as Baggage jumped onto the floor. 'Yes. I believe he was looking for it for some clients. I don't know anything more about it. Kim told us Bill thought it didn't exist. My uncle told her he thought it was a wild goose chase.'

Comby nodded slowly, staring at Albert. 'Maybe, but someone murdered your uncle, and our investigations have come up with nothing. Have you had anyone asking about this Eagle?'

'No.' He looked directly at the policeman.

'Your friends?' Hardman said.

'They haven't mentioned anything.'

Comby stood as Hardman followed his superior's lead. 'If you or your friends get anyone asking about it, I want you to ring me. Do you understand, Mr Jackson?'

Albert stood. 'I do, Inspector.' He watched the two officers leave the room and moved across to the window, waiting until they got into their car and drove off. Sam, Phillip, and Tommo entered from the garage.

'Arrrh!' Albert shouted. 'Baggage licked my face,' he said, sprinting upstairs and into the bathroom to wash it.

Albert returned from the bathroom, two showers and multiple face washes later. The chatter in the room stopped, and everyone looked at him as he entered.

'Happy now?' Sam said. 'We have more important things to worry about than your hygiene.'

Albert screwed up his face. 'I've seen what dogs lick. When I think about where that dog may have had his tongue.' He put his hand up to his mouth to stifle his nausea.

'Forget about Baggage for the moment,' Tommo said. 'What did the police say?'

'They mentioned the Eagle,' Albert said. 'But I told them we knew nothing about it.'

'Did they believe you?' Phillip said.

Albert eyed Baggage as the dog moved closer to him. 'I'm not sure. The police apparently think the Eagle had something to do with Bill's murder.'

Tommo jumped up from his seat. 'We have bodies to dispose of.'

Sam, who had wandered over to the window, spun around. 'There you go again. How the hell are we going to get rid of them? This is ridiculous.'

'We can't leave them here,' Phillip said.

'We can't involve the police, either,' Tommo said.

Sam raced into the hall, returning with the Yellow Pages. 'I've got an idea.' He flicked through its pages. 'Body art, body piercing, body shop repairs. Nope, I thought not. Nothing in here about body removal. There's obviously a niche in the marketplace.'

Tommo looked skywards. 'You're not helping, Sam.'

'Well, you tell me how you're going to get two dead blokes out of here.'

'We need a van.'

Sam sighed loudly. 'A van? Where the hell are we going to get a van from? The hire places will all be shut.'

Tommo raised his eyebrows. 'I know someone with a van.'

Sam looked at him, realising what he was getting at. 'Not Charlie-daft-shite?'

'He's got a van, and he'll be discreet.'

Sam threw the book onto the floor. 'You've got to be kidding.'

Phillip looked first at Tommo and then at Sam. 'Who's Charlie—?'

'My cousin, Ewan,' Tommo said.

'Is that wise?' Phillip said. 'Involving someone else?'

'Ewan's sound. He won't say a word.'

Sam flopped onto a settee. 'He's a tosser.'

Tommo waved a hand at Sam. 'Ignore him. He has a thing about Ewan.'

Sam rubbed his face. 'Albert, have you got any drink in this house? I need a stiff one.'

'I've got some sherry,' Albert said, flinching as Baggage padded closer to him.

Sam jumped up and strode towards the kitchen. 'Where do you keep your pint glasses?' Turning at the threshold, he pointed at Tommo. 'Just keep that dickhead, Ewan, away from me,' he said and disappeared through the open door.

Phillip looked out of the window of Albert's house as a large white van pulled up outside, reversed onto the drive and stopped halfway down. 'Someone's coming.'

Tommo looked at the others. 'Stay here.' Sam sat glumly on one of the settees, sipping at his sherry.

Tommo returned with a ginger-haired man. 'Albert, Phillip. This is my cousin, Ewan.'

Ewan stepped forward, offering his hand to Phillip. 'Hi,' he said as Phillip and Albert took turns shaking it.

Tommo nodded at Sam, who glowered at Ewan. 'You know Sam.'

Ewan turned and stood in front of Sam. 'Sammy-boy. Still shagging any woman with a pulse?'

Sam scowled at him. 'Ewan. Still shagging anything? We passed a horse in the field on the way here. I could get its number.'

Tommo clasped his hands together. 'Now we all know each other, we need to shift these bodies.'

Ewan tossed his van keys in the air and caught them again. 'I've backed onto the drive. Bring them out, boys.'

Sam jumped up. 'Wait a minute. We can't just carry two bodies out. Someone might see.'

'Sam's right,' Phillip said. 'We need to disguise them.'

'Bin bags,' Ewan said.

Sam rolled his eyes. '*Please.* Bin bags?'

'Yeah, well. Have you a better idea, Sammy-boy?'

Phillip pointed towards the garage. 'The rugs. We could roll them up in them.'

Tommo put a hand on Albert's arm. 'Is that okay? You can buy a couple more.'

Albert looked at Tommo. 'They're antique Persian.'

'Worth a bit?' Ewan said.

'About five thousand pounds each.'

Ewan's eyes widened. 'What? For a couple of rugs. I could get you a pair for fifty quid each.'

Sam shook his head. 'Weren't you listening? They're antique, you dickhead.'

Ewan turned to face Sam. 'What's your problem? Still pissed off about Lisa?'

Sam sneered, looking Ewan up and down. 'What the hell did she see in you? You must have drugged her.'

'Not at all, Sammy-boy. She wanted a real man. Not an immature tosser like you.'

The two men squared up. Tommo pushed between them, using his massive arms to force them further apart. 'Will you two give up? Otherwise, I'll knock your heads together.'

Sam slumped onto the settee again. 'Well, keep him away from me,' he said, pointing his finger at Ewan.

'Ditto, Sammy-boy, ditto,' Ewan said.

Baggage came walking in from the garage and made his way across to Ewan. 'Who's this?' Ewan said and rubbed Baggage's ears.

'Ewan, Baggage. Baggage, Ewan,' Tommo said.

'He's mine,' Phillip said.

Tommo marched towards the garage, motioning for the others to follow him. 'I hate to interrupt this, but we need to get moving. Albert, we'll use the rugs and bring them back if you like. You can get them cleaned.'

'I've got a Vax,' Ewan said. 'It'll bring them up a treat.'

Albert frowned. 'They need to be professionally cleaned. There's a specialist company I use.'

Sam shook his head. 'You can't. They'd want to know where the blood came from.'

Albert lowered his eyes. 'Take them. I don't want them back.'

Tommo walked across to him and gave him a man hug. 'Okay, buddy. You stay here with Baggage, and we'll get rid.'

'Why can't I stay?' Sam said.

'You can't. Alberts is still in shock, and we need all the hands we've got. Come on, boys, let's go.'

The white van trundled along the farm track and then off the road. It made its way across open ground before coming to rest near some trees. Ewan turned off the engine, and the four men got out, opened the back of the van and pulled out one of the bodies rolled inside the rug. They had taken the time to wrap the bodies in bin-liners first – to stop any more blood leaking out – and the four men picked up the parcel, hoisting it high on their shoulders before marching deeper into the trees. Finding a suitable spot, they dropped the body onto the ground, returning to the van and repeating the process a second time. They stood, gathering their breath.

Tommo banged his head with the palm of his hand. 'We haven't brought any tools.'

'There's a spade in the back of my van,' Ewan said. 'I'll go and get it.' Ewan disappeared, returning moments later with a small spade.

Sam looked at the implement. 'What good's that? It looks like something Bilbo Baggins would use.'

Ewan dropped the spade at Sam's feet. 'I can't see your spade. All you ever do is criticise.'

Sam kicked the spade. 'If I'd have known what we were planning, I'd have invested in a body burying kit.'

'Hilarious,' Ewan said

'Boys, boys,' Tommo said.

Sam threw up his hands. 'It'll take us all night to dig a hole big enough for two bodies. If we don't want them discovering, that is.'

Ewan turned and looked at Tommo. 'How deep does it need to be?'

Phillip bent and picked up the spade. 'Six feet is traditional.'

'Six feet,' Sam said. 'Jesus, we'll be here until tomorrow night.'

Ewan held up a finger. 'Why don't we cut the bodies up? Then, we can dig a succession of smaller holes. It'll be much easier that way."

Sam stared at Ewan. 'Oh, for God's sake. If we get caught. Sorry when …' He puffed out his cheeks. 'When we get caught. We may be able to convince a jury that we panicked and dumped the bodies, but if we start cutting them up, how's that going to look?'

Phillip looked at Ewan. 'In any case, we haven't anything to cut them up with.'

Sam nodded at Ewan. 'Yeah, Donnie Brasco,' Sam said.

Ewan ignored Sam and looked at Tommo. 'I've got a Stihl saw in the van, and I've got a new blade on it. It'll cut through bone and sinew in seconds.' He made a mechanical noise for effect.

Sam edged nearer to Tommo. 'Tommo. Are you seriously considering this?'

Tommo put a hand on Ewan's shoulder. 'Ewan. It's the middle of the night. If you fired up a Stihl saw, every man and his dog would descend on us. I'm sorry, chaps, but we're just going to have to do it the hard way. We'll take turns. That way, we won't tire out too quickly.'

Ewan grabbed the spade from Phillip. 'I'll go first.'

Sam grabbed hold of the spade's handle. 'No, you won't. The first bit will be easy,' Sam said as the pair wrestled with it.

Tommo grabbed the tool and pulled it from them. 'Enough. We'll draw lots. That'll make it fair.'

The four men carried on digging throughout the night. When they deemed the hole deep enough, they undid the carpet and rolled the bodies inside and then the four began the arduous task of filling it back in. The sun rose in the sky by the time they had finished, and covering the earth with leaves and twigs, they drove across the spot in Ewan's van to flatten the site. Nodding at each other, happy they'd covered it over sufficiently, they got back in the vehicle, slumped into their seats, and headed off.

Ewan pulled the van up outside a café.

'What are we doing here?' Tommo said.

Ewan raised his eyebrows. 'Food. I'm bloody starving.'

Sam rolled his eyes. 'Are you kidding?'

Tommo nodded. 'I've got to be honest, so am I. What about you, Phillip?'

'I could go a breakfast,' he said.

Ewan jumped out of the van. 'Three to one.'

The other three did likewise and followed Ewan into the building. They sat at a table furthest away from the counter, and a middle-aged man made his way over to them.

'What can I get you, lads?' he said.

'Ewan banged the table with the flat of his hand. Four belly-busters, my good man.'

'Anything to drink?'

'Four teas,' Tommo said. 'All with milk.'

The man made a note of their order and walked away.

Tommo looked at Ewan. 'What about your van?'

'Don't worry about that. Its MOT runs out shortly, and a friend of mine is going to make it disappear for me. He knows someone who owns a breaker's yard. This time tomorrow, it'll be a small square of mangled metal. Then I'll report it stolen and claim the insurance.'

Tommo nodded. 'Good. We'll all need alibis for tonight. Just in case the police …'

'Emily will cover for me,' Sam said.

Tommo looked at Phillip. 'What about you?'

'I could ask Kim.'

'Kim? You and her an item then?'

'Not exactly.'

Tommo shook his head. 'Better not involve her. You were at Sam's last night.' He looked at his cousin. 'Ewan?'

'Our lass will vouch for me.'

Sam looked at Tommo. 'And you?'

'I'll give it some thought,' he said as the man returned with their drinks, placing the four mugs on the table before leaving again. 'What did you do with the gun, Sam?'

'I put it in one of the dead guy's jackets.'

Phillip put a hand in his pocket and pulled out some keys. 'What about the car keys?'

Ewan picked them up. 'Are these the cars owned by our two friends?'

'Yeah,' Tommo said.

'Leave them to me. They don't need them anymore. A quick facelift and no one will ever know. It Should pay for a nice little holiday and a new van.' He pocketed the keys with a smile.

After eating the breakfasts, Ewan dropped Tommo back at Alberts so Phillip could collect Baggage. Tommo took Sam home before dropping Phillip and Baggage off. Then Tommo, after making sure Albert was fine, left in his car and drove back to his flat. He pulled up and tiptoed inside, remembering he had left Deb there. Tommo glanced into the bedroom, where Deb snoozed in his bed. Taking off his dirty clothes and getting a duvet from a cupboard, he lay on the settee.

Tommo wasn't sure how long he'd slept, but he suspected it hadn't been long as he opened an eye.
Deb sat in a chair opposite, smiling at him. 'What happened to you last night?'
'It took longer than I thought.'
'The food was great, by the way,' she said. 'What time did you get back?'
Tommo sat up. 'I'm not sure.'
'I waited until about twelve for you and then went to bed. I was out like a light.'
'It wasn't long after that.'
'Why didn't you wake me?' she said.
'You looked so peaceful.'
'So? What did you get up to last night?'
Tommo sighed. 'It's probably better you don't know.'
'Fair enough. I kept some food from last night. If you're hungry?'
Tommo made a face. 'As much as I like Mexican, I don't think I'd enjoy it for breakfast.'
'What about a full English? I noticed you've got bacon and sausage in the fridge.'
'I could do with a shower first.'
'Well, big fella. You go and jump in, and I'll make a start.'
'Yeah, okay.'

Tommo was in the shower and pondered for a moment. Deb had inadvertently given him an alibi. It wasn't exactly ethical, though, but he was so tired and unable to think straight. The thirty minutes of sleep he'd had was nowhere near enough. He desperately wanted to crawl into bed but put his head up against the bathroom wall and closed his eyes. Deb's hands around him roused him. 'If you can wait a little longer for your food,' she whispered into his ear, 'I'll scrub your back.'

Tommo opened his eyes and stared at Deb, who lay next to him, her right hand resting on his hairy chest. 'Whatever you got up last night,' she said, 'it tired you out.'
'Sorry about that. I haven't slept well for ages.'
Deb slowly stroked his chest. 'Well, you certainly did this morning. You've been asleep for hours.'
'Really?'
Deb stroked his chest again. 'Yes. All refreshed now?'
'I feel loads better.'
'Well, let's finish what we began in the shower, shall we?' she said

and stretched up to kiss him.

Robards pulled out his phone and called Tony. 'Have you seen Brendon?'

'No. Why?'

'He was supposed to meet me this morning but didn't show up.'

'He went around to see Jackson, didn't he?'

'He did,' Robards said. 'I've tried ringing his mobile, but it keeps going to answerphone,'

'Shall I pop around to his place?'

'Yeah, do that.'

## CHAPTER TWENTY-SEVEN

Kim strolled along the pavement with Baggage, stopped outside the coffee shop, and fastened Baggage's lead to the metal railings. 'You wait here, Bagsy,' she said, 'and I'll get us a drink.' Baggage looked up, wagging his tail rapidly. Kim crouched and rubbed his ears. 'Good boy,' she said, kissed his head and patted him.

Tony approached her. 'I thought it was you. Whose is the mutt?'

Kim stood up straight. 'His name's Baggage, and he's not a mutt.'

'I didn't mean any offence, Baggage,' he said and patted the dog's head.

Kim folded her arms. 'What do you want, Tony?'

'I thought I might catch you here. Fancy a coffee?'

'No, thanks.'

'Aw, come on, Kim. Don't be like that. I thought we were good?'

'Tony,' she said and unfastened Baggage's lead. 'Leave me alone. We aren't anything.'

He pushed his face closer to Kim's. 'Can't we just have a chat?'

'I don't want a chat. I don't want anything more to do with you. We're over. I've moved on. Maybe you should.'

'You mean your friend, Phillip?'

'It's none of your business.' She turned to walk away.

'Maybe he's not such an angel.'

'Whatever,' Kim said.

'Give Carla a ring if you don't believe me. Ask her about your friend,' he shouted after her as she turned a corner.

Kim marched on with Baggage and tried to ignore what Tony had said, but her interest was piqued. Turning a corner, she stopped outside another coffee shop, tied the dog up, and went inside. Returning moments later with two lattes, she fished in her handbag and pulled out a bowl, pouring one of the lattes into it. She placed it on the floor next to baggage, who eagerly lapped at the liquid. Taking out her phone, Kim searched through her contacts, stopping at the name Carla. She paused, staring at the name, before ringing.

'Hello,' a female voice said.
'Carla? It's Kim. Kim Weatherly.'
'Kim. Long time no hear. Are you well?'
'Not bad. You?'
'Okay, I suppose.'
'I ran into Tony this morning,' Kim said. 'He said I should call you about—'
'Phillip Davison?' Carla said.
'How did you know?'
'I saw you with him the other week when I passed on a bus. A friend of a friend knows his ex.'
'And?'
'And nothing,' Carla said.
'What did this friend of a friend tell you about Phillip and his ex?'
'She said they were going to get married and that he worked for her father's company. He lived in one of those posh apartments on the riverside in Stockton—'
'I know all this,' Kim said.
'They had a big bust up, by all accounts.'
'I know. His girlfriend did the dirty on him.'
'Not how I heard it, Kim.'
'How did you hear it?' Kim swapped the phone to her other ear.
'She found him in bed with her sister. That's how I heard it. She threw him out, and her dad sacked him.'
'I see.'
'Maybe you should ask him? Hear his side of the story.'
'I will. Thanks, Carla.' She hung up and looked at Baggage, who looked back up at her, his mouth covered in froth.
'Oh, Baggage,' she said, rubbing his ears. 'What should I do?'

Carla searched her contacts and dialled. 'It's Carla. I've spoken with Kim. I told her what you said.'
'Good,' Tony said. 'I'll drop that money off later.'
'Did this Phillip Davison actually cheat on his girlfriend with her sister, or did you make it up?'
'Who cares?' he said, ringing off.
Tony phoned Robards. 'Kim knows about Phillip Davison. She's not

playing ball with me, though.'

'She might come around,' Robards said. 'Any news on Brendon?'

'No. There's no answer at his flat. His neighbour hasn't seen him for two days. You don't think Jackson could've ...'

Robards laughed. 'I don't believe so. From what I've heard, he'd have trouble killing a spider.'

'Could Stankovich be involved in his disappearance?' Tony said. 'Or Green?'

'Maybe. I'm supposed to be meeting Stankovich later. I'll see what I can find out. I'm managing to keep him in the dark at the moment.'

'What about Jacobs?'

'I'm pretty sure it wasn't her. I'll ring you later.'

Sam and Phillip sat in the office, and the last pile of paperwork lay in front of Sam. 'I don't think we'll ever find out who killed Bill. Maybe it was one of the two we ...' Sam raised his eyebrows.

Phillip got up and closed the door to the office. 'If it was one of those, they had it coming. You and Emily still not speaking?'

'Sort of. We've moved from notes and texts to the odd word. I wouldn't mind, but I wasn't shagging about. I can't very well tell her what we were actually doing, can I? Sorry I missed our date, Emily. I know you've got yourself all dressed up and made an effort with the food and that, but I've been out all night burying bodies.'

'All right, Sam, someone might hear. Anyway, it's your own fault. Reputations. Easy to come by, hard to shake.'

'Yeah, true, I suppose. Tommo wants us all to meet at the weekend. To discuss what happened.'

'Can't wait,' Phillip said.

Sam leant back in the chair. 'This is bloody impossible. I don't think Bill ever threw anything away.'

'All we can do is keep looking.'

Sam held up his notepad. 'I've got a couple of names here. I'll have to ask Kim if she knows them.'

Baggage came padding into the office carrying a bone-shaped chew, walked over to his bed and lay down with his prize.

Sam nodded towards the dog. 'Someone's happy.'

Phillip got up and strolled into Kim's office. She was sat at her desk, seemingly deep in thought.

Phillip stopped next to her. 'Penny for them?' Kim half-smiled at him. 'I was wondering if you fancied a drink later,' Phillip said.

'Not tonight,' she said. 'I've got a headache. I was thinking of knocking off early.'

'I've got some tablets in the other office,' Phillip said. 'Do you want me—'

'I'm all right.' Kim stood. 'I'll see you later,' she said, walking past him and out of the door.

Phillip wandered back into the office, sat at his desk and rubbed his chin.

Sam looked up. 'What's up, mate?' he said, putting another piece of paper on the pile.

'Kim seemed a little off.'

'Why? What have you said?'

'Nothing,' Phillip said. 'She told me she has a headache.'

'Well, there you go. Time of the month. They're always a bit funny when the decorators are in.'

Phillip rolled his eyes. 'Have you slept with many feminists?'

'Why?'

'I can't see your brand of small talk going down too well, that's all.'

Sam rocked back in his chair, placing his feet on his desk. 'Oh, that. I wouldn't say that to their face. I'm a little more tactful. This is bloke-talk. Even feminists like a man occasionally.'

'Is that you speaking from experience?'

Sam tapped his chin. 'Yep. Gina.'

Phillip held up his hands. 'Go on … Gina?'

'I had an on-off relationship with her. She couldn't get enough of me for two weeks of every month. She'd pull me into a changing room or the toilets in M&S and do unspeakable things, and we'd spend the rest of the time in bed. Then she'd get her period and change completely. What's the female equivalent of a misogynist?'

'A woman.'

Sam smiled. 'Good one. I'll have to remember that. Well, whatever it is, that's what she'd become. Came at me with a knife once.'

Phillip's eyes widened. 'A carving knife?'

'No. One you use to butter bread with. I think it was more symbolic than menacing but a little off-putting. I mean, it could start like that and then escalate.'

'What happened to her?'

'I dumped her. No matter how good the sex is, you can't put up with that. One minute, you've gone to bed with Miss sexual-positions 1999, and in the morning, you wake up next to Lizzie Borden.'

'I never get tired of listening to your sexual exploits, Sam. They are a joy.'

Sam held his notepad aloft. 'It's a pity about Kim. I wanted to ask her about these names.'

Sam sat at his desk, sipping his tea. Phillip had managed to drag Baggage away from his bone and taken him for a walk, so the office was quiet as Sam's mobile sounded. He put down his cup and looked at Emily's name on the screen, sighed loudly and answered. 'Hi, Em.'

'Is Phillip, there?' Emily said.

'No. He's taken Bagsy out. Why?'

'Are you on your own?'

Sam looked upwards. 'Yes, just me here.'

'I've had Kim on the phone. Apparently, she ran into her ex. He told her that Phillip and his ex-girlfriend broke up because she found him in bed with her sister. Is that right?'

Sam rolled his eyes. 'What makes you think I'd know? He doesn't tell me everything.'

'Because you and Phillip are best mates. Bloody men. Always covering for each other.'

'What if it is true?' Sam said. 'It's history. It's in the past.'

'Kim's upset that Phillip led her to believe—'

'I know all about that. It's not as straightforward as you're making out. There were mitigating circumstances.'

'Like what?'

'He didn't know it was her sister.'

Emily sneered. 'Are they identical twins?'

'Well, no, but—'

'So how the hell could he mistake the two of them?'

'I don't know. It was dark. He was half asleep.'

Emily snorted. 'Give me a break. It sounds like the sort of excuse you'd come up with.'

'All I know is that Phillip felt guilty about it. He never wanted to lie to Kim. He was quite cut up about it. He's not like me, and he really likes Kim.'

'Mmm. Well, you had better have a word with her. Use that charm of yours because she's pretty cut up herself. And Sam, this telephone call never happened. Okay?'

'Bloody hell. Now I'm an agony aunt. Why am I getting dragged into this?'

'You are, so get over it. I've done you something for tea. If you can get home on time? Pulled pork and some of my mam's fadgies. You like her fadgies, don't you?'

Sam thought for a moment, his libido stretching and yawning. 'Yeah. I love them.'

Sam pressed the bell to Kim's flat and waited as a key was turned and the door opened. Kim stood there. 'Oh, hi, Sam. I thought for a moment it was Phillip. Come in.'

Sam followed Kim into the living room and glanced at an open case on the settee. Folded pieces of clothing, a toiletry bag, and a hairdryer were next to it.

Sam nodded towards the case. 'Going away?'

'Scarborough,' she said. 'I've got an aunt who lives there. Haven't seen her for yonks. Thought it was time for a visit.'

'Does Phillip know?'

'Er, no. I …'

'Is everything all right?' Sam said.

Kim sat in an armchair and sighed. 'Has Phillip ever mentioned his past?'

'A little. Why?'

'He said he split up with his ex because she was seeing someone else. I got told by someone …' she paused, 'that his ex found him in bed with her sister.'

'I won't lie, he has mentioned it, but it's not as straightforward as it seems.'

Kim folded her arms. 'In what way?'

'His ex's sister had the hots for him, and Phillip kept her at arm's length. One morning he was in bed, and his girlfriend had gone to work. Her sister got into the flat somehow and climbed into bed with him. Phillip thought it was his girlfriend.'

Kim shook her head. 'Please. You don't expect me to believe that, do you?'

'Listen, Kim. Phillip's nothing like me. He's a decent lad. He's not a player. He lost his job – a good job – a flat, everything. I think the boy has suffered enough.'

'Why didn't he tell me, then?'

'He was embarrassed. He really likes you and thought you wouldn't look twice at him if you knew, given what happened with your ex-boyfriend.

Kim nodded. 'He's right.'

'It was before you met. Surely everyone deserves a second chance.'

Kim stood. 'I don't know. I need to get my head straight. I'll have to think it over.'

'What about Phillip? Are you going to tell him about this? Surely, he deserves to know?'

'Not now, Sam, my head's in bits.'

Sam turned to leave. 'Okay.'

Kim followed Sam towards the front door. 'What did you come around for?'

'Oh,' he said, reaching into his pocket. 'I've got a few names here. I was wondering if you recognised any of them?'

Kim plucked the paper from Sam's hand and studied it. 'Rocco,' she said. 'That's the only one I know. He used to do bits and pieces for Bill. A bit of a dodgy character but canny with it.'

'I don't suppose you know where he lives?'

'No. But he drinks in The King William in Dormanstown. I remember Bill mentioning that.'

Sam opened the door. 'Thanks.' He paused at the threshold. 'Don't be too hard on Phillip.'

Kim frowned. 'Don't tell Phillip about this conversation, will you?'

'Scouts honour,' Sam said.

# CHAPTER TWENTY-EIGHT

Sam returned to the office where Phillip was sitting at his desk, Albert was busy dusting his little corner of the room, and Baggage lay dozing on his bed.

Phillip looked up from his paperwork. 'Where have you been?'

'I've been checking on a lead into Bill's murder. A name.'

Albert paused his dusting. 'A name?'

Sam sat at his desk. 'Someone called Rocco. Apparently, he used to do little jobs for Bill. I haven't an address, but Kim told me where he drinks,' he said as Baggage lifted his head on hearing Kim's name mentioned.

'Have you been to see Kim?' Phillip said.

'Yes.'

Phillip stood. 'I need to pop through and see her myself.'

'Never mind that now,' Sam said, tapping his desk. 'We need to follow this lead. Anyway, I think she's gone out.'

'Do you want me to come?' Albert said.

Sam lowered his brow. 'You look like you've got your hands full, and the front of your desk looks as if it needs a wipe.'

Albert moved around to the front of the desk and sprayed some polish on it. 'You're right. It looks as if someone's spilt a drink down it.' He huffed. 'I might need some hot water,' he said, putting his polish and duster down.

'Grab your coat,' Sam said to Phillip, who was deep in thought. 'No time like the present.'

'How are we going to get there?' Phillip said.

Sam opened a drawer and pulled out a set of car keys. 'I've loaned Emily's car.'

Phillip sighed and stood. 'Are you okay manning the phone, Albert?'

'Yes, fine,' Albert said as he busily picked at a piece of dirt with a coin on his desk. 'I'll see you two later.'

Phillip paused with his hand on the passenger door. 'You could have taken Albert, Sam. I really need to see Kim.'

'If you think I'm waiting until he gets himself ready, you've got another think coming.' Sam climbed into the car. 'Come on, Phillip.'

Phillip glanced up at the building towards Kim's flat and climbed into the passenger seat. 'I suppose it'll keep until later,' he said as Sam started up the engine and drove off.

'This guy, Rocco,' Sam said, glancing across at Phillip, 'drinks in The King William, Dormanstown.'

'Isn't that pub notorious?'

Sam winked at Phillip. 'Yeah, but it's an afternoon. The druggies and nutters don't get in until later.'

'How can you be sure?'

'I used to know a lass from there. Quite a while back.'

Phillip sighed. 'I thought there'd be a woman involved, somehow.'

'Linda,' Sam said. 'Quite a looker.' He laughed. 'I dread to think what she looks like now. Probably twice the size she used to be with an army of kids, all with different dads.'

'That's a bit harsh.'

Sam smiled. 'Well, I'm speaking from experience.'

'So, what happened to you and this, Linda?'

'I finished with her when her dad threatened me with a machete.'

Phillip smiled. 'Really?'

'Oh, yeah. And he meant it. So, the lovely Linda and I parted company.'

Sam pulled the car up in the pub's car park, and the pair got out before heading inside. Sam stopped at the bar as Phillip stood a couple of yards behind him.

A barman looked up from his newspaper, folded it and moved across to the two of them. 'Yes, lads?'

Sam pulled a note from his trouser pocket. 'Two beers, mate.'

The barman pulled the pints and placed them in front of the pair as Phillip glanced around the room, which was empty, save for three customers scattered about.

The barman held out his hand. 'Five twenty.'

Sam offered him the note. 'One for yourself.'

The barman smiled, the first sign of pleasantness he'd shown, and

Sam picked up a glass and passed it to Phillip.

He handed Sam his change, picked up his paper and resumed his previous position.

'We're looking for a little information,' Sam said. 'Maybe you could help us?'

The barman stopped reading, raised his head from his paper and narrowed his eyes. 'Oh, yeah?'

Sam glanced at Phillip, who nodded. 'We're looking for someone called Rocco.' Sam said and took a swig of his beer.

'Rocco?' the barman said, putting the paper aside. 'What do you want him for?'

'He did a bit of work for our uncle, Bill Hockney,' Phillip said. 'We were hoping he could help us out.'

'What sort of work?'

Sam wiped the froth from his mouth. 'We run a detective agency and need a spare set of legs. We heard that Rocco does this sort of thing.'

'Haven't seen him for a while,' the barman said, picking up the paper again. 'Rumour has it he's left town.'

'Right,' Sam said. 'Oh, well.'

Phillip pulled a card from his pocket and offered it to the barman. 'If you hear from him. Could you give us a ring?'

The barman scrutinised the card. 'Yeah, no problem.'

Sam and Phillip moved away from the bar and sat in some seats near the window. They finished their pints in silence and got up to leave, nodding at the barman on their way out.

The pair reached the car. 'No further forward,' Sam said.

'Yes. Bit of a waste of time.'

An old man appeared next to them. 'I've got some info,' he said. 'Meet me in Tesco's car park, near the racecourse, in about an hour.'

'You are?' Sam said.

The man ignored the question and disappeared around a corner.

Sam looked at Phillip, who shrugged as the two of them got into Emily's car and drove off.

Robards mobile sounded. 'Yes?'

'Hello, Mr Robards. It's Aaron. From The King Billy, in Dormanstown.'

'What can I do for you, Aaron?'

'You told me I should give you a ring if anyone came around looking for Rocco.'

'I'm listening,' Robards said.

'I had a couple of blokes in earlier. They said they ran a detective agency.'

'Describe them,' Robards said.

The barman described Sam and Phillip. 'That thing we discussed,' the barman said. 'Are we good?'

'Yes,' Robards said. 'Consider it dealt with.'

Sam and Phillip reached Tesco, went inside to buy a coffee, returned to the car with their drinks, and waited.

'How long has it been?' Sam said.

'Just over an hour.'

Sam blew out. 'He's late.'

The pair jumped as the car's rear door opened, and a man dived in. 'Drive,' he said, ducking behind the vehicle's front seats. Sam glanced across at Phillip and then looked down at the man.

'Where?' Sam asked.

'Anywhere.' Sam started up and drove along West Dyke Road, turning left onto Kirkleatham Lane before pulling off the main road and stopping in a layby.

Phillip turned and looked over the rear seat. 'Will this do?'

The man sat up straight, his head scanning left and right. 'Yeah, this will do.' The man continued to glance in all directions. 'I overheard you in the pub. You're looking for Rocco?'

Sam turned to face the man. 'We are. He knew our uncle.'

'Yeah, sorry about what happened to Bill. He was a decent bloke.'

'I'm Sam, and this is Phillip. Your name is?'

The man thought. 'Dave,' he said. 'Rocco's gone to ground. Someone's after him, and he doesn't want to end up like your uncle.'

'Can you get in touch with him?' Phillip said.

'I've got his number. You can have it for a price.'

Sam glanced at Phillip. 'How much?' Sam said.

'Fifty quid.'

'Fifty quid for a number?' Phillip said. 'That's a bit steep.'

'Listen,' Dave said, glancing up and down the road. 'I'm going out on a limb here. That's the price.'

Phillip and Sam each put a hand into their pockets. Sam handed Phillip thirty pounds, and Phillip added the rest.

Phillip held out the cash. 'The number?'

Dave took out an old mobile, searched his contacts, dialled a number, and waited. 'Rocco? I've got those two fellas here.'

Dave passed the handset to Phillip and snatched the money from him in one quick motion. He opened the door, got out and strode off.

Sam opened the door. 'What about the handset?'

'Bin it after you've finished with it. It's nicked, anyway.' And then he was gone.

Phillip put the phone to his ear. 'Hello,' he said as Sam moved his head near the mobile so he could hear too.

'Who's this?' said the voice on the other end.

'Phillip Davison.'
'And your friend?'
'Sam Davison,' Sam said.
'You're Bill's nephews?'
'We are,' Phillip said. 'Rocco?'
'We need to meet. Keep the phone handy, and I'll be in touch.' The phone went dead.
'Hello,' Phillip said.
Sam frowned. 'Do you get the feeling we've been had? Fifty quid lighter and a useless mobile phone.'
Phillip shrugged. 'I don't know. It seems a bit elaborate to con fifty pounds off someone.'
Sam pointed at the mobile. 'Phone him again.'
'He said he'd be in touch.'
'Just try it. He might answer.'
The mobile beeped. 'We've got a text,' Phillip said, opening it. 'The Cod and Lobster, Staithes, ten o'clock tonight.'

Sam and Phillip sat at a table in The Cod and Lobster as Phillip checked his watch again. 'A minute to go,' Phillip said, nodding towards the door. A man came in, stood at the bar and ordered a drink before joining a group of men in the opposite corner.
Sam let out a breath. 'I thought that was him. My heart is beating like a train.'
'Me too.'
The mobile sounded in Phillip's pocket. He took it out, and he answered. 'Hello?'
'Let's take a walk, lads,' a voice said.
'Where?' Phillip asked.
'Around the harbour. Near the café, you'll see a bench. On the bench, there's a newspaper.'
'Newspaper?' Phillip said.
'Newspaper.' The phone went dead.
Phillip looked at Sam. 'Fancy a walk?'
The two finished their drinks and set off, reaching the bench in minutes. Sam picked up the newspaper lying on the seat and opened it, flicking through its pages.
'Anything?' Phillip said.
'No. Just an ordinary newspaper.'
Phillip shook his head. 'Do you get the impression that someone's messing us about?'
'I don't know, but we can't stay here all night.'
The pair headed back to the pub, stopping at the car park, and Sam grabbed Phillip's arm. 'I haven't a clue what's going on here, but

somethings not right.'

Phillip rubbed his chin. 'It's all very cloak and dagger. Maybe he's in the pub?'

'And maybe he's not,' Sam said. 'For all we know, he could be miles away, having a good laugh at our expense.'

Phillip slapped his forehead. 'The car? Maybe it was a ruse to nick the car.'

The pair ran around the far side of the pub, slowing to a jog as they spotted Emily's car parked where they'd left it. They reached the vehicle and opened the doors.

'We'll give it five more minutes and then go,' Phillip said. 'I'm not sitting here all night, waiting for nobody to show.'

'Sorry about that,' a voice said. Sam and Phillip spun around as a man stepped out from the shadows and walked towards the car. 'Shall we?' he said, opening the vehicle's back door.

The three men got in. The man smiled at the pair of them. 'Rocco,' he said and held out a hand. Phillip and Sam shook it in turn, introducing themselves. 'I had to be certain you weren't followed.'

Sam looked at Phillip. 'Followed? By who?' Sam said.

'Have you heard of someone called Robards? Detective Inspector Geoff Robards?'

Phillip narrowed his eyes and shook his head. 'No. We know a copper called Comby.'

'Comby's nothing. It's Robards you've got to be careful of. He's as bent as a corkscrew. I can't prove it, but I think it was him or one of his men who killed Bill.'

'Why would he do that?' Sam said.

'Bill was working on a case. He was looking for something.'

Phillip glanced at Sam. 'What?' Phillip said.

'I don't know. He never told me, but I got the impression it was important.'

'How do you know this?' Sam said.

'Bill told me to get a key for him, which I did. On the night of his murder, I was followed by Robards' men. Luckily, I escaped. I left the key inside the toilets of a pub.'

'Is it still there?' Phillip said.

'Listen, lads, cards on the table. It's obvious you two know more than you're letting on. I'm not bothered about that, but I don't want to get involved. It's your business.'

'We've got the key,' Sam said. Phillip glared at him, and Sam shrugged. 'What does this key open?'

'No idea,' Rocco said. 'Bill never told me.'

'What do you want from us?' Sam said.

'Bill owed me five hundred for getting the key for him. He was supposed to square up later but—'

Sam threw his head back. 'You've dragged us out here for five hundred quid?'

'Get me the money I'm owed plus another five hundred for risking my neck, and I'll give you something.'

Phillip moved his face closer. 'What?'

'The address where I got the key from.' He opened the door, got out of the car and paused. 'I'll ring you in two days.'

Sam opened his door. 'How do we know—?'

'That I won't just run off with the money or give you any address?'

'Exactly,' Sam said as Phillip nodded in agreement.

'You don't.' Rocco rubbed at the bristles on his chin. 'Bill and I went back a long way. He was a decent bloke and helped me out a lot. I'd love to see the bastards that murdered him behind bars.'

'Why not go to the police?' Sam said.

'I wouldn't last five minutes. Robards has already been looking for me, and If I set foot back on Teesside, I'll never make it to court. Get me the money, boys, and I'll give you the address. then it's up to you.' With that, he closed the door and vanished into the night.

Sam arrived late to the office the following morning to find Albert seated behind his immaculately clean desk.

'Morning, Sam,' Albert said.

Sam put his steaming cup of tea down and slumped in his chair. 'Morning.' He picked up the mug and cradled the drink, letting out a long and loud yawn.

Albert brushed an imaginary piece of dust from his desk. 'How did you get on last night?'

Sam puffed out his cheeks and sat back in his seat. 'If I was you,' Sam said, staring at Albert's pristine corner of the office. 'I'd give up those therapy sessions. It's like sharing an office with Howard Hughes.'

'Vanessa thinks I'm improving.'

Sam sneered. 'She would say that, wouldn't she? You're paying her sixty pounds an hour.'

Phillip wandered in carrying a cup of coffee. 'Has anyone seen Kim? I've been to her flat, and there wasn't an answer.'

'No,' Albert said. 'She's usually first in.'

Sam put down his cup and pointed to Phillip's chair. 'Sit down, Phillip.'

Phillip did as he was told. Baggage trotted into the office, stared at the three men in turn, and then looked back towards Kim's office.

'She's gone away for a few days,' Sam said. 'To her aunt's.'

Phillip raised his eyebrows. 'Her aunt's? She didn't say anything about going away.'

Sam glanced at Albert. 'She's found out about you and your ex.'

'How?' Phillip said.

'I'm not sure. Someone told her I think. I tried to put your side of the story, but—'

Phillip jumped up from his seat. 'I've got to talk with her.'

Sam shook his head. 'She's in Scarborough.'

'What happened between you and your ex?' Albert said.

Sam waved away Albert's question. 'She said it would only be for a few days,' Sam said. 'She needs some time, mate.'

Phillip slumped back in his chair. 'Maybe I could ring?'

Sam got up and walked across to him, putting a hand on his shoulder. 'Just give her a little space. Time for her to come to terms with it. If you speak to her now, it could make things worse.'

Phillip stood, pushing his way past Sam, and raced towards the door. 'I'm going for a walk,' he said, slamming the door behind him. Sam sat back at his desk and frowned at Albert.

Albert looked across at Sam. 'What's going on?'

'Phillip's ex-girlfriend caught him in bed with her sister, and Kim found out.'

'I see,' Albert said.

'You don't. This sister did it on purpose. She sneaked into Phillip's flat while he was half asleep and got into bed with him. Phillip thought it was his girlfriend.'

'Does Kim know that?'

Sam shrugged. 'She doesn't believe it.'

'I can understand that.'

Sam glared at Albert. 'Whose side are you on?'

'I'm just saying. '

Sam picked his drink up again. 'Anyway. About last night.'

Sam went on to explain to Albert what had happened. He told him about meeting Rocco and that he wanted money from them to tell them where he'd stolen the key from. Sam went on to say that Robards, Rocco believed, murdered Bill.

'What are we going to do?' Albert said.

'We talked it over last night. I don't think we have much choice. It's a lot of money, but the key is useless without any idea what it opens.'

'Did this Rocco say he knows what it opens?'

'No. He only knows where the key came from. After that, it's up to us.'

'We still might never find out what the key opens,' Albert said.

Sam took a thoughtful sip of his tea. 'That's a chance we'll have to take. But,' he said, raising his eyebrows, 'if we know where he got it from, that's a start.'

# CHAPTER TWENTY-NINE

Sam made his way up the stairs to the office, grabbed a mug of tea en route and smiled at Albert and Phillip as he breezed in. He sat in his chair and put his feet up on his desk. 'Morning chaps.'

Albert looked across at Sam and frowned. 'Do you realise how many germs you carry on your shoes?'

Sam rolled his eyes. 'Lighten up, Albert. You can give it a clean for me later."

'Where have you been?' Phillip said. 'You're normally the first in on a morning.'

'Yeah, sorry about that. Overslept, I stayed up late watching a movie.'

Baggage lay on his bed, his head resting between his front legs. His ears flopping either side of his head. 'What's up with Baggage?' Sam said. 'Is he sickening for something?'

Phillip frowned. 'He's missing you-know-who.'

'Kim?' Baggage stood, wagging his tail, and raced through into Kim's office but returned moments later, flopping back on his bed – adopting his previous position.

Phillip tutted. 'I'm trying not to mention her name. He gets all excited if you do. So, if you could refrain from saying it.'

'I think he's depressed,' Albert said.

Sam rocked back in his chair. 'He's a dog. Dogs don't get depressed. Dogs are, by nature, happy creatures. Give them a walk, a pat and a bone, and they're content.'

'I don't know,' Phillip said. 'He looks pretty sad to me.'

Sam smiled and looked wide-eyed at the other two. 'Maybe we could get him some doggie Prozac.'

'It's all right joking,' Phillip said, 'but I have to live with him. He's not eating his food and hasn't touched his bone-shaped chew.'

Sam got up and walked over to Baggage. 'Oh, fella,' he said, rubbing his ears. 'Cheer up. She'll be back soon.'

Phillip sat up. 'Have you heard anything from her?'

'Not yet. I'll let you know if I do.' Sam put his hands behind his head. 'Anyway, more pressing matters. This money we need to find. How are we going to do it?'

Albert opened his desk and pulled out a wad of notes. 'I've got about five hundred from my last job. Mr Crossley likes to pay in cash,' he said, tapping the side of his nose. He looked across at Baggage. 'I was going to give it to you know who …' He nodded towards Kim's office. 'But ...'

'We should have the other half between us,' Phillip said.

Sam blew out his cheeks. 'Just about. This having a baby lark is expensive.'

'What about this Rocco character?' Albert said. 'Can we trust him?'

Sam threw up his arms. 'Search me, but we've got a key and no idea where it came from or what it opens. It was obviously important to Bill.'

Phillip reached into his desk and pulled out a mobile. 'I'll ring Rocco and arrange a meeting.'

Sam raced Emily's car along the road as Albert sat in the front next to him, with Phillip and Baggage in the back.

Sam glared at Albert. 'We're late, already.'

Albert frowned. 'I've apologised. I was as quick as I could be.'

'Five times we've had to stop because you felt sick, and you haven't thrown up once. If you feel ill again, stick your head out of the window, will you?'

Albert looked out of the side window. 'I did say I wasn't a good traveller.'

They turned off the moor's road, headed towards Staithes, and pulled into the car park of the pub they'd been in on their previous visit. Sam took the mobile from his pocket. 'There's a message … Where are you? It's from Rocco.'

Phillip sat forward. 'Text him back.'

Sam typed a text and sent it, raising his eyebrows at the other two as the trio and Baggage waited.

Half an hour passed, and Phillip put a hand on Sam's shoulder. 'He's not coming.'

'I think Phillip's right,' Albert said.

Sam scanned the car park. 'Five more minutes. We'll give him five more minutes.'

The mobile sounded again and Sam read the text. 'He wants us to take a walk down to that bench again.'

Sam tapped Albert on his arm. 'Albert. You stay here while we go and meet him.'

Albert looked at Sam. 'On my own? What happens if—?'

Phillip patted the dog's head. 'You'll have Baggage. He'll take care of you.'

Albert studied Baggage, who raised his head slightly on hearing his name and then resumed his previous position with his head between his front paws.

Sam and Phillip got out of the car and walked off. 'Will they be all right?' Phillip said, nodding back at the car.

'Someone with OCD and a depressed dog.' Sam laughed. 'Good luck to anyone who stumbles across those two.'

The pair made their way over to the bench, sat and waited. Ten minutes had passed when they heard a noise behind the seat. 'Don't look back,' Rocco said as Sam and Phillip continued to look forward.

Phillip reached into his jacket pocket. 'We've got the money, like you said.'

'What's it in?' Rocco asked.

'An envelope.'

'Put it on the bench next to you.'

Phillip placed the money between him and Sam.

'Don't write any of this down,' Rocco said. 'It's for your own good.'

Sam glanced at Phillip. 'We understand.'

'I got the key from a chest of drawers out of the gardener's shed at the back of *All Saints Church in Skelton.*'

Sam frowned. 'Are you kidding?'

'No. I'm serious. That's where Bill told me it was and where I got it. I had a replica cut and returned the original. I've no idea what it opens or why Bill wanted it, but that's the god's honest truth.'

Albert held onto Baggage's leash and watched Phillip and Sam from a distance.

'What are they doing?' Baggage looked up at him and cocked his head to one side. 'Look at me,' Alberts said. 'Talking to a depressed dog. I'm never going to get out of therapy at this rate.'

Phillip glanced over his right shoulder. 'What now?'

A hand came from out of the bush and grabbed the money. 'Remember what I told you?' Phillip and Sam sat still as they heard a rustle, and Rocco was gone. The pair stood and glanced behind them, but there was no one. They walked back towards the car, and Albert, realising where they were going, followed them with Baggage. He quickened his steps to catch them up, jogged, and tried to close the gap. Sam and Phillip reached Emily's car, got in, and shut the doors.

Sam looked in the back. 'Where's Albert?'

'And Baggage,' Phillip said.

Sam banged on the steering wheel. 'I thought we told them to stay here. I knew we shouldn't have brought him. Don't get me wrong. I like Albert, but boy, he's hard work.'

Albert could see the vehicle about fifty feet away from him and stopped. Two men appeared beside Emily's car and opened the driver's side door as Albert backed behind a wall with Baggage.

Sam looked to his right as the door to the car opened, and a pistol was pushed into his side. The passenger side opened as Sam and Phillip glanced at the men outside the vehicle.

'Get out,' said the man on Sam's side of the car.

'What the hell,' was all Sam could say as the man nudged him in the ribs with the weapon.

Sam and Phillip did as they were told, as the pair were encouraged at gunpoint away from their car.

Albert watched from his vantage point as Sam and Phillip were pushed towards another vehicle. He realised, to his horror, that the men accompanying them had guns. The pair were forced into the back of a van. One of the men got inside with them while the other climbed in the front. Albert looked at Baggage, who cocked his head to one side as the van pulled away. Albert jumped from his hiding place, watching helplessly as the van screeched away from the car park. He jogged across to the car with Baggage, undid the dog's leash and got into the driver's seat as Baggage jumped in next to him. He fumbled in the dark and, realising the keys were still in the ignition, started the engine. He turned the car around while keeping one eye on the disappearing van, then set off in pursuit.

The van travelled back along the moor's road towards Guisborough, with Albert following while maintaining a small distance between himself and the other vehicle. Eventually, the van slowed and then turned off the road. Albert slowed, too, allowing himself a look at the name on the stone pillar outside where the van had turned. It said Heatherview Farm. He pulled up past the entrance and turned off the engine.

Albert looked at Baggage. 'What should I do?' Baggage clawed at the door. 'What are you doing? I'll have to phone someone.' Baggage cocked his head to one side as if not quite understanding what he'd been told. Albert huffed. 'I'm having a conversation with a dog.' He fumbled for his mobile and paused. 'What would Vanessa say?'

Baggage gave a short yelp. 'All right,' he said, showing the phone to Baggage. 'I'm ringing for help. You're so bloody impatient.' He paused again and thought. 'That's probably because dogs don't live as long as humans.' Baggage gave a small bark. 'Yes, yes.' Albert searched his contacts. 'I'm trying to get help. I'm phoning Tommo. He'll know what to do.'

Albert waited as the phone went straight to answerphone. 'He's not answering,' he said, looking at Baggage for help. 'What do I do now?' the dog barked again, this time with more urgency.

Albert raised a finger. 'Emily,' he said. 'No. I'd better not. She's pregnant. I can't tell her Sam's been abducted.'

Baggage barked again, pushing Albert in the side with his nose for good measure. Albert dropped his phone into the foot well. 'Bloody hell, Baggage,' Albert said and opened the door to assist in finding it. Baggage, grabbing his opportunity, jumped from the car as Albert picked up the phone and got out. Baggage raced along the road, stopped at the entrance to the farm and looked back at Albert.

'Baggage,' Albert said. 'Get back here this minute.' The dog ignored him, walking into the entrance before returning seconds later. The pair repeated this process several times as Albert tried desperately to get the dog to come back – Baggage disappearing only to reappear moments later. Albert sighed loudly, locked the car and traipsed after Baggage.

Albert wagged a finger at the dog as he neared him. 'Wait until I tell Phillip about you. Disobedient doesn't begin to describe it.'

As Albert reached Baggage, the dog padded off, stopping every few yards to check that his human companion was still with him. They made their way towards what looked like a farmhouse in the distance. As they neared, Albert could see the van, along with a Mercedes, parked outside. The door to the farmhouse opened, and Albert, fearing he would be spotted, dived over a stone wall to his right. He landed with a mixture of a splash and a splodge in a field. He momentarily lay face down as Baggage, who had walked through an open gate, padded up to him. Albert got to his knees, holding his filthy hands out in front of him. Baggage nudged him, and Albert gingerly got to his feet. Then, he turned to look at Baggage as the thick mud he'd fallen into dripped from his face. His mouth gaped, and he stared at the animal as if the dog would have an explanation for his current predicament.

Phillip and Sam sat fastened to chairs in the middle of a huge barn. A small chink of light shone through a hole in the roof, their only link to the outside world. One of the doors to the barn opened, and three figures walked in. A light was lit, illuminating the large building. Sam and Phillip squinted, allowing their eyes to adjust. The two men who had abducted them and an older man strolled forward.

'Good evening,' the older man said. 'I'm Sidney Stankovich.' Phillip and Sam glanced at each other. 'I see you know my name,' he continued and sat on a seat directly in front of them.

'Not really,' Sam said.

'Come, Mr Davison … Is it Sam or Phillip?'

'Sam.'

'And you must be Phillip?'

'Yes,' Phillip said. 'Look, what's all this about? You abduct us—'

'Mr Davison, Phillip. I'm not a patient man. I had you brought here to answer my questions. Not the other way around.'

'My girlfriend will be worried,' Sam said. 'She's expecting.'

The man smiled and looked across at his accomplices. 'Is it yours?'

'Of course it's mine. What do you mean by that?'

He nodded towards one of his men, who pulled a gun from his jacket pocket and pointed it at the duo. 'Why did you go to Staithes?' he said and lit a cigarette.

Sam smiled at him. 'Fish and chips.'

The man dropped his eyes to the floor as the man with the gun pushed it into Sam's neck. 'I might as well tell him,' Phillip said. 'They've got the gun.' He turned his head to look at Sam and gave the briefest of winks.

The man rose from his seat, glared at Sam and wandered closer to Phillip. 'Your friend has more sense than you.'

'We were supposed to meet someone called Rocco,' Phillip said and looked at Sam, who nodded his approval. 'He told us he had some information about the death of our uncle.'

'I see. Go on.'

'He said Bill owed him five hundred pounds for doing a job but that Bill was murdered before he could pay him.'

'I'm listening,' he said.

'Rocco said that if we gave him this and another five hundred, he would provide us with some information.'

He strolled back to his chair. 'Let me get this straight. You drove out to Staithes to pay a debt and get this information from Rocco?'

Phillip nodded. 'That's right.'

'And what happened?'

'He never turned up,' Phillip said. 'He must have had cold feet.'

'Your guys probably scared him off,' Sam said. 'People walking about waving guns often does that.'

He looked at his man with the revolver. 'Have you searched them?'

'Yes. There's no money on them.'

'We left it in a bush,' Phillip said. 'Behind a bench.'

He sneered. 'Do you have a habit of leaving money about for

strangers? Why not meet Rocco on Teesside?'

'He said he was scared. He said that someone was looking for him.'

'Who?'

'A bent copper,' Sam said.

The man stubbed out his cigarette. 'Robards?'

Sam nodded. 'That's the fella.'

He looked across at his accomplice with the gun and nodded towards the door. 'Go back to Staithes and check for the money.'

'Rocco may have already been for the money,' Phillip said.

'Maybe,' he said. 'What about the Eagle?'

Sam frowned. 'What Eagle?'

'From now on, Mr Davison,' he said, glaring at Sam. 'You keep your mouth shut and let your friend do the talking.'

'Someone asked us to locate it,' Phillip said. 'A fat man called—'

'Rupert Green.'

'Yes,' Phillip said.

'Anyone else?'

Phillip glanced at Sam. 'Eh?'

'What about the lovely Miss Jacobs?'

'Yes,' Phillip said. 'Her too.'

'Tell me,' he said, taking out another cigarette. 'Which one of you two slept with her?'

Phillip glanced at Sam.

'I thought it would be you. You look her type. Quite the lady, isn't she?'

'I've had better,' Sam said.

The man laughed, moving across to Sam and Phillip. 'Cards on the table. I didn't kill your uncle.'

'We've only your word for that,' Sam said.

'You have. I liked Bill. He was a decent sort, but he tried to play us off against each other. That's a dangerous game. I believe Robards may have had him killed. I also believe Bill was close to finding the Eagle. I had another gentleman in my employ – before I took on Bill – to locate the Eagle. He was discovered floating in the Tees near The Riverside Stadium.'

'Did Robards have him killed?' Phillip asked.

'Probably. Rupert Green isn't the type. He wants the Eagle, all right, and will do most things to obtain it, but I think murder would be beyond him.'

'Anne Jacobs?' Sam said.

'I'm not sure about that. I see you've taken to her. How does your partner feel about that?'

'That was before ...'

'What we have ...' He slowly circled the pair. 'Is a situation. Bill believed the Eagle was smuggled across to England from Europe in a statue of The Virgin Mary. He also believed this statue was in a church somewhere in the north-east.'

'The north-east is a big place, Mr Stankovich,' Phillip said.

'That's where you two come in. You must know something.'

Sam rolled his eyes. 'Like what? All we know is that you and Green are looking for the statue. Miss Jacobs employed me to find you.'

'And here I am.' Reaching into his jacket pocket, he pulled out the mobile which his men had taken from Sam. 'Phone Rocco and get him to meet you.'

Phillip shook his head. 'He won't. He's scared shitless. He's probably got the money now, as well.'

'You'll have to persuade him. Otherwise, the future looks bleak for you two. You wouldn't want that child of yours growing up in a one-parent family, would you?'

'No,' Sam said.

'Well. Make the call.' The other henchman moved across to Phillip and started untying him.

Phillip held up the mobile. 'It's gone straight to answerphone.'

'Phone again and leave a message. Get him to meet you back in Staithes.'

Phillip looked across at Sam, who nodded.

Shaken from his shock, Albert made his way over to the wall in front of the farmhouse. He squatted behind it and peered over the top as the door to the barn opened, and a man came out. Albert caught a glimpse of Phillip and Sam before he ducked back down.

'They've got them tied up in that barn,' Albert said to Baggage. 'Trussed up like a couple of turkeys.'

The man got into the van and drove off, heading back along the track towards the main road.

'I've got to get help,' Albert said as Baggage sniffed him – the smell seemingly not unpleasant to the animal. 'I know I stink,' Albert said. 'God knows how many showers I'll need when I get home.' Albert groped for his hip flask, took a large swig and thought for a moment. An idea formed in his head. He reached into his pocket, pulled out his purse, and, taking out the card Inspector Comby had given him, dialled the number.

'Detective Inspector Comby,' said a voice on the other end.

'Inspector,' Albert whispered. 'It's Albert Jackson from The Erimus detective agency.'

'Who?'

'Albert Jackson.'

'Yes, Mr Jackson. What can I do for you?'

'I'm in a field. At a farm.'

Comby sighed. 'Mr Jackson, I'm rather busy.'

'I followed the men here. Well, Baggage did.'

'Baggage?'

'Phillip's ... I mean my dog,' Albert said.

'Your dog?'

'He insisted on me coming here. I didn't really want to, but he wouldn't take no for an answer. He's quite headstrong.'

'Your dog?' Comby said. 'Is this some kind of joke?'

'No. Phillip and Sam are in the barn,' he whispered. The door to the building opened, and two men came out.

'What are you on about?'

'I fell, you see,' Albert said. 'Climbing over a wall, and I'm covered in something awful.' He sniffed himself.

'Are you aware that wasting police time is an offence, Mr Jackson? I'm rather busy.'

'They've been abducted and trussed up inside the barn. I can't see a lot it's dark.'

'Have you been drinking, Mr Jackson?' Comby said.

'A little.'

'Mr Jackson,' Comby shouted, 'I suggest you sober up, and I'll be around to see you in the morning. Good evening.' He ended the call.

Albert frowned as his bottom lip quivered. 'He's hung up, Baggage. What do I do now?'

Baggage padded across and sat next to Albert. 'I'm no good at all this Sherlock Holmes stuff.' He patted Baggage. 'I wish Tommo was here.'

'Who was that?' Hardman said.

'That bloody Albert Jackson. He was drunk. Mumbling about hiding in a field or something.'

'Could it be important?'

Comby grunted. 'Not as important as this Parmo.'

'I always thought he was weird,' Hardman said. 'Who has a settee at an angle like he has it? And that front room. Did you see how everything was so tidy?'

'Yeah, well. We'll run around tomorrow and speak to Mr Jackson. Right now, I'm only interested in this. Nothing gets between a man and his Parmo,' he said. He stuffed a large chunk of it into his mouth and grinned at his partner.

Tommo turned on his phone and checked for messages – there were none. Then, spotting a missed call, he searched his log and noticed it was from Albert.

'Hello,' Albert whispered.

'What's up?' Tommo said.

'I'm in a field between Staithes and Guisborough.'

Tommo rolled his eyes. 'Speak up, Albert. I can hardly hear you. Did you say you're in a field?'

'Yes,' Albert said. 'It's Baggage's fault. He made me come here. I didn't—'

Tommo sighed loudly. 'Baggage is a dog, Albert.'

'He wouldn't do what he was told. I wanted to wait on the main road and phone for help, but Baggage insisted on going after Phillip and Sam.'

'Are they there with you?'

'No. They've got them tied up in a barn.'

Tommo yawned. 'Have you been drinking?'

'Only a little.'

'Albert,' Tommo said. 'I have to close up. I've been run off my feet tonight.'

'But what about Sam and Phillip?'

'Where are they?' Tommo said.

'I told you. Rather, I haven't told you. We were in Staithes, you see.'

Tommo yawned again, slumping on the edge of a stool. 'Yeah?'

'And two men abducted them at gunpoint.'

Tommo jumped up. 'Who abducted them?'

'Sam and Phillip. They were forced into the back of a van. I followed—'

Tommo pressed the phone to his ear. 'Let me get this straight. Someone's got Sam and Phillip?'

'Yes. That's what I said. Baggage insisted on chasing after them. I dived over a wall and landed in some horrible-smelling thing. Probably full of disease or something—'

'Albert? Are you winding me up?'

'No. Some men have them tied up in a barn. I saw them when one of the men came out.'

'Right. Don't move from where you are.'

'What about Baggage?'

'What about him?'

'He's very headstrong. What happens if he—'

'Albert! For God's sake. He's a dog and you're human. Keep hold of him and tell him he hasn't to move. Promise him a juicy bone, anything, but stay where you are. Have you got that?'

'Yes.'

'Right.' He lowered his voice a little. 'Tell me where you are.'

Albert gave Tommo the address of the farm as Tommo jotted down the information before ringing off.

Albert looked at the dog. 'Did you hear that, Baggage? You have to stay here with me. Don't go running off, or you'll be in big trouble.'

The dog cocked his head to one side, digested what Albert had said, yawned, and wandered back over to Albert to sit next to him.

Albert patted his head. 'Good boy.'

Tommo searched through his contacts and phoned.

'Heh, big fella,' Ewan said. 'What's up?'

'Ewan. Have you got any transport yet?'

'Yeah. I've got myself a Mercedes Sprinter. You should see it. I bought it with the proceeds of you know what.'

'I need you to come around here, pronto.'

'You're kidding. I've ordered a pizza.'

Tommo rolled his eyes. 'Never mind that. This is a matter of life and death.'

'Really?'

'Really. As quick as you can.'

'What's up with your car?' Ewan asked.

'It's in the garage. Failed its MOT.'

Ewan chuckled. 'I don't know why you don't scrap it. That car is a piece of junk.'

'Have you been drinking?' Tommo said.

'Not a drop.'

'Yeah, well, okay. As quick as you can.'

'Yes, sir,' Ewan boomed.

Tommo looked at the mobile, shook his head and dialled Deb.

'Hello, gorgeous,' she said.

'Deb. I may be late.'

'Oh. I was going to order some food.'

'Can you keep it warm for me?'

Deb laughed. 'What about the food?'

Tommo put his hand over the phone. 'If this is a wind-up, Albert, I'll swing for you. Sam and Phillip have been abducted.'

Deb burst out laughing. 'Good one, Tommo.'

'I'm serious. Albert rang. Two men forced them into a vehicle at gunpoint.'

'Oh, my, God,' Deb said. 'Should I ring the police or Emily? It could be dangerous?'

'No. Not yet. It may be a wind-up.'

'Albert wouldn't do that, would he?'

'I don't think so. Just sit tight. I'll be in touch. I rang Ewan, and he's on his way around.'

'Ewan? Are you sure? He's not the most—'

Tommo sighed. 'I know, I know, but he's got a van. My car's in the garage. I'll have to go. See you soon.'

'Be careful, Tommo. I'm starting to like you.'

'Thanks.'

Tommo paced up and down Baker Street, waiting for Ewan. He leapt into the road as a white van turned into the street, and Ewan pulled the van up next to Tommo. 'Hey, big fella.'

'Where the hell have you been?'

'Massive queue at McDonald's.'

Tommo shook his head. 'You've been to McDonald's? Didn't you understand what I told you?'

'Chill, man. I'm starving. And with me not getting the pizza—'

'I don't believe you.' Tommo jumped in the passenger seat and buckled up.

'You need to take a chill pill. You're way beyond uptight, man.'

Tommo stared across at Ewan. 'Are you sure you haven't been drinking?'

'No. I've had a bit of blow. To loosen my strings.' He winked.

Tommo pushed Ewan in the chest. 'What the hell are you doing driving? You idiot!'

'I didn't intend to, but then someone phoned and said it was an emergency.'

'Get out,' Tommo said. 'I'm driving. You'll kill us before we get past Guisborough.'

'Are we going to Guisborough? Because if you are, can you stop at the Woodhouse services on the way? I'd kill for a coffee,' he said as he swapped seats with Tommo.

Tommo rolled his eyes and set off, and Ewan motioned around the vehicle with his hands. 'What do you think, Tommo?'

'Of what?' Tommo said.

'Of the wheels, man. It's only done 15,000 miles. Absolute bargain. A bloody steal.'

'Ewan, eat your chips,' Tommo said, thrusting the carton across to Ewan.

They travelled along the Guisborough road before turning off onto the Moors Road.

Ewan held up a chicken nugget. 'Do you want one?' he said, holding it towards Tommo.

'No.'

'Oh,' Ewan said. 'Wait until you see this. The van's got Bluetooth.' He dialled a number and waited.

'Hi,' said a female voice on speakerphone.

Ewan winked at Tommo. 'It's your hubby. Are you in yet?'

'Just come through the door, lover boy.'
'I'm doing Tommo a favour. I've ordered a pizza and—'
'I know. I met the delivery man on the drive.'
'It's all yours, sweetie,' Ewan said.
'Oh, thanks, honey,' she purred. 'Love you.'
'Love you too. I don't know what time I'll be in, so don't wait up.'
'Give me a nudge when you do. I might have something for you.'
Ewan raised his eyes at Tommo. 'Like what?'
'You know that outfit you like me to wear?'
'The nurse's?'
'Yeah. Well, I might put that on. You can be Dr Feelgood again.'
Tommo stared at Ewan. 'Ewan, I am here.'
'Who's that?' the female voice said.
'It's only Tommo. He's getting embarrassed. You know what a prude he is?'
'Hi, Tommo. How are you?'
'I'm good, Steph.'
'I'll let you two boys get on with it then,' she said. 'This pizza isn't going to eat itself.'
'Love you, sweetie,' Ewan said.
'Love you too,' she said and then rang off.
'What about that, then?' Ewan said. 'Hands-fucking-free.'
Tommo banged his head on the steering wheel and accelerated.

Tommo stopped the van next to Emily's car, quickly unbuckled his seatbelt and jumped out. 'This must be it.'
'Thank God,' Ewan said, getting out of the van to relieve himself. He finished and, delving into his jacket pocket, pulled out a joint, lit it up, and sucked greedily at it.
'Ewan, for Christ's sake,' Tommo said. 'We've come here to rescue Sam and Phillip, and you're getting off your tits.'
'It's great shit.' He held out the joint. 'Do you want a drag?'
'No, I don't. You can stay here and watch the van. I can't be putting up with you while I'm doing this.'

Albert was slumped against the wall with Baggage between his legs, the pair dozing as his phone sounded. Albert grabbed it from his pocket and quickly answered.
'Albert, it's Tommo. Where are you?'
'In a field about fifty yards from the barn. There's an entrance on your right.'
'Stay where you are. I'm at the top of the lane. I'll be with you soon.'
'Okay,' Albert said.
Tommo glanced back at Ewan, who was leaning against the side of

the van and blowing smoke rings. Tommo rolled his eyes, turned and set off along the track. As he neared the farmyard, he noticed a gate to a field. Assuming this was the one Albert had mentioned, he entered through it and headed for the far wall. Tommo froze as a shape moved towards him but realised seconds before it reached him that it was Baggage. The dog pirouetted around his legs, and Tommo grabbed him in a bear hug.

'Good boy,' he said as the dog licked his face.

He crept towards the wall, and Albert clambered to his feet. 'Is that you, Tommo?' Albert whispered.

'Yes.' He reached Albert and put Baggage on the floor. 'Where are they?'

'Over in that barn.' Albert pointed, and Tommo looked over at the building. 'They're tied up,' Albert said.

'Where are the men?' Tommo said.

'One of them left. The other two are in the farmhouse.'

'You stay here and keep hold of Baggage. I don't want him running over.' He turned to face Albert and caught a smell as a gust of wind brushed past them.

Albert looked at Baggage. 'I'm not sure I can handle that dog. He's got a will of his own.'

Tommo wrinkled his nose. 'You stink.'

'I fell in something over there. I could do with a shower. Well, several, actually.'

'We'll sort that out later. Just keep hold of Baggage. Remember who the master is here?'

Albert looked at Baggage, who cocked his head to one side. 'I'll try.' Albert took a swig from his hip flask and held on to Baggage with his free hand.

Tommo leapt the wall and crept towards the barn, trying to remain in the shadows, out of sight of the farmhouse. He reached the doors and peered through the crack between them. Sam and Phillip sat on two chairs in the middle of the barn, securely fastened with a rope. He opened the door a little and peered in.

'Sam, Phillip,' he whispered. The pair looked up towards him, peering through the gloom.

'Is that you, Tommo?' Sam said.

'Yeah. You two all right?'

'We're okay,' Phillip said.

Tommo crept inside, headed across, squatting behind the pair, and untied them. Freed from their restraints, the duo stood. 'Follow me,' Tommo said, and Sam and Phillip hurried after him.

The three men jumped the wall and landed in the field. Baggage broke free from Albert's grasp and ran towards them.

Sam grabbed Baggage. 'Okay, boy,' he said, trying to fend off the dog as Baggage danced around. 'There's plenty of time for that later.'

Baggage jumped at Phillip, who placated the dog. The four men made their way along the track and emerged onto the main road. Ewan sat slumped against the van wheel, staring up at the sky. Next to his van was a second vehicle.

Tommo ambled forward and pointed at the van. 'Where did that come from, Ewan?'

'Hey, big fella.' Ewan hugged him. 'You missed all the fun. This bloke pulls up in a van and starts shouting the odds at me. Asking me what I'm doing here. Cheeky twat. It's a free world, and I can park where I like, I said. You know what he did?' Ewan staggered backwards. 'He only pulls a gun on me. A fucking gun.'

Tommo glanced back at the other three. 'What did you do?'

'I caught him a beauty with this tree branch.' Ewan bent forward and picked up the piece of wood. 'Bam,' Ewan said. 'Right across the napper.' He swung it around his head. The weight of the branch caused Ewan to lose his balance and fall backwards onto the ground.

'Where is he?' Tommo said.

'I tied him up and put him into his van.' Ewan giggled. 'Wow! Look at those stars,' he said. Lying on his back, he stared upwards.

Tommo pulled open the door and looked at the man, trussed up. He put a finger to the unconscious man's neck. 'He's alive. At least you haven't killed him.'

Ewan clambered to his feet. 'Hey, Phillip. Sam. What's up, dudes?'

Sam looked at Tommo. 'What's up with Charlie-daft-shite?'

Tommo shook his head. 'Ignore him. He's been on the wacky backy.'

Sam glanced in the back of the van. 'He's one of the men.'

'I guessed that much,' Tommo said. 'You three take Emily's car, and I'll follow you with Keith Richard's here.' Tommo grabbed hold of Ewan and pushed him forward.

Albert handed the keys to Sam, and Phillip and Baggage jumped into the car, closely followed by Sam and Albert. Tommo bundled Ewan into the passenger seat and sped off, following the other vehicle.

Ewan fumbled in his pocket, pulling out his mobile. 'Have I told you that this van has Bluetooth?'

Tommo rolled his eyes and sighed. 'Yes, Ewan, you have.' Tommo grabbed the phone from him. 'Why don't you have a sleep?'

'Oh, you're a moody get.' Ewan leaned his head against the window and closed his eyes. 'Can we stop for a pizza,' he slurred sleepily. 'I'm famished.'

# CHAPTER THIRTY

Phillip, Albert, Sam and Tommo sat in the office contemplating the previous night's events as Baggage snoozed on his bed.

Tommo clapped his hands together. 'Right, gents. We have a decision to make. Do we involve the police?'

'No,' Sam said.

'I tried ringing last night,' Albert said. 'But that Inspector Comby didn't believe me.'

Phillip looked at Albert. 'When was this?'

'When I was in the field. I tried ringing Tommo, but it went to answerphone. I was panicking and didn't know what to do.'

'Let's not worry about that,' Sam said. 'Stankovich told Phillip and me something interesting last night.'

Tommo leant forward and sipped his tea. 'Oh, yeah?'

'He said Bill told him that he thought the Eagle was inside a statue of The Virgin Mary.' Sam raised his eyebrows. 'And this statue was in a church somewhere around here.'

Tommo frowned. 'That's a lot of churches.'

'Phillip,' Sam said, nodding at his friend. Phillip opened his drawer and pulled out the book of churches. He tossed it across to Tommo, who opened the book where Sam had placed a marker.

Tommo looked up. 'All Saints Church, Skelton?'

Sam rocked back in his chair. 'Yep.'

'But how do you know—?'

'Bill hid that book and other things under the floorboards over there. I think that proves their importance.'

'And …' Phillip said, 'Rocco gave us the same address. He did a job for Bill.'

Sam sat forward in his chair, lowering his eyes at Tommo. 'He obtained a key from the gardener's shed at the back of that church, copied it and returned the original.'

'And the key?' Tommo said.

Sam pulled it from his drawer and held it aloft for Tommo to see.

Tommo rocked back in his seat. The seat groaned as if resenting having to endure Tommo's massive frame. 'Wow. This Eagle could be there, then. Inside the church?'

'Absolutely,' Phillip said.

Tommo rubbed his beard. 'It doesn't alter the fact that the people trying to find it are willing to go to any lengths to obtain it.'

'Sell it to the highest bidder,' Sam said.

'There is a fly in the ointment,' Phillip said. 'Rocco also warned us about a bent copper called Robards. Stankovich mentioned him too.'

Tommo nodded slowly. 'So that rules out the police, then.'

Comby and Hardman entered. 'Did someone mention us? Mr Jackson,' Comby said, moving across to Albert's desk. 'Have we sobered up yet?'

Hardman eyed Sam and Phillip. 'I see your friends are here, too. The two you mentioned last night. Weren't they abducted or something?' He allowed his stare to linger on Sam and Phillip.

'Yes,' Albert said.

Comby sat on a chair. 'My colleague and I will have a cup of tea. Milk and three sugars each, and then you can tell us all about it.'

Comby sat cradling his tea. 'What happened last night? Tell me everything, and don't leave a thing out.'

Albert looked across at Sam and Phillip. 'Tell him, Albert,' Sam said.

Albert sucked in a deep breath and began. Recounting how the three of them had gone up to Staithes. How Sam and Phillip had been abducted at gunpoint and taken to the farm, and how Tommo had come and rescued them.

Comby glanced across at Hardman, who was taking notes, before looking back at Sam and Phillip. He leant forward and, picking up a biscuit, dipped it in his tea before biting the dunked end off. 'And this gentleman said he was called Sidney Stankovich?' Sam and Phillip nodded in agreement. 'Why did you two go up to Staithes in the first place?' Comby said.

Sam rubbed his eyes. 'To meet someone called Rocco.'

'Thomas Rock?' Hardman said. Sam and Phillip shrugged. 'AKA, Rocco,' Hardman continued.

Comby smiled. 'Thomas Rock is a petty criminal. My colleague and

I are well aware of him. Why did you meet with him?'

Phillip leant forward. 'He said Bill owed him money and that he had some information about his death. He said if we paid the money Bill owed him and another five hundred, he would give us this information.'

Comby sighed, picking up a second biscuit. 'Didn't I warn you, gentlemen, not to try running an investigation of your own? What did he tell you?'

Sam glanced towards Phillip, raising his eyebrows. 'He didn't turn up,' Sam said. 'We think Stankovich and his men may have scared him off.'

Comby slurped his tea, putting the mug on Phillip's desk with a loud thud. 'Right then. Let's go and see what Mr Stankovich has to say for himself.'

Comby looked at Tommo as Sam, Albert, Phillip and Tommo all stood. 'Mr ...,'

'Thompson,' Tommo said. 'Howard Thompson.'

'Well, Mr Thompson. You can stay here and look after the dog. You three, follow us.' Tommo watched the five disappear as Baggage padded across to Tommo, slowly wagging his tail.

'It's you and me, pooch.' He patted the dog on the head. 'What about if you come over to my place and help me open up? I'll stop off and buy you one of those bone-shaped chews you love.' Baggage pirouetted and wagged his tail wildly before following Tommo out.

The police car ground to a halt outside Abandon nightclub, and the three cousins followed the policemen as they made their way around to the side. A man, stacking boxes onto a sack barrow, stopped when he saw the five men approach.

'Can I help you?' he said.

Comby halted close to the man. 'We're here to see Mr Stankovich?'

'And you are?' the man said.

'Detective Inspector Comby and Detective Sergeant Hardman,' he said, and the officers flashed their credentials.

The man nodded and went inside, returning moments later. 'This way,' he said, and the five men followed him inside.

They carried on through the building and up a flight of stairs, stopping at a door marked private. The man knocked.

'Come in,' a voice from within shouted. The man opened the door and ushered them inside before leaving.

Stankovich looked up from a pile of money he was counting. 'DI Comby and DS Hardman,' Stankovich said. 'Long time, no see.' Stankovich studied Phillip, Sam and Albert in turn. 'And you've brought some friends with you.'

Comby stepped forward. 'I believe you've met my friends?' he said, pointing at the cousins.

Stankovich shrugged. 'Never seen them before in my life.'

'Wait a minute,' Phillip said. 'This isn't Stankovich.'

Comby sighed. 'Mr Davison, this is getting tedious. This man here is Sidney Stankovich. Owner of the establishment we're standing in.'

Phillip looked across at Sam. 'That's not the man from last night,' Sam said. 'It looks nothing like him.'

Hardman turned to face the cousins. 'What do you mean, not the man from last night?'

Sam held out his hands. 'I mean … That's not the man who abducted and tied us up.'

Stankovich laughed. 'Is this really what I pay my taxes for? Isn't there a bacon butty out there with your name on it, Comby? I'm really quite busy. I haven't got time to sit here while you bring strangers to gawp at me.'

Comby rolled his eyes. 'It appears, Mr Stankovich, that we've got crossed wires. I'm sorry for bothering you.' He turned and marched towards the door, glaring at the cousins. 'You three follow me.'

They exited the building and marched towards the car. 'He said his name was Stankovich,' Phillip said.

Comby spun around. 'Well, apparently he was fibbing. Get in the car.' He nodded at Hardman. 'Let's go and have a look at this farm.'

Phillip and Sam got into the back of the vehicle, stepping over umpteen fast-food cartons and plastic cups. Phillip nudged Sam. 'This is the first car I've been in that I've had to wipe my feet when I got out,' Phillip whispered.

'It's like a skip with wheels,' Sam said.

Phillip smiled. 'It's a good job they left Albert at the station. He'd be in shock.'

Stankovich picked up his phone and dialled a number. 'Robards,' said a voice on the other end.

'Geoff, it's Stankovich. I've had your lot around here with two of those idiots from the Detective agency. What the hell is going on?'

'No idea. What did they want?'

'Don't give me that,' Stankovich said. 'You were up to something last night. I want to meet. If you're trying to cross me—'

'Sid,' Robards said. 'I was just trying to scare them, that's all. I thought they might be holding out on us.'

'Then why use my name?'

'It was a joke. They can't pin anything on you. Comby and his sidekick are useless. Those three, though, know more than they're letting on. They were meeting Rocco.'

'Rocco? Have you got him?'

'He never showed. They know something, I'm sure.'
'I want to meet,' Stankovich said. 'Eight in the morning, here.'
'I'm not sure I can make it.'
'You'd better,' he said and hung up.

Robards dialled a number. 'Geoff,' Miss Jacobs said.

'Those idiots went to the police, and I've had Stankovich bending my ear.'

'I told you it would backfire,' she said. 'You couldn't resist using his name, could you?'

'It could work in our favour,' Robards said. 'He wants to see me tomorrow.'

'And?'

'I think our three-way split may have to become two-way.'

'Isn't that a little dangerous?'

Robards snorted. 'Leave it to me. I'll sort it. Abandon will have to find a new owner.'

Tony sat in his car as his phone rang. 'Yeah?'
'It's Sid. What happened last night?'
'I don't know. He didn't take me with him. Used two of his other lads.'
'Does he suspect you're working for me?' Stankovich asked.
'I'm not sure,' Tony said. 'Maybe we should meet?'
'Robards is coming here at eight in the morning. Come at six. Make sure no one sees you, and I'll leave the fire exit open.'
'What are you planning?'
'Robards might be more trouble than he's worth. Maybe we should create a vacancy within Middlesbrough Constabulary. After all, who likes a bent copper?'

The car drove along the farm track and stopped in the farmyard. The men got out, and Hardman marched across to the front door, stopped and knocked. There was no answer. 'No one in, guv.'

Comby looked at the cousins. 'Show me this barn,' he said as the three of them walked across to it, stopping outside the door.

'In there,' Sam said.

Comby pulled open one of the doors and stared into the barn at the Hay bales stacked floor to ceiling. He turned and glared at Sam and Phillip in turn. 'Well?'

Phillip stepped forward. 'I don't understand. It was definitely here.'

'In the car,' Comby said, 'while I decide what to charge you two and your friend back at the station with.'

# CHAPTER THIRTY-ONE

Ewan tottered into the Sidewinder and crept towards the bar, clumsily clambering onto a stool. 'Man, my head's in bits, Tommo.'

'Really?' Tommo said, polishing a glass as he looked up.

'Last night's a blur. I remember you calling me. The next thing I woke up on the kitchen floor with half a pizza on my chest.'

Tommo placed the glass under the pump and started filling it. 'And you don't remember anything else?'

'No. The truth is,' he lowered his voice to a whisper, 'I got some blow off Billy the buzz, and man, was it some heavy shit. I think I'm going to stay off that stuff in future.'

'Pint?' Tommo said, handing him a glass of beer.

'Yeah. Legal highs from now on.' He pushed a note across the counter towards Tommo.

'What did your lass say?'

Ewan widened his eyes. 'I found her lying on the top of the bed wearing a nurse's outfit. Not sure what that was about.'

Tommo raised his eyebrows. 'Really, Dr Feelgood?' he whispered.

'What?' Ewan said.

Tommo fake smiled. 'Nothing.'

'I had a really bizarre dream last night, too. I was outside a farm near Guisborough. Looking up at the stars.'

Tommo smiled. 'That is strange.'

'And another thing. I've lost my new van. I was so out of it last night I must have driven it somewhere. I've looked all over for the keys, but I must have left them in the van. Some scally has probably nicked it by now.'

Tommo reached under the counter and pulled out a set of keys, dangling them under Ewan's nose. 'Are these them?'

Ewan plucked them from Tommo's hand. 'Where did you find them?'

'Long story, mate. The van's parked out back.'

'Sound, Tommo.' Ewan grinned. 'Did I mention that my van's got Bluetooth?'

Tommo patted him on the shoulder. 'Yes, Ewan, you did.'

Phillip, Sam and Albert walked in, stopped at the bar, and Phillip pulled out a note. 'Usual, Tommo.'

Tommo held out his hands. 'Well? Have they arrested him?'

'It wasn't him,' Sam said.

Tommo frowned. 'Wasn't who?'

Sam climbed on a stool next to Ewan. 'The man who said he was Stankovich last night wasn't the same man we met today. He apparently lied.' He glanced at Ewan, who was now asleep with his head on the bar and frowned. 'What's up with Charlie-daft-shite?'

Tommo waved a hand towards Ewan. 'Forget him. What about the farm?'

Sam rolled his eyes. 'We had a lovely drive out there today, and guess what …?' Tommo shrugged, and Sam continued. 'The barn was full. And when I say full, I mean from floor to ceiling with hay bales.'

Tommo rubbed his beard. 'They must have put them back when we escaped.'

Sam sighed. 'No shit, Sherlock. I need to drown out this whole sorry episode.'

Albert moved forward. 'We all looked rather foolish.'

'What do you mean, we?' Sam said, spinning on his stool. 'You weren't even there. You were happily drinking tea with that pretty WPC.'

Albert lowered his eyes. 'DI Comby said he needed someone to give a statement.'

Sam nudged Phillip. 'She could take down my particulars any day,' Sam said.

Tommo rolled his eyes and took down three glasses from the shelf above him. 'What are we going to do about the church?'

Sam accepted the first pint and took a large swig. 'What can we do?'

Tommo pushed Sam playfully. 'Go up there and check it out. There could be a priceless statue waiting to be discovered.'

'I don't know,' Phillip said. 'This case is getting complicated.'

Albert sniffed himself. 'Do I still smell, guys?'

Tommo handed a pint to Albert. 'How many showers did you have when you got home last night?'

'Ten,' Albert said.

Tommo chuckled and shook his head. 'I don't think anyone would smell after ten showers.'

Albert sighed. 'But I keep getting a whiff of something.'

Sam blew out hard. 'Albert. We've more important things to think about than your personal hygiene.'

Phillip took his pint from Tommo and took a sip. 'What if we get followed? It's incredibly dangerous.'

'Yeah,' Sam said. 'By whoever abducted us? The bent copper Rocco mentioned.' San glowered. 'Maybe Comby and his sidekick are corrupt as well.'

'Stop being paranoid,' Tommo said.

Sam stared wide-eyed at his friend. 'Paranoid? Of course I'm paranoid. Getting abducted at gunpoint late at night and driven to a remote farm, then, being trussed up by some thugs ... That would make anyone paranoid.'

'But we can't just leave it,' Tommo said. 'It could be worth millions.'

Albert sniffed his clothing again. 'What about Mr Green? He promised us a good deal of money to find the Eagle. Maybe we should hand it over to him and take what he's offering.'

'We could try and get him to go higher,' Phillip said.

Sam held up a finger. 'Wait a minute. Miss Jacobs.'

Tommo shook his head. 'Stop thinking with your dick for a minute.'

'No,' Sam said. 'She employed me to find Stankovich, but he didn't seem that hard to find today.'

'I thought you said you'd asked about him?' Phillip said.

'I did,' Sam said. 'Apparently, he was out of the country. Maybe I should tell Miss Jacobs that he's back?'

'Good idea,' Phillip said. 'But that doesn't help us with the Eagle.'

Baggage came padding across from under a table, yawned and stretched before pushing his nose into Phillip's leg. 'You hungry, boy?'

'He shouldn't be,' Tommo said. 'He's had a steak pie and a sausage roll.'

Sam shrugged. 'Maybe we should sleep on it. I'm going to head home soon. Emily's in a mood with me.'

'Why?' Tommo said. 'What's up with her now?'

'She thinks I'm seeing someone.'

'But I told her about last night,' Phillip said. 'Doesn't she believe me?'

'She said she does, but I can see suspicion in her eyes. If I'm late back again ...'

Tommo looked at Phillip and waved him closer. 'What about K.I.M?' Tommo said.

Phillip frowned. 'She's still at her aunt's.'

Tommo chuckled. 'So only me happy in my relationship? I think I'll have a pint to celebrate.'

Baggage sniffed Albert. 'I'm sure I still smell,' Albert said. 'Baggage can smell it, too. Dogs have a tremendous sense of smell, you know.'

Phillip rolled his eyes as Sam slowly began banging his head on the bar counter.

Sam wandered into the kitchen, where Emily stood washing up some pots. He put his arms around her and kissed her cheek. 'Morning, darling. Are you still mad at me?'

'No. I'm sorry about shouting.'

'And throwing things at me?' Sam said.

'Yeah. And throwing things at you. Do you want a cuppa?'

Sam sat at the table. 'Have we got any mugs left?'

Emily sighed. 'Sam. I'm huge. Look at me. I swear I've put a stone on overnight.'

'Eating all that chocolate won't help.'

She turned to face him. 'Cheers.'

Sam smiled. 'Sam Davison, telling it how it is.'

She pushed out her bottom lip. 'Where's the tact and diplomacy?'

'You used to say you liked my honesty.'

She pulled on the straps of her dungarees. 'That was before I morphed into a beached whale. I'm running out of stuff to wear. I've had to put these on.'

'They make you look like a proper dyke. Where did you get them from? Lesbos are us?'

'There are some women out there, Sam, that would take offence at that,' she said. 'They're Stella's. She left them here ages ago. I found them in the back of the wardrobe on top of a huge dildo.' She puffed out her cheeks.

'I thought pregnant women wore those pregnancy thingies,' he said, flicking through the newspaper. 'Smocks or something.'

'Sam,' she said, opening the oven. She pulled out a plate and placed it in front of him. 'It's not the 1970's, you know. Pregnant women these days are still elegant. They're just—'

'Elegant and massive,' Sam said as he tucked into his breakfast.

'Cheers for that,' Emily said, sitting opposite him, her eyes now glistening.

Sam stretched a hand across the table and took hold of Emily's. 'This is just banter, Em. We always did banter.'

'I know, it's my hormones. They're all over the place. I keep crying at silly things.' She sighed. 'The other day, I saw a bird with a worm in its mouth, and I just started blubbing. Poor little thing, I thought.'

'Hold on,' he said. Getting up from his seat, he walked out of the room and returned moments later with a small box which he held out in his hand. Emily took it from him and opened it. Inside was a chain with three hearts hanging from it. One of the hearts was engraved with an

'S', on the second, an 'E', and the third one was blank. Emily looked at Sam, frowning.

Sam grinned. 'S and E for us, and I thought we could get the baby's initials engraved on the third.'

'Oh, Sam, it's wonderful,' she said, fanning her eyes.

'You know, Emily Simpson,' he said, taking hold of her hand again. 'If this baby's a girl, it will look just like her mother, and she'll be absolutely gorgeous. A real heartbreaker.'

'And if it's a boy?'

'Well,' he said and held his hands wide, a huge grin on his face. 'What can I say? He'll look like me.'

'Sometimes, Sam Davison, I hate you.' She smiled and looked at the chain again. 'But most of the time, I love you.' She placed a hand on his cheek and stared lovingly at him.

'It's the cross I've had to bear,' he said, stuffing half a sausage in his mouth. 'Any more beans?'

Tommo rolled onto his back and opened his eyes, looking to his left, where Deb lay on her side smiling at him.

'What are you smiling at?' he said.

Deb rubbed a hand through the thick mat of hair on his chest. 'It's called contentment.'

'And that's good?'

'Certainly is.'

Tommo put a hand on Deb's arm. 'How about a spot of breakfast?'

'I'm sure that breakfast can wait.' She snuggled in closer.

Tommo raised an eyebrow. 'You're not going to use me and abuse me like you did last night?'

'I most certainly am.' She climbed on top of him. 'Feel free to struggle, Tommo, but I'm like the Borg. Resistance is futile.'

'Will I end up a mindless cyborg?' He said, adopting a mock horror face.

'Yes, you will. However,' Deb said, licking her lips, 'the important parts will remain human,' she said, allowing her hand to slip lower.

Albert, having showered twice and resisting the temptation of a third, got dressed. After straightening the cushions and everything in the living room, he prepared his breakfast – a small bowl of organic muesli and half a grapefruit washed down with two cups of Lapsang Souchong. He spent the next hour cleaning – scrubbing the already obsessively clean surfaces. His appointment with his therapist was at eleven. After going through his regular routine of leaving the house, which, much to his delight, had only taken him twenty minutes – a personal best – Albert set off on his walk to Marton shops and his meeting with Miss Waltham.

The spring in his step perfectly matched the weather as the bright morning sunshine bathed him in warmth, and Albert waved at neighbour after neighbour on his way along the road.

Phillip sat staring out of the window of the offices at the detective agency and viewed the people on Redcar High Street going about their business. Not really registering much, he turned sharply as he heard a noise from Kim's office next door, and Baggage, who was dozing peacefully on his bed, opened a sleepy eye. The dog stood and shot off out of the room. Phillip got up himself and followed the animal, stopping in reception.

Kim bent over and hugged the dog. 'Hello, you,' she said as Baggage covered her with licks and spun around furiously. 'Look what I've got for you.' She handed Baggage a dog chew shaped like a stick of rock. Satisfied with his prize, he accepted it and headed back to his bed.

Phillip forced a smile at Kim. 'Hello.'

'Hi,' she said.

He walked forward. 'I'm sorry, Kim. I didn't mean to lie to you. It just came out. When you told me about your past boyfriend, I didn't want anything to jeopardise us. I know it was wrong. I like you. I like you a lot, but I'll understand if you don't want anything more to do with me.' He held up a hand as Kim started to speak. 'But even though this time last year I had a smart car,' he continued, 'a good job and a fantastic apartment in Stockton, I'd still give it all up for a chance to meet you. I really would.'

Kim smiled and held out a rock dummy. 'I got you this.'

'Thanks,' he said and took it from her.

Kim held out her arms and waved him closer. 'Come here,' she said as the two of them embraced.

Albert sat in Miss Waltham's office, holding a freshly made steaming cup of green tea. He turned his head as the door opened.

'Good morning, Albert,' she said, positioning herself opposite him.

'Morning, Miss Waltham.'

'Vanessa. I thought I told you to call me Vanessa.'

'Yes, Vanessa,' he said.

She opened her notebook. 'So, what have you been getting up to this week?'

'Phillip and Sam were abducted.'

'Oh, my, God,' she said. 'By whom?'

'They don't know. He said his name was Stankovich, but it turns out that wasn't true.'

'Have the police been informed?'

'They don't believe us. Tommo came and rescued them.'

'That's terrible.' She tutted. 'Is this related to …' she flicked through her notes. 'The Eagle?' she said.

'Yes, the Eagle,' Albert said. 'We think so.'

'This seems extremely dangerous. Surely you should inform the police?'

'We can't. Phillip and Sam think it's best if we keep it to ourselves.'

'But what happens if they abduct …, these people, I mean. If they abduct them again?'

Albert thought for a moment. 'I'm not sure. There's also a corrupt policeman. A bent copper, Sam calls him. So, if we go to the police, he may find out.'

'Albert,' she said, peering atop her glasses. 'Are you making this up?'

'No, Miss … Vanessa. Detective Inspector Comby and Sergeant Hardman don't believe us.'

'Is this Comby the bent—?'

'No. That's Robards,' Albert said. 'But we've never met him.'

'So, this Comby and—'

'Hardman,' Albert said.

'They're?'

'Investigating our uncle's murder.'

'I see.' She laughed. 'This all sounds like an Agatha Christie novel.'

Albert smiled. 'Baggage and I have been getting on a little better. Although he is quite willful.'

'Baggage is—'

'Phillips dog. The one Kim loves.'

'Phillip?'

'No, Baggage. Kim likes Phillip. Although they have had a fallout. She's in Scarborough. At her aunt's.'

Miss Waltham removed her glasses, put one of the arms in her mouth, tapped it against her teeth and then put them back on before pushing them up the bridge of her nose. 'How on earth are you going to solve this, then?'

'We're having a meeting today at the office. To plan our next move. Between you and I, Vanessa,' he said, moving closer, 'this time next week, we could be a whole lot richer.'

Miss Waltham raised her eyebrows. 'Oh yes?'

'Phillip and Sam believe they know where the Eagle is.'

Tony parked his car a couple of miles away from Abandon nightclub, completing the remainder of his journey on foot. Stopping periodically to check that no one was following him, he reached the road leading to the back of the building and crept along the side. Halting at the entrance to the rear yard for one final look, he entered, opened the door to the fire escape and mounted the stairs to Stankovich's office. Stankovich sat behind his desk as someone tapped on the door. He pulled a gun from his drawer and pointed it towards the door. 'Come in.'

Tony entered, and Stankovich lowered the weapon and replaced it in the drawer. 'You're a bit nervy, Sid,' Tony said, sitting on a seat on the opposite side of Stankovich's desk.

'You're sure Robards men haven't followed you?'

'Certain,' Tony said. 'Are we alone?'

'Yes. I've given a couple of the lads an early finish, and the evening lot won't be in until this afternoon.'

Tony smiled. 'Robards is sending someone to kill you.'

'I see. So, I was right.' Stankovich banged the desk. 'He was going to double-cross me. Who's he sending?'

'Me.'

Stankovich laughed. 'He's going to be disappointed.'

'Why?' Tony said, pulling a gun with a silencer attached from his pocket. He levelled it at Stankovich.

'Is this a joke, Tony?'

'No. This is as far as we go, Sid.'

'Hey, Tony.' He held up a hand. 'If this is about money? If Robards has offered you more, that's not a problem.'

'He thinks the Davison pair and Jackson are close to finding the Eagle. He's sure of it, in fact.'

'Well, that's great. I've struck a deal with Green, and he's offered me a cool five million. You and I can go fifty-fifty. Remove Robards, and we'll split it.'

'What about Miss Jacobs?'

'Jacobs and Robards are having a thing. I've known for some time. Drink?' Stankovich said, rising from his seat, he moved slowly across the room.

Tony lowered the weapon but kept it pointed at Stankovich. 'Why not.'

Stankovich poured two drinks and handed one to Tony. 'You see,' Stankovich said, 'the way I look at it if we remove Robards, we could pin it on her. Someone has to carry the can.'

Tony half-smiled. 'You've obviously given this some thought.'

'I have. You and I could be very wealthy. It would set you up for life.'

Tony took a sip from his glass. 'There's only one problem?'

'What?'

'Hector Williamson.'

Stankovich sat back down with the bottle still in his hand. 'Hector Williamson?'

'He was a friend of mine.'

'I see.'

Tony sat back in his chair and sneered. 'I know you had Hector killed.

It's pointless denying it.'

Stankovich shrugged. 'Hector got greedy. He was trying to cut another deal. He would have double-crossed me.'

Tony drained his glass and placed it down. 'Maybe he would. But you shouldn't have killed him.'

'What about Hockney?' Stankovich said.

'Bill was greedy too,' Tony said. 'He was seeing Jacobs and was also working for Green. He would have done the same.'

'So, you're just like me.'

'No, not really. Hockney wasn't your mate.'

Stankovich held up his glass. 'Another?'

'One's enough,' Tony said, levelling the gun again. He smiled. 'Robards says, hi.' And then he fired, hitting Stankovich square in the chest. He slumped back against the wall and fell to the floor, dead. A small trickle of blood ran from the side of his mouth as Tony picked up the glass he'd used with his gloved hand and deposited it inside his jacket pocket. He strolled towards the door, turned and looked at the dead Stankovich once more before leaving.

## CHAPTER THIRTY-TWO

Comby sat in his office behind his desk, where paperwork and empty plastic cups lay scattered across the surface.

Hardman entered and handed Comby a polystyrene carton. 'Breakfast bun, with brown sauce.'

Comby opened the box and pulled out the sandwich. 'I've been thinking,' he said as his two chubby hands precariously manoeuvred the huge bun towards his mouth.

Hardman flopped into his seat. 'Oh, yeah?'

'I think we should put a tail on those three.' He took a large bite of the sandwich, and bits of sausage and bacon fell onto his desk. 'See what they're up to.' Comby wiped the sauce from around his mouth.

Hardman bit into his bun, chewing for a few seconds. 'I don't think the Chief Inspector will go for that. It'll cost a small fortune to watch all three. We don't have any evidence, only suspicions.'

'I know that,' Comby said, 'but I'm convinced they know something about the Eagle. The Eagle is the key to Hockney's murder, I'm certain.'

'It'd take a lot of manpower to keep tabs on all three of them.'

'That's why I was thinking of following only one of them,' Comby said.

'Jackson?' Hardman said. His mouth crammed with the sandwich.

'No. One of the others. That Howard Thompson is interesting.'

Hardman wiped his mouth and took a swig of tea. 'The big bloke who runs the pub?'

'Indeed. He has something to do with this, I'm sure. Whatever they do, they'll do it together.'

'When were you thinking?' Hardman said.//
'We'll start tonight.'//
'Oh, guv. I was going out this evening.'//
'Sorry, Mick. Work comes first.'//
Hardman frowned. 'All week?'//
Comby's phone sounded. He held up his hand at Hardman, put down the bun, wiped his mouth and hands, and then answered it. 'DI Comby.'//
'guv,' a male voice said. 'We've had a phone call. Sidney Stankovich has been found dead. Shot through the chest.'//
'Where?'//
'His nightclub.'//
'Any CCTV footage?'//
'No, guv. Whoever it was must have come up the fire escape. The camera there had been turned off.'//
Comby sat back in his chair. 'Who by?'//
'The manager says only he and Stankovich could have done that.'//
'And he didn't, I suppose?' Comby said.//
'That's what he says, guv.'//
'We'll be ten minutes.'//
Hardman paused with his sandwich in front of his mouth as a sausage slowly slipped from within. 'What's that about?'//
'Someone's shot Stankovich.'//
'Oh, dear,' Hardman said as he picked up the fallen sausage and pushed it into his mouth.//
Comby picked his bun back up. 'We'll finish these and go over there. Then we'll pop across and see Phillip and Sam Davison and their odd friend Jackson. '//
'You don't think they had anything to do with it, do you?'//
'Who knows,' Comby said. 'Bit of a coincidence, though, Stankovich, getting himself killed and the palaver we had with those three.'//
Hardman nodded. 'True enough, guv.'//

Phillip and Albert sat in the detective agency's office. Sam entered carrying a mug of tea, closed the door behind him, and sat at his desk.//
'Kim's back,' Phillip said.//
Sam winked. 'I thought you had a smile on your face.'//
'How's Emily?' Phillip asked.//
Sam sat back in his chair, rocking it back on two legs. 'Up and down.' He sipped his tea. 'She's all over the place at the moment. Hormones. Getting bigger by the day as well.'//
'Sit, Baggage, sit,' Albert said to Baggage, who cocked his head at him.//
'What are you doing?' Phillip said.//
'I'm trying to teach him some obedience.'

'I'd give up, mate. I tried that once. He has a mind of his own, that dog. I don't own Baggage. I just happen to live with him.'

Seemingly bored with Albert, Baggage tramped over to Sam, who gave him a pat on the head. 'Good boy,' Sam said. 'Don't listen to Albert. He'll have you doing all kinds of stupid things.' Baggage satisfied with his stroke, padded back to his bed. He performed two quick circles before settling down and closing his eyes.

Sam rocked back in his chair again. 'Right. Now that Bagsy's happy, we can crack on. A thought crossed my mind today.'

'Short journey, was it?' Phillip said and winked at Albert.

Albert chuckled and picked up his cup. 'Very witty, Phillip,' he said and sipped his chamomile tea.

'I think I liked you better when Kim was away,' Sam said. 'This new, happy Phillip will get irritating, very quickly. As I was saying, I think we should visit the church.'

'I thought we discussed this last night,' Phillip said. 'We're probably being watched.'

Albert looked around the room. 'Maybe we've been bugged.'

'Yes,' Phillip said. 'Someone crept in here last night and planted one.'

Sam slurped his tea. 'If you two are going to be silly, I'm going home. I've got a nursery to decorate.'

'Sam,' Phillip said. 'If we go up there and the bad guys follow us—'

'I know all that. I've got an idea. We'll go in the middle of the night when no one's about.'

'Right,' Phillip said. 'With you so far.'

'We all act normally.' He glanced at Albert. 'Well, as normal as we can. We go to bed at our usual time, but then we get up around two or three and meet somewhere. We then travel to Skelton—'

'And break into a church,' Albert said.

'Smash open a statue of The Virgin Mary,' Phillip said.

Sam held out his hands. 'And the Eagle's ours. Cue loads of money and a holiday of a lifetime.'

Phillip laughed. 'What can go wrong?'

'A lot,' Albert said. 'It's breaking and entering.'

Sam tutted loudly. 'Jesus, Albert. Sometimes in life, you have to step out of your comfort zone.'

'Why doesn't Albert get in touch with Green and tell him where we think it is for a large reward?' Phillip said. 'Then there's no risk to us.'

Sam sighed. 'We've been through this. How do we know it wasn't Green who had us abducted?'

Albert nodded. 'We don't.'

Sam slurped his tea again. 'We can't go to the police because of Robards. And Miss Jacobs is also looking increasingly dodgy, even though she's a bit of a babe,' he said, closing his eyes momentarily.

'The only people we can trust are us, and I'm not that sure about you, Albert.'

Albert looked at Phillip. 'And Tommo. We can trust Tommo.'

Sam pointed at Albert. 'And Tommo,' Sam said.

'And Ewan,' Phillip said.

'Ewan,' Sam said. 'That knob-head. He was smacked off his tits the last time we saw him. We can't trust that tosser.'

Albert nodded his approval.

'Okay,' Phillip said. 'Let's keep it between us three and Tommo.'

Sam stood, racing across the office. 'Did you hear something?' Opening the door, he wandered outside just as Comby and Hardman entered the reception. Sam turned and looked at Phillip and Albert. 'Best behaviour, lads. The old Bill's here.'

Comby stepped forward. 'Ah, Mr Davison.' He followed Sam into the office. 'And your cousins are here too. Splendid.'

Sam held out his hands in a mock gesture of having handcuffs fitted. 'What have we done now?'

Comby looked sternly at him. 'I wouldn't make jokes, Mr Davison. Your other friend, Mr Thompson? The one who wouldn't look out of place on the pitch at Twickenham. Where is he?'

Phillip shrugged. 'In his pub, I suppose.'

'Can I ask you, gentlemen, where you were between the hours of 05:30 and 08:00 this morning?'

Sam frowned. 'In bed. I don't do early mornings.'

'Me too,' Phillip said.

'And you, Mr Jackson?'

'I was in bed as well.'

Comby plodded towards the window and looked out into the street. 'Together?'

'What is this?' Sam said.

'Are you sure you weren't abducted again?' Comby said. 'By aliens this time?' Hardman laughed. 'They didn't whisk you away in a spacecraft and probe you all night, did they?'

Sam sat back at his desk, rocking back in his chair. He picked up his cup and loudly slurped his tea. 'You've lost me, Inspector.'

Comby turned. 'Mr Stankovich.'

'The real one or the pretend one?' Sam said.

Comby strolled across and stopped at Sam's desk, moving bits of paper about. 'You tell me. It's hard to say what's real and what isn't in your fertile imagination.'

'Inspector,' Phillip said. 'Is there something we can help you with? We're all rather busy.'

Comby plodded towards Phillip. 'Mr Stankovich. The one we visited yesterday. Was found dead by the cleaner this morning, a little after eight.'

Sam pointed at Comby with his mug. 'Probably a disgruntled reveller?'

'You may joke, Mr Davison,' Comby said, walking back across to Sam. 'But I'm not laughing. You three are hiding something. I can smell it.'

Sam nodded towards Albert. 'That's Albert. He was up to his neck in shit the other night.' Albert frowned and sniffed himself.

Comby glared at Sam. 'Hardman. Let's take these three jokers down to Middlesbrough Nick and test how watertight their alibis are.'

Albert, Sam and Phillip trudged into the Sidewinder, where Tommo was already pulling pints for them. 'Where have you three been?'

They reached the bar and Phillip nodded at Sam. 'Ask laughing boy, here,' Phillip said, leaning against the bar.

Sam hopped on a stool. 'Down the nick. Stankovich was murdered this morning.'

'Someone shot him,' Albert said.

Tommo popped the first pint on the counter. 'The real one?'

Phillip sighed. 'Yes. The real one.'

Tommo placed the other two pints down. 'And the police think you had something to do with it?'

Sam pushed a note across the bar as Maria came in from the cellar. 'One for you and one for the lass with the bright green hair.'

'Oh, cheers, Sam,' Maria said.

Phillip slumped onto a stool next to Sam. 'Sam didn't help. Constantly winding Comby up.'

Sam rolled his eyes. 'No one can take a joke these days. We got out, didn't we?'

'Only after the girls verified our alibis,' Phillip said. 'Three hours later.'

Sam picked up his pint. 'I like the way they believed Albert and not us.'

Albert edged forward and collected his drink. 'Inspector Comby said he didn't think I'd hurt a fly, never mind shoot someone.'

Sam rolled his eyes and mocked Albert as he spoke. 'You need to get the polish out,' Sam said. 'For that halo of yours.'

Phillip waved Tommo closer. 'We need a chat,' he said, nodding to the corner.

'Yeah, sure,' Tommo said. 'Watch the bar a minute, Maria, will you?'

Maria nodded. 'Okay,' she said and handed Sam his change.

Sam followed and sat with the others, leaning forward towards Tommo. 'We need to talk before the girls turn up.'

'Where are they?' Tommo asked.

'Gone for a coffee and a caramel slice,' Phillip said.

Tommo leant forward. 'So? What have you got?'

'We're going to the church tonight,' Phillip whispered.

Sam waited until a customer who'd come in moved out of earshot. 'We're going to act normal, well as normal as we can,' he said looking across at Albert, who was sniffing himself again. 'Go to bed and rendezvous early in the morning.'

Phillip glanced around. 'We'll have to creep out of our homes, the back way, and make sure we're not followed.'

Albert lifted his arm up to his nose and sniffed. 'We'll need transport.'

Tommo got up, retrieved Ewan's van keys from behind the bar, and sat down with the others. 'Look what I've still got. Ewan's van is parked out back. I ended up putting him in a taxi.'

Rupert Green sat in his suite, reading The Times. There was a light knock on the door, and a man entered, stopping in front of Green. 'Yes, Billy?' he said, without lifting his head from the paper.

'We've just had word, Mr Green. The listening device we placed at the pub has come up trumps. Apparently, they're moving tonight. The three cousins and the big guy who owns the bar are going to meet up.'

Green dropped his newspaper. 'Where exactly are they going?'

'A church was mentioned but not the address.'

Green folded his hands across his stomach, nodding slowly. 'Good, good.'

'Should Sandy and I come armed, sir?'

'Of course, Billy. This could turn ugly.'

Tony answered his mobile. 'Geoff?'

'The bug we planted in the agency picked up a nice little conversation. Unfortunately, that fat idiot Comby turned up before we could find out where they're going.'

'Is it tonight?' Tony said.

'We're not sure. But we've planted a tracking device on Sam Davison's car. We may have to watch the others, too.'

'I know Stankovich is no longer a worry, but what about Green?' Tony said.

'As far as I know, he doesn't know anything about this. Just in case, I'll bring along the boys that I used to abduct the cousins the other night.'

'And Miss Jacobs?' Tony said.

Robards scoffed. 'I think we can leave her out of this, as well.'

'It's still fifty-fifty?'

'Absolutely,' Robards said.

'Will I need my gun?'

'You will. If this turns nasty, I want to be prepared.'

Comby and Hardman sat in their car, parked at the end of Baker Street. Comby screwed up his face. 'These chips are a bit manky.'

'You said to be quick, so I went to that kebab shop over the road,' Hardman said.

'Did you get a drink?'

'Diet Coke or Fanta?' Hardman held out the cans.

'Fanta.' Comby said. 'I don't hold with any of those chemical sweeteners. I once read an article in the paper about them.'

'Really?' Hardman said and stuffed a large piece of fish into his mouth.

'That's them,' Comby said. 'Coming out now. Samuel Davison, Phillip Davison and Albert Jackson. Oh, and the lovely Kim Weatherly. Plus, Emily Simpson. The one who alibied Davison.'

Hardman jotted the names in his notebook. 'Shall I follow them, guv?'

'No,' Comby said. 'What time is it?'

'Ten.'

Comby picked up a piece of fish. 'I have a plan. I think Howard Thompson, AKA Tommo, is the key. We'll wait here and see what he does. He'll be closing soon. Let's see where the big fella goes.'

## CHAPTER THIRTY-THREE

Phillip and Sam sat in the lounge of Sam and Emily's flat as Sam stood and wandered towards the kitchen, stopping at the door. 'Another beer?' he said to Phillip.

Phillip placed his empty can down. 'This will have to be the last. We don't want to be pissed when Tommo turns up.'

Sam stopped and turned, popping his head back through the threshold. 'Do you think the girls believe our stories?'

'I spoke to Kim on the phone earlier, and she didn't seem to have a problem. Anyway, Albert verified it as well. For some reason, no one ever thinks he lies.'

Sam opened the fridge. 'What are they doing?' he shouted.

'Girly night. Deb's going around, and they're watching chick flicks.'

Sam rolled his eyes, collected the beers and returned to the lounge. 'We dodged a bullet there, mate,' he said, handing Phillip a can. 'What time is it?'

Phillip cracked open his can and held it out towards Sam. 'Quarter past two.'

Sam raised his can. 'Not long now,' he said.

'No,' Phillip said, clinking his can against Sam's.

Tommo had locked up around eleven-thirty, and rather than go back to an empty flat to wait, he had decided to stay at the pub. He filled the time by doing the jobs he usually did first thing in the morning – restocking and checking the gas on the pumps, putting the dirty glasses through the dishwasher and stacking them under the bar. He even tidied and wiped the tables and bar top, saving his cleaner the trouble in the morning. Tommo looked at his watch, checked outside – the street empty but for a couple of cars parked further along the road along with Ewan's van outside the pub – and readied himself as the time neared. He smiled to himself and sat on a stool as the clock crawled towards two-thirty.

Comby nudged Hardman, who woke with a jolt. 'He's moving,' Comby said, looking at his colleague and nodding towards the van.

Hardman yawned. 'What time is it?'

Comby rubbed his hands together. 'Half two. I knew he was up to something.'

'Maybe he's off home.'

Comby scoffed. 'They shut hours ago,' he said, nudging Hardman to follow Tommo as he pulled away in Ewan's van – the police car travelling at a discreet distance as the roads were devoid of traffic but for the odd taxi scurrying by.

'Did you see the speed that taxi was going?' Hardman said.

'We've bigger fish to fry than taxis, Mick.'

Hardman shook his head. 'Must have been doing sixty.'

Comby grabbed hold of Hardman's arm. 'Stop here, don't get too close.'

The van waited for a moment before two figures, one of them holding a dog, emerged from the darkness and got into the vehicle.

Comby banged the dashboard with his fist. 'Bingo!'

Tommo got out of the van and opened the side door. 'Why have you brought Baggage?' he said, giving the dog his usual pat. 'We're not the famous five.'

Phillip shrugged. 'He doesn't like being left alone, and with the girls being over at Kim's place, I thought I'd bring him along.'

Sam patted Baggage on the head, and the dog jumped onto a seat. 'He'll be all right,' Sam said. 'He can be our lookout, can't you, boy.'

Baggage cocked his head to one side, digesting this information as his tail wagged frantically. The dog turned and pressed his nose to the window, looking out into the street-lamped semi-darkness.

Tommo drove the short journey to Albert's house, pulling up on a side road some distance away. 'I'll go and get Albert. You two stay here, sound the horn if anything happens.'

Phillip grabbed his arm. 'You're not going around to the front, are you?'

'Albert's leaving the back door open,' Tommo said. 'There's a couple of fences to negotiate, though. Don't worry. No one's following us. I'm certain.'

Sam closed his eyes and put his head against the window. 'I'll have a sleep. It'll take you half an hour to get back here with all that rigmarole Albert goes through locking up.'

Tommo shook his head, got out, and looked around, slowly scanning the area before disappearing down the side of another property.

Robards answered his mobile, yawning. 'Yes, Tony?'

Tony looked through his binoculars. 'The big fella from the pub has just arrived in a van, and it looks like Sam and Phillip Davison are with him.'

'Those two are still supposed to be at Sam Davison's flat. I bet Bennie and Jamie have fallen asleep.'

'Well, they're definitely here, Geoff.'

'Follow them,' Robards said. 'I'll rouse the other two, and we'll be along soon.'

Robards hung up and dialled. 'Yes, Geoff?'

'Don't *Geoff* me! Are you still outside the flat?'

'Yeah, why?'

'Are the Davison's there?' Robards said.

'No movement. Neither of them has left. We've been watching all night.'

Robards grabbed his coat and headed towards the door. 'Well, how come they're in a van outside Jackson's house in Nunthorpe?'

'They must have slipped out the back,' Bennie said.

'Oh, must they. Didn't you think of having one of you wait there? You're a couple of half-wits. Get your arse over to Nunthorpe, and don't make a scene. I'll ring when I know where they're heading.'

Rupert Green sat snoozing in an armchair. An empty brandy glass and a half-full decanter on the table by his side. There was a light tap on the door, and Green opened an eye and yawned. 'Yes, Billy.'

'One of the boys has phoned. The guy who owns the pub has gone into Jackson's.'

'And the Davison's?'

'They're in a van outside.'

Green hauled his corpulent body out of the seat and chuckled. 'This is it, Billy. I'll phone Miss Jacobs on the way. Fire up the Batmobile.'

The door to the van opened, and Albert got in as Sam peeped out of one eye, glancing at his watch. 'Twenty-two minutes, Albert,' Sam said. 'It must be a personal best.'

Albert frowned, looking at the house. 'I'm sure I've left a window open.'

Tommo jumped into the driver's seat. 'Albert, for Christ's sake, we've checked.'

Albert stared outside. 'What about the front door? I'm not certain—'

Tommo started the engine. 'Albert. Belt up.'

Albert sat back in his seat as Baggage jumped across next to him, and Albert patted the dog affectionately.

'Are you two friends now?' Phillip said.

'It comes out of adversity, Phillip. Spending hours in that field together.' Albert shuddered. 'He was the only thing that kept me going.' Albert sniffed himself as memories from the farmhouse arrived, put his hand in his pocket, pulled out his hip flask, opened it, and took a large swig of sherry.

The van travelled along Guisborough Road, stopping at the Woodhouse services. Tommo pulled the car up to a pump, got out, moved around to the side to fill up and opened the passenger door a little. 'Are you sure we're being followed?' he said.

Sam nodded across the forecourt. 'Certain. They've pulled into the Subway over there.'

Tommo motioned his head, looking in the direction Sam had indicated. 'I can't see them.'

'They've parked down below. You'd have to walk over to the wall to see them.'

Phillip sat forward. 'Shall I have a look?'

Tommo nodded. 'Yeah, but don't let them spot you, though.'

Phillip got out and crept over to the wall on the side of the forecourt. He peeped over the top and glanced below before making his way back to the van. He threw open the side door. 'It's our friends, the fat coppers,' he said, jumping back in.

Albert sat up straight, taking another mouthful from his hipflask. 'What now? Should we call it off?'

Tommo paused for a moment, stroking his beard. 'I've got an idea.' He headed inside to pay for the fuel.

Phillip watched Tommo as he disappeared into the shop. 'What's he planning?'

Sam closed his eyes, leaning his head against the window. 'No idea.'

Tommo returned carrying a plastic bag. 'I've got some drinks and snacks to keep our strength up.'

Sam altered his position in an attempt to find a more comfortable one. 'Yeah, why not? Let's have a party while Bill and Ben, the fat policemen, watch our every move. You don't have a pillow in that bag, do you?'

'Ignore him,' Tommo said to Phillip. 'He's always grumpy when he hasn't had his sleep. What I did get was these.' He pulled out a bag of nails.

Phillip frowned. 'Nails?'

'We're going to scupper our two friends over there?'

Albert sat forward. 'Isn't that against the law?'

Sam opened an eye. 'Albert. We're on our way up to Skelton, where, on arrival, we'll break into a church and start smashing religious icons.'

Albert shook his head. 'We won't be breaking in, though. We have a key. Technically, that's not breaking and entering.'

Sam opened the other eye. 'One. We don't know if the key's going to fit yet. Two, what are we going to say if someone catches us inside? Even if we've used a key. *We were only doing a brass rubbing, your honour.*'

'Will it work?' Phillip said. 'The nails?'

Sam took hold of the packet of nails. 'They look a bit small.'

Tommo grabbed them back. 'I'm sorry, Sam. It's a twenty-four-hour service station. They only have a limited range of things in their tiny DIY range. Had I known, I'd have brought some three-inch, flat-head, galvanised ones.'

Sam closed his eyes again and put his head on the side window. 'Now who's getting grumpy?'

Tommo held out a nail. 'If we put the nail like this,' he said, holding it between his thumb and index finger. 'Wedge it between the tyre and the ground, when they drive off, Bob's your uncle. Trust me, it will work. We have a history. Don't we, Sam?'

Sam grinned. 'Mr Murphy, the geography teacher?'

Tommo chuckled. 'Yep.'

'How do we get close enough to do the deed?' Phillip asked.

Tommo rubbed his beard. 'I'm not sure.'

Sam opened his eyes again and sat up. 'Have you seen those two? Both of them are huge. I can't imagine the pair of them sitting outside a Subway and not being tempted.'

'He's got a point,' Albert said.

Sam indicated across the forecourt. 'Park over there. Far enough away but near enough so they can still see us from inside. Turn off the lights as if we're waiting for someone, and watch the fat buggers crack.'

'That's brilliant,' Albert said.

Tommo smiled. 'He does occasionally come up with something useful.'

Tommo parked where Sam indicated, and Albert and Sam went inside to buy some sandwiches, trying to tempt the policemen. After sitting for five minutes, Phillip sneaked from the van and, out of sight of Comby and Hardman, crept around the back of their vehicle and waited ten feet away with a handful of nails in his pocket.

'What are they doing, now?' Hardman asked.

'Waiting. They must be meeting someone. Maybe our friend, Rocco?'

'I'm starving,' Hardman said. 'Do you fancy a foot long, guv?'

'I thought that myself, but if we go in, and they drive off?'

Hardman tapped his phone. 'We've still got the tracking device I planted on Baker Street.'

'You're right. I'd forgotten about that,' Comby said. 'We'll take a chance. I need the toilet as well. You order the food and give me a shout if anything occurs.'

'I need the toilet, too.'

'Seniority,' Comby said. 'When I come out, you can go in. How's that?'

'Sounds like a plan, guv.' The duo lumbered out of their vehicle and plodded inside.

Phillip jumped back into the van. 'I've done it.'

'Two wheels?' Tommo said.

'All four. I wanted to make sure.'

Albert handed Baggage a piece of sandwich, which the dog eagerly devoured. 'Won't they know it was us that did it?' he said.

Tommo laughed. 'Let them prove it.'

Sam leant forward. 'Are we going then?'

'Not just yet,' Tommo said. 'Let them get back in their car and start eating, and then we'll head off.'

Comby came out of the toilets. 'Anything?'

'Nothing, guv. They're still parked over there.'

'Good. You go to the bog, and I'll sort out the food and drink.'

The two policemen left the building and got into their car, making sure to keep out of sight of the van. Comby handed Hardman his sandwich and coffee, putting his own coffee in the holder.

Comby opened the foot-long and smiled. 'Let's hope that we'll have time to eat these,' he said, lifting the sandwich to his mouth and taking a huge bite.

Hardman put his coffee down, spilling half of it. 'Oh, shit. They're moving.' He turned on the ignition, took a quick bite of his sandwich and waited. The van turned left towards Middlesbrough, then performed a U-turn at the roundabout, accelerating away and heading towards Whitby. The policemen watched the vehicle and then did the same manoeuvre as the van, and keeping a significant gap between them, they headed after them.

Albert peered out of the rear window. 'They're following us.'

Phillip put a hand on Tommo's shoulder. 'How long, do you reckon, Tommo?'

Tommo looked in the rear-view mirror. 'With nails in four tyres? Not long.'

Tommo accelerated further. The speedometer hit 70 mph before he slowed at another roundabout and carried on. They rapidly approached a second roundabout – the signpost indicating Skelton was to their left and turned.

Tommo glanced back at Albert. 'Anything?'

'No sign. I think we've lost them.'

Comby wiped barbeque sauce from his chin as the car came to a bumpy stop by the side of the road. 'What's up, Mick?'

'A flat, guv, I think.' Comby sighed as Hardman got out.

Comby put down the window and popped his head through. 'Have we a spare?'

'Wouldn't matter if we did,' Hardman said, walking around to Comby's side. 'We've got four flats. It looks as if someone's put nails in our tyres.'

Comby looked through the windscreen along the empty road. 'They've mugged us, Mick. Good and proper. I'll have those bastards. I'll throw the bloody book at them!'

# CHAPTER THIRTY-FOUR

Rupert Green sat in the back of a car with two men in the front. He took out his mobile and called.

'Rupert, darling,' Miss Jacobs said. 'How are we?'

'I'm well. We are at present following our friends towards Redcar.'

The driver glanced back. 'It looks like they're heading for Skelton, Mr Green.'

'Strike that, my dear. They're travelling towards Skelton.'

'I'm on my way,' she said.

'Has our friend, Robards, been in touch?' Green asked.

'No, he hasn't.'

'It appears you were right. Robards can't be trusted. Does our deal still stand?'

'It does.'

'Good, good,' he said.

'Robards and his men?' she said.

'Leave them to me. My people will deal with the untrustworthy Mr Robards. We will have the element of surprise.'

'What about the cousins?' she said.

Green chuckled. 'I can't see those three and their friend causing too many problems. Especially with a gun pushed into their faces.'

The van pulled up around the corner from All Saints church. Tommo turned off the ignition and swivelled in his seat to face the others. Baggage pushed his head between Sam and Phillip as if he wanted to be in on the conversation.

Tommo looked at Sam. 'You did remember the key?'

Sam pulled out his set of keys and held the key to the church aloft. 'Right here. I've had it on here for days. I thought it would be better to hide it in plain sight.'

Tommo nodded behind Albert. 'Hand me that bag, Albert. I think it may be better if we leave one at a time and wait in the churchyard until we're all there.'

'I'll go first,' Sam said. 'I've got the key.'

Sam climbed out, raced towards the church, and glanced around, surveying the street – no one was about. Satisfied, he entered the grounds of the church and made his way towards the entrance. The doors were set back in an alcove, and Sam slipped into the shadows, pressing himself against the wall, out of sight of anyone walking past. One by one, the other three made their way over to join him – Phillip, the last with Baggage on his lead. Tommo nodded at Sam, who took out the key and inserted it into the lock, slowly turning. Grasping the ironwork handle, he pushed – the door swung open with a loud groan, deafening in the silence. The five went inside, with Tommo, carrying his bag, the last to enter. Sam allowed himself one final glance along the road before he closed the door and locked it.

Robards sat in the front passenger seat of Tony's car, directly behind a vehicle containing his two other men.

Tony nudged Robards. 'They're in the church. What shall we do?'

'Sit tight. We'll give them a couple of minutes before we go over. Get them as they're coming out.'

Robards mobile sounded. He held a finger to his mouth, and Tony nodded, indicating that he understood. 'Anne,' Robards said. 'It's a bit late for you to be calling.'

'I'm at a bit of a loose end, and I thought you might be interested in coming over.'

Robards raised his eyes at Tony. 'I can't. I'm on a job. A stakeout.'

'Not our friends, is it?' she said.

'No. Some druggies. No movement on that lot. Perhaps tomorrow?'

'Sounds good to me. Phone me in the morning, and I'll get a bottle of bubbly put on ice.'

'I can't wait.'

Tony nodded towards the phone. 'Jacobs?'

'Yes. We don't want that silly cow turning up. More for us, Tony.'

'Absolutely,' he said.

Miss Jacobs searched her contacts and dialled. 'Robards was going to renege, and Green still thinks I'm going along with him. I'm on my way over to Skelton now. Keep your head down until the last minute.

We want to know who all of the players are and what they intend before we show our hand. I've decided we'll get more for the Eagle on the open market. I have a Russian contact – more for me and you. See you soon. Love you.'

Green sat in the rear of his car behind his two men. He leant forward and put a hand on the driver's shoulder. 'What's happening now?'

'The cousins, that Tommo guy and bizarrely, a dog have gone in the church.'

'And Robards?'

'He's in the back of the car with Tony. His other two men are in the car in front.'

'Good, good.' He patted the man on his arm, and Green sat back. 'Wait for them to make their move. When Tony's inside with them, we'll make ours.'

The man nodded.

Tommo banged the torch with his hand. 'I checked this before I left.'

'Is it the batteries?' Albert said.

Tommo opened the base. 'New ones.' He took out the batteries and replaced them, more in hope than anything. 'I've got another torch in the van, in the glovebox.'

Sam held out his hand and sighed. 'Give me the keys and I'll go and get it.'

Tommo handed Sam the van keys, and he headed off. The others edged their way along the aisle towards the altar, moving carefully in the darkness, and then they spotted it in the gloom – the statue of the Virgin Mary. They all looked at each other and gasped as Baggage, who had padded forward, sniffed at its base. Tommo took a lighter from his pocket and lit a candle near the statue, bathing the small corner of the church in light.

Sam rooted about in the front of the van, finding what he sought, and grabbed the torch. He pressed the button, and thankfully, it worked. He turned swiftly as he heard a noise behind him.

'Mr Davison,' Robards said. 'We meet again.'

'Stankovich?'

Robards smiled. 'Robards, actually. Mr Stankovich couldn't make it.'

Sam turned and searched in the van again. 'I'm just looking for something. It's in here, I'm sure.'

Robards took hold of his arm. 'We know why you're here, so cut the pretence.' He pushed Sam towards the pistol carrying Tony. 'Shall we join your friends?'

Sam sighed. 'Yeah, why not? I've nothing else on.'

Robards, Tony and the two other men marched Sam back towards the church. Robards paused at the door, quickly scanning the street and followed them inside. They entered the darkness of the church, Tommo and the others turning as Sam was pushed forward towards them.

Robards shone the torch towards the three men, deliberately blinding them. 'Good evening, gentlemen. What have we here?'

'We're—'

Sam was pushed forward by one of Robards men. 'It's pointless lying, Tommo. They know why we're here.'

Robards pulled a packet of cable ties from his pocket. 'Fasten them up, boys, and then we can have a little chat.'

Green and his men headed across to the church, and stopping briefly at the threshold, they crept inside.

Tommo, Sam, Phillip and Albert sat on a pew at the front with Baggage, sitting obediently at his master's side, watching Robards and his men.

Robards stood in front of Tommo. His face was now visible for the first time. 'Geoff,' Tommo said.

Robards grinned. 'Now then, Tommo.'

'You're Robards?'

'I am. It might be better in future if you learn a man's surname.'

'So, we still have a future?' Phillip said.

Robards strolled over, stopping in front of Phillip. 'Sit quietly, and we won't have a problem, Mr Davison.'

'The police are on their way,' Albert said.

Robards let out a laugh. 'Who? Comby and Hardman? The useless duo. The last time I saw those two, they were parked on Guisborough Road with four flat tyres. Good move that.' Robards turned and looked at the statue. 'Now, what have we here?' He strode across to it and placed his hand on the head. 'And this is what we've all been searching for.'

Green, a gun in his hand, stepped out of the gloom into the light. 'Just hold it there, Robards. That statue is mine.'

Robards drew his gun and pointed it at Green. 'It appears we have a standoff, Rupert.'

Green lumbered his massive frame behind a pillar. 'There's no way out. My men have got your other two goons at gunpoint. Nowhere to run, I'm afraid, and we don't want this to end badly.'

Robards edged away from the statue and into the semi-darkness. 'There's still two of us. If you want a gunfight, I'll give you one. You'll have to kill us to get the statue.'

Green laughed. 'Really? That's not a problem.'

Robards froze as he felt the muzzle of the gun pressed into the back of his neck. 'Drop it, Geoff,' Tony said.

Robards glanced over his shoulder. 'I thought we had a deal.'

'I know you wouldn't keep to that, and I'd only end up floating in the Tees, like Hector Williamson.'

'That was Stankovich's doing,' Robards said. 'I had nothing to do with his murder.'

Tony took the weapon from his hand. 'But you knew about it.'

Green stepped from behind the column and into the light. 'Fasten him up with the others.'

Tony secured Robards' arms with a cable tie and pushed him onto the pew next to Sam. Sam winked at Robards. 'It's getting crowded in here, Robards. That didn't exactly go to plan, did it?' He glowered back.

Green lumbered along the aisle and stopped at the statue, his two men following him, one carrying a large crowbar. Green held out his hand and took it from him. 'You two check outside and make sure we're not disturbed.' The men nodded and disappeared down the aisle into the darkness. Green looked at the assembled people, smiled and then smashed the statue.

Sam nudged Tommo. 'Not a Catholic, then.'

Tommo shook his head. 'Bloody sacrilege. I was only going to break the base. I even brought some super glue to repair it.'

Sam's mouth dropped open. 'Are you for real?'

Tommo nodded. 'Once a Catholic, Sam, always a Catholic.'

'Well, I'm an atheist now,' Sam said. 'So they can smash it as much as they like.'

Tommo raised his eyebrows at Sam. 'It wouldn't matter anyway. You're going to hell with all the shagging about you've done.'

Footsteps on the stone floor broke the silence, and all eyes turned as Miss Jacobs made her way out of the darkness. 'Is it there?' she said.

Tommo nudged Sam. 'Christ,' Tommo said. 'Everyone's been invited.'

Sam rolled his eyes. 'A fantastic set of detectives we are. There doesn't appear to be a person connected to this case who didn't know we were coming here tonight. We might as well have put an announcement in the Gazette.'

Tommo nudged Sam again. 'I hope all your girlfriends don't show up,' Tommo said. 'We won't have the room in this little church.'

Sam smiled. 'Yeah, good one, Tommo.'

Green beckoned Anne forward. 'So nice of you to join us. How did you get past my men?'

'They're busy trussing up Robards' guys.'

'I see.' Green nodded at Tony and then towards the broken statue. Tony took the hint, walked over, and dropped to his knees, searching amongst the bits. He stood upright, holding something wrapped in sacking, and handed it to Green.

Albert nudged Phillip. 'Is it the Eagle?' he whispered.

'I can't see,' Phillip said.

Green unwrapped the sacking and allowed it to fall to the floor. Gazing at the Eagle, he turned to the assembled throng. 'It's beautiful,' he said, taking out a little eyeglass. He turned it over and checked the base. 'It's genuine. My life's work.'

Miss Jacobs joined him at the altar and, pulling a gun from her coat pocket, held out her left hand. 'I'll take that, Rupert,' she said, pointing the gun at his head.

'Dear, dear, Anne. How disappointing. We had a deal, but now you'll get nothing.'

She motioned with the gun. 'You wouldn't have kept your side of the bargain.'

Green pulled the Eagle close to his body. 'You're forgetting my men.'

'Your boys are tied up outside. They really are slow on the uptake.'

'Tony,' Green said, continuing to look at Miss Jacobs. 'Shoot her.'

Tony stepped forward. 'I would, but unfortunately ...'

Tony stood with his gun-carrying hand by his side. The figure of another person wearing a ski mask stood behind him. A gun was pressed into the back of his head, and the masked figure leant forward and plucked the pistol from his hand. Then they picked up a cable tie and, securing his hands behind his back, led him over to the pews and pushed him down next to Robards.

Sam leant forward and looked along the pews at Tony. 'Groom or Bride?' he said as Tony glared back at him.

Miss Jacobs slipped closer. 'I'm waiting, Rupert, darling. I could put a bullet in your head if you prefer.'

Green scowled and handed it over. 'I'll pay whatever you ask. I must have it.'

The masked woman walked across and secured Green's hands. She led him over to the pews, sat him down with the others, and then joined Miss Jacobs and pulled the ski mask from her head.

Albert gasped. 'Miss Waltham.'

Miss Jacobs smiled. 'Oh, I forgot, Albert. You and Vanessa have already met.' The two women embraced and kissed – a long, passionate kiss.

'Christ, Sam,' Tommo said, glancing at his friend. 'Your magic's backfiring. You're turning straight lasses gay now.'

Sam stared at the pair. 'She's a good actor in bed. I'm going to have visions about these two for months. This is going straight into the memory bank.' Tommo turned his head and stared at Sam – his mouth wide open. Sam shrugged. 'I'm just saying.'

'How could you, Miss Waltham?' Albert said. 'You're my therapist.'

Miss Waltham sauntered forward. 'Oh, Albert. I'm sorry about that. The truth is, I'm not a therapist at all. Didn't you think it was a bit strange? Me finding you? Normally, patients seek out medical help and not the other way around. We were amazed when you fell for it. A flyer through your door.' The two women giggled.

Albert lightly shook his head. 'Well … I …'

Miss Waltham edged closer. 'Put it down to experience, Albert. Your OCD is much better. I'm not bad for a novice.' She looked at Tommo. 'And Tommo,' she said, moving closer to him. 'I even tried to get to know you, but that Deb woman put paid to that. I may even have slept with you.'

Sam nudged Tommo. 'Hard luck, big fella. She's got a great arse.' Tommo shook his head.

Miss Waltham turned and looked along the pew. 'Poor Albert there told me everything. Anne and I have tracked your progress week by week. You were quite helpful.'

Tommo, Sam and Phillip glared at Albert as Baggage, following their stare, looked up too, his head slightly tilted at an angle. 'I didn't know,' Albert said. 'She had certificates and everything.'

'Marvellous what you can achieve with a fake office and an inkjet printer.' The two women laughed loudly.

Miss Jacobs glided across to Sam. 'The lovely Sam. Thanks for the memories, handsome. Have you thought of charging for your services?'

Sam smiled. 'Once or twice.'

She laughed. 'You're rather good at it. Bill would have been proud.' Miss Jacobs threw back her head. 'I love that wit of yours. I'm almost tempted to bring you along,' she said as Phillip, Albert, Tommo and Baggage all stared across at Sam.

'It's a cross I have to bear,' Sam said. 'What's the story with you and Miss Waltham?'

'That's the trouble with men. You're so naïve about sex. Sex is not about male and female. It's subtler than that.' Miss Waltham joined her, putting an arm around Miss Jacobs.

Sam winked. 'You know my address. Send me a postcard.'

Miss Jacobs laughed and, bending, kissed him passionately on the lips. The bright red lipstick she was wearing covered Sam's mouth.

Miss Jacobs stepped back, juggling the Eagle in her hand. 'Sorry, we can't stay any longer, boys. We've got an Eagle to sell.'

Green tried and failed to get to his feet. His face now a bright red. 'I'll track you down,' he said, getting redder by the second. 'The world's a small place when you're being hunted.' He gasped as his breathing became heavier.

Miss Jacobs waved. 'Have fun, guys,' she said and turning with Miss

Waltham, the pair fled.

Phillip sighed. 'Well, that was fun.'

Baggage yawned, performed a couple of circles, and lay on the floor while the others sat back in the pew.

Sam looked at Tommo. 'What would you have done with the money, Tommo?'

'What money?'

'The money we would have got for the Eagle?' Sam said.

'New car, mate. Mine's ready for the scrappy.'

Sam smiled. 'A house for Emily and me. What about you, Phillip?'

Phillip sighed. 'Holiday for Kim and me. I fancied Mexico.' He frowned. 'I've always wanted to go to Mexico.'

Sam nodded and looked at Albert. 'Albi?'

Albert slowly shook his head. 'I can't believe she did that. I even bought her chocolates. Expensive ones, too.'

The door to the church burst open, and the room was bathed in light as several armed policemen entered, followed by the breathless Comby and Hardman.

Comby stepped forward, stopping in front of the pews. 'Well, well, well. Fancy meeting you lot here.'

Sam nodded towards Robards. 'That's Stankovich. The one who abducted us.'

'Inspector Robards,' Comby said. 'Would you like to explain?'

'Fuck off, Comby.'

'Charming,' Comby said. 'The Eagle?'

Phillip nodded towards the door. 'You've just missed it, Inspector. It was last sighted in the hands of a couple of gay lasses.'

Tommo half-laughed. 'If one of them tells you she can cure your fear of heights, Inspector. Don't believe her.'

Comby turned to the officers. 'Don't just stand there, you idiots. Get after them.' He took a couple of strides along the aisle and stopped, turning to face the pew again. 'By the way, you lot,' he said, pointing at Tommo and the three cousins. 'You owe Cleveland Constabulary for four new tyres and a pickup truck.'

'What about us,' Green said. 'You can't leave us trussed up like this? I don't feel well.'

Comby marched down the aisle and, stopping at the door, he turned. 'You lot can wait. Say a prayer or something. It might come in handy later.'

Tommo, Sam, Phillip, and Albert emerged from Middlesbrough police station, where Emily, Deb, Kim, and Baggage stood waiting.

Emily approached them. 'Well?'

'They're not charging us,' Tommo said.

Sam put an arm around Emily. 'Yeah. We told them everything. They're all in there selling each other out.'

Tommo shook his head. 'There's no honour among thieves.'

Phillip nodded back towards the station. 'That Green bloke had been rushed to the hospital. It doesn't look good.'

Sam rolled his eyes. 'Did you see the size of him? I thought Comby and his mate were big until I clapped eyes on him. Heart attack waiting to happen. All the excitement must have pushed him over the edge.'

Phillip ambled across and put his arm around Kim. 'It was Tony who killed Bill. Robards spilt the beans.'

Kim dropped her head down. 'Oh, I see.'

Sam put a hand on Kim's arm. 'I think, Kim, we should go to Tommo's and have a few drinks in memory of Bill.'

'I'd like that,' she said.

Tommo nodded. 'Yes. You can tell us all about him.'

Kim smiled and linked Phillip with her right arm while holding Baggage's leash in her left hand.

Sam kissed Emily and took hold of her hand while Deb linked Tommo.

Albert edged towards Kim. 'Can I hold Baggage?' Albert said.

Kim passed him the lead. 'Of course.'

Albert squatted. 'Now, you behave yourself, and I might just buy you one of those bone-shaped chews you love.' Baggage cocked his head to one side as his tail wagged wildly.

# EPILOGUE

Tony sat on the edge of his bunk, reading a paper, and looked at the headline: Millionaire Businessman Rupert Green dies. He glanced up as a man entered the cell.

Tony stood, walked across to the man and raised his eyebrows. 'Where have you been?'

'Bit of business,' the man said.

'Did you get the stuff?'

'Yeah.' Tony stood, holding out his hand as the man moved closer. The man thrust forward. 'Robards says hello,' he said, plunging the blade into Tony's chest. Tony staggered back as the man struck again, pushing it deep into his neck. Tony fell to the floor, blood oozing out in a large pool around him. The man grabbed a towel and, wrapping the knife within it, raced from the cell. Walking quickly along the landing, he handed it to another prisoner before heading down some stairs.

The car sat silently by the side of the country road as the tree canopies above cast dappled shadows onto it. Its driver's side window shattered, and the lifeless body of a woman slumped over the steering wheel with thick globules of red dripping from a bullet wound in her forehead. Her companion, her head slightly turned towards her friend, pressed up against the headrest, her blood and bits of cerebral matter clinging to the roof of the car. A small hole where the bullet had exited the vehicle allowed a small shaft of light to penetrate the interior. A squirrel outside scurried past the open boot as birdsong broke the silence of a warm summer day.

He picked up the telephone and placed it to his ear. 'Ballinovich,' he said.

'Sir. We have the Eagle.'

'You have done well, Alexei. I will reward you handsomely for this. Did you have much trouble?'

'Nothing we couldn't handle.'

'When will I have it?' Ballinovich said. 'I long to hold it in my hands.'

'We have a chartered flight booked tonight. We expect to be in Moscow by midnight.'

'We will toast with vodka on your arrival.'

The plane levelled, travelling across the sea as the strong winds battered the small aircraft as it battled to maintain altitude.

The cockpit door opened, and a breathless man pushed his head inside, looking wide-eyed at the pilot. 'What's happening?'

'We may have to turn back. One of the engines is struggling. Make sure our passenger is comfortable and strapped in,' he said. The man nodded and closed the door behind him, made his way along the aisle and stopped at the only passenger on the plane, who sat puffing wildly at his cigarette.

'Sir,' the steward said. 'The pilot says we may have to turn back. Please fasten your belt as it may get rough.'

The man nodded. 'Yes, I see.' He stubbed out his cigarette and lit a second.

'Would you like me to stow that in the overhead locker?' the steward said, pointing at the parcel beside the man.

The passenger shook his head, picked up the object and clutched it tightly to himself. The steward nodded politely and returned to his seat, fastening himself in.

The plane, buffeted by the strong wind, dropped further as the pilot struggled to maintain control, and the aircraft plummeted towards the sea.

# THE AUTHOR

John Regan was born in Middlesbrough on March 20th, 1965. He currently lives near the sea in Redcar.

This was the first book he wrote and fulfils his life-long ambition. He is currently enjoying early retirement, having worked as an underground telephone engineer at BT and Openreach for the past twenty-five years.

This book was re-edited in 2024 to reflect how the author's writing has improved since its original publication.

November 2024.

Email: johnregan1965@yahoo.co.uk

# OTHER BOOKS BY THIS AUTHOR

**PERSISTENCE OF VISION** – Seeing is most definitely not believing!

**Amorphous:** Lindsey and Beth separated by thirty years. Or so it seems. Their lives are about to collide, changing them both forever. Could a higher power intervene and re-write their past and future?
**Legerdemain (Sleight of hand):** Ten winners of a competition held by the handsome and charismatic billionaire – Christian Gainford – are invited to his remote house in the Scottish Highlands. But is he all he seems, and what does he have in store for them? There really is no such thing as a free lunch, as the ten discover.
**Broken:** Sandi and Steve are thrown together. By accident or design? Steve is forced to fight not only for Sandi but for his own sanity. Can he trust his senses when everything he ever relied on appears suspect?
**Insidious:** Killers copying the crimes of the dead psychopath, Devon Wicken. Can Jack save his wife – Charlotte – from them? Or will they stay one step ahead of Jack?

A series of short stories cleverly linked together in an original narrative with one common theme – Reality. But what's real and what isn't?
Exciting action mixed with humour and mystery to keep you guessing throughout. Altering your perceptions forever.
Reality just got a little weirder! Fact or fiction…You decide!
Seeing is most definitely not believing!

## THE SPACE BETWEEN OUR TEARS

If tears are the manifestation of our grief, what lies within the space between them?

After experiencing massive upheavals in her personal life, Emily Kirkby decides to write a novel. But as she continues her writing, the border between her real life and fiction begins to blur.

Sometimes, even the smallest of actions can have far-reaching and profound consequences. When a pebble is cast into the pool of life, there is no telling just how far the ripples will travel.

A rich and powerful story about love in all its many guises. A story about loss and bereavement. A story about guilt and redemption, regret and remorse. But mainly, chiefly, it's about love.

## THE LINDISFARNE LITURGY – The Erimus Mysteries

The boys from The Erimus Detective Agency are back in the funniest adventure to date. The search for an ancient Celtic Cross – The Lindisfarne Liturgy – saved from the marauding Vikings and missing for centuries. Could this cross have somehow ended up on Teesside? Sam, Phillip and Albert, assisted by their friends, attempt to discover its whereabouts while simultaneously trying to wrestle with the vicissitudes of everyday life.
A hilarious romp containing canine offspring and Pilates. Spikey auras and misaligned chakras. Orange shirts and cravats. Monogrammed flip flops, waders and fishing flies. Irate coppers, monocles and puppy pads. A side-splitting adventure from beginning to end. Will the boys find the cross, or will they be thwarted by a collection of individuals intent on owning it?
Mystery and intrigue have never been more enjoyable!

## THE FALLEN LEAVES – Detective Inspector Graveney Series

One of the most perplexing cases Inspector Peter Graveney has worked on. After twenty years, a car is dredged from the bottom of a deep pond. The grisly remains of two bodies locked inside. Why is Graveney certain this discovery is linked to a dubious businessman and the murders of the men working for him? And why does a young woman's name keep surfacing within the investigation after her release from prison for murder? As Graveney digs deeper, he finds more missing pieces to the puzzle and faces his biggest struggle yet – his own mind. As the body count escalates, Graveney battles with his own demons. Desperate to solve the case, he allows himself to be guided by an unlikely source from his past. A gruesome and provocative sequel to the author's first novel, 'The Hanging Tree'. The Fallen Leaves takes the reader on a breathtaking journey, from the graphic opening chapter to the emotionally charged denouement.

**If you bury the past, bury it deep.**

## THE WHITBY WAILERS

Six friends, each with a story of how they ended up in the seaside town, find that some secrets won't stay hidden forever.
Deep in the past lies a story of deceit and betrayal. A chance conversation opens up a can of worms which threatens to expose a long-buried crime and set in motion devastating consequences.
When history comes looking for payment, who will suffer the ultimate price?
A gripping read that will leave you hooked from the first page and carry you on a breath-taking journey to the end. Culminating in a nail-biting climax.


## THE HANGING TREE – Detective Inspector Graveney Series

Sandra Stewart and her daughter were brutally murdered in 2006. Her husband disappeared on the night of Sandra's murder and is wanted in connection with their deaths.
Why has he returned eight years later? And why is he systematically slaughtering apparently unconnected people? Could it be that the original investigation was flawed? Detective Inspector Peter Graveney is catapulted headlong into an almost unfathomable case. Thwarted at every turn by faceless individuals intent on keeping the truth buried.
Are there people close to the investigation, possibly within the force, determined to prevent him from finding out what really happened?
As he becomes more embroiled, he battles with his past as skeletons in his closet rattle loudly. Tempted into an increasingly dangerous affair with his new Detective Sergeant Stephanie Marne, Graveney finds that people he can trust are rapidly diminishing.
But who's manipulating who? As he moves closer to the truth, he finds the person he holds most dear threatened.
Graphically covering adult themes, 'The Hanging Tree' is a relentless edge-of-the-seat ride.
Exploring the darkest secrets and the depths that people will plunge into to keep those secrets hidden. Culminating in a horrific and visceral finale, Graveney relentlessly pursues it to the final conclusion.

EVEN THE DARKEST SECRETS DESERVE AN AUDIENCE

## NEARHOPE – The Rise of the Demons – Book One

Felix has lost everything. On an ordinary evening, he meets a lonely figure at a service station who needs his help. How can Felix be of any assistance to this man, and where is he taking him? Plunged into blackness and faced with demons from his past, he must fight to help save the future of humankind.

Nearhope, a place populated by the damned, acts as a buffer between the demon's realm and our world. But the first incursion has occurred. Can the chosen twelve and their leader return evil to where it came from? If they fail, He who reigns over all the darkness will claim the prize he has long sought, and the consequences for the human race will be devastating.

A fantasy horror, where the fight between good and evil rises to a new level and takes the reader on a journey to a place like Hell… only far, far worse.

## POETRY COLLECTIONS

**Poetry in the key of life**
**Keeper of the Memories**
**The Stranger in all of us**

Three wonderful collections of poetry covering a variety of subjects, including Loss, love, and memories.

Printed in Great Britain
by Amazon